Entangled

Also By Graham Hancock

Supernatural: Meetings with the Ancient Teachers of Mankind
Underworld: The Mysterious Origins of Civilization
Fingerprints of the Gods
Lords of Poverty
The Sign and the Seal

(with Robert Bauval)
Master Game: Unmasking the Secret Rulers of the World
The Message of the Sphinx
The Mars Mystery

(with Santha Faiia)
Heaven's Mirror

www.grahamhancock.com

GRAHAM HANCOCK

ENTANGLED

THE EATER OF SOULS

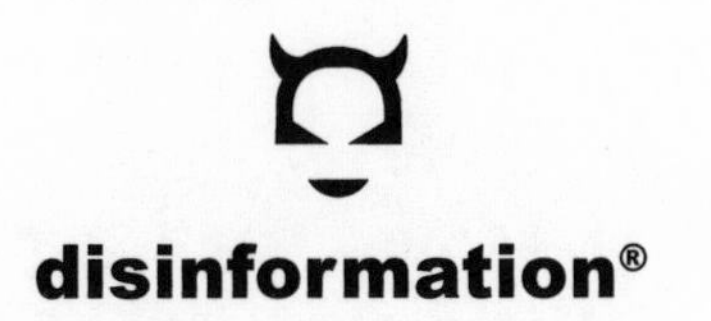

Published by The Disinformation Company Ltd.
163 Third Avenue, Suite 108
New York, NY 10003
Tel.: +1.212.691.1605
Fax: +1.212.691.1606
www.disinfo.com

First U.S. edition; previously published in Great Britain by Century

Library of Congress Control Number: 2010935119

ISBN: 978-1934708-56-9

Cover Design by Greg Stadnyk

Distributed in the U.S. and Canada by:
Consortium Book Sales and Distribution
Toll Free: +1.800.283.3572 Local: +1.651.221.9035
Fax: +1.651.221.0124
www.cbsd.com

Printed in USA

10 9 8 7 6 5 4 3 2 1

Managing Editor: Ralph Bernardo

For Santha, always, forever, my light, my inspiration, my love, my hope. Without you there would be no words here.

Acknowledgements

I'd like to thank my wife Santha for her long hours of reading and commenting on the manuscript of *Entangled* as it has evolved over three years, and for her many inspired suggestions, but most of all for giving me the moral support and encouragement to attempt it in the first place. She was with me every step of the way as we researched the background in the U.S., northern Spain and the Amazon jungle, and has watched over me on some difficult inner journeys.

Thanks also for the encouragement and enthusiasm of our children, Sean, Shanti, Ravi, Leila, Luke and Gabrielle, who all followed the development of the story from its earliest chapters and were a mine of information and good ideas. Deep appreciation to my friend Ileen Maisel who did so much to boost my confidence when I was at a low ebb and helped me to see there was merit in this book. Thanks also to my mother, Muriel Hancock, and uncle, James Macaulay, for their readings and suggestions, and to Debbie and Rodney, Jan, Elizabeth, Sue, Mark and Adrienne, who were kind enough to comment on various drafts of the manuscript.

Very special thanks indeed go to Mark Booth, the brilliant editor of the UK edition of this book, who championed *Entangled* and gave it light when it was still less than a hundred pages long and who helped me in so many ways to bring out the best in it at every stage in its creation. I several times found that suggestions Mark had made, which at first seemed to involve only small changes on one or two pages, went to the heart of some deeper problem that might require me to rework dozens of other pages. The end result was always hugely beneficial to the story.

Thanks to Gary Baddeley of The Disinformation Company in New York, the publisher of this U.S. edition, for his excellent advice and friendship, and to Disinformation's Managing Editor Ralph Bernardo for seeing the book through this publication so efficiently.

There is a considerable research background to *Entangled* in fields as diverse as neuropsychology, consciousness, quantum physics, shamanism and palaeoanthropology. I have drawn on this background at a number of points but I make no claim to factual accuracy. *Entangled* is a work of fiction –

indeed of fantasy – and I have never hesitated to depart from the facts when that was what the story required.

The "machine elves" introduced in Chapter Twenty-Nine are of course a homage to the late, great Terence McKenna, an unrivaled explorer of non-ordinary realms. Amongst other scientific researchers whose work I have studied I want to give special thanks to Rick Strassman, MD, Clinical Associate Professor of Psychiatry at the University of New Mexico School of Medicine. Rick's groundbreaking research with DMT and human volunteers does not provide a model for the DMT research project described in these pages (which I fictitiously located at UC Irvine); however it does show that such a research project is possible. Moreover, Rick's utterly stunning and disturbing findings, published in his book *DMT: The Spirit Molecule* (Park Street Press, Rochester, Vermont, 2001) provide strong scientific support for the central proposition of *Entangled* – namely that non-ordinary levels of reality, including freestanding parallel worlds, may become accessible to us in altered stated of consciousness.

Rick kindly read *Entangled* in manuscript and gave me his comments. I'm very grateful. Thanks also to Luis Eduardo Luna, Ph.D., and Ede Frecska, MD, for their readings and comments, and to all at Wasiwaska in Brazil who sat round with me and gave me encouragement and feedback during evenings in 2007 and 2008 when I read aloud from the evolving manuscript of *Entangled.*

Needless to say none of the individuals named above, whose advice I sometimes ignored, are responsible for any of the faults or errors of the book which are entirely my own doing.

I will close by expressing my gratitude and respect to sacred Ayahuasca, the visionary brew of the Amazon, which plays a part in *Entangled.* Ayahuasca (the "Vine of Souls") has been used by shamans for thousands of years to make out-of-body journeys to what they believe are the realms of spirits. Unexpectedly, some Western scientists who have drunk Ayahuasca themselves (rather than simply read about it) are inclined to agree. They speak not of spirit worlds but of a secret doorway in our minds that Ayahuasca can open, through which we may project our consciousness into parallel realms or dimensions.

I first drank Ayahuasca in 2003 while researching my non-fiction book *Supernatural,* and I have continued to work with the brew ever since. In 2006, during a series of sessions in Brazil, in a ceremonial space overlooked by an image of a blue goddess, my visions brought me the basic characters, dilemmas and plot of the novel that would become *Entangled.*

I felt I had been set an assignment – and this is not unusual, for it is often said by shamans and Western researchers alike that Ayahuasca is a school. Three years of hard work followed, and the result I now set before the reader.

Graham Hancock
Bath, England, September 2010
www.grahamhancock.com

This web of time – the strands of which approach one another, bifurcate, intersect, or ignore each other through the centuries – embraces *every* possibility. We do not exist in most of them. In some you exist and not I, while in others I do, and you do not, and in yet others both of us exist. In this one, in which chance has favored me, you have come to my gate. In another, you, crossing the garden, have found me dead. In yet another, I say these very same words but am an error, a phantom . . . Time is forever dividing itself toward innumerable futures . . .

Jorge Luis Borges, *Ficciones*

Note on characters and plot: Set in parallel in the twenty-first century and the Stone Age, *Entangled* tells the story of a cosmic conflict between good and evil fought out on the human plane. The heroes are exceptional young women, but by no means too young for the adventure in which they find themselves swept up. Both **Joan of Arc** (who was also guided by voices) and **Alexander the Great** had led troops into battle and won stunning military victories by the age of seventeen.

Note on Stone Age setting: The archaic human species known as the Neanderthals lived on in Spain alongside anatomically modern humans – our own direct forebears – until as recently as 24,000 years ago. Soon afterwards the Neanderthals (who are the model for the "Uglies" in *Entangled*) became extinct. Archaeologists suspect it may be the first example of ethnic cleansing in history.

Note on modern setting: Where modern locations such as the city of Los Angeles, the city of Iquitos, the UCLA Medical Center, the UC Irvine School of Medicine, etc., etc., are mentioned they are used entirely fictitiously. Their geography and physical layout as described may vary from reality since they are intended to be understood as the fantastic counterparts of these locations, in what is effectively a parallel realm, and not as the locations themselves. In particular it should be emphasized that no scientific study using dimethyltryptamine (DMT) and human volunteers has ever been conducted at UC Irvine School of Medicine. Such a study was, however, conducted in the 1990s at the University of New Mexico's School of Medicine. The research was led by Associate Professor of Psychiatry, Dr. Rick Strassman. His remarkable findings are set out in his book *DMT: The Spirit Molecule* (Park Street Press, Rochester, Vermont, 2001).

Note on dialogue: We can't know how people spoke 24,000 years ago. But whatever their style of speech it is a reasonable supposition that it could be translated into the idiom of any other time and place – just as Ancient Egyptian hieroglyphs can be translated into modern English, and Classical Greek into modern Japanese. Indeed, rendering the idiom of one culture into the idiom of another is an important part of the translator's job. Rather than contrive a "Stone Age" style of speech for my characters of 24,000 years ago, I have generally expressed their dialogue in the modern idiom. The exception is the thought-talk of the Uglies which I represent in pidgin in the early parts of the book. As I conceive them, these are telepathic creatures forced to compress the complex multi-layered imagery with which they normally communicate into the narrow boundaries of another species' language – so it's reasonable, I think, that they would express themselves in a clumsy way. Later, when Ria receives the magical gift of languages, she is able to understand the Uglies perfectly and their speech is thereafter no longer rendered in pidgin.

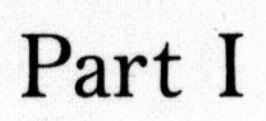
Part I

Chapter One

Northern Spain 24,000 years ago, late summer

Ria was stalking a plump rabbit halfway up the side of a winding valley bright with pink saxifrage and thyme, coarse grasses and patches of yellow gorse. She kept low, crawling on her belly as she got closer, until she was in range. Then, stone in hand, her right arm already drawn back, she rose to a crouch and let fly – only to see her target bolt, startled by the sounds of shouts and loud whoops.

Who the *fuck* had spoiled her shot? She whirled in the direction of the noise, shading her eyes against the morning sun, and spotted a young Ugly male with a gimpy leg hopping and stumbling in terror along the valley floor a few hundred paces below and behind her. He was pursued by Grigo, Duma and Vik, youths of her Clan. Bellowing at the tops of their voices, waving stout wooden clubs, their bloodlust was up and Ria saw they meant to kill the helpless subhuman. On a whim, mainly because she disliked Grigo so much, she decided to stop them.

The winter before, Grigo's overbearing father Murgh had approached her brothers Hond and Rill and proposed she should marry his son. She would rather marry a head louse so she had refused. Hond and Rill, who loved and adored their younger sister, had supported her decision. But there had been bad feeling between the two families ever since and Grigo had found countless ways to annoy and offend her.

Now it was payback time.

The valley side was steep and strewn with boulders, but Ria ran down it with sure feet and soon the distance closed to two hundred and then just a hundred paces. Although they were charging straight towards her, neither the fugitive – intent on avoiding pitfalls at his feet – nor any of his pursuers – intent on murder – seemed to have seen her yet.

Grigo, tall and raw-boned, his lumpy features contorted with malice, was leading the pack. At seventeen he was a year older than Ria, but age-mates with Duma and Vik who looked up to him with such subservience it made her want to vomit. Vik was the fat boy of the gang. His body juddered like a big slab of seal blubber as he pounded along twenty paces behind Grigo. Then came Duma, last as ever, his spindly legs pumping under his scrawny buttocks, his flat unpleasant face covered in ripe pustules, and a look of fanatical stupidity in his eyes.

Ria scooped up a fist-sized rock without breaking her stride and, at thirty paces, flung it with a fluid overarm motion. Just as he was about to bring his club down from behind on the Ugly's head, the projectile struck Grigo in the mouth and knocked him sprawling. In the same instant, evidently overcome by exhaustion and fear, the Ugly collapsed and lay helpless with his two remaining pursuers bearing down on him fast.

But Ria was faster. She sprinted forward, jumped over the Ugly's body and confronted Duma and Vik with such ferocity they skidded to a halt: "Leave him alone," she panted. "Shame on you, picking on a crippled kid like this."

"None of your business, Ria," responded Duma, his face seething. "Just fuck off *now*, or . . ."

"Or what?" she taunted. "Or you'll beat me up? Oooh. I'm afraid. I'm very, very afraid. Really I am."

Out of the corner of her eye Ria saw that Grigo was no longer on the ground where she'd knocked him down. Then, without warning, he threw himself on her from behind. Somehow she'd failed to anticipate this even though she'd known from the beginning he was much more of a threat than his two spineless slaves. She felt his thick muscular right arm circle her neck, pressing on her throat, saw his chunky big-jawed face looming over hers, and smelled his foul breath as he forced her head back and hissed in her ear: "You think you can mess with us because of your brothers but your brothers aren't here to protect you now." He spat a gob of blood into her hair and added: "We have to kill the Ugly first. We're going to torture him to death; you can watch if you like. After that . . ." He giggled – "Hey, Duma. Hey, Vik. Why don't we all take turns to enjoy Ria and then kill her too?"

Grigo said it in such a casual way that at first she didn't get the seriousness of the threat. *Enjoy*? What could he mean? Then his stranglehold tightened and she struggled, scratched and bit but couldn't break free. She felt her eyes begin to glaze over, gasped for breath and tried to reason with him – but no words came out through the tight grip on her vocal cords. As she choked and coughed she heard him persuading Duma and Vik to join him in raping her, murdering her, and dumping her body where it would never be found.

Vik sounded doubtful: "Sulpa might not like it. He told us to kill Uglies. He didn't say anything about Clan."

"Are you kidding?" Grigo laughed. "You don't know him as well as I do. He's gonna love it."

Ria had no idea what they were talking about. She'd never heard of this Sulpa guy.

Then Duma asked: "What about Hond and Rill? If they find out they'll kill us . . ."

"They won't find out," said Grigo with flat confidence. He shoved his left hand down the back of Ria's deerskin leggings and began to explore her ass and crotch. As he groped her he shifted his grip on her neck, allowing her just enough slack to reach the big sinew in the crook of his elbow and attack it with her teeth.

Grigo screamed, spraying blood and bad breath into her ear, and tried to jerk his arm free. But she clung on, biting hard, grabbed a handful of his face and tore at his flesh with her nails, seeking an eye to gouge. More oaths and bad breath. Then Grigo started punching her as well as strangling her. Her vision began to dim for a second time, but she kept on struggling until Duma and Vik pinned her legs and arms, dragging her to the ground. Finally Grigo lost his balance, all three of the hefty teenagers tumbled on top of her, and Ria thought, *Shit, I'm going to die.*

She felt as though she'd been crushed beneath an avalanche and blacked out for a moment. But as consciousness seeped back she found things were changing for the better. For a start, the weight on her chest was much less now. Duma and Vik had been lifted off her by someone and hurled in opposite directions. Then it was Grigo's turn. Descending from what seemed like a great height, she saw one of a pair of huge hairy hands seize his crotch; the other gripped his neck, and he was hoisted into the air and shaken so hard his teeth rattled.

Still on her back on the ground, Ria discovered with mixed feelings of alarm and satisfaction that what was holding Grigo aloft was a truly immense Ugly male with gigantic brow ridges – and massive yellow teeth bared in a terrifying snarl. The creature seemed poised to break Grigo's back across his knee, but for some reason he relented, tossed the teenager away and stepped over Ria to attend to the crippled Ugly youth whose rescue had got her into this mess in the first place.

Ria was calming down, taking in more and more of the scene unfolding around her. It wasn't just the big guy with the teeth. He'd brought along about sixty of his friends – *Where did they come from*? – males and females dressed in stinking, badly cured animal skin's. Some of them carried clunky wooden spears like small tree trunks hafted to huge, crudely knapped stone blades. Others were armed with clubs and axes. Several had decorated their bodies with stripes of red and white paint. One of the females wore a necklace of bat skulls.

Moans and groans from Duma, Grigo and Vik told Ria they were still alive. She would be having words about them with her brothers very soon, she thought. Or she would be if they all survived. The Uglies looked furious, which was understandable not only because they'd caught three humans hunting one of their kids but also because of all the other shitty things the Clan had done to them recently. They had a thousand reasons for a revenge attack and this was a perfect opportunity. So the only question that really mattered to Ria was . . . *had they seen her heroic and selfless rescue attempt*?

But the Uglies didn't seem interested in revenge on Duma, Grigo and Vik, or in showing any special favors to Ria for putting her life on the line for one of them. They stepped past her and gathered round the cripple in a circle, arm in arm, emitting low hooting sighs. Very soon he shook himself like a wet dog and stood up.

They made him better, thought Ria, amazed by the kid's quick recovery. But then she corrected herself: *Of course they didn't.*

Like all his kind this youth looked strong. He could probably have outrun Grigo and his posse if he hadn't been hobbled by a deformed foot, turned inwards and downwards at an unnatural angle. He was about Ria's age, perhaps a little older, and what was weird – even disturbing – was that he wasn't bad-looking. His brow ridges weren't fully formed yet and the brown eyes beneath them gazed at her with unexpected warmth and intelligence.

The Uglies were supposed to be mindless animals, like aurochs or rhinos, lacking in smarts and incapable of any of the finer emotions. But the eyes of this youth, staring at her with such urgency, were entirely human and filled with sensibilities she had no difficulty recognizing. The Clan had always believed the Uglies were too stupid to talk but with a flash of insight she understood this one was already communicating with her – somehow. She knew he was grateful to her for helping him out, for taking his side without thought of herself, and the moment she grasped this she heard a voice – not out loud but inside her head – that spoke her language and said, simply, "Thank you."

This was absolutely astonishing and strange but Ria was already convincing herself she must have imagined it when the Uglies began to move away, taking the club-footed youth with them. He shuffled along with his elders, shoulders hunched, head down, and she saw she would soon be left alone with Duma, Grigo and Vik. They were *certainly* going to finish what they had started with her.

She jumped up. "Hey, Uglies!" she shouted. "Take me with you."

Chapter Two

California today, late summer

Leoni was seventeen and no longer kept count of her lovers. A few stood out as being sensationally good, a few she remembered for being dismally bad, but most were just . . . forgettable.

Like this one bouncing up and down on top of her now. He was so forgettable she'd already forgotten him. Was he called Mort? Hmm . . . Could be. But then again, maybe he was a Michael, or a Matthew? Or perhaps his name didn't even begin with an M. Perhaps he was a John or a Jim or a Joe? Might even be a Bill or a Bob.

Whatever.

Leoni waited with barely disguised impatience for him to finish. Then she stifled a yawn, dabbed herself down with his Versace T-shirt, made her excuses and left.

He lived in a mansion with lots of complicated corridors that kept bringing her back to his bedroom like one of those nightmares where you can't escape. Then, when she found a door and stepped out into the warm Malibu night, she couldn't remember where she'd parked her blue convertible SL500. She spent several frustrating minutes pressing the remote buttons on her key until she realized the car must be at the other side of the house.

As she trudged around the massive building in her high heels she thought: *What did that bastard slip in my vodka?* She felt stupid, like her head was full of bubbles. And where was the Merc? *Beep beep.* Ah, there it was. She crawled in behind the wheel and started up the engine. Better. Much better. Now all she had to do was find her way out. She flicked the control to put the top down. *Whirr . . . hiss . . . click.* Then it was Jimmy Choos off, full beams on, right foot down on the gas, and a satisfying spinning of wheels and splatter of gravel. She drove a couple of times round the big house to get her bearings, then tore down the main driveway and pulled to a screeching halt in front of the tall iron gates that barred her exit.

Leoni was beginning to feel thwarted. All she wanted to do was go home and sleep for, like, three days. But she couldn't get out. She put her palm on the car's horn, pressed hard and revved the engine. Deafening din. Then she backed up and charged at the gates, skidding to a stop just before hitting them. She backed up and charged again. On the third attempt her lover of the night must have pressed a button somewhere because the gates swung open and she shot out onto the road in her little blue car like a cork from a bottle, weaving from left to right before regaining control.

Pacific Coast Highway coming up. With the wind in her hair, struggling to light a cigarette, Leoni executed a spectacular left turn at about a hundred miles an hour towards Santa Monica, cutting sharply across the path of a shitty-looking black-and-white Ford traveling in the opposite direction. She made eye contact with two startled faces – both male, one with a moustache – staring out at her from behind the windshield. Then she saw the seven-pointed gold star painted on the Ford's door beneath the words CALIFORNIA HIGHWAY PATROL, also in gold.

Leoni floored the gas pedal and was soon skimming along at around a hundred and forty, but in seconds the black-and-white loomed up in her rear-view mirror with its sirens blaring and its lights flashing. *Jesus, those boys had turned fast.* And their shitty Ford was *hot.* Accepting that she wasn't going to get away, Leoni cut her speed, pulled into the emergency lane and stopped. Her heart was pounding and she had stomach cramps. *Jesus*!

The officer with the moustache appeared at her side, scowled down at her and demanded to see her licence. He was in his mid-twenties, with short black hair and a Latino look, and he had a big Smith & Wesson strapped to his butt. Fumbling for her ID, Leoni spilled the contents of her purse all over the passenger seat and burst into tears to create a distraction when she saw, under the unforgiving glare of the street lights, not only her driving licence, credit cards, money, tampons, condoms and lipstick but also a dozen bulging wraps of cocaine.

"Ma'am," said the officer, "I need you to step out of the car NOW."

Her father's attorney posted bail for her in the morning and whisked her out of a side door with a blanket over her head to avoid the press and camera crews waiting at the front. By lunchtime Leoni was back in Beverly Hills, slouching in the palatial kitchen of the parental home.

She had never hated mom and dad with such intense and personal revulsion as she did right here, right now. Her flesh was actually *creeping* with disgust.

Dad was a short, stocky middle-aged guy, running to flab, wearing a ten-thousand-dollar suit and a buffed Beverly Hills tan. He had blonde hair, cut short, receding sharply at the temples, the cold blank eyes of a fraud investigator, and a long, suspicious nose that didn't seem to belong on the same face as his wet, fleshy, very red lips. He was a bully, the loudest voice in the room, but this morning his wife was doing all the talking and he stood near the door searching his teeth with his tongue as though trying to dig out morsels of food.

Mom was the taller of the two by four inches, skinny, hatchet-faced and mean as a rattlesnake. "We've been fielding calls all morning from the rival channels and press," she spat at Leoni. "Even the *National Enquirer*, for Christ's sake." She mimicked the headlines: "MEDIA TYCOON'S RICH-BITCH DAUGHTER ON BAIL AFTER NIGHT OF DRUGS AND BOOZE." Her upper lip trembled. Tears spilled through her eye make-up: "You've shamed us again" she yelled, spraying spit. "Shamed your father. Shamed me. Worst of all, you've shamed your brother in his first week in middle school" – she was triumphant now she'd managed to bring Adam the miracle child into the conversation – "and I'll never forgive you for that."

It was a big deal that Adam had skipped a grade and moved up to middle school. The precocious brat had just turned ten, making him more than a year younger than most of his classmates, and his brilliant performance was in stark contrast with his big sister's drop-out academic status – as her mother liked to remind her. "Everything comes down to Adam for you, doesn't it?" Leoni sobbed. "Adam this. Adam that. It's always about Adam. Never, ever, *ever* about me."

But Mom yelled right back: "What do you mean, it's never about you? You selfish little bitch. I JUST DON'T GET IT. Haven't we always given you everything you've ever wanted?"

You didn't even give birth to me, Leoni wanted to say, *so how would you know*? Part of her really wanted to get into all the big hurtful issues . . .

(*right now*).

But she still wasn't sure if what she thought had happened to her was real or imagined.

"Look," she said finally, "I'm sorry, OK? This is a difficult time for me. I'm adjusting. Dealing with a whole lot . . . I haven't felt right about . . . *anything* for, like, the whole of this *year* . . ."

"Well, let's see how you adjust to having no car." Mom cut her short. "And no allowance. And how about we don't pay for an attorney to represent you when this gets to court? I guess the state can provide one for you. Some kid, fresh out of law school, still wet behind the ears, who won't be able to keep you out of jail. THIS TIME YOU EARNED IT, YOUNG LADY."

This time you earned it, young lady. What a jerk, Leoni, thought, *what a jerk you are, Mom.* Her self-control broke. She uttered a short high-pitched scream at the top of her voice, ran from the kitchen, colliding with her father on the way out, knocked over a lamp stand in the hall, pounded up the stairs to her bedroom and slammed the door so hard behind her that two of its wooden panels cracked and flakes of white paint showered to the floor. She stalked forward, snatched up her sketch pad and Magic Marker from the bedside table and with stabbing, slashing strokes scribbled a cartoon featuring her mother being mounted by a donkey. Then she tore the drawing into confetti and collapsed on the big pillow-strewn bed sobbing, feeling like a three-year-old throwing a tantrum. Why was it that Mom always managed to reduce her to this?

Five minutes later Leoni was still so angry she was shaking. But then she remembered she had just the thing. Kicking off her shoes she padded across the room to her underwear drawer and fumbled around in it for a rolled-up sock she kept way at the back. She could just make out her parents' voices down in the kitchen, faint and indistinct. They were shouting about something. Probably about what they were going to do with her. She retrieved the sock, unrolled it, and counted out five white OxyContin pills stolen, amongst other goodies, from her mother's drugstore-sized stash of legal prescription highs.

Leoni had not used OxyContin before but she had heard good things about it, excellent things, and now seemed like the time. The pills were ten milligrams each. Were five too many? Too few? She'd seen her friend Billy, crystal-meth addict and heir to a billion-dollar fortune, knock back a big blue hundred-and-sixty-milligram torpedo of OxyContin and suffer no obvious ill effects – so a teensy fifty milligrams wasn't going to do her any harm, was it? And did she actually care if it did? On impulse she upped the dose to eighty milligrams and then remembered Billy's advice that the effects could be intensified by crushing the pills and snorting the powder. Snorting was definitely something Leoni knew how to do.

With much effort and impatience, using the end of a steel nail file, she ground the eight pills down to a fine powder. Then she rolled up a hundred-dollar bill and took a gigantic sniff. Hmm. Not bad. Instant rush. Leoni snuffled up the rest of the powder and lay back on her bed to enjoy the euphoric glow suffusing her whole body. God, this was better than sex. Her mind drifted. At first she felt like she was submerged in a pool of warm jelly. But soon she started to shiver and her skin turned cold and clammy. The room seemed to be spinning round and something was suffocating her.

She tried to get off the bed, shuffle towards the door, call for help, but she couldn't coordinate her movements and fell to the floor. The sense of being smothered worsened until Leoni could no longer draw breath and slipped into deathly unconsciousness.

Chapter Three

Ria had no intention of staying with the Uglies a moment longer than necessary. She wanted to put a safe distance between herself and Grigo, Duma and Vik. After that it would be goodbye to her big hairy yellow-toothed protectors, a tough hike through the backcountry, and then hello again to the safety of the Clan and the righteous vengeance her badass brothers Hond and Rill would soon be meting out.

She was still shaking with anger and shock at how close she'd come to being raped and murdered.

But there was something else. The three youths, Grigo in particular, were renowned assholes. Even so, their behavior had been strange. There were few grown men in the Clan, let alone untested boys like these, who would risk the anger of Ria's lean and lethal elder brothers. So what had changed?

She guessed it was their connection with "Sulpa" that was making them stronger. And for some reason this Sulpa wanted them to torture and kill Uglies.

It was an idea that seemed to be catching on. Since the beginning of summer a powerful faction of the council of braves, led by Grigo's father Murgh, had been hunting the Uglies like wild animals, slaughtering whole families at a time, inflicting terrible tortures on those they captured alive, driving them out of their ancestral hunting grounds.

But none of Murgh's bullies, nor anyone else in the Clan, was called "Sulpa." The name had a suspicious alien ring to it. Ria decided it must belong to an outlander.

Why were Grigo, Duma and Vik taking orders from an outlander? They'd spoken about him in fawning and awestruck tones. Vik had sounded afraid of him, and Grigo had proudly claimed to know him better than the other two.

Why were they all so impressed?

Why would Sulpa have "loved it" if they'd succeeded in raping and murdering her?

The whole thing gave Ria the creeps.

The Uglies lumbered forward at a good pace. The males were so heavily muscled their bodies bulged like rhino skins stuffed with large, irregular rocks. The females were almost indistinguishable from them in size and general appearance but, if anything, even more hideous and disgusting to look at. In recent years the sorry creatures had begun to imitate the dark eye paint and red-ocher lipstick used by Clan women of childbearing age – accessories that Ria herself had worn since her first menstruation three years before. But Ugly females just weren't designed for make-up.

Still, their misplaced effort at self-beautification was interesting. Like the fiercely intelligent and strangely human expression in the eyes of the boy she had saved, the amateurishly applied make-up of the women – seen now in close-up for the first time – had a most unexpected effect on Ria. She found herself feeling sorry for the Uglies, identifying with them somehow, and realizing again in a very direct and immediate way that they couldn't possibly just be dumb mindless animals. *They walk on two legs, just like we do,* she reflected. They have hands with five fingers, feet with five toes. They have ears like ours, eyes like ours. *Just like ours.* The mothers hold their babies to their breasts to feed them, just like we do. They use tools and weapons just like we do – even if most of their stuff is crap.

On the other hand, no matter how well-disposed she was feeling towards them, there were differences that were hard to ignore. Ria glanced about, absorbing details of the Uglies who had surrounded her on the march. For starters those famous brow ridges of theirs were . . . well . . . not very human. They had almost no chins and their heads, which lolled forward, seemed to sprout directly from their hefty shoulders. There were matted patches of coarse red hair all over their bodies, which gave them a mangy look. Also, they *smelled* like shit.

Just then Ria became aware of a new presence limping along by her side – the Ugly youth with the club foot. He was looking at her with something like devotion and again, as their eyes met, she was shocked to hear a voice inside her head, clear like a mountain stream, speaking her language. What it said this time was: "Protect you . . . Protect . . . Ria . . . I will protect Ria."

So it hadn't been her imagination before. The kid's lips hadn't moved, but she knew, totally knew, that it was his voice she'd heard – that he had somehow figured out a way to talk to her inside her head. Like seeing the sun rise in the west or a river run uphill, this was so surprising it made her dizzy.

"How come you know my name? she asked, feeling spooked. "And, by the way, sorry that I have to speak out loud like normal humans." She rallied: "You heard Duma call me Ria, didn't you? That's how you know my name."

The reply inside her head was instant: "Don't need words of Duma. I *know* your name. Without speak, I know your thoughts. There is a rope between us, you and me. From now, always, I will protect you. You are my . . . sister."

"I already have enough brothers, thank you very much. What's this about a rope between us? And – hang on a minute – did you just say you know my thoughts?"

"Uglies are mangy. Smell like shit. Weapons crap. Can't wear make-up."

Ria gasped: "Oh. I see. So there's no privacy, then? Doesn't matter if I speak or not? Every random thought that crosses my mind I have to share with you? Is that how things work with you guys?"

"When we have a rope between us we can share," Ria heard inside her head. "Share feelings, thoughts, pictures. Clan has words. We listen. Learn your words, but don't like. Clan people speak: '*blah bar, blah bar, blah, blah, blah*' . . . Say one thing, mean another. We can't do spooky speaking out loud like Clan." As though to emphasize this point the kid opened his mouth – like his elders he obviously hadn't cleaned his teeth since the day he was born – and emitted a low grunt followed by a hoot, which he repeated several times: "*Rugh . . . agh . . . Rugh . . . agh . . . Rugh . . . agh . . .*"

What was this? What was *Rugh . . . agh*? With a stifled giggle Ria got it. The Ugly youth was trying – and failing – to speak her name, even though, inside her head, he could already say it perfectly. Now he pointed to his throat – or at least to where his throat would've been if he'd had a neck – and grunted some incomprehensible gibberish that sounded like a wild animal chewing stones.

"OK," said Ria, "I get it. You actually *can't* speak. Your throats won't make words. So you get straight inside each other's heads instead. Cool trick. Wish I could do it. Must save a lot of time."

"Can hurt," came back the kid's thought-voice. "What's inside other's heads can hurt."

Ria nodded in immediate agreement: "I expect it can. I don't think I'd have many friends left if they knew what I was thinking about them all the time. Now listen . . . You know my name, so you should tell me yours. Fair?"

"Is difficult."

"What's difficult?"

"My name. For you will be difficult."

"Go on . . . Don't be shy."

"Brindle-phudge-tublo-trungen-apciprona."

"Ah. I see what you mean. Would you mind saying it again? I'm sure I'll get used to it."

"Brindle-phudge-tublo-trungen-apciprona."

"OK. Brindle it is, then."

Ria looked back over her shoulder. The entrance to the valley could no longer be seen and they were climbing the slope of another of the many low hills characteristic of this area. Once they were over the summit and down the other side, she calculated, Grigo, Duma and Vik would be far enough behind for her to outrun them.

Brindle's voice invaded her head again: "You will run? Not such a good idea. Boys who hunt will hunt you. Better you stay with us this night. Maybe tomorrow go back to Clan."

You must be joking, thought Ria.

"Not joking. This night you stay with Uglies. Be safe." And with the thought of safety came pictures and sensations – cave walls, something cooking within a flickering fire, a musky aroma of woodsmoke and roasting venison, a ledge with thick, warm furs spread over it that seemed to invite her to sleep.

"NO!" Ria yelled at the top of her voice, causing Brindle to flinch and the other Uglies nearby to grunt and hoot. "YOU MUST BE JOKING, OK? NO WAY AM I GOING TO STAY WITH YOU. NOT TONIGHT. NOT EVER." Suddenly she broke to her left, shouldered past a couple of hefty females and, her heart pounding, sprinted towards the summit of the hill. None of the Uglies pursued her, which was good. In fact, with the exception of Brindle whose exclamations of alarm rang like bird calls inside her head, the rest of the group showed no interest in her departure and just continued to plod ahead.

Soon Ria reached a big boulder just below the summit where she paused for breath. She looked back with a sense of triumph at the column of Uglies now two hundred paces below her. *Phew. What a relief.* For a moment she'd been certain they meant to keep her prisoner. Or that Brindle did.

Not prisoner, came Brindle's thought-voice. *Never prisoner*!

Ria shrugged. *Fuck this.* She was out of here. She scrambled the last few paces through thick gorse and bracken to the summit.

What she was expecting was a long downhill run to freedom. Instead, thirty paces below her, on the other side of the hill, hidden from view until now, she saw Duma, Grigo and Vik, climbing hard, with clubs in their hands.

Grigo had a glint in his eye. "Hello, Ria," he gloated. "Ready for your gang-bang?"

Chapter Four

Leoni was hovering in her bedroom, close to the ceiling, like one of those helium-filled party balloons. Hmm . . . There were cobwebs up here that Conchita must have missed when she cleaned yesterday. Left dangling amidst threads of dust and lint, a fat black spider and half a dozen paralyzed bugs swayed back and forth in the gentle afternoon breeze that drifted in through the open picture window. Avoiding the wildlife, Leoni tried to brush the webs away with her fingers but couldn't do it. Her hands just seemed to pass through them. Poor Conchita was going to get her ass fired when Mom noticed this mess.

In a detached way, and without fear, Leoni knew that something odd was happening to her but didn't want to deal with it right now. Then she looked down and . . . *Oh . . . my . . . God*! There on the floor was her body, sprawled like roadkill, coke-snorter's nose buried deep in the thick pile carpet, skirt hitched up over her left butt cheek. On the table beside her bed was a glossy magazine dotted with a few telltale flecks of OxyContin powder – so she hadn't got it all, then – a steel nail file and a rolled-up hundred-dollar bill. Might as well have a sign on the door saying "DRUG ABUSER LIVES HERE," she thought.

She zoomed down for a closer look at . . . herself. Was she dead? In a coma? The questions weren't urgent and Leoni was surprised to discover how little she actually cared about the fate of this prone, intimately familiar and yet somehow alien body which seemed reduced already to skin and bones, meat and offal. Besides – and this was totally fucked-up – she had some other kind of body now. She had transparent hands that could not sweep away cobwebs. She could see her limbs, feet and flesh but they were not solid. Overall there was a strange sort of diaphanous insubstantiality about her – an aerial quality, as buoyant and ephemeral as a glistening soap bubble. She found nothing threatening or fearful in this. Quite the opposite. She felt she was floating on a wave of light and joy.

Still, surely she must summon help? While there was even the faintest hope, surely she couldn't just let her meat body expire? Could she? And what would happen to her aerial body if she did? Perhaps she would just go *pop*! and disappear?

With that thought Leoni floated up and out of the bedroom window, down into the sunlit garden and through the open French doors into the kitchen where her parents' shouting match had ceased. Now they were seated at the table in their usual positions, Mom at the head, Dad at the side to her right, talking in lowered, serious voices.

"Listen, guys," Leoni told them, "I'm dying upstairs. You've got to get me to a hospital right now."

They paid no attention.

"Dad!" She reached out to shake his arm, but it was as though her fingers had closed on air. She made a grab for Mom and was able to push her hand right through her chest and through the back of the chair behind her.

Fucked *up*!

Leoni ascended and hovered over the middle of the table, looking down at the two of them. They seemed uglier than usual, like Komodo dragons in human masks, and their whispers had harsh, sinister undertones. She felt a mild but insistent force tug at her. She surrendered, and began to drift towards the garden, when her father said something that drew her right back: "Leoni's putting us at risk. Pretty soon she's going to blurt it all out to some reporter."

"My daddy made sex with me," Mom mimicked in a high-pitched childish tone before adding, in her own voice: "Little bitch. It's going to hurt the business."

"We drove her to this." Just for an instant Dad sounded remorseful until Mom butted in with a fervent look in her eye: "It's what Jack wanted," she said.

"Exactly," Dad replied, brightening. "It's what Jack wanted."

"He delivered his side of the bargain," Mom said. "We delivered ours. Now it's time to clear up the dead wood."

Leoni's mind reeled. She'd been plagued with doubts for years about the sick things she remembered her dad doing to her in two widely separated episodes of sustained attacks during her childhood.

Had any of it happened?

She'd so much wanted to believe it was just mad sexual nightmares and her imagination running wild, as Dad had told her again and again, but now here was Mom seeming to confirm that it had all been real – and that she'd been raped because that was what some guy called Jack wanted.

So who was Jack?

And what did Mom mean about clearing up the dead wood?

As Leoni struggled to find answers, the force pulling on her aerial body grew stronger – much stronger. For an instant it was like riding the lead car of the roller coaster at Santa Monica Pier, only a thousand times faster, plunging and soaring through vast domains of sky until – *WHOOMF*! – she was back in her bedroom again, hovering directly over her meat and bones. There was someone else on top of her as well – Conchita! She'd come back with a broom to dust the cobwebs – screaming for help between bouts of mouth-to-mouth resuscitation.

With a hair-raising plunge of the roller coaster Leoni drew a huge gasping breath and was impelled back into her body. The last thing she heard before she lost consciousness was Conchita dialing 911.

Then Leoni was hovering at ceiling height again but not in her bedroom. This was more like it. They'd got her to a hospital at last. It looked like an operating room with lots of sexy male doctors in green scrubs scurrying around. And in the middle of all the action, stretched out on a gurney, hooked up to an amazing array of tubes, wires and bags, was Leoni's poor pale body.

The docs were working at a frantic pace, doing things to her, and all of it was mildly interesting, of course. Then . . . what was this? Mad panic all round. Shouted commands. Whine of an electric-shock machine charging up. Looked like her heart had stopped. Over on the array of monitors Leoni could see the flat line on the ECG, heard the high-pitched buzz of the alarm and became aware again of that powerful gravitational compulsion that had drawn her back into her body earlier – only this time it seemed to be pulling her in the opposite direction, away from herself and into a staggering and awe-inspiring vortex of light that opened, like a tunnel, at her side. She just had time to think . . .

(*Oh . . . my . . . God! This is really interesting.*)

. . . when she found she was already inside the revolving tunnel and floating through it.

At intervals its walls were marked with large geometric grids, something like windows with multiple panes, in each of which faint images of people and places glowed.

Leoni was able to slow her forward motion to examine the images and discovered that if she concentrated on them they first sharpened and then dissolved into vivid memories.

Except the image she was concentrating on now couldn't be a memory because nobody could remember what happened to them when they were only a few hours old. Could they?

Instead, the panel showed her a scene that she had tried to imagine all her life, but somehow it was now infused with all the solidity and shadow of an observed event.

It is night. Rain spits down. A single street light casts its orange glow into a mean alley. The alley is closed at one end by a high brick wall topped with jagged shards of glass. A barred and rusted iron door is set into the wall and piled on either side are heaps of bulging plastic trash bags, slick with rain. A young woman, blonde, pale, a livid bruise on her cheek, dark circles under her eyes, slips into the alley. Furtive, she looks back over her shoulder as though she fears she is being followed or observed. Dangling from her hand is a black plastic bag containing some small object and now, with further hunted glances, she places it amongst the rest of the trash and hurries off without a backward glance. The bag is not tied closed, merely gathered at the top, and as the woman's footfalls echo away something stirs within it and utters a feeble cry. The bag flops open and rain leaks onto the wrinkled face and blue eyes of a newborn babe.

The babe, Leoni knew, was herself.

The child nobody wanted.

In the next panel she had reached two years of age. She was wearing a little print dress and was seated on the floor looking up at a TV set in a Los Angeles orphanage where all her first clear memories began.

Here she was at three, out for the day with a family, hoping they might adopt her. She so much wanted to live in a real house, with toys that were hers and with real parents. But it didn't happen.

Another panel, another visit, another rejection. The child nobody wanted.

Now she was nearly five, quiet, withdrawn, friendless amidst the crowd of other children. She sat alone with a crayon and a sketch pad. She always loved to draw.

The next panel showed her big moment, a few months later when, after a sudden rush of interest, she was adopted by Herman and Madeleine Watts. They weren't rich – the meteoric rise of Dad's business began right after Leoni's adoption – but she remembered how the house they'd lived in then in East Hollywood had felt to her like a fairy-tale palace.

Here she was at seven in their first Beverly Hills home, her best year. Mom and Dad must have wanted her otherwise they wouldn't have adopted her. Would they? They gave her so much. A tree house. All the pets in the world. A little car with a real engine to drive around the grounds. Closets full of clothes. Make-up. Zillions of pairs of shoes. She felt like Cinderella at the ball.

Now she was eight, the beginning of the bad times. She was asleep in bed in her cozy room. Suddenly someone grabbed her hair, jerking and shaking her, and she awoke with a scream. It was Dad. He had no clothes on. In the glow of the night light his eyes were blank as stones as he clambered on top of her, still gripping hold of her hair. She struggled, screamed – "*What's happening? What's happening? Dad? No!*" – and he cuffed her face hard with his free hand, making her head spin. He was heavy. He sprawled over her, forced his knee between her legs and groped her. She screamed again – "*Mom! Mom! Mom!*" – very loud.

But Mom didn't come to her rescue. She didn't come once during that whole year of terrifying night-time visits.

Now Leoni was nine. She was in the car with Dad. He was explaining to her that the rapes had never happened, and at some level she did believe they were just bad dreams and her imagination. The other problem – the damage to her body – was because she went a little crazy sometimes and hurt herself in her private parts.

In the next panel she was ten, on a family day out with her parents. Adam, their own biological child (they called him the "miracle child" because of Madeleine's previous infertility) was celebrating his second birthday. As she reviewed the scene Leoni experienced again the pangs of envy and hatred she had felt that day at the way Mom doted on Adam, giving him all her attention, and was cold and neglectful towards her.

Now she was eleven. There had been no more rapes. Or dreams. She was in the schoolyard, mercilessly bullying poor Janet Lithgo, a smaller girl with a hair lip who later committed suicide.

Now Leoni was twelve. The bad times were back. She saw herself lying in her bed, as though paralyzed, with her dad's body, sweaty, face averted, humping away on top of her.

(*"It's what Jack wanted."*)

There had been thirty rapes that year and she hadn't screamed. Not once. She just shut her eyes and let them happen, did any positions he wanted, and never complained. It didn't hurt so much that way and while he was inside her she just pulled herself out of her body the way the Blue Angel had taught her.

The Blue Angel, who started to visit her in dreams around that time.

Her secret friend who she never talked about.

Not to anyone.

Just the way she never talked about what her dad did to her.

In the next panel she was fourteen, on a shopping spree in Rodeo Drive. Mom and Dad had been showering possessions and money on her, she hadn't been raped for nearly two years and there had been no more dreams.

Here she was at fifteen, naked, down on her hands and knees in a big bathroom at a party. Five guys she didn't know were taking turns to screw her.

Now she was sixteen, on the floor of some other bathroom, sniffing up lines of cocaine, her nostrils red and her eyes stinging.

And finally here she was at seventeen, overdosing on Oxycontin in her bedroom . . .

Leoni could still see the operating room behind, and sense the rush and chaos surrounding the body on the gurney in there; but all that was fading . . . fading. Ahead, getting closer, the other end of the tunnel was filled with an illuminated swirling fog through which tantalizing vistas of green sunlit meadows dotted with trees appeared and vanished again.

Looks good, Leoni couldn't help thinking. *Is it heaven?*

Then the figure of a woman materialized out of the fog filling the mouth of the tunnel, a tall, very beautiful woman, beckoning to her, surrounded by a cascade of white robes – a smiling woman with jet-black hair and indigo skin whose face was hauntingly familiar like an old friend not seen for many years.

The walls of the tunnel dissolved, full remembrance dawned, and Leoni found herself in the presence of the mysterious being she called the Blue Angel. They were standing barefoot on grass wet with dew, in the midst of a vast meadow. A herd of strange animals unlike any she had ever seen before grazed in the shadows of a nearby clump of trees and there were two suns in the sky, one almost at the zenith, one low down towards the horizon.

"Where are we?" asked Leoni.

"This is the land where everything is known," replied the woman. "Shall we walk a bit?"

Chapter Five

Ria skidded to a halt on a patch of scree at the summit and in the blink of an eye had hefted two good throwing rocks. She hurled the first at Grigo, now just twenty paces below her, and saw it strike the middle of his forehead, felling him like a speared bison. The second rock glanced off Duma's right ear. It reamed out a chunk of cartilage but he was still coming at her. Then Vik was upon her in a full charge, catching her with his hefty shoulder and sending her sprawling into a thorn bush.

An urgent whisper from Duma: "Hey, Vik! Behind you! Uglies!"

Morons, Ria thought. *Shit for brains.* Hadn't they even considered the possibility that the Uglies might still be close? Struggling to free herself from the thorns, she enjoyed a comic moment as Vik's jaw dropped and Duma turned around and fled down the hill in the direction he had come from, pursued by two enormous braves from the Ugly column. They caught him in less than fifty paces. One reached out and pinched his torn right ear, then dragged him back by it, squealing and protesting, to the top of the hill. Vik had been knocked to his knees by a third big male. A fourth menaced Grigo as he regained consciousness.

Assholes.

"Definitely assholes," agreed Brindle's thought-voice. Together with the rest of the Uglies he had scrambled up to the summit. Now he limped over to stand beside Ria and sent her a vivid image of herself running away from the column: "Protect you. Told you I would."

Ria was getting used to not having to speak aloud. Because she and Brindle had a "rope" between them – whatever that meant – she could simply think and he would know. She tried it out: "OK, so I guess that makes us even . . ."

"Can never be even. What you did before, fought the hunter boys, saved my life – that was . . . magnificent. You are hero. Brindle useless cripple. Can't fight. Just tell braves to help you."

"You mean if you hadn't told them they wouldn't have helped?"

"No. Why help? No rope between them and you. And you ran away from us. Your decision – so Uglies think: better stay out of it. Better not get mixed up with Clan." Pictures exploded in Ria's mind of the massacres, tortures, thefts, burnings, beatings and insults that Murgh's followers had recently been inflicting on the Uglies – the whole range of ruthless techniques used to annex their traditional hunting grounds. With the pictures came a huge wave of sadness and loss and Ria understood in a flash that Clan braves had killed Brindle's mother, brother and sister just two moons before, catching them in the open while they trekked from a distant camp. With more images he showed her that almost every one of the sixty or so Uglies now gathered round the hilltop had suffered similar losses.

It made sense to stay out of the Clan's way. It made sense to avoid getting mixed up in Clan business. But now, with Grigo, Duma and Vik on their hands, the Uglies were mixed up with the Clan whether they liked it or not. "What's going to happen to them?" she asked Brindle.

"Feels like problem."

"Will they be killed?"

"Clan are people like us. Are spirits . . . like us. Better let them go . . ."

"If it was the other way round and the Clan had captured three Uglies who'd been hunting one of our boys, we wouldn't hesitate. We'd kill you guys on the spot. Without mercy . . ."

Brindle looked pained and, for a few heartbeats, Ria received nothing from him at all: no words, no feelings, no emotions. Then, very still, serious and emphatic, his thought-voice was back inside her head: "Uglies would *not* hunt one of you. Uglies are not Clan. Don't kill if don't have to. Never kill for fun."

Ria wasn't impressed. "If you let them go," she said, "they'll just follow us and grab me again as soon as I'm on my own."

"We are going to Secret Place. Half-day march from here. Many of us hiding there now since Clan started to attack us. Not only for your sake but for our sake also we must not be followed there."

The four braves guarding Grigo, Duma, and Vik stayed on duty. The rest, including Brindle, gathered into a tightly packed circle nearby and began to hoot. Coming from these massive, stinking brutes in their ragged skins it was a weird and eerie sound, halfway between an owl call and the cough of a mountain lion, that sent chills up Ria's spine.

She wondered what purpose it could serve for them when they already had the power to see into each others' minds.

She was also curious about Brindle. He described himself as a useless cripple yet he was respected by the other Uglies, including the toughest braves. It seemed that when he told them to do something – like rescue her – they obeyed. In Clan society gimps got no respect at all and certainly didn't give orders. In fact, most of them didn't even live past the age of five.

As suddenly as it had started, the chanting stopped, the scrum broke up, and Duma, Grigo and Vik were prodded to their feet. A brave wearing a reindeer-skin backpack walked over to them, took off the pack and pulled out a big coil of fine flexible rope woven from grass fibers. Lengths of the rope were cut and used to tie the three scowling youths' wrists tight together behind their backs, and then to bind their legs equally tight at the ankles – Vik's right to Grigo's left and Grigo's right to Duma's left. Only Vik's left leg and Duma's right leg remained untied and free to move. Grigo was in the middle, hobbled on both sides.

Ria stood close to them on the hilltop, picking thorns out of her leggings and jerkin and feeling spiteful. After what they'd tried to do to her she had no pity for them. As Brindle walked over to join her again she asked: "So is this the plan? Just tie them up?"

"Yes. Not perfect, but better idea than killing them. This way they cannot follow us and we'll make it to Secret Place before they can get back to Clan . . ."

The three-bodied man that Duma, Grigo and Vik had become began an awkward shuffle away from the Uglies. When no one stopped them they seemed to take heart and tried to move faster, cursing and complaining with every tottering hop and skip, but they lost their balance and fell over in a tangle of limbs and profanities. Vix's fat ass ended up in Grigo's lap, pinning him to the ground.

Ria giggled and yelled: "Hey, Grigo, I know you guys like each other a lot, but please, go behind a tree or something . . ."

With a grunt Grigo shoved Vik aside and forced Duma into a painful contortion so that all three of them could stand. Grigo's face was flushed with anger and exertion, his lips split and bruised, his teeth broken, his forehead bloody. "I'm going to kill you, Ria," he hissed through the wreckage of his mouth. "The next time I see you you're dead."

"Big words, Grigo. Only maybe it won't be me who gets killed the next time you see me." She whipped back her arm as though about to throw another rock at him and he cowered.

"See that, Vik?" Ria couldn't resist gloating. "See that, Duma? Your lord and master is afraid of my empty hand." She held up her hand to them, palm outward, fingers extended, and Grigo glared at her with such an intensification of hatred that she knew she'd made an enemy for life.

"Who's Sulpa?" she asked suddenly, hoping to catch him off balance.

A sly look crept over Grigo's face, but he said nothing and when Duma started to speak he silenced him with a snarl.

Chapter Six

Leoni walked in silence for some minutes, just looking around at the peculiar wildlife, trees and scenery, trying to understand what had happened to her, and sneaking glimpses out of the corner of her eye at the Blue Angel walking by her side.

Before, when she had come to her in dreams – and that had not happened for many years – the Angel had been a motherly, gentle, and reassuring presence, with just a hint of some great power held in reserve. On her first visits she had been winged, like the angels painted on the ceilings of Italian churches, and sometimes golden stars had spangled her body. But as Leoni encountered her more often she came to look more and more as she did today – a splendid, imposing but wingless woman.

In dreams, though, it had been as if Leoni were seeing her through a soft filter, or twenty feet of water, whereas now she was revealed in a brilliant radiance and glory, terrible as an army with banners.

Her indigo skin was the color of earth's oceans seen from space. Nobody had skin like that.

Then there was her incredible charismatic presence. She was six feet tall, maybe a little more, and she was dressed in figure-hugging robes that seemed to have been sewn from incandescent threads of white metal. Her jet-black hair had a wild satiny sheen and hung thick and straight to below her waist.

She was beautiful in a spectacular and ethereal way, with the high cheekbones, large heavy-lidded almond eyes, arching eyebrows, fine straight nose, full sensual lips, delicate chin, and long elegant neck of an Ancient Egyptian goddess.

Leoni was doing her best to act nonchalant but inside she was freaking – and it wasn't just because of the Blue Angel.

Everything she could see around her – absolutely everything – was utterly strange and weird.

First problem: wherever this was . . .

(*the land where everything is known?*)

. . . it certainly wasn't Planet Earth.

There were two suns, for fuck's sake.

Second problem: what was the deal with those animals – there seemed to be about twenty of them – grazing close to the trees? They looked very much like a herd of cows. They were cow-sized. They had udders like cows – one was even suckling a calf. And they had leathery hides. But they also had six legs, stubby wings folded up over their backs, and heads like beetles.

Third problem: were those really trees? From some angles they looked more like a dozen tall spindly birds that had disguised themselves as trees with elaborate contortions of wings and leafy feathers. Every now and then Leoni got the sense they were inching closer to the grazing cow-beetles.

Fourth problem: what the cow-beetles were grazing on – and she was walking on – was not dew-sprinkled grass, as she had supposed, but a carpet of little green flowers into which she sank up to her ankles with each step. The flowers were wet because they exuded fragrant sap when pressed down underfoot and, although there was no breeze, the surface of the whole mass of them, as far as the eye could see, rippled and undulated in a beautiful yet somehow disconcerting manner.

Fifth problem: feeling all these things, seeing and experiencing all these things, was she herself alive or dead? Back at home after her OxyContin overdose, later in the emergency room, and passing through the tunnel of light, Leoni had felt as though she had acquired some sort of transparent and insubstantial aerial body – and, accompanying it, a certain inexplicable joy of freedom. But here things were different. Every sense told her she was in a body of flesh again, weighed down by gravity, no longer a creature of the air. She was wearing a sleeveless knee-length tunic of rough plain cloth, knotted at the waist with rope. She couldn't remember putting this garment on, so where had it come from? Some place with no style was the only thing that could be said for sure.

"You used to come to me," Leoni told the Angel. She realized it sounded like an accusation. "You saved my life that year, when I was twelve . . ."

"When your father was raping you . . ."

"I think I would have gone mad if you hadn't been there. But then you never came back." Leoni couldn't keep the hurt out of her voice. "Why didn't you come back?"

"I couldn't reach you any more. Your parents suppressed your ability to leave your earthly body."

"But you've reached me now . . ."

"Because you have left your earthly body again. In fact, Leoni, as things presently stand, that body is dead . . ."

"Dead?"

"Dead," the Angel repeated. Her expression changed, becoming stern and forbidding. "To be born in the human form is a precious gift, and you have squandered it. Even though it is not your time. Even though I have a purpose for you to fulfill." Her beautiful features softened a little and there was a note of disappointment in her voice: "I had such plans for you, Leoni, and now they hang in the balance. Doctors are trying to restart your heart. If they have the skill to revive you, and if your own will is strong, then you may return to the land of the living. If they cannot do so, or if your will is weak, then I am here to guide you onwards . . ."

Leoni felt blind panic overtaking her, making her want to scream and stamp her feet. "I'M NOT READY TO BE GUIDED ONWARDS," she shouted. "I don't even want to *hear* about onwards! My will is strong and it isn't my time, OK? You said it. I have things to do. Please, lady, if you're really an angel I'm begging you – PLEASE send me back."

As though Leoni's wish were a signal, there came a peal of thunder out of the clear sky and two things happened.

First, one of the trees under which the cow-beetles were grazing became animated and bent double. The scissor blades of a huge beak revealed themselves amidst the camouflage of leaflike feathers, and the suckling calf was seized from beside its mother and lifted high into the air, mewling and bleating. The beak tilted skywards and closed with a loud *clack*. Two of the calf's six legs were severed and fell to the ground, spouting a clear fluid, its body disappeared with a gulping sound into the open maw of the monstrous predator, and the twenty cow-beetles, bellowing in terror, stampeded towards the horizon.

The second thing that happened was that the whirling tunnel of light that had brought Leoni to this strange and scary place reopened right beside her and she felt herself being drawn towards it. The Blue Angel held up one hand in salutation: "Well done," she said. "You're going back." Her expression became urgent: "But I must see you again. Make the veil between worlds thin and I'll show you Jack."

Jack!

Leoni was inside the mouth of the tunnel now and being pulled through it. "How do I make the veil between worlds thin?" she yelled.

"Ask your doctor," came the faint answer. Then Leoni was swept away and the Angel was gone.

The return journey through the tunnel was much faster than the outbound trip. In fact, it was a bit like being flushed down a gigantic toilet. After some final nauseating swirls and a long drop through empty space, Leoni found herself back in the emergency room, hovering near the ceiling, as light and transparent as a soap bubble once again. Her first thought was that this was so much better than being marooned in a world with horrible tree-sized birds of prey, and she was filled with an ineffable sense of joy and a tremendous surge of light and restless energy.

A quick glance at the monitors. *Hooray.* Her ECG wasn't flatlining any more. The docs were still working on her, though. Hmm, one of them – in his mid-thirties, *really* good-looking – was charging up the paddles of the electric-shock machine . . . *Wham*! As her meat body writhed and jumped she sensed its breath and warmth and felt its pain.

Leoni recoiled in surprise and flew straight through the wall of the emergency room, down a maze of corridors, and found herself in what seemed to be the main reception area of the hospital. There she dodged behind the desk, obeying an irrational desire to hide, and floated a few inches above the floor. She noticed that the receptionist, a model of efficiency in a severe charcoal business suit, was wearing incongruous orange sneakers with striped purple and green laces.

Whoomf! The doc must have zapped her with the paddles a second time and she was impelled back to the emergency room where she hovered right over her body.

She could hear the high-pitched tone of the electric-shock generator charging up and then *wham*! – another painful jolt – and she was back inside her body, like a fish returning to water.

Her eyes fluttered open. "Hello, Leoni," she heard the doctor saying. "Welcome back to the land of the living."

She examined his face and tried to speak, but her voice was slurred, as though she were drunk. She tried again: "The land of the living?"

The doctor's soft brown eyes turned quizzical: "Yes?"

She was bone weary. "You're not going to believe me," she said, "but five minutes ago I met an angel who called it the exact same thing."

Chapter Seven

As Grigo, Duma and Vik continued their slow and undignified descent of the hill, the Uglies lost interest in them, reassembled and resumed their march. Ria followed Brindle as he shuffled over to join the column and fell into step beside him.

She had no particular plan. Probably she'd head home soon. She just needed to think a few things through first.

She glanced at the huge shambling creatures marching all around her. They'd been heading roughly west and continued to do so at a faster and more urgent pace than before. Now it was obvious who the leader was – the giant yellow-toothed male who had rescued her in the valley. His gray hair and grizzled white beard marked him out as an elder, although he had the knotted muscles of a brave in his prime. He radiated fierce physical power but it was coupled with the same gentleness and delicacy of manner she'd found in Brindle.

Ria decided the Uglies made a poor first impression because of how they looked and smelled. But, once you saw past that, they were, in fact, quite amazing.

She'd never paid much attention to the outlandish claims put about by Murgh's faction. She knew from her own (very infrequent) encounters with Uglies on her – very frequent – rabbit-hunting trips that there weren't many of them around. Certainly not thousands of them as Murgh claimed. She knew they weren't wiping out all the game. She had never known them to be violent or in the least bit threatening, even when she'd once passed a big male in a remote spot where he might easily have attacked her. And for all these reasons, though she had no proof, Ria was also sure the Uglies weren't bloodthirsty cannibals who relished human flesh. It was just another phony excuse for murdering them and stealing their hunting grounds.

She had forgotten that Brindle could read her mind, but now he replied to her thoughts with a great wave of anguish: "You know truth!

So why do you accept? Why let Clan murder Uglies?"

Ria was quick to object: "Hold on, Brindle. What just happened this morning? I saw three of my Clan trying to murder *you* and I stopped them. Remember? I risked my *life* to stop them. You told me I was a hero for doing that."

Brindle looked contrite: "Yes. You are hero. Very sorry. What you saw with own eyes you stopped." Then he frowned: "But I mean why stay silent when you know Clan are killing Uglies – not just one Ugly, but every Ugly they find? Why not stop that?"

"Because I can't stop it, Brindle. I'm female and sixteen. No one gives a fuck what I say about anything."

When Brindle made no reply Ria returned to her thoughts, and to the second problem that was bothering her, namely Sulpa.

He was an outlander for sure, so how had he gained influence over three high-ranking youths of the Clan?

With Grigo involved it was a safe bet that something underhanded was going on. And Grigo's mission to kill Uglies made it very likely the whole thing was also connected to his father. It was well known that Murgh had challenged the traditional leadership of the assembly of elders. Could his son's loose talk of Sulpa hint at an alliance with another tribe – not only to kill Uglies but also to snatch overall power within the Clan? With men like Murgh and his thugs, Ria thought, the possibility of such treachery couldn't be ruled out.

She had to get back to camp and tell Hond and Rill what she suspected.

The Uglies were streaming along the floor of a glen she'd never explored before, reminding her she was getting further away from camp with every step. She checked the sky. High sun had already passed. She was about to tell Brindle of her decision to turn back – although of course he knew all her thoughts – when he put a warning hand on her arm and pointed to the ridge a few hundred paces above them.

Two savage-looking men stood there, huge and naked, with shaggy shoulder-length hair. Ria saw both of them were smeared with fresh blood and knew from their pale skin and strange weapons they weren't from the Clan or from any of the neighboring tribes.

Were the splashes of gore glistening on their hard muscular bodies from Grigo, Duma and Vik? The three youths had been hobbled and defenseless, Ria reflected. They would have been easy to kill.

In a smooth whirl of motion one of the bloodstained men unslung a wooden baton and a bundle of short spears hanging across his shoulders, locked a spear into the baton, drew back his right arm, rolled at the hips and launched the missile down the slope of the valley. It made an eerie whistling sound as it flew. Tipped with a heavy flint spike it crunched with horrible force into the side of a big Ugly in the third rank of the column, passed straight through his body amidst gouts of blood, and lodged itself deep between the ribs of the brave next to him.

Both Uglies went down, dead in an instant, and the entire column stopped in its tracks as though stunned.

Taking his time, looking relaxed and confident, the second naked warrior on the ridge unslung his own baton and spears and coiled his muscular body to throw.

Chapter Eight

When Leoni spoke of the Angel she thought she saw a strange expression cross the doctor's face; it lasted a few seconds before he got it under control. "I do believe you," he said, "but right now you need to take it easy. We nearly lost you in here . . ."

"I died and went someplace else . . ."

"It was touch and go, Leoni, but you're a fighter and we got you back."

She smiled and suddenly sleep stole up on her, overwhelming her like a superior force.

The next twenty-four hours passed in a blur as Leoni progressed through the recovery and critical care units and thence into a plush convalescent suite overlooking the leafy gardens of the hospital. If Mom and Dad had spent any time at her bedside right after she came out of the ER she hadn't noticed them, but now a smiling middle-aged nurse brought her the happy tidings, they were on their way.

Leoni felt physically sick at the prospect. In the days leading up to her overdose she'd been in turmoil over what to do about her father. The big question was . . . had he really raped her – repeatedly – when she was eight, and again, inexplicably, when she was twelve? It had always happened in the dead of night, and on each occasion he had snatched her without warning out of deep sleep. Before her thirteenth birthday the attacks had stopped as suddenly and mysteriously as they had started, but she had been tortured ever afterwards by night terrors and dreamlike memories of these ordeals.

The last time she'd plucked up the courage to accuse him was a couple of years ago. But, as always, he had denied everything, told her she was an evil liar, and claimed the rapes had only happened in her overactive imagination.

He made her question her own sanity.

He made her wonder whether the blood she recalled trying to scrub off her sheets after each attack could, after all, have come from some sort of self-harm.

For a long time he had kept her quiet with such brainwashing. But, in recent months, the horrible and disgusting memories had come flooding back – no longer as dreamlike sequences but shatteringly graphic, specific and real – and Leoni had regained some certainty that it was not she but her father who was the evil liar in the family.

That had been her state of mind when she'd quarreled with her parents yesterday afternoon, and she could see with new insight how her incredible rashness and stupidity with the OxyContin tablets had been directly connected to the rage and hate she felt towards her dad.

So far, so bad . . . But now, after her brush with death, there were other, even more agonizing and confusing matters to ponder. Although she didn't understand the mechanism, she had somehow witnessed Mom admitting, in a very horrible way, that she'd known about the rapes all along. And there had been the strange talk about someone called Jack, and clearing up the dead wood – whatever that meant.

This was all new and worrying, but what made it more problematic was the peculiar way Leoni had come by it. Was her out-of-body eavesdropping just a hallucination cooked up in her druggie mind, or had her mother really known about the rapes when they were happening? If she had known, and encouraged them, then what kind of set-up was that?

And who was "Jack"?

Leoni had asked for a sketch pad and half a dozen Magic Markers when she'd been moved into the convalescent suite, and now she was sitting up in bed, her back propped against a pile of pillows, working on a drawing of the Blue Angel. She was struggling to get the likeness of that perfect face, the high cheekbones, the almond eyes, the indigo skin, when her parents appeared in the doorway. For some reason she felt guilty and closed the pad, sliding it beneath her covers as they advanced.

To her irritation, they had brought Adam the miracle child sulking in tow. The obnoxious ten-year-old scowled a reluctant greeting, made a beeline for the sofa by the window, switched on his Nintendo and was soon slaughtering aliens in *Metroid Prime.*

Mom and Dad settled in the armchairs on either side of Leoni's bed.

No one spoke for some minutes, and the tension in the room began to rise.

Finally Mom leaned forward and hissed: "Adam knows you overdosed. He couldn't miss it. It's been all over the TV news. I need you to apologize to him."

Leoni's blood boiled: "Apologize? To Adam? What for?"

"For the distress and embarrassment you've caused him at school."

"Well, maybe he'd be even more distressed and embarrassed if I told him where I got the OxyContin tablets I overdosed on . . ."

Dad cut her off: "Let's not talk about your drug habits today." He flashed a warning look at Mom. "This is just meant to be a nice family visit."

"Nice for who?" Leoni retorted. "Nice in what way?" She lowered her voice to a whisper: "Would it be so nice if Adam knew what you used to do to me?"

Adam had ears like a bat and was curious about ugly, disturbing and contentious matters. "Dad," he asked. "What was it you used to do to Leoni?"

"Nothing, Adam," Dad snapped. "Leoni's suffering from an illness. It's called false memory syndrome . . ."

"Fuck OFF!" Leoni screamed, "I'm up to HERE with your bullshit. My memories aren't false. It really happened . . ."

"But WHAT happened, Dad?" wheedled Adam. "I wanna know."

"You wanna know?" mimicked Leoni. "OK, spoiled brat, I'll tell you. Dad used to get into bed wi—" *THWACK*! Stunned, she realized that Mom had just slapped her face – hard – and now stood over her, panting and flushed. Leoni's right ear was hot and ringing where the blow had struck. At once her anger brimmed over and she bellowed: "You KNEW about it, Mom. You even ALLOWED it." She saw that this accusation had hit the mark. Mom's face fell and, just for an instant, before she got herself under control, she had a hunted, almost frightened look in her eyes.

Leoni pressed home her advantage: "You BITCH. You DID know about it. You KNEW!" She lunged forward and tried to claw her mother's face but her father got between them, shouting: "This is madness, Leoni. Stop it! Stop making things up."

Leoni wasn't about to stop anything: "Oh yeah?" she shrieked. "If I'm making things up then how come I know about JACK?"

The startled expression on both her parents' faces told her once again she'd scored some sort of point. That was when the good-looking doctor who'd saved her life in the emergency room walked in.

Dad and Mom jumped back and the doctor strode across the floor to stand at the foot of the bed. "What's going on here?" he demanded.

Mom gave him her constipated-gorilla look: "Who's asking?"

"Dr. Bannerman. I attended Leoni in ER."

"Well, Dr. Bannerman, we're Mr. and Mrs. Watts, Leoni's parents, and we're having a private family discussion that's none of your business. OK?"

"No, Mrs. Watts. It's not OK. I heard the shouting halfway down the corridor, and I also think I heard somebody getting hit." He paused, seemed to reconsider something he was about to say, and added: "But let's not go there right now. Your daughter is my patient. My responsibility is to ensure she makes a proper recovery and she isn't going to do that if she has to deal with this kind of . . . 'discussion.' Please just leave at once and let her get some sleep . . ."

"You're telling us to leave?" screeched Mom. "You don't have the right. We're her parents. We're paying her bills here."

"As it happens," said Dr. Bannerman, "I do have the right, and I don't care who you are or what you're paying. The patient comes first and this patient needs peace and quiet."

Mom turned to Dad: "Herman! Didn't we give a big capital gift to this hospital last year?"

"You bet we did. Five million dollars for the building program."

"There!" yelled Mom. "And it's not the first time. Check it out, doctor! How do you think Chancellor Edelman will feel if we withdraw future support because of your behavior? WE'RE NOT GOING ANYWHERE."

"I've had enough," said Bannerman. "I'm calling security."

Mom glared at him as he moved to the bedside to pick up the telephone. He had already started dialing when Dad capitulated. He marched over to the sofa and grabbed his son's hand: "Come on, Adam, time to go home. Come on, Madeleine. Let's get out of here."

For a moment Mom was speechless. She had been defeated! Something she could not abide. As the three of them headed in disarray towards the door she looked over her shoulder and flashed the doctor her poisonous-lizard look: "There's going to be consequences" she said. "You'll be hearing from our attorney."

In the last second she turned her eyes on Leoni and beamed rays of hatred at her. Then they were out of the room and marching down the hallway under a barrage of shrill questions from Adam.

Chapter Nine

"MOVE, YOU IDIOTS!" Ria screamed, startling the Uglies out of their inertia and sending them running in all directions as the second spear came whistling in. It shot past her and buried itself in the face of an old hunched female in the seventh rank, dropping her in a heap.

Still nobody seemed to know what to do. Ria sought around, found that Brindle had stuck close to her, and pointed to the men on the ridge three hundred paces above. "WE'VE GOT TO CHARGE THEM," she yelled in out-loud speech – there was no time to risk thought-talk not working – "CROWD THEM. GET THEM OFF THE HIGH GROUND OR THEY'LL SKEWER US ONE BY ONE."

She'd already snatched a jagged stone out of the sodden earth and was sprinting up the steep side of the glen. She could see one of the attackers aiming a shot at her, waited until he let fly and threw herself to the ground. The whistling spear missed her by a hand's breadth and as she sprang to her feet twenty Ugly braves pounded past her, their heavy footsteps shaking the earth, roaring incoherent defiance at their attackers.

More spears smashed into their ranks, bringing down four more Uglies with horrific injuries. Blood spurted, bones broke, there were cries of pain and shock, but still the tough uphill charge didn't falter. The big yellow-toothed leader was ten paces ahead of everyone else, waving a massive war axe, but before he reached the ridge Ria hoped to kill one of the spearmen herself. Her grip tightened on the stone she'd picked up. It wasn't of ideal size and weight. But it would do. She was less than fifty paces away and already drawing her arm back to throw when the spearmen turned and were gone. By the time she reached the ridge they were nowhere to be seen, as though some sorcery had concealed them.

Ria didn't believe in sorcery.

The men were there, slithering on their bellies like snakes through the bracken, gorse and tall tussocky grasses packing the downslope below.

"Put your guys out in a long line," Ria yelled to Brindle, still using out-loud speech. "Beat the bush. We'll find them."

There was some confusion but soon almost the whole Ugly column, still more than fifty able-bodied males and females, plunged into the thick undergrowth in a ragged line, each separated by only an arm's length from the next. They beat the bracken with spears and clubs, stabbing and probing, but the two attackers could not be found.

Finally Brindle called off the search. "Not good waste more time here," he said. "Better get to Secret Place fast."

Ria considered her position.

She'd been about to head back to the Clan camp but now it wasn't so simple. The moment she left the protection of the Uglies she would be vulnerable to the two killers lurking out there. They'd be watching and if they saw her alone they'd hunt her down.

On the other hand, if she stayed with the Uglies then the important intelligence she bore – that armed strangers with devastating new weapons had infiltrated Clan lands – would be delayed. She wasn't clear yet on the fate of Grigo, Duma and Vik. Were they working for the strangers, as she suspected? Or had they been murdered by them? Both alternatives were possible but, whatever the answer, something bad was happening and she had to warn her brothers.

"Won't be able to warn them if you dead, Ria," Brindle's thought-voice reminded her. "You must stay alive. Come with Uglies to Secret Place. Will figure out how to get you home safely tomorrow."

What Brindle was saying made sense. Earlier, Ria had been horrified when he'd asked her to spend the night at the Ugly hideout. But everything had changed since then, and she had to adapt. "OK," she said after only a brief hesitation, "I'll come with you. Just don't kill me and eat me when we get there!"

Brindle's brow ridges puckered, his deep-set eyes clouded over, and a look of horror crossed his face.

"Well, I don't mean it, of course! It's a joke!"

However, it wasn't exactly a joke, and Brindle's ability to peer inside her mind meant he must know that. The truth was Ria couldn't quite rid herself of a nagging fear that the Uglies could still turn out to be cannibals.

* * *

Three males and a female had been killed by the strangers' spears. There was nothing more to be done for them. Three more were injured. Now separate circles of Uglies, eight or ten to a group, gathered arm in arm around each of their wounded comrades where they lay and began a rhythmic, hooting chant much like the one they had sung for Brindle earlier.

Inside the first circle an old female crouched down beside an injured brave. Blood was spurting from his mouth – a spear had struck him in the cheekbone below his right eye, smashed his teeth and half-severed his tongue. Doubting that anything could be done about such a horrible injury, Ria watched in growing astonishment as the aged female held out her hands and a mysterious blue light began to pour from her open palms into the bloody wound. More of the same light streamed forth from all the Uglies standing in the circle, converging on the fallen brave and enveloping him in an eldritch radiance. The hooting became much louder and vibrated uncomfortably in Ria's ears. She gasped as the brave's body rose a handspan into the air and floated without any supports. The blood flow from his mouth reduced from a torrent to a trickle and Ria could almost believe the wound in his face had begun to close when the Uglies' song reached a peak, and stopped, and his body sank back to the ground.

In the second circle it was a grizzled elder who poured the uncanny blue light into a deep wound in a brave's back, and in the last it was Brindle whose big hands channeled it into the body of the third injured brave where a spear had smashed his collarbone.

While these rituals unfolded other Uglies got to work with spear shafts and ropes and as each of the circles broke apart the injured were lifted onto improvised stretchers ready for the march. The brave with the wounded face was sleeping. He looked peaceful and his breathing was clear. The other two were alert and even seemed energized in some way despite their injuries.

The whole column gathered around the bodies of the four who had been killed by the strangers. "Saying goodbye," Brindle explained to Ria as they marched off. "When Uglies die we must give proper funeral ceremony. But now is time of war. Have to leave them."

After walking deep in her own thoughts for some while, Ria asked Brindle about the circles of braves, the hooting and the blue light she'd seen pouring from his hands.

"When put heads together and sing," he explained, "all become one mind. Stronger that way. Use to make light for healing, use to figure out problems. Make big decisions."

That was when Ria noticed with a jolt that the brave with the wounded back and the brave with the broken collarbone were already on their feet, disdaining their stretchers.

"Blue light is a kind of magic," Brindle told her. "Needs much power. Helps if many Uglies make circle. Sick person must be close or healing doesn't work."

"Can you heal all injuries?" Ria asked. After what she had just seen she was ready to believe anything.

"No. Not all. If heart, lungs or liver are pierced is very difficult."

"Difficult? Or impossible?"

"Very difficult. Not impossible."

"Amazing!" Ria said. "Now tell me about talking inside our heads. That's a kind of magic too. How far apart can we be before that stops working?"

"Maybe three bowshots. Maybe five if rope strong. Then can't reach each other any more."

"And this rope you keep mentioning? You said there's one between you and me. What is it? What does it mean?"

"Means . . . something like love. Something like friendship. Ria saved Brindle's life. Took risk for Brindle. Saw Brindle is human, not dumb animal. Brindle saw Ria not like rest of Clan. Doesn't hate Uglies. Is human too. I open heart to you, you open heart to me. This way we get rope between us."

As the afternoon of hard marching wore on, Ria's familiar hunting grounds were left far behind, she found herself in regions she had never ventured into before and she grew more and more uneasy. She began to memorize landmarks – an old dead tree, a rippling flowing stream, an unusual boulder, a barren hill, a distant craggy peak – as she talked to Brindle.

Scouts had been posted around the fast-moving Ugly column to forestall any further surprise attacks but there were no sightings of the savage spearmen. The worst possible outcome, Ria thought, would be if they were part of a much larger force. The best hope was that they were loners passing through.

But in her heart she didn't believe this and was unable to rid herself of the suspicion that they were following. Several times the hairs on the back of her neck stood on end as they traversed a high, wide-open, almost featureless plateau. It was dead flat, but the ground underfoot was soggy and a cold wind howled across it from the ice deserts far to the east.

Ria glanced over her shoulder and just for an instant she thought she saw something move. It might have been no more than wind in the marsh grass, but it spooked her. "I'm certain we're being followed," she pulsed to Brindle as they reached the lip of the plateau and entered the shelter of a steep valley. "I don't want to walk into an ambush when I head back to the Clan tomorrow."

"Uglies send big war party with you tomorrow. You be safe."

"What about Secret Place? You didn't want to take the risk of Grigo, Duma and Vik following us there. So it doesn't make sense to allow these two savages to follow us, either."

"But what can we do?" Brindle asked.

"We have to kill them," said Ria.

Chapter Ten

She'd thought the doctor was good-looking but now Leoni decided he was movie-star handsome – lean athletic build, six foot three or four, mid-thirties, dark hair with just a hint of premature gray about the temples, warm, walnut-colored eyes, firm chin, good lips. "Thank you, Dr. Bannerman," she whispered as the sounds of her departing family faded. "Thank you for saving my life in the ER. Thank you for taking my side."

He smiled. "Not a problem. Shall we switch to first names, by the way? I know that you're Leoni." He gave her a warm, firm handshake: "I'm John."

Over the next five minutes she was relieved that he did not pry into the fight with her parents but asked her questions about how she was feeling, peered into her eyes with a bright little light, tested her reflexes and checked her respiration, pulse and blood pressure. "All in good order," he pronounced. "I don't see any reason why we need to keep you in hospital much longer. Stay tomorrow for another day of observation, we'll do a few more tests and discharge you the following morning." Suddenly he shifted gear: "Now . . . tell me about the drugs."

"You mean the OxyContin I overdosed on?"

"Well, yes. For a start. How much did you take?"

"I snorted eighty milligrams. Stole the pills from my mom's medicine cabinet. Ground them into powder with a nail file. I've seen friends of mine take much bigger doses and none of this shit happens to them."

"That'll be because they've built up tolerance. OxyContin is an opiate and if you take it a lot, like your friends must do, then your body gets used to bigger and bigger doses. You were using it for the first time, I bet?"

"Yes . . . and the last time."

"What about other drugs?"

"You want me to be honest?"

"Of course."

"I do quite a bit of cocaine."

"How much is quite a bit?"

Leoni shrugged: "Thirty, maybe forty lines – on a night out clubbing, or at a party. Then I'm clean for a few days. Then I might have another binge over a long weekend, get through ten or fifteen grams. You know how it is."

"Would you say you're an addict?"

"No. I wouldn't. I snort a lot of coke, but I think I can take it or leave it." Leoni paused: "I'm planning to leave it in the future."

"Have you used heroin?"

"Ugh! NO. Never. Not my thing."

"Crystal meth?"

"Couple of times. Maybe three. Liked it a lot but I won't be going back for more."

"You sound pretty sure of that."

"I am. Some things happened to me when I was dead . . ."

"Which made you want to fix the problems in your life?"

She was surprised. "How did you know that?"

"Right after you came round in the emergency room you told me you'd met an angel . . ."

"Yes. She's got indigo skin!" Leoni retrieved her sketch pad from its hiding place under her covers and opened it at her drawing of the Blue Angel. "This is what she looks like."

Bannerman leaned forward and poured over the sketch. "Very interesting," he said. "Tell me . . . did she give you a lecture about how much you'd screwed up?"

"Now you're *really* freaking me out. She said I'd squandered my potential. I don't understand how you know this stuff."

"My guess is you went through what we call a near-death experience – and people who've had NDEs very often come out of them with a whole new attitude." A look of boyish enthusiasm had spread over Bannerman's face: "Actually, this is a special research project of mine. I've been investigating NDEs for five years. If you'd like me to, I may be able to help you understand a bit more of what you went through."

To her surprise, Leoni found she was crying and blurting out what she wasn't yet sure she should reveal. "The Angel told me something really weird. She told me I have to make the veil between worlds thin to see her again. Do you have any idea what that means?"

"I think I probably do have an idea," Bannerman answered after a moment, "but I also think you need a good night's sleep. Why don't we pick up this conversation again in the morning?"

Leoni dabbed her eyes with a Kleenex. "If you know anything that can help me deal with what happened to me then I need to hear about it right away."

"Why so urgent?"

"I was . . . out of my body. For a long time. Seemed like forever. I was able to move about – like I was flying. I could go through walls. I could see and hear other people but they didn't know I was there. Can I say that without you thinking I'm crazy?"

"I don't think you're crazy. The near-death state most often involves two stages. In the first you're out of your body, much as you describe – in fact we call this an 'out of body experience,' OBE for short – but you're still very much in this world. You can move about at will; lots of people describe it as flying. You see everyday life going on around you but nobody can see you. Then comes the second stage when you leave this world behind. You go through a tunnel, or a corridor, or it could be you're carried down in a whirlpool, and you find yourself . . . somewhere else . . . Not here. Not the Earth. You're in another world. Very often you'll meet . . . entities there. Sometimes deceased friends and relatives who've come to welcome you or to send you back. Some people report meeting an angel. Sound familiar?"

Leoni nodded: "There's scientific studies, right? Which prove all this?"

"Plenty of scientific studies. The phenomenology of NDEs and OBEs has been thoroughly documented. These are truly universal human experiences."

"Never mind phenomen – whatever. And I don't care about universal. I only want to know one thing . . . Is this stuff real? Or isn't it? Because it felt real to me – more real than real, in fact – and I got some information, and it's just blowing my mind."

"What sort of information?" Bannerman asked.

"I left my body right after the overdose hit me. Flew out of my bedroom window and down into the kitchen. I wanted my parents to rescue me. Fat chance. They didn't have a clue I was there. They were talking and they said . . . they said some things to each other about me that I didn't know before."

"And these things. Did they make sense?

"Yes. In a horrible sort of way what they were saying made perfect sense. So what I'm asking is – could I really have heard them say that? Or do you think it was just some kind of hallucination made up by my brain?"

"Well, that's actually the million-dollar question." Bannerman's face was animated. "First off, you have to rule out the possibility that what you heard reached you in the normal way through your physical senses. Where did you take the OxyContin?"

"In my bedroom."

"OK, from your bedroom – maybe with the window open? – are you able to hear people talking in the kitchen?"

Leoni thought about it: "Sometimes I know when there's a conversation going on there. Sometimes I hear voices, but they're faint. Even if they're yelling I can't hear individual words or sentences. Besides, what happened wasn't just about hearing. I was down there in the kitchen with them. I could see their faces. I just wasn't in my body. My body was on the floor upstairs."

"I know that's how you experienced it, Leoni," said Bannerman, "but skeptics would say that you weren't a hundred percent unconscious up there on your bedroom floor. They'd argue that you heard what you heard through your ears in the normal way and then hallucinated or fantasized the rest of it."

"Is that what you think?"

"Not necessarily. A lot of new work has been done in this field and some of us are willing to consider other explanations for these sorts of experiences. Consciousness is one of the big mysteries of science. Maybe the biggest mystery. The dominant view is that it's a function of the brain, that it's somehow generated by the brain the way a factory makes cars, but actually there's no proof of that."

"But if consciousness doesn't come from the brain then where *does* it come from?"

"I don't know. No one does. Maybe it just *is*. Maybe it's a fundamental force of the universe like electromagnetism or gravity, free-floating everywhere, residing in everything. And maybe the essence of consciousness isn't physical at all – in which case our brains might not be generators of consciousness but simply vehicles or receivers that mediate consciousness at the physical level . . . It would explain a lot – not least, OBEs and NDEs."

Leoni thought about it: "OK. I guess I can see that. If my consciousness isn't generated by my body and brain, and if it doesn't depend on them to exist – if it's like the TV *signal*, rather than the TV *set* – then there's no reason why it should die when my body and brain die."

"No reason," Bannerman affirmed. "On the contrary, you'd expect it would continue to have experiences separate from the body. So maybe that's what OBEs are – non-physical consciousness, liberated from the body and brain, continuing to witness and overhear events in the physical world."

"In which case that conversation between Mom and Dad could have been real?"

Bannerman shrugged: "I'm not saying that. I'm saying we – I mean doctors, scientists – actually don't know what OBEs are. They're mysterious. Unexplained. Most of my colleagues would reject the idea that you really are out of your body when you have these kinds of experiences . . ." A pager attached to his belt began to bleep: "And they'd think you were delusional if you tried to tell them that you'd accessed real information in such a state. But honestly, after what I've seen and heard in the ER I'm not so sure . . ." He silenced the pager and picked up the telephone by Leoni's bed: "Excuse me for a second. I've got to respond to this, OK?" He dialed a number, listened and hung up. "I have to go," he announced. He was already heading for the door. "Get some sleep, Leoni, and I'll see you tomorrow. I still want to hear about that angel you met."

"Wait. Dr. Bannerman . . . John . . . Orange sneakers. Purple and green laces."

He paused: "Sorry . . . I don't understand."

"Something else I saw yesterday while I was out of my body. There was a receptionist. Behind a desk in the main lobby of this hospital. She was wearing a dark suit. Looked very prim and proper. But she had orange sneakers on her feet, with striped purple and green laces . . ."

"So . . . ?"

"If that person exists, then it means I saw real things, doesn't it?"

"Not necessarily . . . Look, I've got to go . . ." Bannerman gave her a nice smile. "But I'll check it out, OK? I mean, about the receptionist. I'll be in to see you around ten a.m. Now sleep."

* * *

Just after six a.m. Leoni awoke with a start to find a crowd in her room. Mom and Dad were there, a janitor pushing an empty wheelchair, two men in suits and several nurses. Without a word one of the nurses got hold of her arm and began prepping her for a shot. Leoni screamed and struggled to pull free, but in an instant she felt the needle pierce her skin. The last thing she saw, as her vision blurred, was the look of absolute triumph and vindication on Mom's face.

Chapter Eleven

"You know where we're going," said Ria to Brindle. "I don't. So help me find a place where we can set an ambush." She experimented with a thought-picture, envisaging a forest with open country beyond it. Eight of the Uglies and Ria herself would hide amongst the trees to await the men following them. But the main column, still numbering more than forty, would continue on out of the forest where they should be in plain view for a long while as they crossed the open country. "Is there somewhere like that?" she asked.

Brindle's eyes lit up: "Yes!" He hesitated: "But near Secret Place. Maybe not good to let them get so close . . ."

"It doesn't matter how close it is. We have to kill them and then they won't be telling any tales. The more important thing is, are you ready to murder these strangers? Because that's what we're going to have to do."

Brindle hesitated again and Ria felt herself becoming irritated at his instinctive gentleness: "I don't want to hear any crap about them being spirits and people just like us," she prompted. "They're killers. They slaughtered four Uglies for no reason. Just because they could. So now it's their turn."

"I know," said Brindle. "Uglies must kill or be killed. Clan already teaching us this lesson every day. But hard for us to learn."

After reaching the lip of the plateau they hiked down a steep densely forested slope, in the lee of the wind. Ria loved all forests and this one was beautiful, silent and lit up at intervals by glints of golden sunlight thrusting down between the branches.

At the bottom of the valley they emerged from the trees onto the rocky shore of a narrow gleaming lake and began to trek four abreast alongside it.

Ria and Brindle were in the second rank, right behind the lumbering, grizzled leader. Now Ria noticed, as she had not when he had intervened to drag Duma, Grigo and Vik off her this morning, that three deep parallel scars ran down the outside of his right arm to a point below the elbow, the token of some violent encounter with a wild beast – bear? lion? – many years before.

Brindle's voice popped up inside her head: "Ten winters ago, hungry bear came into our camp and tried to grab Grondin's wife. Wanted to eat. Grondin had other ideas. There was fight . . ."

"And?"

"Bear lose. Grondin's wife got fancy necklace from teeth and claws. Wears all time."

"Is Grondin part of a longer name, like Brindle?"

"Ha! You really want to know? OK. Here goes: Grondinondin-grand-inadin-apciprona."

"The 'apciprona' bit on the end sounds familiar."

"I am Brindle-phudge-tublo-trungen-apciprona, remember? Grondin is my father's brother."

Again Ria shared a wash of sorrow and pain with Brindle and knew that thinking of his father had led him to recall the death of his mother and siblings at the hands of the Clan. She also received strong imagery of an Ugly elder, looking quite a bit like Grondin, but even taller and more massively built.

"You're showing me your father, aren't you?"

"Yes. I love him! He's a great guy. Best friend as well as father and King of all the Uglies."

"Hang on. You're joking, right? Your father is the king?"

"Not joking."

"So that means one day you're going to be . . ."

"King of the Uglies? Yes. If any Uglies left."

Ria looked puzzled.

"We are last Uglies in world," Brindle explained. "Five hundred of us now at Secret Place. Maybe seven hundred more still living in camps outside. Can't protect from attacks of Clan there. Trying to bring all to Secret Place."

"There are no others?

"No more Uglies after we gone. All dead."

At once many things about Brindle that had puzzled Ria began to make sense, and she understood why he had so much authority amongst a large group of elders and braves. It wasn't just some no-account crippled kid she'd rescued but the only surviving son of the King of the Uglies! She decided she would help him when she returned to the Clan. Murgh's sinister campaign to wipe out these gentle creatures was all wrong and she had to try to stop it. It might not even be too difficult if she could prove what she suspected – that he and Grigo were taking their orders from ferocious outlanders like the two who followed them now.

Ria had spent almost her entire life in the open air, gathering fruits and nuts in the forests, using her skill with stones to hunt rabbits, birds and small deer. She thought she was nearly as strong and skilled, as wily and tough, as many of the full-grown braves of the Clan. Even so, the relentless non-stop pace set by the Uglies – since they left the lake almost all their route had been up the side of what seemed to be an interminable mountain – had given her a persistent stitch low down in her side. This was embarrassing because she didn't want to appear weak, and what made it worse was that none of the Uglies – not even the injured, or the stretcher-bearers, or crippled Brindle – showed any sign of slowing down.

It was late afternoon when they entered a swathe of ancient forest growing right across the flank of the mountain and continued to wind their way upward under the shelter of huge pines. "We coming to place where must make ambush," Brindle warned. "Not far from here."

Ria peered back over her shoulder. The Uglies – despite their losses, there were still more than fifty of them – were leaving a clear trail amongst the thick layers of brown pine needles smothering the forest floor. Even a child would be able to follow them. But that was the whole point of her plan.

Now they entered an immense grassy clearing, hundreds of paces from side to side, and marched straight across it, trampling the grass underfoot. When they passed back under tree cover on the opposite side of the clearing Ria saw that the edge of the forest lay close, and that beyond it reared a huge amphitheater of emerald-green mountain meadow, lit up like a promise in the declining sun, hemmed in far above by a spectacular array of high and forbidding cliffs.

Armed with flint knives, war axes and each carrying two heavy spears, Brindle, Grondin, and six other big braves stayed behind with Ria to set the ambush. She noted how they all seemed to be waiting for her to tell them what to do. "We not good at this sort of thing," Brindle admitted.

Ria, who had filled her pouch with throwing stones at the lakeside, didn't hesitate to take charge. Using Brindle to communicate with the others, she showed how the men behind them would be following the broad and conspicuous trail of the column. "If we're lucky they won't notice that some of us have turned back," she said. She pointed to the others hiking up the steep slope towards the still-distant wall of cliffs. "It's just going to look like we marched straight through the forest and carried on climbing the mountain on the other side."

There was no time for elaborate tricks or traps. Ria ordered her ambush party to take shelter behind trees on both sides of the track, ready to rain down spears and stones on the killers on their trail.

But a worm of doubt nagged at her.

With their fatal gentleness, would eight Uglies be enough to win victory against such hard and violent men?

Chapter Twelve

As Leoni emerged from sedation she discovered, to her horror, that she was strapped down in a metal-framed, high-sided cot in an unfamiliar room. She was groggy but she knew what had happened. Mom and Dad had pulled strings and had her committed to a mental hospital – something that they had threatened to do before.

It hit her that this must be what Mom had meant by "clearing up the dead wood."

She screamed and struggled against the restraints holding her wrists and ankles, and thrashed her head from side to side. Then, realizing that she must be under video surveillance, Leoni forced herself to calm down. Acting mad was the last thing she needed to do in here.

She looked around the room. It was quite large, and luxuriously furnished, but the door had three locks and an inspection hatch, and the windows were barred on the inside. Basically she was in a jail. "Hey," she yelled, "I need to use the bathroom."

Silence.

"Hellooo. Is anybody out there? I need to use the bathroom."

Silence.

"Look. Take me seriously. I'm going to wet the bed if someone doesn't get me to a bathroom pretty soon."

Silence.

Was this some kind of test? Leoni sighed and waited. She was, she realized, in very deep trouble. Mom and Dad had all the money in the world and in sunny LA, where money mattered so much, how hard would it be for them to find a psychiatrist willing to certify she was insane? The hospital was no doubt being well paid to accommodate her and would also have an interest in keeping her where she was – sweetened perhaps by the promise of one of Dad's multi-million-dollar capital gifts.

She dozed for a few moments. The next thing she heard was the sound of keys turning in the locks. Then the door swung open and two beaming beefy nurses marched in. "Hello," they said in unison, and introduced themselves: Deirdre and Melissa. They fussed around Leoni, removed her restraints and helped her into a sitting position. "You were given quite a strong sedative," Deirdre explained. "You've been out for most of the morning so your legs are going to be a bit wobbly. We need to help you walk over to the bathroom."

"Wobbly" was an understatement. Leoni's legs felt like jelly. Still, at the bathroom door she insisted that she would manage the rest of the operation by herself. "No," said Melissa. "You have to be supervised."

"What for?"

"Suicide watch. You're under twenty-four-hour supervision. Dr. Sansom's orders."

Leoni was so embarrassed at having an audience that she couldn't urinate. "Look, give me a break," she protested, "I'd like a bit of privacy."

"Sorry, sweetie," said Deirdre. "Can't do that. But don't worry. In cases of shy bladder syndrome we usually catheterize."

"On the other hand you could just unclench and pee," added Melissa.

The two of them were still beaming, but it wasn't nice.

Twenty minutes later, humiliated and furious, Leoni finished in the bathroom. She allowed Deirdre and Melissa to help her to her bed and was halfway across the floor, with her ass sticking out of the open back of her hospital smock, when a big man walked in. "Hi there, Miss Watts," he said. "I'm Dr. Sansom. I'm in charge here." He ogled her as the two nurses lifted her onto the mattress and placed her between the sheets. "You can go," he told them.

Sansom was a tall, florid Texan in an expensive business suit. He was aged around sixty, Leoni guessed, and had the authoritative, domineering air of a man used to getting his way. His hands, which were enormous, were rough and calloused – the hands of a laborer, not a physician. A spider's web of broken blood vessels decorated the bulbous tip of his nose.

"Welcome to Mountain Ridge Psychiatric Hospital," he said. "Do you know why you're here?"

"Because my parents have paid you to say I'm mad?"

"Quite a paranoid answer, Miss Watts, but then we get used to that sort of thing. Your parents love you very much and they are *very* concerned about your mental health. Your persistent drug abuse, your rampant promiscuity" – he leered – "your fantasies about your father . . ."

Leoni stared him down: "I don't know what you mean. I have no fantasies about my father."

"I think you know exactly what I mean. False memories, crazed accusations. All this, culminating in your suicide attempt, amounts to obviously delusional behavior."

"What suicide attempt?" Leoni gasped.

"You took an overdose of OxyContin. You would have died if your parents hadn't rescued you in time—"

"Bullshit. It wasn't even my parents who rescued me. It was Conchita, our housemaid. If it had been up to my parents they would just have let me die."

"Paranoia again, Miss Watts. Frankly, the more I hear the more certain I am your overdose was a suicide attempt. That's why you've been involuntarily confined at Mountain Ridge under Section Fifty-One-Fifty of the California Welfare and Institutions Code."

"Confined here for what? I don't get it. Why have I been confined?"

"For your own good, of course."

"I can't believe this is legal. Last night I was a patient at UCLA Med Center recovering from a drug overdose, this morning I was sedated, kidnapped and imprisoned here. How can that be right?"

"*Kidnapped*, Miss Watts? *Imprisoned*? Just more paranoid delusions. Your mother and father were worried – rightly, in my view – that you might make a second attempt to kill yourself. They decided it was irresponsible to leave you in an open-access hospital without the best psychiatric care and a suicide watch round-the-clock. So they went through due legal process and had you committed. Your declaration was written up by an accredited LA County clinician in the normal way. It allows us to hold you here at Mountain Ridge for seventy-two hours to evaluate your mental state and make sure that you aren't going to pose a danger to yourself in the future."

"After seventy-two hours I can go?"

"In your dreams," Sansom boomed. He leaned closer and lowered his voice to a confidential whisper: "Between you and me, when the seventy-two hours are up I'm certain we'll have no shortage of reasons to renew the hold and keep you here for . . . well . . . as long as we want to. I'm looking forward to treating you for several years at least."

"Not a chance, asshole. I'm out on bail for drug and driving offenses. There's going to be a court hearing in a couple of months so you can't just make me disappear."

"Already dealt with. California Highway Patrol have dropped the charges against you. They agreed with us that the stress of a court appearance might just make you crazier. So it looks like we really do have you all to ourselves. I think you're going to be a very challenging case." He pressed a buzzer by the bed and moments later Deirdre and Melissa bustled into the room.

"Restrain the patient again, please," Sansom ordered, and left without a backward glance.

Chapter Thirteen

Leoni's next human contact came when Deirdre delivered her lunch and removed her restraints to allow her to eat it. Half a dozen pills of various sizes and colors had also been set out on the tray and Deirdre made her swallow these when she had finished her meal. Finally Leoni accepted the offer of another toilet visit and then was strapped down in her cot again.

The pills made her sleep. When she awoke it was dusk and a weedy, weaselly man with thinning gray hair and stained teeth was hovering over her bed like a wraith. She recoiled and gasped – "Ugh!" – and he flapped his arms and fluttered his pale little hands in a gesture that fell far short of being reassuring. "Who're you?" Leoni croaked.

"Er . . . ah . . . Dr. Grinspoon. I've come to ask you some questions."

"I don't want to answer questions. I'm tired. Go away."

"It's part of your psychological evaluation, Miss Watts. It's not optional."

Grinspoon turned on all the lights, removed her restraints and had her sit up in bed, propping her back against a heap of pillows. He then handed her a pen and a huge sheaf of paperwork attached to a clipboard. "This should take you no more than ninety minutes to fill out," he said.

"Ninety? What is it?"

"It's called the Minnesota Multiphasic Personality Inventory. There's . . . let me see . . . five hundred sixty-seven test items . . ."

"Whaddya mean, five hundred sixty-seven test items?"

"Ah . . . er . . . five hundred sixty-seven questions. Each one you answer either true or false. It's extremely straightforward and if you're honest it'll give us a clear snapshot of your mental health problems." He smiled, exposing his rat teeth. "It's a *good* thing, Miss Watts. Once we know what's wrong with you we'll be able to treat you and get you well again . . ."

Leoni couldn't help herself: "This is such bullshit," she hissed. "You guys aren't 'treating' me. You're keeping me prisoner here" – she indicated the straps and buckles that Grinspoon had just freed her from. "I'm a prisoner! Admit it . . . I'm not even allowed to take a piss without somebody watching me."

"Well, this is because you are on suicide watch, of course. When we're satisfied that you're no longer a danger to yourself these restrictions can be lifted. I know that Director Sansom wants you to be comfortable here . . . Now, please fill out the questionnaire."

A cellphone began to croon the Brahms Lullaby and a furtive look crept over Grinspoon's face. He fumbled in his pockets. When he found the instrument, after some pantomime, he answered in a low voice and scuttled from the room, leaving Leoni unrestrained.

Her first impulse was to run at once, but that made no sense. She could hear Grinspoon mumbling right outside the door but even if she could evade him, or any other staff who might be passing, she had no idea which way to go. If she was going to escape she needed a plan, possibly allies, preferably a knight in shining armor to come to her rescue.

Like John Bannerman, for example. Leoni's beautiful savior from the emergency room had seen how things were between her and her parents. Surely he'd be suspicious – wouldn't he? – about her sudden overnight transfer from his care. He was interested in her experiences and he hadn't for a moment seemed to think she was mad or a danger to herself, so she hoped that even now he might be moving heaven and earth to get her out of Mountain Ridge. Having witnessed him in action she didn't think all the Watts' lawyers and money would be enough to divert him if he wanted to help her. On the other hand, if he was going to help her then why wasn't he here now?

With a sense of the inevitable, Leoni plumped up the pillows behind her back and began to go through the questionnaire that Grinspoon had given her.

Whatever she said it was obvious that Mountain Ridge were going to spin her answers to prove she was mad: "I see things or animals or people around me that others do not see." True or False? "I commonly hear voices without knowing where they are coming from." True or False? "At times I have fits of laughing and crying that I cannot control." True or False? "My soul sometimes leaves my body." True or False?

"At one or more times in my life I felt that someone was making me do things by hypnotizing me." True or False? "I have a habit of counting things that are not important such as bulbs on electric signs, and so forth." True or False?

Other questions seemed much more ordinary but also had to contain hidden lures and traps: "I am bothered by acid stomach several times a week." True or False? "I am easily awakened by noise." True or False? "I like to read newspaper articles on crime." True or False? "I am neither gaining nor losing weight." True or False? "I have never been in trouble with the law." True or False? "I am inclined to take things hard." True or False? "I get all the sympathy I should." True or False? "I never worry about my looks." True or False? "People generally demand more respect for their own rights than they are willing to allow for others." True or False?

After half an hour of this Grinspoon reappeared at the door. He folded his cellphone, advanced towards Leoni's bed and stood over her: "Is all clear on the questionnaire, Miss Watts?"

"It's OK," Leoni replied, "I'm getting it done." Out of the corner of her eye she noticed he had not yet pocketed his cellphone and sensed an opportunity: "But there's one thing you could really help me with. Would you hold these for me for a moment? I need to scratch an itch." She pushed the clipboard and pen into his hands, making him juggle them with the cellphone. He grunted with surprise and tried to thrust the objects right back at her. Leoni squirmed away and, as he lunged again, she grabbed his wrists. His jaw dropped, his eyebrows shot up and in the moment of fumbling confusion that followed she palmed his cellphone along with her clipboard and pen.

Her heart was hammering in her chest – she couldn't believe she was doing this – but the horrible little man had become so flustered he didn't notice the loss. To create a further distraction Leoni now dumped all three items on the bed, taking care to cover the cellphone with the clipboard, turned round on her knees and pointed her bare buttocks at the doctor. "I just need to scratch myself here," she grunted, letting her smock drop forward and reaching for a point between her naked shoulder blades.

Grinspoon looked at the ceiling and then at this feet. "You're out of line, Miss Watts," he spluttered. "Cover yourself, please."

"Oh, come on, Dr. Grinspoon – you *are* a doctor, aren't you? – haven't you ever seen a woman's ass before?"

“That’s irrelevant. Now, please, get back under the covers or I’ll have you restrained again.”

Leoni shrugged, arranged her pillows, maneuvered herself into a decorous seated position, picked up the clipboard and pen where she had left them and hoped that she had managed to conceal the cellphone in a fold of the bed sheets in the process. Not daring to look down to confirm this, she returned to the questionnaire and ticked “True,” “True,” “False,” “False,” “True . . .”

Chapter Fourteen

The two grim warriors who'd stalked the Uglies all day materialized, pale as ghosts, from the gloom of the forest. Their shaggy hair clung lank around their shoulders and their powerful heavily muscled bodies were slick with sweat. They were moving at a fast jog, their eyes to the ground, intent on the trail, silent and focused. Then one pointed ahead where the track led under the last trees and out onto the steep open meadow beyond. The mountainside here was already in deep shadow but a ray from the setting sun burst through a gap in the surrounding peaks and showed the Ugly column still climbing far above.

Risking a quick glance round the trunk of the tall black pine she'd taken cover behind, Ria saw the outlanders jog forward. They were peering up through the trees for further glimpses of the column and didn't seem to suspect that a force might have been left behind to deal with them. The simple plan, when she gave the word, was that she and her eight Uglies would step out and rain spears and stones down on them from point-blank range, catching them in a lethal crossfire.

They came on, their bare feet falling quiet as leaves on the forest floor. Closer . . . Closer . . . Ria was about to give the order to attack when the Uglies stepped into plain view, surrounded the outlanders and threatened them with their big clunky spears.

This was fucking unbelievable. "What's happening, Brindle?" Ria pulsed.

"Make them surrender" – his thought-voice was stubborn, like he knew she wouldn't agree but had decided anyway. "Take prisoner. Don't want to kill."

"No way they're going to surrender," said Ria. She'd stayed hidden: "Get those spears into them now!"

But still no spears flew and for an instant the two groups faced off in silence.

Ria could see the outlanders had recovered from their initial surprise.

They turned and grinned at each other, exposing mouths full of yellow teeth filed to sharp points. They must have thought the Uglies mad not to have slaughtered them already.

Time seemed to stop, and Ria heard the sounds of the forest – the rustle of wind through the treetops, the creak of branches, the call of a nightbird, the distant howl of a wolf. She noticed that one of the outlanders was carrying a sack made of coarse woven cloth. There was something bulky inside it, staining the fabric. He held the sack dangling from his left hand, bumping against the ground. His right hand moved towards the hilt of a flint knife sheathed at his waistband.

Surging out from behind the tree, Ria snatched a stone from her pouch and hurled it at him. The light was bad, but not that bad yet – the stone whizzed across the track and there was a solid *CLUNK*! as it hit him square in the brow. He staggered, his eyes rolled up in his head, and he fell on his face. From the opposite direction, out of the corner of her eye, Ria glimpsed the blur of a tomahawk whirling towards her, dived to escape it, and somersaulted back to her feet, shocked to see two more outlanders, whose presence she hadn't even suspected, running in to attack out of the gathering darkness.

She could throw well with both hands and pulled two more stones from her pouch as the outlanders shouted terrible war cries and clashed with the Uglies, hacking and stabbing in a frenzy of violence. The whole scene was chaos. In a heartbeat she saw three of the Uglies slaughtered, their bodies bloody and battered underfoot as the fight rolled over them.

Ria threw with her right hand first, hard and fast, fetching a tall outlander a vicious blow to the back of the head, felling him in a heap just before he got a knife into Brindle. She saw another of the Uglies killed, and chose his attacker for the left-hand shot but Grondin stepped in on him first, thrusting his big spear through his chest and splitting his heart in a splash of bright blood. The surviving Uglies beat the last outlander to death with their clubs and axes. As suddenly as it had begun it was all over.

Ria darted forward. The men she'd hit lay close together, unconscious but alive. She didn't want them on her trail again.

She looked around. The scene of the ambush was littered with fallen weapons. She plucked up a flint knife and tested its edge. Good enough. She'd done this to rabbits and deer more times than she could remember.

Ria dropped to her knees beside the big brave who she'd seen carrying the sack; he'd fallen on his face when her stone hit him. He stirred, groaning and muttering as she straddled his back, grabbed a handful of his hair with her left hand and jerked his head up off the ground. Reaching under him she stabbed the point of her knife deep into his neck just below his left ear – a roar of pain now, thrashing and struggling – and sawed its blade sideways through the gristle of his throat, releasing jets of hot reeking blood.

When she was sure he wouldn't get up she climbed off him and turned to the second outlander, slumped in a half-seated position against a tree. He was still unconscious. She felt no pity for him and slit his throat too.

Both men gurgled, hissed and bubbled as their blood drained into the ground. For the count of ten Ria sat on her haunches between them, watching them die. It was the first time she'd killed humans. But it was no big deal.

Then her eyes fell on the sack.

She hefted it, found it was heavy, and upended it on the forest floor. With dull thuds and a bounce, two battered and bloody but still recognizable heads rolled out.

Duma and Vik.

Two sets of freshly severed male genitals followed.

It was a long march up the mountainside. They would never have made it in the dark, with four dead to carry and three of the others injured, if the whole Ugly column hadn't returned to help them. Even so it was a tough climb.

At last, in moonlight, they reached the dense stand of bushes and small trees that grew all the way along the base of the wall of cliffs towering at the summit. Grondin turned to his right with the rest of the Uglies pacing along behind him.

Ria still hadn't spoken to Brindle about the bungled ambush, or whose fault it was. She wasn't going to tonight. "What's happening here?" she asked, pointing at the cliffs.

"Secret Place has secret entrance. Watch. You will see."

A few moments later Grondin stopped in front of an unremarkable section of undergrowth and began to move the branches and thorns aside revealing that a path, invisible to passers-by, had been cut through the thick trees and bushes leading all the way to the cliff face. He entered with Brindle and Ria and the rest of the group followed. The last ones through closed up the gap in the undergrowth behind them and they all surged forward into the shadows of the thicket.

Because her eyes had not yet adapted to this deeper darkness, Ria didn't understand what happened next. One minute they were in amongst undergrowth, with gnarled roots and dry leaves underfoot, then suddenly the atmosphere changed. It was damper, there were sounds of dripping and running water coming from several different directions, and she found herself slipping on smooth wet rock.

"Cave," Brindle informed her. "Very long cave. Runs all the way through mountain. Comes out on other side."

Then flints were sparking and tinder flared into flame that was transferred to little fat-burning stone lamps in the hands of several of the Uglies. The flickering light sparked a fantasia of reflections from thousands of stalactites that hung poised overhead like glittering icicles.

Ria had been in a cave before, just two years previously. Though quite different, it had been every bit as spectacular as this one. She'd been hunting with Hond and Rill and they'd pursued a wounded deer through a narrow opening in a hillside into a huge echoing chamber. There they lit their lamps and found themselves confronted in all directions by breathtaking images, painted in red and black: humans who were part bison, others who were part lion, and outlandish animals combining the heads, bodies, legs and teeth of many different species – the denizens of another world bursting through into this one, emerging out of fissures and from behind bulges in the rock.

It had been one of those caves that had been decorated in the long-ago by the Painters, an ancient people ancestral to the Clan. According to old myths told around the campfires they had discovered a way – now forgotten – to enter the spirit world and afterwards had painted these images of the strange and terrifying beings they met there.

"Not forgotten." Brindle said. "Uglies still know way to spirit world."

There were no paintings in this long eerie passage through the body of the mountain. Whenever the flickering torchlight reached its walls Ria saw only bare, polished limestone dripping with water and overgrown with calcite deposits – here resembling a mammoth, there a serpent, here a bear, there a bison. Sometimes stalactites descending from above joined up with stalagmites rising out of the floor to form pillars, and forests of pillars, through which they had to thread their way. Sometimes the roof was so far above their heads it could not be seen; at others it was so low that they had to drop onto their bellies and wriggle, becoming smeared with thick, wet mud. At one point the side walls also closed in around them to form a tunnel so narrow that Grondin had great difficulty getting his bulky shoulders into it, and so long that Ria thought she would never emerge and must end her life here entombed in the mountain. There were ledges poised above roaring underground rivers, treacherous potholes and deadfalls, and a labyrinth of side passages in which, Brindle assured her, those who did not know the correct route could wander until they starved without finding their way out.

"But you guys do know where you're going, right?"

"Yes. Our Lady of the Forest led us to Secret Place. Showed us the way."

"Our Lady of the Forest? Who's she?"

"She's a great spirit, Ria. Watches over us." And he sent into her mind an image of a group of Uglies passing through the cave system led by a beautiful, very tall woman with blue skin.

A little later the dank, almost stifling, mineral atmosphere that had enveloped them for so long began to freshen and Ria felt a rush of night air. Then she was clambering over fallen rocks and debris to emerge at last on a moonlit hillside, under blazing stars, the peaks of snow-capped mountains gleaming in the distance and the cheerful glow of campfires visible just a few bowshots below. She looked to Brindle for an explanation but he had become morose and lost in thought. "Secret Place?" she asked.

"Yes. Secret Place. But something wrong." He began to run down the hill, stumbling and falling, picking himself up, stumbling again. The other Uglies also broke into a run and Ria was carried along in the stampede. "What's happening, Brindle?" she cried out: "Why are we running?" But there was no reply.

As all this was unfolding a weird, dejected mood descended on her, she began to tremble as images of the fighting in the forest flashed before her eyes, and she suddenly felt alone and full of misgivings about the Uglies.

How did she really know she could trust them?

Maybe she'd made a terrible mistake coming with them into their own territory. There wasn't a hope she could find her way out through those caves without their guidance.

She slowed to a walk, cursing under her breath, and steered a course towards a group of solemn, shadowy figures standing round a large fire that had burned down to its embers. Something was going on at the fire that seemed to be attracting a lot of attention.

Maybe something cooking?

As Ria came closer she recognized with horror that a human body was roasting in the embers and now, as she watched, it was dragged out by the Uglies. The females fell upon it in a frenzy and began to tear loose and consume great handfuls of its burnt and blackened flesh. With a single blow from a flint axe one of the males hacked off its head and another – Brindle! – smashed the base of the skull with a stone bludgeon and reached inside to extract the brains.

Ria's shock at Brindle's betrayal was so huge it left her reeling. *You had me fooled all the way,* she thought.

Then she turned to run.

Chapter Fifteen

Ria ran helter-skelter down the darkened hillside, her heart pounding, breathing in short heaving gasps. She ducked and dodged around boulders and between trees, careening off unseen obstacles, gasping with shock and pain. She was repulsed by the thought that her body would be next for the fire, her brains next for the cannibal feast.

What a fucking betrayal.

She hadn't condemned the Uglies' near-catastrophic stupidity during the ambush, because she'd wanted to believe such faults stemmed from their good and gentle nature.

When all along, as she'd now seen with her own eyes, everything that Murgh and his thugs had said about them was true. She cursed the wayward streak that had led her to trust CANNIBALS over Clan. She swore, if she survived the night, that she'd never make the same mistake again.

Without warning the ground opened beneath her and she tumbled, somersaulted and landed on her feet with a jarring thump in some kind of pit. Terrified and disorientated in the darkness she rushed to climb out, but the sheer sides were at least twice her height and she fell back in. She tried a second time, digging her hands and feet into the cold, crumbling earth, and hauled herself almost to the surface before again falling back. As she sat winded in the bottom of the pit, gathering her strength for a third attempt, she heard a cacophony of grunts, high-pitched squeals and horrible snuffling noises. There was a wild beast trapped with her! *A badger? A bear?* She jumped up and backed into a corner, fingers hooked like claws, before she realized she was alone in the pit and that all the sounds were coming from herself.

Shit. She was losing it. In a total funk. If Hond and Rill could see her they'd tell her to pull herself together, take control of her situation, stop cowering. With an effort Ria slowed her breathing, gritted her teeth to stifle the pathetic babble that kept bubbling up in her throat, straightened out of the crouch she had adopted and moved into the center of the pit.

Silence fell, but not complete silence. As the panic left her, she found she could hear the sounds of the Uglies combing the hillside for a nice fresh human snack. A group of them were close, crashing through bushes and trees, but she reasoned that Brindle must not be with them, or that the "rope" between her and Brindle had been broken by his betrayal – because if he could still get inside her head they would have found her already.

Ria waited until the hunters had passed by. Then, with ferocious energy, she threw herself again at the wall of the pit, again sunk her hands and feet into it, again climbed by sheer force of will, and again reached nearly to its lip before falling. But her landing was bad – there was an agonizing *crack*! and she couldn't stifle a gasp of pain and shock as her left leg buckled under her.

Braving the hurt, she rolled onto her back. If her leg was broken she was fucked. She looked up. Framed by the square mouth of the pit, the cloudless sky was dazzling with the glitter of a host of stars. Then a grizzled head and shoulders appeared, silhouetted against the starlight, and – with surprising agility for so massive a figure – Grondin jumped in beside her.

Ria didn't struggle – she couldn't beat this guy – but the first thing Grondin did surprised her. He dropped down on his knees and ran his hands over her injured leg, massaging the point where the pain was most severe. There was nothing predatory about his touch and at once she began to sense a warm, healing glow.

When Grondin seemed satisfied with his work he placed his strong arms under Ria's thighs and shoulders, hoisted her over his head, passed her up into the calloused hands of other Uglies waiting above, and leapt out of the pit himself. A stretcher was improvised from branches lashed together and they laid her upon it. Then, with one Ugly in front, one behind and Grondin walking by her side, she was carried away from the pit, through scattered stands of trees and back up the hill towards the fires of the distant camp.

Now that she was truly their prisoner, with no hope of escape, Ria began to relive the events that had led her to flee earlier: the body in the fire, the females tearing at its flesh, the decapitation and – horror – Brindle smashing the base of the victim's skull in order to feast on his brains. Once again, despite Grondin's gentleness, she was racked by a spasm of disgust for the Uglies. She was injured, helpless, and surrounded by stinking subhuman cannibals who were going to kill her and eat her.

Preferably in that order.

They were closer to the fires, climbing steeply, and suddenly, as though out of nowhere, Brindle's voice was back inside her head: "*Not cannibals*! *Not way you think*!"

Ria formed a thought and threw it at him as though it were a rock: "Liar!"

"Told you before. Uglies don't lie."

"But I saw you. *I saw what happened to that body in the fire* . . . Was he Clan?"

"Maybe in death Uglies and Clan look same—"

Brindle's thought-voice was full of some intense emotion that Ria was too furious to identify. "I'm not interested in your maybes," she interrupted. "Just answer my question."

"He was not Clan. He was my father, King of the Uglies. Died last night."

That was when Ria recognized Brindle's emotion for what it was. Sadness. Deep, aching sadness. But she was still so angry that it didn't stop her saying: "You ate your own father's brains? That's such a gross thing to do!"

"Maybe gross to you, but we do not put dead in hole in ground like Clan and leave to rot. For us that is very bad thing. By eating, we bury dead . . . inside our own bodies. Is how we respect them. Is how we keep them with us. Is not . . . 'cannibalism.' Uglies never, never *kill* other Uglies or Clan to eat."

"It *is* cannibalism, Brindle. What you're saying is that it's not murder as well . . ."

"No! Not murder! I love my father."

This time Ria's rage drained away and she shared the young Ugly's pain and loss through the openness of thought-talk. It made her ashamed. "I'm sorry," she said as the full force of his grief hit her. "Oh Brindle, I'm so sorry I misjudged you . . ."

A few more steps up the incline and her stretcher-bearers lifted her onto a spacious terrace, wide and flat, leading to a looming cliff wall. The glow of fires was all around her and there were Uglies everywhere, males and females, young and old, with matted hair and wild, uncouth looks, gazing down wide-eyed as she was carried by. Many were covered from head to toe in stripes of yellow, red and black paint. Several carried clunky spears or flint knives.

Brindle's voice again: "We look wild, but our hearts are pure. Will not hurt you. I promise."

Craning her head over the side of her stretcher, Ria saw that she was already halfway across the terrace and being carried towards the base of the cliff where a massive overhang and fallen boulders almost concealed a dark opening in the rock. As she came closer she saw that it was a tunnel about as high a man and ten paces wide. She was carried through it – twenty paces, thirty paces, it was hard to estimate the distance in the dark – and emerged into a cavern so vast that she gasped with surprise. Around its walls the Uglies had positioned a huge number of their fat-burning lamps, a thousand at least, as many as the stars in the sky. The reflected light of their guttering flames revealed a roughly circular chamber that seemed – was it possible? – to be hundreds of paces across in some places. She looked up. Far above her head the soaring dome of the ceiling disappeared into lofty darkness.

There were a lot of Uglies in the chamber already and more were pouring in through the entrance all the time. Their burly forms, looming up out of the faint glow cast by the lamps, seemed alien and monstrous. Grotesque shadows played across the walls, unfamiliar smells assailed her and Ria found that her stretcher and its bearers, with Grondin still by her side, had been swept into the midst of a large crowd moving across the floor.

She struggled to sit up. "What's going on, Brindle?" she pulsed. "What's this crowd about? I don't like it. Why am I being brought here?"

She had a sense he was very close and as she sent out her thought-voice she caught a glimpse of him in the flickering light. He was seated, enthroned between two stalagmites, on a natural rocky platform jutting out from the side of the cave.

"When old Ugly king dies," he said as she was carried forward, "new Ugly king must make journey to spirit world to speak with him. I have to go tonight." He paused: "You can make journey to spirit world too, Ria."

Her stretcher-bearers brought her in front of him and stopped. The platform was about waist-high and he was looking down at her.

She pointed to her injured leg: "I don't think I can even walk . . ."

"Not that kind of journey."

Chapter Sixteen

Grondin lifted Ria onto a comfortable cushion of ibex skins piled up for her beside Brindle. The hysterical way she'd run – totally freaked at the thought of being eaten – was really shameful now she'd had a chance to review it calmly.

Of course the Uglies were never going to eat her. Only dumb fear and prejudice had made her imagine such a thing.

"Don't feel bad," said Brindle. "You been hero all day, kept courage strong, saved lives of many Uglies, didn't freak when it mattered."

"I guess . . . But I still freaked."

Ria very much wanted to stop talking about herself. "Do you know what happened to your father?" she asked. "Did he die suddenly? Was it an accident?"

Through a mixture of images and thought-talk Brindle made her understand how proud he had been three days ago when Grondin had asked him to join the expedition from which they had just now returned – an expedition to persuade outlying communities of Uglies to take refuge in the sanctuary of Secret Place. His father had seemed well then, and had sent Brindle off with his blessing, but it seemed that soon afterwards he had sickened with some mystery illness, begun to stumble and fall, lost the ability to walk, talk and eat, and very rapidly died.

"I angry with Father," Brindle now confessed. "First time I ever go away he dies. Now suddenly I responsible for everything. Don't know what to do."

Ria too was an orphan. Her mother and father had passed on together seven winters ago. She'd been nine years old then, on the worst day of her life, when the two people she loved most had left her without saying goodbye, and for a long while afterwards all she'd been able to feel towards them was the same sort of bitter, cheated anger that Brindle was dealing with. "You won't be angry forever," she promised. "And you'll figure out what to do."

As if it had happened yesterday Ria found herself reliving the whole sequence of events that had stolen her own parents from her – that stupid, stupid accident, so avoidable and unnecessary that even now the memory of it made her choke.

Through the broad valley where the Clan pitched its principal summer camp flowed the great river called the Snake. It was deep and wide, filled to the brim with leaping, succulent fish but – like its namesake – it was also dangerous and unpredictable. It could bite.

On a sunny morning under a clear sky, with no intimation of impending doom, Ria had walked and skipped beside her parents along the banks of the Snake at the start of a day's fishing. Father had been twenty paces ahead when Mother had seen the ideal spot. "Shush," she whispered, "let's catch one before he turns round." She told Ria to stand back, then lowered herself onto her stomach and leaned out over the rushing water, reaching into the hollows under the bank to snatch sleeping fish. Her arm was submerged to the shoulder when she made a sudden grab and brought up a fat, glistening brown trout, flapping and wriggling in her firm grip. But just then the undermined bank gave way beneath her weight and pitched her, and the trout, head first into the river, with a mighty splash.

At first Ria laughed. It hardly seemed serious – more like a joke – but it stopped being fun when Mother didn't resurface. Then Father was pounding along the bank, yelling to Ria to stay where she was, and when Mother's head at last bobbed up amongst the roiling waters, gasping for air, he jumped in after her. That was when Ria started to scream, with tears rolling down her cheeks, as she too ran along the bank as fast as she could, for a short while keeping pace with her parents.

Father was a strong swimmer. He reached Mother, grabbed hold of her and lifted her face above water. No doubt he believed he could save her. But, instead, the two of them, clinging to one another, were whirled into the main torrent, pulled under the surface, and lost forever. Left alone on the bank Ria sank down on her haunches, buried her head in her hands and wept. Much later that was where her brothers found her, no longer crying, just staring out at the river with vacant eyes.

Brindle was tuning in: "Afterwards your brothers became your parents," he said.

"Hond and Rill. They're much older than me. They were already men when the accident happened . . . They're good hunters and they've looked after me well. I can't complain . . ." – Ria touched her heart – "but the pain is still here."

"Maybe help if you can meet mother and father again," said Brindle.

"Maybe it would, but it's not very likely is it?"

"Told you, Uglies know way to spirit world. This is the Cave of Visions, and I will talk with spirit of my father tonight."

Ria felt uncomfortable when Brindle spoke of spirits and the spirit world. She believed in them, of course; everyone did. But at the same time she'd never seen any solid evidence for their existence.

What happened next only added to her conviction that the Uglies were getting everything upside down.

Grondin had quietly left the platform while she'd been talking to Brindle but now he returned carrying a broad woven basket filled with hundreds of small mushrooms of the vile and obnoxious "Demon's Penis" variety. By age-old lore the collection and consumption of these mushrooms was forbidden to the Clan under penalty of death, so Ria spat and made the sign of the evil eye. "You're not planning to eat those, are you?" she asked.

"Of course we will eat them," said Brindle. "How else you think we get to spirit world?"

"But those who eat Demon's Penis turn into demons!" Ria exclaimed. "Don't you know this? I can't believe you don't know this! They grow long tiger teeth. They go mad. Their mouths foam. Blood drips from their eyes. They run about trying to kill everyone. If they are pregnant they give birth to monsters. These mushrooms are very, very bad, Brindle."

"You are intelligent person, Ria, but right now being kind of stupid – I'm sorry. You don't know anything. Have just been told these things by other know-nothing people and you believe. Have you ever with your own eyes seen somebody eat these mushrooms and grow tiger teeth, go crazy, like you say?"

"Well, no. I haven't. But everyone knows it's true."

"No, Ria! Not true! Uglies know these mushrooms very well. They are sacred to us. Very special. Very good. We don't call them bad name like you do – 'Demon's Penis' – which makes you think bad thoughts, puts horrible idea inside head. We call them 'Little Teachers' – because they teach us. We call them 'Little Doctors' because they heal us. We call them 'Little Guides' because they show us how to enter spirit world, and return to land of living."

"Well, maybe they do all that for Uglies, but I am Clan and if I were to eat them I'd turn into a demon with long teeth."

"Let me ask you question, Ria. The Painters – they were your ancestors, right? If you go back to your father, and your father's father, and your father's father's father – all the way back to the long-ago – then no more Clan, only Painters, right?"

"Yes. We came from the Painters."

"Means Clan and Painters same thing but at different time?"

"I guess."

"Then safe for you to eat the Little Teachers."

"Why?"

"Because Painters ate the Little Teachers in the long-ago. Made ceremony with them. Traveled to the spirit world. Uglies showed them how."

In front of the ledge where Ria was perched with Brindle the rock floor was flat and open. Here, with much shuffling and hooting, all the Uglies – hundreds of them, males and females, young and old – found places for themselves, settling down cross-legged or reclining on improvised cushions of skins. Grondin and three other elders moved amongst them distributing more of the woven baskets overflowing with Demon's Penis. Despite everything Ria had been taught it was obvious that the Uglies weren't in the least bit afraid of the disgusting fungi.

"Why should I believe you," she asked Brindle, "that the Painters ate Demon's Penis?"

"Please don't call bad name like that, Ria!" he protested. "Hurts my head. Please show respect to the Little Teachers."

"OK. Why should I believe you that the Painters ate the . . . Little Teachers?"

"Should believe me," Brindle said, "because Uglies can't tell lies – we share our thoughts. Don't forget past. Uglies were here in the long-ago, welcomed first people who looked like you to come into this land. Showed them many things – good hunting grounds, good shelter, good water. Fed them when they were hungry. Gave healing when they were sick. When my ancestors gave your ancestors the Little Teachers, that was when they became the Painters. When your ancestors turned against the Little Teachers that was when they became the Clan."

Brindle reached into the basket of mushrooms that Grondin had set down between them, took a handful, pushed them into his wide mouth and made a great show of chewing.

Ria watched, bewildered. How could the Uglies just sit here and feast on these obnoxious mushrooms while enemies with terrible spears roamed free in the world beyond? Who knew how many more of them there were than the four they'd killed today?

"I will ask spirit of my father about the spearmen," Brindle said, picking up her thoughts. "He will tell me what to do."

"You should ask him about Sulpa as well," Ria remembered. "Grigo, Duma and Vik said he'd told them to kill Uglies. Whoever he is I think he's part of this."

A strange, irregular beat began to echo round the Cave of Visions, growing in volume, an amazing, hair-raising, exhilarating sound, the like of which Ria had never heard before. In the lamplight, with its play of flickering shadows, she found it difficult to pinpoint the source of this mysterious, complicated reverberation, which seemed to come from everywhere at once. But soon she traced it to three Ugly males, spaced far apart amongst the crowd, hunched with batons in their hands over knee-high cylindrical sections of tree trunk. Each of these wooden cylinders had a deerskin stretched tight over both ends and the braves seemed to be producing the sounds she was hearing by beating on the deerskins with their batons. Awesome. Ria began to keep time with them, sitting up on her cushions and swaying her head and shoulders from side to side.

Then a small, very ancient and wizened female Ugly rose to her feet in the middle of the floor, brought a length of cave-bear femur to her mouth and blew through it while the fingers of both her hands danced over holes drilled into the bone. The result was another sound, so heart-rending, so plangent and so energized with emotional power that Ria found tears – of joy, of sorrow, she didn't know which – running down her face.

"What's that incredible sound?" she asked. She felt dazed. A little giddy. "What's it for? Why does it make me feel so weird?"

"We call it the bone song," said Brindle. "It goes out into the spirit world. It's like a serpent, winding here and there." He made sinuous hand movements. "It becomes a road for us to follow when the Little Teachers bring us through to the other side . . ."

Brindle was eating more mushrooms as he sent her these thoughts. Just about everyone in the room was eating mushrooms, even the kids. Everybody looked . . . calm. Kind of relaxed and thoughtful. No one growing tiger teeth. No one going insane. No atmosphere of threat or violence at all.

Still swaying to the unfamiliar rhythms, Ria took one mushroom from the basket and placed it in her mouth.

It was bitter, tasting of roots, of earth.

Chapter Seventeen

"False." "True." "False." "False . . ."

Leoni was filling out the questionnaire on autopilot while her mind was busy with a more pressing problem. Who was she going to call?

All her friends' numbers were stored on speed dial on her own cellphone and she didn't remember any of them. Not one. Her coke snorter's Swiss-cheese brain didn't hold on to little details like that.

As this realization sank home Grinspoon hailed a passing colleague and stepped into the corridor again. Through the open door all Leoni could see was his back, the dirty gray hair straggling over his collar, the dandruff on his shoulders, the way he nodded his head and moved his hands as he talked. It was the perfect opportunity for her to call . . . Information!

With shaking fingers she dialed 411 and asked in a stage whisper for the number of the UCLA Med Center.

The operator wasn't helpful: "I don't hear you clearly, ma'am. Say again, please."

"UCLA Med Center," Leoni breathed.

"Ma'am – in which city would that be?"

Under normal circumstances Leoni would have been spitting buckshot by now, but these were far from normal circumstances. "Los Angeles, of course," she hissed.

"And which bed center did you say in Los Angeles?"

"Not *bed* center. *Med* Center. I . . . want . . . the . . . number . . . for . . . the . . . UCLA . . . Medical . . . Center. Surely that can't be so difficult?

"Do you wish me to connect you, ma'am?"

Leoni was picking up hints from Grinspoon's body language that his conversation in the corridor was ending, and she was forced to lower her voice still further "No. Please just give me the number," she hissed. "Just give me the number, OK?"

"310-861-8251."

Leoni scrawled the figures on the palm of her hand, hung up and shoved the cellphone under her bedclothes just as Grinspoon turned away from his colleague and walked back into the room.

"Have you finished the questionnaire, Miss Watts?"

"Umm. Not yet."

"Well, get on with it, then" – he looked at his watch – "I haven't got all night." There was a chair by the bathroom door which he now sat down in. He crossed his legs and began to examine the fingernails of his right hand.

Another ten minutes passed. Leoni was sweating under the covers, and giving ever more random responses to the annoying, persistent, repetitive questions on the form. She could feel Grinspoon's cellphone nestling against her thigh and it was driving her crazy. She was terrified that he would make another call, or receive one – either way her entire escape plan would go down the tubes. But she didn't dare reach down and switch the instrument off; if it was password protected she wouldn't be able to activate it again later.

Five more minutes. "False," "False," "False," "True." She glanced over at Grinspoon. He had finished with his fingernails. Now – hopeful sign – he tilted his head back against the wall and yawned. Tick, tock, tick, tock. Never had Leoni felt more aware of the passage of time, or more fervently willed another human being to fall asleep. "True," "False," "True," "False." Grinspoon's eyelids were drooping closed, his neck muscles relaxed and his head flopped forward, pulling his upper body with it. He began to topple off the chair, then jerked awake at the last moment, sat upright, and gazed around, blinking in apparent confusion.

"I'm nearly finished with the questionnaire," Leoni offered. "Just give me another few minutes, OK?"

Grinspoon yawned and made an exasperated sound. "I've got a call to make," he said. "I'll be right outside in the corridor." And he stood up, patting his pockets.

It was now or never. Her heart thudding, Leoni started punching in the number before Grinspoon was even through the door. She figured she had thirty seconds – tops – before he realized what had happened to his phone.

An operator answered: "UCLA Med Center, who would you like to speak with?"

"Er . . . um . . ." – Leoni was momentarily tongue-tied – "Bannerman. Dr. John Bannerman."

"He's unavailable right now . . ."

"But I have to talk to him! It's urgent!"

The operator was unimpressed. "He's in surgery and he can't be disturbed. Would you like someone else, or shall I connect you to Dr. Bannerman's voicemail?"

Leoni was shaking with stress and fear. She felt as though she was about to burst: "Voicemail? OK. Yes. Put me through."

For a moment the line went dead but then, without any announcement, there was the kind of tone that normally invites you to leave a message. Was this really Bannerman's voicemail? Perhaps the operator had put her through to another extension entirely? Since there was no way of knowing, she just had to go for it. "John?" she yelled into the phone – she was no longer making any effort to keep her voice down – "This is Leoni Watts. I've been kidnapped by my parents. They've locked me up in a fucking mental hospital called . . . um . . . er – shit, I can't remember. Mountain something or other" – she racked her brains – "Mountain Ridge Psychiatric Hospital, that's it. The director is a guy called Sansom . . ." She sobbed, peered at the door, took a deep breath: "You've got to get me out of here, John. I don't have a friend in the world who can do this for me except you."

As Grinspoon came pounding back in with a thunderous look on his face Leoni hung up his phone and held it out to him. "Look what I've found," she said.

Chapter Eighteen

Despite her worries, it wasn't too long before Ria was having a good time. On Brindle's further encouragement she had feasted on the mushrooms – she had forgotten how hungry she was – and now she was just hanging out, tuning in to the strange rhythms that the Uglies were producing. Her thoughts flew and soared on the bone song's sad notes, swirled and dived amongst rivers of flowing colors, waterfalls of brightly hued dots, dazzling starbursts, rotating spirals.

Meanwhile Brindle was out of it. Not communicating. Silent. It wasn't like he was asleep. It was like he was somewhere else. Maybe he really had gone through the veil into the spirit world. If so, he obviously didn't need his big gangly body to make the journey because his body was still here, stretched out on the floor, breathing slow and deep.

And had eating the mushrooms made any difference to her? Ria did a quick inventory. She hadn't been turned into a tiger-toothed demon. She hadn't been driven insane. Clan lore on these matters was obviously full of shit. Still, if she was honest, she had to admit that she was beginning to feel a little . . . peculiar.

It wasn't just the patterns she'd never seen before, or the starbursts, or the way she could now taste sounds and hear colors. Everything else had gone queer as well.

For example, her arms and hands. Why were they glowing? Why were they steaming like the flanks of a hot reindeer on a cold day? She moved her left hand from side to side, laughing at the ghostly smear of scintillating light that trailed behind it through the air. She held up the hand for closer inspection. Six fingers. Odder and odder. She flexed her fingers. Each one was outlined by a soft, radiant, pulsating aura.

"Wow," said Ria, to no one in particular. "So beautiful." She let her hand drop and began to lever herself upright, at length getting to her feet. She was clumsy but her leg, though still painful, was not broken.

She grabbed another handful of the little mushrooms, crammed them into her mouth, flung a couple of ibex skins around her shoulders, picked up a stone lamp and limped out into the throng of Uglies.

Most of them were flat on their backs in the same silent, withdrawn state as Brindle. Maybe it was just an effect of the guttering lamplight, or maybe it was because they were very dirty, but she also noticed that some had green skin. *Green.* Totally gross. There seemed to be some changes under way in the shapes of their faces, too, that she preferred not to look at. Bit scary, really. But interesting at the same time.

She decided to check out a patch of the cave wall fifty paces away. It had caught her eye for some reason and she felt drawn to it. But the floor was an obstacle course of prone and seated Uglies and now she saw a big male staring at her. He was sitting cross-legged, holding a stone lamp that lit his face luridly from below, transforming his nostrils into the black gaping holes of a death's head. His beetling brows were knitted into a thunderous frown. His glinting eyes, reflecting the flame, were guarded and hostile.

Shit, Ria thought as she walked past him. *What's that about?* She'd started to believe all the Uglies were gentle and good-willed but this guy gave her a different feeling. When she looked back he was still staring at her. She considered returning to the comfortable and reassuring pile of skins beside Brindle but rejected the idea. *No way*! She wasn't going to be bullied.

The patch of wall that had attracted Ria proved, when she reached it, to be no taller than herself, no wider than the span of her outstretched arms. It was bone white and its surface, which was damp, mirrored her lamp's yellow flame. There was something . . . compelling about these rippling reflections, something inviting about their glitter and shimmer.

Ria glanced back over her shoulder but the hostile-looking brave was lost in the shadows amongst the crowd on the floor. She didn't think he was still staring at her and dismissed him from her mind. Brindle would not allow any harm to come to her here and she needed to give the wall her full attention. Holding out the lamp, she stepped closer, her eyes darting from side to side as she followed the dance of the reflections.

Except – and this was suddenly very obvious – these weren't just reflections. With a flash of clarity and absolute conviction, Ria understood that the rock had become transparent through some strange sorcery, like a limpid pool on a hot summer's day, allowing her to see through it . . . into another world.

It seemed to be a world that was very much like her own, full of sierras, of forests, of rivers, stretching away into a vast and incalculable distance. But it was also different, overlaid with an eerie and sinister glamour.

She stepped closer again. Could she see movement through the rock, in that enticing realm beyond? Were there figures there? She was beginning to get the creepy feeling that she was being watched. She frowned, narrowed her eyes. *There. What was that?*

For a moment the scene clouded over. When it cleared two specks were visible in the sky of the otherworld, moving towards her, and Ria found that she was standing with her nose pressed against the cave wall, gazing into it with fascinated intensity. The two dots grew in size and began to take recognizable form – wings, feathers, talons, beaks. These were birds of prey, big ones, flying fast. Could they burst through the rock? Could they cross over from their world into this world?

Ria braced herself. Her heart was racing. But she didn't turn and run.

She could see now that the birds were white owls. Ghostly white owls. Specters of the night. They came closer, right up to the other side of the rock wall, and hovered in front of her. The slow, powerful beating of their wings was lulling . . . hypnotic . . . She felt their eyes – huge, dark, filled with intelligence – boring into her.

Did they want to talk to her?

Maybe the same way Brindle talked to her?

"OK," Ria said. "I know how to do that."

She set down the lamp, laid the ibex skins she had brought with her on the floor, and sat carefully, stretching out her injured leg. All the while she continued to gaze into the rock surface where the two owls stared back at her through the wet, glistening sheen.

"Do you wish to pass through?" a thought-voice chimed inside her head. And at that, as though commanded by a magic spell, the owls vanished and a jagged vertical crack opened with a groan in the surface of the bone-white cave wall.

The crack expanded into a wide fissure.

Then a dwarf appeared in the gap and beckoned Ria.

Chapter Nineteen

Grinspoon snatched back his cellphone, retreated to a safe distance, looking furious, and pecked at the keys with an extended forefinger to check which numbers Leoni had dialed. Since there was no point in hiding what he would discover anyway, Leoni confessed: "I made a couple of calls. One to Information. One to UCLA Med Center."

Grinspoon pressed more keys and held the phone to his ear: "Hello, yes. This is Dr. Silas Grinspoon, Mountain Ridge Psychiatric Hospital. A patient of mine just called this number and I'd like to know who she was put through to . . ." Pause: "What do you mean?" Longer pause, then: "I see . . . Yes . . . Yes . . . But that's ridiculous . . . Our director will be calling your chancellor about this. Goodbye!" And he hung up.

Grinspoon glared at Leoni: "I need to know exactly who you called at UCLA Med Center," he demanded.

"That's private information," Leoni spat back. "I've got rights. Ask my lawyer."

"You're a patient here. You have been *committed.* Don't you get that? There is no private information. You have no rights. You have no lawyer. You don't call anyone without our say-so . . ."

"You should have thought about that before you loaned me your phone, asshole."

"I did *not* loan you my phone," Grinspoon spluttered. "You stole it from me!"

"Sure . . . Whatever."

Leoni's mind was working overtime. Now they knew she'd made calls, and perhaps summoned help, they couldn't risk keeping her here in Mountain Ridge. They'd move her. Perhaps out of the state – perhaps even get rid of her altogether, if her parents wanted that. How about another "overdose"? This time fatal? She was already on suicide watch, after all. And then no more risk of embarrassing revelations from the adopted daughter of a very rich man.

Grinspoon was red in the face and yapping at her: "I'm not going to ask you this again, Miss Watts. Tell me who you spoke to or you'll spend the next twenty-four hours in a straitjacket."

Leoni had a quick temper, and she lost it now – at the sheer ludicrous unfairness of her situation, at Grinspoon's soiled and unwholesome presence, and at the catalog of multiple indignities that her life had become. Without giving the matter any further thought she bounded off the bed, pounded across the room in her bare feet, shoved Grinspoon hard in the chest with both hands and bolted out through the open door.

A long empty corridor lit with neon and painted clinical white.

No windows, no natural light, just a vanishing perspective of door after door to either side of her extending into the distance.

Did any of them offer an escape route? Or just access to other rooms?

Leoni hesitated for a fraction of a second then darted to her right and sprinted towards what she hoped was a fire-exit sign glowing red at the far end of the corridor, maybe two hundred feet away. She could hear Grinspoon just behind, yelling something. A klaxon began to sound.

In front, to her left, a door burst open and a man and woman in green overalls rushed out. The man was small and had Oriental features. Leoni barged into him when he tried to block her and sent him sprawling. The woman executed a clumsy flying tackle at her legs, missed and collided with the man. When Leoni glanced back she saw that both were on the floor and Grinspoon had tripped over them. If it hadn't been so serious it would have been comical. She could hear what Grinspoon was yelling now: "ESCAPED PATIENT! STOP HER! STOP HER!"

Leoni covered half the distance to the exit in a few seconds but by then there were people everywhere, pouring out into the corridor from the side rooms, grabbing at her as she hurtled by, and she felt panic bubbling up inside her chest, shutting down her reasoning.

(*Not gonna make it. Don't stand a chance.*)

Now another threat loomed – young guy in a white coat, wire-frame spectacles, earnest expression. He got her in a bear-hug but she bit his ear, which crunched like raw cabbage . . .

(*Yecch!*)

. . . until he screamed and let her go.

Spitting the salt taste of his blood from her mouth, Leoni ran again, dodged a foot stuck out to trip her, and slalomed left and right. Her breath was coming in shuddering, wheezing gasps, her heart was thudding in her chest but she had just twenty feet to go . . .

(*Maybe I can do this.*)

. . . when she realized, with a sinking heart, that she really wasn't going to make it, really didn't stand a chance.

She'd been right about the fire exit. But now it was guarded by Deirdre, Melissa and three other brawny nurses. Panting, Leoni skidded to a halt and faced them.

"You don't want to fight us, girlie," said Deirdre. There was menace in her voice.

Leoni knew she was right but was so far beyond reason that when they tried to grab her and pin her down she fought back anyway, biting, scratching and kicking, drawing blood, pulling out a fistsful of hair. Someone punched her in the head so hard she saw stars. A beefy elbow pummeled her kidney. Finally they managed to turn her face down on the floor and one of them knelt on her back, pulling her arms out behind her in a sweaty wrestling lock. Her ankles were pinned under what felt like a ton of lard, and out of the corner of her eye she could just see Melissa prepping a large syringe.

"What's that?" Leoni protested, close to tears.

Melissa leaned down, stabbed the needle into her thigh and pushed in the plunger: "Four hundred milligrams of ketamine intramuscular, baby! It's all I had to hand at such short notice. Let me tell you, this is *really* going to calm you down."

Soon after Melissa had administered the drug, and before it had fully taken effect, there was a commotion in the corridor. Leoni heard Grinspoon's voice, wheedling, and Sansom's confident bullying tones. "I'm not worried," Sansom was saying.

"But she might have talked to someone."

"Even if she did, so what? What can they do? The girl's here legally. Her own parents had her committed. Nobody can touch us."

Leoni was barely conscious and had lost control of her limbs when the nurses lifted her onto a gurney and wheeled her back to her room. They strapped her into her bed. When they left they turned out all the lights and triple-locked the door.

Complete darkness and complete silence fell.

Chapter Twenty

The dwarf beckoned again, but Ria hesitated. She wasn't sure she liked the look of this little fellow. He wore colorful knee-length leggings, one side red, the other yellow, his jerkin was green, and he was no taller than a child, yet his face was ancient, sallow and grim. In his right hand he held a long thin wand made of some pliant, gently glowing material.

Another gesture, this time betraying a definite hint of impatience, and the dwarf's thought-voice rang inside Ria's head: "Come quickly. I'm here to send you on." As he spoke he reached towards her with the rod and touched her lightly on the shoulder. At once she felt reassured and became conscious of a steady, insistent tugging, as though some invisible force were drawing her towards the gap that had opened in the cave wall. But that couldn't be what was happening because even as these sensations were at their most intense Ria could see that her body, seated on ibex skins on the floor, wasn't going anywhere.

Then she realized that she had never actually seen *all* of herself in quite this way before – even the bits she couldn't normally see, like her own eyes! It wasn't like looking at her reflection in a river pool. This was a completely new perspective – somehow *outside* herself, separated from and able to look down on her body.

Ria had heard of such things before when tales of the Painters were told around the campfires. Like everyone else in the Clan she had been taught that these mysterious ancestors of theirs had discovered a way to send their souls out from their bodies – and thus to travel to the spirit world and return alive. She had also been taught that this way had been closed, and forgotten by mankind, since the long-ago. But now, through happenstance and adventure, Ria possessed a devastating secret unknown to even the most senior elders of the Clan. The way to the spirit world was not closed at all. Its long-lost entrance could be found, at will, by eating the forbidden mushrooms that Brindle called the "Little Teachers."

The dwarf beckoned one final time, then turned his back on Ria and disappeared through the cave wall. His thought-voice in her head urged "*Hurry*!" and she felt herself drawn further away from her body and into the jagged crevice – no more able to resist than smoke carried on a strong breeze.

Inside there was darkness ahead. She moved forward – where was that dwarf? – and the cave wall behind her closed up with a crash, shutting her off with horrible finality from her own body.

Now there was only darkness everywhere and Ria found herself adrift with no reference points.

Was she in motion or was she still?

At first she had no way to tell, but little by little the level of light began to grow, like a slow dawn, and soon there were hints of form and substance – a brief flash here, an illuminated grid there, sparkling zigzags, a swirl of dots. From such clues, in the rising light, she came to understand her predicament better.

She was being swept through an immense tunnel. Its walls – within which the patterns appeared and disappeared – were not rock but some other substance, a bit like water, a bit like sky, slow and majestic, wheeling round her. Sometimes, as though through mist or cloud, she thought she caught glimpses of that other country that had beckoned to her from beyond the cave wall.

The darkness had been banished and it was full daylight, dazzling and unearthly. The walls of the tunnel became thinner, more transparent and finally invisible. Then there was a sudden deceleration and a clap like thunder and Ria found herself standing in a meadow of green flowers beneath two suns.

Two suns! *What the fuck*?

Her first thought was to ask the dwarf, but he had vanished.

Another mystery was her body. She was quite certain that she had left it behind in the cave but she was equally confident that she was now in a body again. It felt like her own familiar body – but her injured leg was healed, and she was dressed in a fine fabric smock she'd never seen before.

How all this could have come about was a great puzzle but she decided she could leave its solution to another time.

She was here, now, and she wanted to explore.

* * *

The mantle of green flowers sloped upwards and away from Ria in all directions, and was ringed by the horizon, suggesting she must be standing at the lowest point of a huge shallow basin. There were no other features to break the view – not a tree, not a river, not a hillock – and the flowers exuded a sticky, richly scented sap that bathed her feet as she walked.

She had never in her life seen such flowers. They were the iridescent green of a kingfisher's feathers – quite breathtaking in such a mass – and the entire expanse swayed and bowed as though agitated by a gentle continuous breeze, yet no breeze was blowing. It was like looking into the shimmering surface of a brilliantly colored ocean.

Then there was the little matter of two suns in the sky. How great was that? Before, when Ria had thought of the spirit world – which was not often – she had pictured it as a murky place filled with ghosts and monsters. She had hated the idea that her parents had passed on to an eternity of gloom and shadow. But now the little mushrooms had brought her here it was obvious it wasn't like that at all and she even began to hope, as Brindle had hinted, that in this place of marvels she might find her mother and father alive once again.

It was difficult to judge distances because of the absolute lack of landmarks and the ceaseless swirling patterns of the flowers at her feet. But Ria didn't care. This was all much too exciting to allow caution to slow her down.

Ria was uncertain how long she'd been walking and couldn't track the passage of time. At home the sun moved through the heavens along a predictable path at a predictable speed, measuring out morning, noon and night. But here in the spirit world there were two suns and both seemed fixed in their places. If they were moving at all it was at a rate too slow to be perceptible.

The rays given off by the twin suns, bearable or even pleasant at first, were now almost scorching, the air was hot, dry and utterly still, and for the first time Ria began to wonder . . . *Where do you go to get a drink in the spirit world*? She was very thirsty and longed to bury her face in a mountain stream, but there was no water to be had anywhere. She reached down and trailed her hand through the green flowers, brought a finger to her lips. Despite their pleasant fragrance their sap tasted so alien, bitter and salty she was repelled.

A new thought occurred to her: if she didn't climb out of this basin soon and find shelter or water, or preferably both, then things could go very badly for her. Ria was just beginning to wonder if she could actually *die* of thirst in the spirit world when she felt something small and fierce bite her ankle and discovered that there was pain here as well – at least as bad as the pain of a polecat bite she'd suffered the previous summer. Only this wasn't a polecat. A hideous little beast, something like a cross between a rat and a cockroach, had clambered onto her foot and sunk its fangs into her. She hopped about on one leg trying to brush it off, lost her balance, and crashed down on her bottom amongst the flowers, unleashing a further splatter of the bitter sticky sap.

The beast still had its teeth in her and wasn't letting go. The little fucker was drinking her blood! Ria gripped it behind the head with her finger and thumb and pinched hard. It squealed in protest, scrabbled at her with its rat claws, and made threatening buzzing sounds with its cockroach wings. Ria pinched harder. She could see the mechanism of its jaw now. She shifted her grip, increased the pressure to the maximum strength of her hand, forced the jaws apart and pried the jagged razor-sharp teeth out of her flesh. Then she got hold of the creature's neck and with a sharp twist and a wet plopping sound she tore the head away from the scaly body. She threw both parts down amongst the flowers where they continued to jerk and writhe as though trying to reunite.

Ria examined her ankle. She had suffered a savage and bloody bite. She was lucky the rat-roach had been alone or she would have been in trouble. She picked herself up, looked around feeling spooked, and began to hurry. She had always imagined that spirits were insubstantial and ghostly so it worried her that she could suffer physical harm in the spirit world. If she could be bitten, if she could be thirsty, what else might happen to her here?

The bite felt hot, and Ria was growing sure some poison had been injected into her system when she came at last to the rim of the basin of green flowers. The flowers continued beyond the rim – for all she knew this whole world was covered in flowers. But at a distance that looked like a morning's hard march the peaks of lofty mountains revealed themselves. Much nearer, just a few hundred paces away, an inviting river meandered through a broad valley. Nearer still – almost close enough to touch – two utterly outlandish creatures examined Ria through segmented black eyes. The creatures were about the size of aurochs, but they had six legs each, and they had stubby beetle-wings folded up on their backs. Judging from the clumps of flowers dangling from their mouths they had been grazing, but now, startled, they turned away and began to canter towards a copse of a dozen trees by a bend in the river.

Ria followed, limping.

There was, she decided, something odd about the trees. For a moment she considered avoiding them, but checked herself. This was ridiculous. They were just trees. And their shade was most inviting. Because she was now in so much pain, and because she wanted to drink and then lie down and rest out of the glare of the two suns, she overruled the instincts honed in years of hunting and gathering – instincts which signaled danger – and continued to approach.

Fingers of shade reached out to caress her.

Ah. Bliss.

Ria passed the first tree, noticing the curious feathery texture of its long green leaves, and stepped into the midst of the copse, luxuriating in the deep shadows as she made for the river just a hundred paces ahead. Above her, branches creaked and leaves rustled.

Then she heard a voice, shouting in a language she didn't understand. This was not a thought-voice. It was out-loud speech. Ria turned, and was shocked to see that a young woman of about her own age had somehow materialized right behind her – a beautiful young woman, dressed as she was, with golden hair. She was pointing and gesticulating and it was she who was the source of the incoherent yelling.

"What manner of spirit are you?" Ria asked, also using out-loud speech.

The other girl rolled her eyes, yelled some more, then raised her arm and one outstretched finger.

What was she pointing at?

Could it be the trees?

Ria looked back over her shoulder.

Fuck! They weren't trees.

Chapter Twenty-One

They weren't trees. They were monsters, three times Ria's height, and she'd walked right into the midst of them. She looked left and right trying to figure out an escape route, but they were all around her – in front of her, behind her, towering over her – blocking her way to the nearby river. She could see their beady red eyes now, like poisonous fruits amongst the weird foliage, and their long pointed beaks, big enough to cut her in half or swallow her whole. These features made them look like birds – perhaps some gigantic species of stork. But their legs really resembled tree trunks, their feet were clumps of tangled roots, their feathers were a mass of dirty green leaves, and a network of large and small bones resembling branches and twigs supported the stubby rudiments of wings.

Could they fly, jump, run, like birds? Or were they – *please let it be so* – fixed in place like trees?

Ria spun on her heel hoping for answers from the spirit girl, but she had vanished. One moment she was there, signaling and shouting, seemingly flesh and blood. But a blink of an eye later she was . . . just gone.

Ria had no time to be mystified. Moving with exaggerated care, she took a couple of experimental steps towards the river a hundred paces away.

The monsters responded with muted clucks.

A third step brought an ear-splitting squawk from just over her head, accompanied by a disconcerting rustling of leaf-feathers.

As she took her fourth step the rustling increased to a crescendo and she was already breaking into a run when a huge beak scissored down.

Ria dodged rapidly to her left and ducked. The beak snapped closed where her head had been an instant before. She stumbled, almost fell, threw herself forward to evade another murderous lunge and then was up and running again.

Glancing back she confirmed that the weird tree-birds were not, as she had hoped, rooted to the ground. The good news was that most of the flock seemed to have no interest in her, but the bad news was that two were in hot pursuit, only paces behind, and closing the distance fast. They were so big and heavy that the ground was shaking under their feet.

Whoosh!

One of the great beaks was swinging towards her. She tracked it out of the corner of her eye, ducked – *Clack*! – and carried on running.

Faced by danger Ria's natural instinct was to snatch up stones and throw them at whatever threatened her, but she could see no stones amongst the endless green flowers of the spirit world. So her only plan was to get to the river and find something to defend herself with, or dive in and swim for it.

The bank was close but the two huge birds were agile and fast-moving and forced her to run the indirect zigzag course of a startled rabbit. They were right on her heels, crowding her, stabbing at her back and legs with their scything, snapping beaks. But it seemed that neither wanted its rival to get to her first so they lunged and stabbed at each other as well, uttering furious clucking squawks.

While they were squabbling, Ria stopped zigzagging and made a break for the river, now only fifty paces away, but in an instant one of the tree-birds caught up with her again, squawking and shrieking. *Clack*! Its wickedly sharp beak stabbed down at her head. *Clack*! *Clack*! She sprinted forward the last few paces and reached the bank. There was a drop of about twice her height to a shingle beach below – a beach covered with rounded cobbles.

Whoosh! *Clack*! Another near miss. Ria was already in the air. She went into a forward roll as she landed, grabbed a couple of stones and ended on her feet facing the tree-bird as it flapped down onto the beach twenty paces from her and began to pick its way across the shingle.

The stones were larger and heavier than she would have liked, but there was no time to find substitutes. They would just have to do. Scanning the top of the riverbank for the second bird, she drew back her right arm, took aim and let fly at the first, which had closed the distance between them to just ten paces. There was a distinct and absolutely satisfying *thwack*! as the missile found its target. The creature's head split open, spilling its brains, and it crumpled on the spot in a heap.

One down, one to go.

She scanned the riverbank again and the second bird hopped into view, its disproportionately small wings thrashing before it crashed down to the shingle a dozen paces in front of her. It stood still for a moment, clacking its beak and sizing her up with its greedy red eyes. Hoping she could throw as well with both hands in this world as she did in her own, Ria hefted her second stone.

If she took just three steps backwards she knew she would be in the river. It looked as deep and fast-flowing as the Snake, in which her mother and father had drowned, and she wasn't getting into it unless there was no other way to avoid being eaten. She aimed and threw again, but lost her footing. The stone flew wide of its mark, bouncing off a wing, and at once the tree-bird was on the move, screeching its rage, lurching towards her.

Ria waited a little too long to dodge its charge and was sent sprawling by a kick from one of its massive rootlike feet. As she struggled to pick herself up, the tremendous momentum of the creature's onslaught carried it past her, skidding on the wet sand. It was unable to stop itself and plunged into the river with a stupendous splash and flapping of wings. At once the water around it seethed and boiled and the monster began to call out with a repeated piteous ear-splitting screech.

What was happening?

Ria peered closer and saw that a host of small reptilian-looking fish with mouths full of long serrated teeth were swarming over the tree-bird, bearing it down under the surface of the swirling river, eating it with astounding efficiency and attention to detail. The teeth flashed and glittered in the sunlight, the water boiled and splashed in a mad frenzy, and within moments there was nothing left of the huge predator at all except trails of blood in the water and its strangely beautiful skeleton, now stripped clean like a dead tree, sinking into the depths.

"Well done, Ria" said a thought-voice in her head. It was a voice so thrilling and ethereal that it made her hair stand on end. "You have passed the first test."

She looked up from the bloodied water and saw three figures standing watching her less than a bowshot away on the far bank. One was a tall woman with long black hair and deep blue skin. The others were her mother and father, waving, looking just as they had on the last day of their lives.

Forgetting everything in her love and excitement, Ria ran out into the river.

Chapter Twenty-Two

As the waking sleep of deep ketamine sedation wore off, Leoni began to be troubled by memories of a strange dream.

If it had been a dream.

It came back to her in fragments, not in a connected whole, and with the sense that she had forgotten large parts of it.

It began with a vivid and convincing rerun of her near-death experience, and she found herself out of her body, drawn into a vortex of light and returned to that strange world that the Blue Angel had called the "land where everything is known." She was in a body again and – exactly as before – she was dressed in a simple sleeveless tunic that didn't belong to her. She was sure that she'd had another encounter with the Blue Angel, one laden with significance, but she couldn't remember anything that had passed between them.

Next came a tremendous rush and noise, everything around her blurred and refocused, and she materialized in the midst of a group of the sinister tree-birds. Right in front of her walked a young woman dressed in a tunic identical to her own. She seemed oblivious to the imminent danger.

Leoni's powerful instinct to run away was not so strong as the deep and immediate connection she felt to this girl, and she knew she had to warn her even at risk to her own life. Besides, there was no *risk*, right? Because at one level of consciousness she understood she was lying on a hospital bed tripping out on ket and this was all just a crazy dream. Wasn't it?

Still she yelled: "Hey, you! We gotta get out of here. These things aren't trees."

The young woman spun on her heels. She was more of a girl, really – maybe sixteen – quite short, wiry, very pretty in a tough tomboyish way, with nut-brown skin and chestnut hair. She stood facing Leoni with her hands clenched into fists and shouted a challenge in a strange language. *Dumb bitch.* She was so up for a fight she was missing the bigger picture – namely, a flock of monster predators with beaks the size of cars looming right over her head.

Leoni rolled her eyes and tried again: "RUN! OR WE'RE BOTH GOING TO BE BIRDFEED!" She raised her arm and pointed. The kid looked back over her shoulder and saw the danger. Then – *whoomf*! – the scene went blank and Leoni was emerging from her ketamine haze in California, strapped down to her bed, locked up tight in thick darkness.

It was as though her mind were running on two parallel tracks. One continued to give her glimpses of that strange and compelling other-world that she had been immersed in on the edge of death and seemed somehow to have entered again under the influence of ketamine. The other dwelt on her predicament as a prisoner in a psychiatric hospital where her parents intended to keep her permanently out of their way.

Leoni had done a lot of drugs in her short life and once at a club had been persuaded to snort a bump of K. It made her eyes sting and burn, left a horrible taste in the back of her mouth and turned her bones to rubber. Far from speeding her up, as ecstasy and cocaine usually did, ketamine had locked her in a lugubrious and incoherent world of her own where everything moved in slo-mo and simple physical tasks like lifting a wine glass became daunting obstacle courses. It also gave her the feeling that she had somehow been sitting about a foot away from herself for most of the evening. She realized now that this might have been a kind of low-level out-of-body experience.

The dose Melissa had injected into her must have been larger than the amount she'd been able to snort. Much larger. And it had produced different effects – including a weird and spectacular return journey to the land where everything is known.

Here was the problem. Leoni's very strong instinct about her bizarre experiences in the near-death state was that they were *real* – and the one good conversation she'd had with Dr. Bannerman had reinforced her in this view. But, courtesy of Melissa, she had now discovered that she could repeat elements of those experiences, get the out-of-body feeling, even encounter the same beings – such as the Blue Angel and monsters like the tree-birds – simply by shooting up a drug.

Didn't that prove that *all* such adventures, whether induced "artificially" by ketamine or "naturally" in a near-death coma, were just hallucinations – and thus completely *unreal*? And if that was so then wasn't it likely that the devastating conversation she'd overheard between her parents while supposedly out of her body must also have been unreal?

Alone in the darkness, fearful, strapped so tight to her bed she couldn't move, Leoni began to lose her newfound confidence in her flashbacks of being raped by her father. Suppose the rapes were just hallucinations too? Suppose they had never happened, as Dad had always claimed? Suppose they were no more "real" than her ketamine dreams and near-death delusions of a non-existent otherworld?

Suppose her memories really were false?

Leoni heard the sound of keys turning in locks and bolts being drawn. Then the door was flung open, lights came on and Sansom strode into the room, scowling and red-faced.

Right behind him was John Bannerman.

Chapter Twenty-Three

Before her feet touched water, Ria felt herself lifted as though on a windstorm, and carried into the sky far above the river.

She heard the sound of cicadas singing and felt the force of a powerful intelligence – far more powerful than Brindle's – probing and knowing her mind. Finally the beautiful thought-voice that had addressed her before was back inside her head, a voice like a soft wind blowing through pines, speaking the Clan language: "You have passed the second test, Ria. Now you must return to the land of the living. Use the Little Teachers again. I will await you."

Then Ria was no longer in the sky but rushing at great speed through a rotating tunnel of light. Everything was moving so fast she felt dizzy and lost consciousness. When she awoke she was back in her earthly body, inside the Cave of Visions, slumped on the cold stone floor on a couple of ibex skins, surrounded by sleeping Uglies.

It was very dark in the cave. Almost black. None of the lamps that had illuminated the scene the night before were still burning and only the faintest trace of daylight filtered through the distant entrance passageway.

Ria turned on her side and reflected on everything that had happened since the mushrooms had taken her to the spirit world, culminating in that brief tantalizing encounter with her mother and father and then this abrupt return to her earthly body.

She sobbed. Seeing her parents for a fleeting moment after seven long years was almost too painful to bear. Yet it had convinced her that death was not the end. In some way she could not understand it seemed her mother and father really did live on in the spirit world.

Other mysteries were equally bewildering to contemplate. For example, who was the bewitching blue woman who had stood beside her parents on the river bank? She looked like the spirit whose image Brindle had shown her on the way into Secret Place – the spirit he had called Our Lady of the Forest who he said watched over the Uglies. Was it she who had rescued her? And was it her thought-voice she had heard inside her head?

The thought-voice had spoken of tests. Which tests?

Then there was the problem of the mysterious girl who had appeared just in time to warn her of the monstrous tree-birds, then vanished again. And there was the bigger problem of life and death in the spirit world. She'd been in a body in that world – she was sure of it. So, what would have happened if the tree-birds had eaten her? She had bled and felt pain in their realm so presumably she could die in it – and if she had would her earthly body have lived on? Or died as well?

Ria reached down to touch her right ankle where the rat-roach had sunk in its fangs. Though there was no hot festering wound she could feel the scars of two puncture marks in the spot where she had been bitten. She turned her attention to her left leg. It should have been stiff and sore from her fall the night before but was free of pain and felt healed.

Thinking about what all this might mean, but coming to no immediate conclusions, Ria stood up and picked her way amongst slumbering Uglies towards the faint light of the entrance passage. Outside she saw Brindle sitting amongst the rocks, watching the sun rise over jagged mountains that soared up to touch the sky far away across the valley. She sent him her thought-voice: "The Little Teachers were amazing, Brindle. Thank you for getting me to try them. I had the most incredible journey. I actually did see my mother and father!"

"Saw my father too," Brindle replied.

"That's what you were hoping for, right?"

But he didn't answer. Instead he sent a picture into her mind of the wild braves who'd attacked them the day before. "They are scouts of a great army," he told her. "Father gave me secret knowledge of this." The pictures changed showing Ria throngs of the savages swarming into the Clan's hunting grounds. "They are called the Illimani. Their homeland is in the east, beyond the ice deserts . . ."

"No one can cross the ice deserts," said Ria. She was simply stating a fact.

"They *have* crossed! You must believe this! Illimani scouts already been here many moons, learning these valleys, preparing the way. Now thousands more are coming, killing all in their path."

"But why?"

Brindle's expression grew darker: "Because of the one called Sulpa. They have fallen under his power . . ."

Ria gasped.

"The Eater of Souls," Brindle continued. "That is what his name means. He is King of the Illimani but he is not a human being. He is a demon from the spirit world who has taken an earthly body. On the outside he is handsome – men and women worship his beauty – but within all is foul, all is evil. He is a mighty sorcerer, Ria. He delights in causing suffering. He glories in pain. He feeds on the misery of others. That is why his horde is marching . . ."

"And Grigo, Duma and Vik?"

"They too fell under his power."

"Then why were they killed?"

"Father showed me Grigo not killed. Only Duma and Vik. Scouts followed us. Grigo went other way. See Sulpa."

"But why? I don't get it . . ."

"Something bad going to happen."

With Brindle's words came images of smoke.

Images of fire.

And though the morning sun was growing warm, Ria shivered.

Chapter Twenty-Four

Two nurses, not Deirdre and Melissa but of the same general build, followed Sansom and Bannerman into the room. One of them was carrying a bag; the other marched to the window and drew back the thick blackout curtains. Somehow the entire night had passed and bright morning sunshine flooded in through the bars.

Leoni looked to Bannerman for recognition and gave him a wavering smile but his expression was stern and he seemed surrounded by an invisible armor.

Sansom approached her bed, tight-lipped and surly, and began to unfasten the buckles of her restraints with abrupt, jerky movements. "You're free to go, Miss Watts," he told her as she sat up. His small piglike eyes glittered above the busted blood vessels in his nose: "My nurses here have your clothes. Get dressed, please."

And that was that.

Five minutes later, Leoni and her rescuer were following Sansom's broad well-tailored back out of Mountain Ridge.

Leoni kept glancing up at Bannerman. She couldn't help it. She was in awe of him. First he'd saved her life. Now he'd broken her out of a secure mental hospital. What would he do for an encore? Leap tall buildings in a single bound? Stop runaway trains in their tracks? Fly through the air faster than a bullet? Alongside everything else that had happened in the last couple of days, she realized, she was falling for this dashing, mysterious, totally hot guy!

"You got my message," she whispered out of the corner of her mouth.

He nodded: "Yup."

"You moved pretty fast. I'm impressed."

Sansom led them into a plush office with leather furniture, a power desk and a bubbling coffee pot. Bannerman hunched over the desk to sign a couple of forms and then they were back out in the corridor again and headed for the elevator. As they descended, Leoni noticed that the two doctors were locked in some kind of weird staring contest. At one point Bannerman's upper lip actually curled.

The elevator opened into a public vestibule and Leoni and Bannerman stepped out. Sansom stayed put. The doors slid closed in front of him and he was gone.

"Phew!" said Bannerman. "That felt like sharing a cubicle in hell with the devil."

"He's really gross," Leoni said. "I hate him." She paused: "Listen . . . John . . . I owe you big time for this . . . I mean," she laughed, "it's not as though I *don't* owe you big time already. Seeing as you saved my life! But now I owe you even more . . ."

Bannerman looked embarrassed. "No problem," he said. "What your parents and this pissant psychiatric hospital did to you was beyond wrong. Their lawyers had covered their tracks pretty well and I couldn't find out where they'd taken you, so it was just great to get your voicemail."

They were walking across the parking lot now. The sun felt good on Leoni's skin and she couldn't believe how amazing this guy was. "You mean," she said, "you started looking for me even before I called you?"

"You bet! I had an attorney working on your case from the minute I knew they'd grabbed you off the ward."

At this she threw her arms around Bannerman's neck and attempted to kiss him on the mouth.

He returned her embrace, but kept his lips tightly closed.

Being rebuffed sexually by a good-looking man was not a common experience for Leoni. She stepped back: "I'm sorry," she said. "That was brazen of me."

"No!" he replied. "It's me who should apologize! I must seem ungallant. But you see . . . I'm gay. It was my partner who did your legal work. That's him over there . . ."

John Bannerman's lover was yet another spectacularly good-looking man. *What a waste*! "Hi," he said, "I'm David Temple. Good to meet you, Leoni."

"Hi, David. I'm really grateful to you for getting me out of there." Leoni made a vulgar gesture at the hospital with her middle finger. "I don't know how you did it, because my dad has swarms of killer lawyers working for him, but you must be brilliant and amazing. So . . . thank you!" And she leaned forward and hugged him.

"It wasn't such a big deal," David told her. "I think Sansom probably was convinced he was holding you legally, but it turns out he was wrong. They did have a qualified clinician write up your declaration – bribed him or blackmailed him, I'd bet. But I found so many holes in the paperwork there was no way it could be enforced. Once I brought the county magistrate up to speed he ordered you freed at once."

"Does that mean I'm safe? My parents won't be able to do this to me again?"

"The original declaration has been thrown out," said David. "They could try for a new one but I'm sure we'd nail them in court if they did. So, yes, short of them kidnapping you again, I'd say you're safe . . ."

While talking they'd climbed into a beat-up, late-'90s model Chevrolet Impala looking like it hadn't been washed since it came off the production line. Bannerman was driving, and he'd ushered Leoni into the front passenger seat. David was sprawled in the back: "Even so," he continued, "we figured you'd want to get off your parents' radar for a while."

"You figured right."

"And I know you want to understand more about what you went through during your near-death experience," Bannerman added.

"I have to find out!" Leoni agreed. "Because it's driving me nuts. One minute I think everything I saw and heard was real, the next I convince myself it was just some kind of hallucination. I go back and forth on it fifty times a day."

"So I have a proposal for you," said Bannerman. "Remember what I told you about my research into near-death and out-of-body experiences?"

Leoni was immediately alert: "Yes."

"I'm running a very hush-hush clinical study at the UC Irvine School of Medicine that's looking into these sorts of experiences right now. My proposal is that you join the project for the next couple of weeks as a volunteer. You're an ideal candidate and I'm pretty sure you'd get spectacular results."

Leoni was curious: "What makes me so ideal?"

"Lots in general, but one thing in particular. When you described your NDE to me you said you had an encounter with an angelic being . . . You showed me a sketch you did of her."

"The Blue Angel . . ."

"You said she gave you a lecture about how you'd squandered your potential?"

"She did." Leoni nodded. "But that was just the start. There was so much other weirdness that I didn't get a chance to tell you about. She said I had come to a place called the 'land where everything is known.' There were green flowers everywhere, strange-looking bugs the size of cows . . . and there were monsters there, John . . . Real monsters."

Bannerman turned slightly as he drove, glanced at David in the back seat and gave him a *look* – something of a knowing, I-told-you-so look.

Leoni bristled: "Hey, you guys don't think I'm crazy, do you? I'm up to here with people trying to make out I'm crazy."

"No!" David reassured her.

"No way!" said Bannerman. "It's just that David knows I've had other recent cases of people who've been through NDEs and claim to have met a blue woman – also in extraordinary surroundings. Most of them described her as an angel. None of them can draw as well as you but their sketches of her have obvious resemblances to the figure you showed me. Two of the volunteers in my project have reported encounters with her – "

"Which means," David interrupted from the back seat, "when we add your testimony to what John already has on file it starts to look like there's something very strange going on here. If enough different people experience the same supposedly non-real things then you begin to wonder whether what they're experiencing might be real after all . . ."

"And is it?" asked Leoni. "Is it real?"

"We have to be cautious about this," said Bannerman. "It's difficult to verify what people say has happened to them – in what might effectively be other dimensions of reality – in ways that would be accepted by scientists who don't believe in other dimensions. All the volunteers in my project have reported out-of-body experiences of other worlds, but I narrow down the field by only using those who've also had veridical experiences in this world while they were out of body."

"*Veridical*? What's that?"

"It means truthful and real – in other words people who've had experiences that can be verified. If I can confirm even one level of this phenomenon then it helps to increase confidence that the other levels could be real as well. You had one of these experiences – an experience while you were out of body that I've been able to verify . . ."

For a moment Leoni wasn't sure what he was talking about and must have looked puzzled. Bannerman jogged her memory: "Remember you told me you were out of your body inside the hospital – just before we revived you in the ER?"

"Yes . . ."

"You saw a receptionist. You said she seemed very prim and proper but that she was wearing orange sneakers with striped purple and green laces?"

"Exactly! Above her desk all you could see was this stiff charcoal business suit. Made her look like a headmistress or something. But under the desk she had on this crazy footwear."

"Which was definitely orange sneakers with purple and green laces?"

"For sure. I was looking right at those shoes when you zapped me back into my body."

"Well, here's the thing. That receptionist exists. She told me she was on duty the afternoon you were admitted and she was wearing a pair of sneakers exactly like the ones you described – right down to the purple and green striped laces."

Leoni objected: "The scientists you want to convince aren't going to accept that as evidence of anything, are they? They'll just say I must have seen her when I was being brought into the hospital."

"Well, obviously I've checked. Turns out you were brought directly into the ER from the helipad on the roof of the Med Center – straight down in an express elevator. You didn't go anywhere near the reception area. So there's no way you could have seen that receptionist's shoes while you were in your body . . ."

"Unless I'd been to the Med Center before and seen her then . . ."

"Obviously I've checked that, too" – Bannerman was looking vexed. "*Have* you been to the Med Center before, by the way?"

"No. Never."

"Well, it wouldn't matter if you had because this receptionist was new there. The day you were admitted was her first day on the job and the sneakers weren't even hers. She'd had to borrow them from a colleague who goes running because she broke a heel on her own shoes that morning."

"It's a cut-and-dried case," David chipped in from the back. "You saw something real that you couldn't possibly have seen if your consciousness was confined to your body."

"That's what I'm afraid of," said Leoni. "Some of the places I saw, and some of the things I heard . . . It's going to be pretty scary in lots of ways if it's all real."

"But you agree it's worth trying to find out?" Bannerman asked.

Leoni bit her lower lip and thought about everything that had happened. "Yes," she said at last. "Let's find out. I'm going to help you every way I can."

Chapter Twenty-Five

"Father also spoke of you," Brindle said. "Told me you been chosen to fight Sulpa. That why you in valley yesterday to save me from Grigo, Duma and Vik. Not accident."

Ria frowned at more of Brindle's mystical talk. "What do you mean, I've been chosen to fight Sulpa? Who chose me?"

"There is good and evil in spirit world. Good interested in proper order of things. Balance. Harmony. Love. Life. Sulpa part of evil. Interested in confusion, chaos, hate, death. Our Lady of the Forest kept him chained up long time. Stopped his wickedness. But he got away, turned proper order upside down, took human body, came into our world. Now good spirits need you to fight him."

"But that's ridiculous. If he's a demon they should fight him themselves."

"In spirit world they can fight him. In our world they cannot. Not allowed for them to take human bodies. That why they need you. Me as well. Uglies and Clan must make strong rope together to fight Sulpa."

"A rope? You're talking about friendship between the Uglies and the Clan? Not a chance, Brindle. Our leaders would shit mammoths at the idea."

"OK. Let them shit mammoths. Doesn't change anything. We the ones who have to fight Sulpa. Our responsibility. Our job. This our time."

"We will lose against Sulpa," Ria said, "if you go on trying to be merciful to the – what did you call them? The Illimani? The way you handled the ambush yesterday was really stupid."

"We trying to do right thing, Ria."

"I understand. And it's noble. But it cost lives. Remember what your father told you. These Illimani do the bidding of a demon. The only right thing is to kill them."

Last night the large expanse of flattened earth in front of the Cave of Visions had been lit with a score of lurid fires, and the wild uncouth looks of the Uglies had been terrifying. But now as those very same

Uglies began to emerge from the cave in ones and twos, blinking at the sun, yawning, stretching, in several cases farting, Ria discovered that she shared a strong bond with them.

Indeed, in her head, faint as a whisper, she imagined she could now hear the thought-talk of the whole multitude.

"Not imagining, Ria," Brindle interrupted. "When you ate the Little Teachers with us last night they made rope between you and all the Uglies . . ."

Ria was shaking her head from side to side, scratching her ears. "You mean everyone can speak to me now, not just you?"

"Sure. Why not? Every Ugly is your friend." He stood up, rested his hand on her shoulder: "Soon time for you to go back to Clan. Before go, Merinabob-grundle-nupro-atrinkam has present for you." He stood and walked off, beckoning her to follow.

"*Who* has a present for me?"

"Merinabob-grundle-nupro-atrinkam. Our Sorcerer."

"You mean you're taking me to see a magic man?"

"Not man. Woman. Very old. Very powerful. She going to help us fight Sulpa."

Ria had long ago checked out the Clan's magic men and discovered they were all total fakes. "Powerful?" she demanded. "How? In what ways? Give me examples."

"Can turn herself into wolf, find lost things, talk to animals, heal sick, make storms, fly like bird."

"Oh come off it, Brindle!" Ria scoffed. "You don't really *believe* that crap do you?"

"You mean same way you believed Clan crap about the Little Teachers turning people into demons?"

Ria hesitated: "OK, you were right about that, I admit."

"Right about this, too. You will see. Sorcerer's magic real."

The slope behind the Cave of Visions was rocky and precipitous, rising up to an immense wall of sheer cliffs. But in front, where Ria had fled in terror the night before, the ground fell away in a series of wide terraces; birch and oak grew in scattered stands and numberless huge boulders lay about in tumbled disarray amongst tussocks of coarse grass. Below the last terrace the stony banks of a clear alpine stream marked out the bottom of the valley which rose steeply beyond into mixed forests of alder, willow and pine. Higher up these were succeeded by patches of open moorland and, in the distance, a daunting vista of jagged snow-clad peaks.

"I can see why Clan scouts never found this valley," said Ria. "Cliffs that can't be climbed on one side, mountains that can't be crossed on the other. It's the perfect hideout when you know the secret way in."

A narrow but well-trodden path connected each terrace to the one below it. As Brindle led the way down, Ria saw that clusters of lean-tos made of branches roofed with skins nestled under almost every tree and up against the fallen rocks, and Uglies of all ages were going about their daily chores. With the morning sun warm on her back she realized this could be any camp, anywhere, a Clan camp just as much as an Ugly camp, united by multiple common bonds of humanity – females cooking, curing hides, and weaving grasses, males setting out on the hunt, knapping flints, building shelters, groups of children playing games.

The lowest and widest of the terraces, not far above the stream, was overgrown with a thick coppice of ancient oaks. Here there were no dwellings and small herds of red deer grazed amongst occasional clearings. It was amazing to Ria, who knew the skittish temperament of this species, that they did not run away when she and Brindle approached; one powerful buck even allowed her to stroke him and fondle his ears.

She laughed in delight: "I don't get this, Brindle. What's the matter with these animals? Why aren't they afraid of us?"

"Sorcerer has magicked them."

"But how is that possible? I've never heard of such a thing."

"Told you. Sorcerer very powerful."

In the heart of the coppice, just where it seemed to be at its most tangled and overgrown, they came to a little dome-shaped tent made of skins stretched over a framework of curved branches. It stood in a circle of shelter beneath the outstretched boughs of three gigantic oaks. Beyond lay a broad open meadow where many different kinds of herbs, fruit bushes and brightly hued flowers had taken root in ordered and regular rows. Waist deep in all this abundance, with a cloud of butterflies fluttering around her, a very small, very old Ugly female dressed in a loose smock of woven hemp was working on a bush, removing its flowers and placing them in a bag slung from her shoulder. "She is Sorcerer," confided Brindle.

At this the woman turned and began to walk out of the meadow towards them. She was frail, tiny and wizened, her gait was painful and stooped and Ria recognized her as the player of the bone song in the Cave of Visions. Clumps of pinkish-gray hair protruded from her large head, giving her a disconcerting babylike appearance. But in the shadow of her prominent brow ridges, narrowly set above her broad nose, her gray eyes sparkled with wisdom and experience. Her breathing was shallow as she approached, with many wheezes and gurgles, her hollow chest rising and falling beneath her smock, and yet she radiated invincible inner strength.

Ria found that her heart was pounding, as though she faced some powerful animal, and fought off an impulse to back away. Then a warm and gentle thought-voice addressed her: "Greetings, Ria of the Clan. I am Merinabob-grundle-nupro-atrinkam."

"I shall call you Merina," Ria replied. "I loved the sound you made last night with the bone."

Merina looked impressed: "You've learned how to thought-talk fast! Brindle told me you're very special."

For some reason the compliment made Ria feel uncomfortable: "I'm just a rabbit hunter," she objected. "There's nothing special about me."

"But I've heard you have a special gift with stones," said Merina. Then, with surprising speed, she took hold of both Ria's arms just below the elbows and began to knead and prod her flesh, working her way down to her hands, tugging at her fingers, and popping each of the joints in turn.

"Ow!" Ria protested. "What are you doing to me?"

"Giving you magic," whispered Merina with a mischievous smile. She turned, leaving Ria's arms tingling, and hobbled towards the little dome-shaped tent. "Follow me, rabbit hunter," she said.

Brindle pulled back the tent's entrance flap to allow Merina to step inside. A beam of light falling through the opening illuminated the scene in the cramped dark space beyond as Ria followed, her heart still thudding. Hanging from the curved branches forming the tent's framework, suspended on finely woven grass threads, hundreds of little quartz crystals danced, casting back a myriad of dazzling reflections like stars. Bundles of fragrant herbs and dried fungi were stored in wicker baskets on the floor.

Merina was feeling her way around the walls of the tent, setting the quartz crystals jingling above her head. She picked up and discarded various objects. Finally she announced "Here they are," and turned, holding out a deerskin pouch: "Five good throwing stones for Ria the rabbit hunter."

Ria took the pouch from her.

It was heavy.

She put her hand inside and counted one . . . two . . . three . . . four . . . five stones, all of perfect throwing weight. She drew one of the missiles out and examined it in the beam of light at the entrance flap. It was, without a doubt, the most beautiful thing she had ever seen – a cold and deadly egg of milky quartz.

She took the other stones from the pouch and laid all five on the floor of the tent side by side so she could study them. All were exactly the same shape, size and weight. All shared the same outer shimmer and the same strange inner opacity, like swirling mist or clouds. All were flawless and smooth to the touch.

"I've had them half my lifetime," said Merina. "I found them by the Snake River, lying in a circle on the bank, still wet as though someone had just fished them from the water. But no one else was there. Beautiful, mysterious stones. They have some power about them – any fool can see that. I picked them up and carried them away with me. All these years I've kept them safe . . ."

"Then you mustn't give them to me. They're much too precious a gift . . ."

"All these years I've kept them safe," Merina repeated, "without ever knowing why. But last night Our Lady of the Forest visited me and told me to give them to you."

With the words came an image of the beautiful, exotic, thrilling woman whom Brindle had called by the same title and whom Ria had seen on her journey with the Little Teachers. The tall woman with long black hair and deep blue skin who had stood with her long-dead parents by a river in the spirit world.

Ria was dumbfounded: "Last night, after I ate the Little Teachers, I also saw this blue woman . . ."

"She is not a woman, Ria! Do not be deceived, for she does not belong to humankind at all. She is one of the eternal spirits. One of those to whom all the worlds and every time and place are open. Past, present, future – nothing is hidden from her."

"But what does she want me to have the stones for?"

"Why, my child! Is it not obvious? She wants you to *throw* them, of course."

Chapter Twenty-Six

Thanks to a stopover at a Starbucks in Santa Monica, heavy morning traffic on the 405, and the beat-up engine in Bannerman's decrepit Chevy, the fifty-mile journey from Los Angeles to UC Irvine was now well into its second hour. In such circumstances Leoni should have been fuming. She couldn't bear to be delayed or frustrated – by anything. But having just escaped from Sansom's creepy lunatic asylum she felt differently. Every mile that crawled by on the freeway was a mile further away from Mountain Ridge and a mile closer to Bannerman's project – and maybe to some answers to the big questions now swarming all over her life.

"It's a residential program," Bannerman was explaining as he drove. "Part of the deal is that all the volunteers – there are thirty of them – live in at our research facility on campus and don't have contact with the outside world for the duration. The whole project runs for four weeks but the other volunteers have been there for nearly two weeks already, so you'll be joining halfway through."

"And what is it? Like some sort of dorm or something? I'm not sure how good I'll be at living with thirty other people."

"You'll have a small private room. You can be left alone, or you can socialize. It's up to you. The only commitment is that approximately once every two days you come down to our lab – it's in the basement of the same building – and we give you a shot and you report the effects to us . . . Sometimes we'll ask you to have two or three shots in the same day – which can be tough."

"These shots . . . they're not ketamine, are they?"

"Ketamine?" Bannerman sounded surprised, even affronted. "Certainly not. Where did you get that idea from?"

"At Mountain Ridge. Last night I tried to escape . . ."

"That was gutsy of you," commented David from the back seat.

"I just got so mad with the way they were treating me," said Leoni.

"Anyway, it didn't do any good. They caught me in a minute and sedated me with a huge hypodermic full of K. Then they strapped me back on my bed and that's where I stayed until a certain shining knight named John Bannerman rode in and rescued me this morning . . ."

Bannerman's face had clouded with anger: "That's so irresponsible of them," he exploded. "Sansom ought to be behind bars for using ketamine like that. It's not a tranquillizer – unless you're a horse."

"So what is it, then?"

"Lots of things. It's used as an anaesthetic for certain kinds of surgery. It's also a powerful hallucinogen – that's why it's popular on the club and rave scene."

Leoni nodded in agreement: "I snorted it in a club once. It's a heavy trip. But what it did to me at Mountain Ridge was way beyond that."

"Any idea how much they gave you?"

"The nurse said something about 'four hundred milligrams intramuscular?'"

"That would do it!" Bannerman whistled: "You could have open-heart surgery on four hundred milligrams IM and you wouldn't feel a thing."

"Yes, I was knocked out – or at least my body was. But my mind felt like it had been set free and I traveled to the same place I was in when I had my near-death experience. It was the land where everything is known again, and the Blue Angel was there. The green flowers were there. The monsters I saw before were there, too – they're trees but they have these huge beaks like birds – and I met this girl who they were going to attack. I tried to warn her, then the next thing I knew I was yanked out of there and stuffed back inside my body in Mountain Ridge."

"You told me your near-death experience felt, what did you say, 'more real than real?' Did all this feel that way too?"

"A thousand percent. But ketamine's just a drug . . ."

"Not necessarily. Remember we talked about how our brains might not be so much generators of consciousness as vehicles or receivers that mediate consciousness at the physical level?"

"The idea of the brain being like a TV set?"

"Exactly. And most human brains are tuned, by default, into Channel Normal – everyday reality, in other words."

"Makes sense," said Leoni. "We'd be pretty messed up if they weren't."

"But that doesn't mean that there aren't other channels broadcasting at us all the time which are all also equally real but not normally accessible to our senses. Perhaps what happens in NDEs is that there's a natural release of hormones into the brain that retune its wavelength setting and allow us to perceive those other realities."

"But what's it got to do with illegal drugs like ketamine?"

"A lot, if I'm right. In fact, my whole research project's based on an illegal drug."

Leoni grinned: "You've got to be kidding me. You're pushing an illegal drug at UC Irvine? Which one?"

Bannerman was obviously uncomfortable: "Look . . . there are about half a dozen substances that affect the brain in much the same way that the near-death state does and make it possible for us to induce the same kinds of experiences. To a certain extent, ketamine is one of them – as you discovered – but it's far from ideal. It's unpredictable. Too hard to control. Maybe even dangerous."

"So what do you use?"

"We get good results with dimethyltryptamine . . ."

Leoni frowned: "Dimethyl – what? Never heard of it."

"Dimethyltryptamine – DMT for short."

"OK, now I know what you're talking about. Friends of mine have smoked it. I hear it's pretty full-on."

"Yes. It's full-on," said Bannerman. "And we give it as an intravenous infusion which makes the onset of the experience even stronger and faster."

"How come you're allowed to do this?" Leoni objected. "I mean DMT's a Schedule 1 drug, right? People go to jail if they're caught with it. What makes you so different?"

Bannerman sighed: "Because we're administering DMT – which isn't addictive, by the way – as part of a properly constructed scientific project. We went through all the correct channels and procedures. It took years but eventually we got full approval from the DEA, so we're completely legit. The next problem was raising money to pay for the research. We didn't get anywhere with that until about six months ago when one very rich guy stepped in and gave us everything we need."

"Who is this guy? Maybe I know him . . ."

"I have to keep his name confidential. It's part of our deal. He's very imaginative and open-minded . . . We sold him on the idea that if he backed our project we'd find the holy grail of quantum physics for him . . ."

Leoni felt stupid but asked anyway: "The holy grail of quantum physics?"

"I mean proof of the existence of parallel universes and a reliable method for getting volunteers into them and then back out again in one piece."

When Leoni still seemed confused, Bannerman said: "OK, look . . . It's what we've been talking about. We're using DMT to simulate the brain chemistry of the near-death state in a large group of volunteers. Right?"

"Right."

"We hope to get some insights into the visions of other worlds that NDE-ers report – the same sort of realistic and convincing visions that you yourself experienced in the near-death state. Established medical opinion is they're 'just hallucinations' but the hypothesis we're testing is they could be part of an alternate system of human perception – a sort of sixth sense that might be harnessed to explore other dimensions of reality."

"So the realm of the Blue Angel is a parallel universe? And I can enter and leave it with DMT? Maybe that's what she meant when she said I had to make the veil between worlds thin if I wanted to see her again. Perhaps that's exactly what DMT does."

"Maybe," Bannerman agreed. "But I'm only saying that it's possible. If we do the science properly we might get a bit closer to certainty on this . . ."

"I'm not a scientist," David interrupted. "So I can call it like I see it. The Blue Angel is real. She has to be, otherwise different people wouldn't see her. She wants something from us and we need to find out what it is."

Chapter Twenty-Seven

Before high sun Ria and Brindle had climbed the terraces of Secret Place again and returned to the flattened platform in front of the Cave of Visions. Carrying the deerskin pouch from a strap slung around her shoulder, hefting the reassuring bulk and weight of the five quartz throwing stones inside it, Ria felt more like a warrior queen than a rabbit hunter. She had weapons! Given to her by a real Sorcerer. What could be cooler than that?

All around her there were Uglies armed to the teeth with spears, hand-axes and clubs. A war band of fifty braves had assembled to escort her safely back to the Clan. Grondin and Brindle would once again be leading and Ria saw many other familiar faces.

Most radiated friendliness and warmth. The single notable exception was the brave who'd stared at her with such hostility and anger during the night in the Cave of Visions. He stood at the front of the crowd with his shoulders hunched, his swarthy features knitted up into a frown, his chinless jaw thrust forward, and dark and thunderous thought-imagery emanating from him like a noxious vapor. Then his gruff voice was inside her head: "I am Garn-garnigor-shengo-aptenjen," he said, "and I oppose this mission. I will do as my king orders but I fear that only grief and loss will come of it."

Ria kept her eyes fixed on Garn: "I agree with you," she said. "Fifty men is too many. It's just going to attract attention. Five will be enough to get me home."

Brindle jumped into the conversation: "War party going out anyway, Ria. Still seven hundred Uglies living in outlying camps, remember? They in great danger now. Have to bring all of them back to Secret Place before Illimani reach them."

"Not that part of mission I oppose," interjected Garn. "Don't like taking Ria back to Clan, that's all. Not necessary. Just asking for trouble."

Again Ria could only agree. Brindle's plan *was* asking for trouble. Never mind the Illimani. If the Clan caught her with fifty Uglies there'd be a fight.

But now others were also expressing their views.

She recognized two brothers, twins with identical bushy brow ridges, prominent pock-marked noses and goofy buck teeth. They'd joined Brindle in disobeying her in the near-disastrous ambush yesterday. They stepped forward one after the other and hugged her. She sensed that, in their clumsy way, they were trying to apologize. "I am Trenko-wirtagorn-marny-apciprona," said the first. "I am "Krisko-wirtagorn-marny-apciprona," said the second. "We are your friends and we are for the mission."

Next it was the turn of a small fat Ugly with a bushy red beard and wrinkled leathery features. "I am Oplimar-sendo-wulshni-atrinkam and I am for the mission."

"I too." This time it was Grondin who spoke. "Ria is one of us now."

"Yes, one of us!" declared a tall gangling brave with a badly broken nose. "I am Brigly-jengle-jarlsteed-wulprasnik and I am for the mission."

"And I . . ."

"And I . . ."

Garn turned slowly where he stood, glaring at each of the braves as they spoke up for Ria. "She is *not* one of us," he protested. "Can't you see that? She is *not* our friend. She is Clan! Why should we risk our lives for any woman of the Clan?"

"Yesterday Ria saved *my* life," Brindle said. "Fought on side of Uglies, very brave, very clever. Last night she ate the Little Teachers with us. Today we bring her safely home. Hope she will make strong rope between Clan and Uglies. Good things come from good things, so I am for the mission."

By now many of the Uglies had linked arms and there was a strange mood in the air. Some began to make the low hooting sighs they used when they were trying to reach a group decision or heal the sick.

Garn's chest puffed out, his face swelled with anger and for a moment it seemed that he might burst like an overfilled water-skin. Instead he exclaimed "Enough of this!" He turned his back and stamped off, soon disappearing from view on the path amongst the terraces.

"What happened?" Ria asked Brindle. "Why did he just give up like that?"

Brindle shrugged: "Nothing else for him to do. Whole group against him. Uglies not good at being different."

The little fat guy called Oplimar fell into step behind Ria, and the twins Trenko and Krisko took up station on either side of her, as the war band set off uphill to the cave system connecting Secret Place to the outside world.

The entrance, from which they had emerged last night in darkness, was low and mean, little more than a slit in the rock. Beyond lay the vast and confusing labyrinth of corridors and passageways, echoing galleries and dark deadfalls, but Grondin was as sure-footed guiding them out as he had been bringing them in.

It was afternoon when they emerged amongst the undergrowth on the other side and made their way out on the hidden path, covering up its opening with branches and leaves as they exited so that it was once again invisible to passers-by.

Yesterday they'd thought only two men were following them but ended up having to kill four. Were there others coming behind? Perhaps even preparing an ambush for them right now?

Had the spirit of Brindle's father spoken true when he'd said there were thousands of these "Illimani"?

The sun was still high overhead when they approached the tract of thick woodland halfway down the mountain's flank. After the fight here last night the Ugly wounded and dead had been brought to Secret Place but the bodies of the Illimani had been left where they'd fallen at the edge of the trees.

The bodies were no longer there.

At once Ria heard Brindle's thought-voice: "Looks like trouble."

"If it comes to a fight," she reminded him, "show no mercy."

Brindle grimaced but said nothing as they entered the shadow of the trees. If there was to be an ambush it would be soon. But instead of the stealthy approach of enemies they heard shouts and screams, faint at first but horrible and utterly blood-curdling. Grondin and Brindle stopped in their tracks and the whole war party of Uglies came to a halt.

"What do you make of it?" Ria asked.

"Don't know," Brindle replied. "Gives me bad feeling. Has to be Illimani. Better get out of here fast."

"Let's go," Ria agreed – no point in seeking out violence when it could be avoided – and at once the Uglies were off again, threading through the trees, the sound of their footsteps muffled by the covering of brown pine needles lying ankle-deep on the forest floor.

The screams rose in volume and soon Ria was getting glimpses, a few hundred paces to her right, of the edge of the very large grassy clearing they'd crossed yesterday. Whatever was happening was happening there. All she had to do was ignore it and she'd be home free.

But as they hurried away she began to feel restless and uneasy: "I'm sorry, Brindle," she said at last. "I've got to find out what's going on." She ran back, quiet and fast. Just before the edge of the clearing she dropped onto her belly and wriggled forward.

What she saw were twenty Illimani performing a bizarre circular dance and shouting in their barbaric language. The nearest of them were two hundred paces from her. They all carried the familiar wooden spear-throwers slung across their backs but they were otherwise naked. Many were smeared with blood. All of them seemed furious and agitated. The whole scene was charged with an atmosphere of unspeakable violence and savagery.

Ria wriggled forward a little further.

She could see now that two men were tied to stakes, facing one another about ten paces apart in the midst of the circling mob. One was struggling to break free. The other, the source of the screaming, had been gutted like a fish. As Ria watched, a huge savage, towering head and shoulders above the rest, thrust his arm deep into the man's open belly, shouted with glee, and began to haul forth his glistening entrails to the sound of more horrifying screams.

Ria crept forward again, and risked breaking cover by rising to a half-crouch because a dreadful suspicion had dawned on her.

Was that screaming voice Rill's?

She peered out from the edge of the clearing and suddenly she was sure. It was her own dear brother Rill who was being murdered before her eyes. The man tied to the other stake was Hond.

Keeping low, Ria stepped out into plain view, reached into the pouch Merina had given her, selected two of the perfectly balanced quartz hunting stones, and began to run towards the dancing mob. They were all so focused on the torture that they failed to notice her at first, but she was still more than a hundred paces out, much too far for a sure kill, when the executioner, his arm drenched to the shoulder in Rill's blood, snatched a long flint knife from his waistband and turned on Hond.

There was no time for fine judgements. Closing the gap at breakneck speed, Ria drew back her arm for the throw of her life.

Part II

Chapter Twenty-Eight

The UC Irvine campus is a sprawl of modern low-rise buildings laid out across rolling terrain in a series of concentric rings around the green bull's-eye of Aldrich Park. In one of the outer rings, off Academy Way and Medical Plaza Drive, lies the Department of Health Sciences, dominated by the futuristic Biomedical Research Center. A few minutes' walk west of the Center, across California Avenue, is the University Research Park. It was here, in a white-painted, two-story rectangular building backing onto the San Joaquin Hills Toll Road, that the DMT project was housed.

While David waited in the Chevy, Bannerman showed Leoni to her room on the upper floor of the building. It had a small window overlooking the green lawns of the research park. There was a simple pine-framed single bed, a matching desk and chair, and a small cupboard for hanging clothes. She didn't have her own bathroom and would have to share communal facilities down the hall.

Leaving her bag, Leoni followed Bannerman out into the hallway and down by the stairs to the lobby floor of the research building. As they walked he said: "I'm going to introduce you to two colleagues who're running the DMT project with me. In fact, they're here a good deal more than I am so they'll be looking after you when I'm gone."

"Gone?" Leoni was a little stunned. Until now she had assumed that Bannerman would personally supervise her participation in his project from beginning to end.

"Yes, I'm afraid so. I have to divide my time between the research and UCLA Med Center. The deal is I put in four days a week there and three days a week here, but I have to return to LA right now – I'm already running late – and I won't be able to get back to Irvine until Friday."

"What day is it today?"

"It's Tuesday."

Leoni thought about it and began to put the recent high-speed blur of her life into some sort of order. Last Friday night she got wired on cocaine, drunk on vodka, had bad sex with some rich nonentity, and was arrested by the California Highway Patrol. Saturday afternoon she overdosed on OxyContin. Saturday evening and night, while she traveled out of body to the realm of the Blue Angel, John Bannerman battled to save her life in the ER. Sunday night was Mom and Dad's visit to her hospital room in UCLA. Monday morning she was abducted to Mountain Ridge. Monday night she tried to escape, was treated to an involuntary ketamine experience and had another visit with the Angel. Tuesday morning, bright and early, John Bannerman arrived to rescue her.

Today was therefore indeed Tuesday, and, in fact, it was still morning: "Tuesday . . . Wednesday . . . Thursday . . . Friday . . . That means I have to sit around here doing nothing for three days until you come back?"

"Not necessarily."

Leoni was beginning to realize this was one of Bannerman's favorite phrases. "What do you mean, 'not necessarily?'" she mimicked.

"Well, for example, you could just go ahead and have your first round of shots, guided by one of my colleagues. They're both very good at this work."

As he spoke he led her into a conference room where an earnest young male with fresh features, extremely thin lips, a crew-cut and tiny glasses was waiting beside a large, lumpy olive-skinned female in her mid-forties with a prominent nose and three dark hairs growing out of her chin. Bannerman introduced the woman as Dr. Shapira and the man as Dr. Monbiot.

Shapira's manner was brusque, verging on unwelcoming, and she seemed nervous. "John's told us all about your recent near-death experience," she said as soon as Leoni was seated, "and we've agreed – under duress – to accept your late entry into our DMT program. But I have doubts about your candidacy and it's my responsibility to put them on record."

"Sure," said Leoni, not really knowing how she was expected to respond. "Go for it."

Shapira leaned forward, planted her elbows on the table, and arranged her thumbs and fingers into a triangle: "DMT is a blunt instrument for breaking open certain areas of the mind that might be better kept closed. It can lead to disturbing experiences. It can be terrifying."

"Yes . . . ?"

"So my question to you, so soon after you've gone through a full-blown NDE, is whether you've thought through the risks of plunging yourself back into such realms again?"

"Risks?" Leoni cast a puzzled glance at Bannerman. "What risks?"

Shapira's stare locked onto her. "Some people, and from what John has told me you are one of them, have a strong inborn ability to make contact with 'spirit worlds' and 'spirit beings' – whatever these things are. An effect of DMT can be to open them up even further to these other realms – perhaps real, perhaps illusory, we do not know – to the point where they become vulnerable. Some begin to wonder if they are going mad and if they will ever be able to live a normal life again."

"But in all fairness," interrupted Monbiot, "they *don't* go mad and they *are* able to lead normal lives again."

"Well, so far, yes" – Shapira looked skeptical – "but in the future who knows? The more I do this work, the more I'm convinced that DMT is capable of inflicting immense psychic harm . . ."

"That's not very reassuring," said Leoni.

"It's not meant to be," snapped Shapira. "I want you to be fully aware that you're getting yourself into a very serious business with us here . . . DMT's got nothing to do with 'highs,' or 'kicks,' or 'fun' like other drugs you've experimented with."

Leoni bristled: "Look, I know it's going to be tough and it won't be 'fun,' OK? I accept there might be some risks – thanks for warning me. But this is something I need to do and I've made up my mind." She turned to Bannerman: "I guess you're right. I don't have to wait for you to get back to start the DMT. If you say I'm ready, then I'm ready."

Bannerman passed the buck: "You're ready only if you feel you're ready."

"Then I guess I'm ready. Let's do it."

At ten a.m. on Thursday, with her heart beating a little faster than normal, Leoni reported to the lab in the basement of the research building.

Her only "duty" in the previous two days had been to undergo tedious medical tests of her respiration, liver function and blood pressure, as well as an ECG and seemingly endless requests for samples of her blood and urine. Otherwise she was free but felt so terrified and alarmed at the prospect of socializing that she contrived to keep herself to herself, even avoiding the restrooms if another volunteer was present. She also acted hostile and monosyllabic at communal meals. There was one guy, maybe eight or ten years older than her, a mature student taking courses at UC Berkeley, who dressed like a hippie and tried to get her talking a few times. He had a nice voice – sounded British – but on each occasion she'd cold-shouldered him. The only thing she wanted to do was stay in her bare, quiet room filling the pages of a sketch pad with scenes and details from the land where everything is known. The two suns in the sky, the strange green flowers, the Blue Angel, the cow-beetles, the tree-birds and the girl with chestnut hair – all were there.

Who was the girl? How had she come to be in the Angel's realm? And why had Leoni felt such a strong connection to her? As though in search of a coded message she'd made a dozen different sketches of her, recalling every detail of her pretty, tomboyish face, but was none the wiser.

Perhaps DMT would take her to a place where she could find answers?

Both Monbiot and Shapira were waiting for her in the lab. They had her sign a wad of consent forms and ushered her down a long corridor lined with plastic chairs and into a curtained-off treatment room fitted out with a hospital bed, IV stands, medicine cabinets and a handbasin. She lay down on the bed and looked at the ceiling. Then Shapira rolled up Leoni's sleeve, prepped her arm with surgical wipes and inserted an IV line into her forearm vein. "DMT fumarate," Monbiot explained. "We're starting you off on a low dose – 0.2 milligrams per kilogram of body weight. Some people don't even experience any effects at that level but it gives you a chance to get familiar with the general set-up and prepares you for a larger dose tomorrow."

Out of the corner of her eye Leoni could see Monbiot flushing a syringe into the IV line. Fifteen seconds later she heard a loud buzzing and crackling in her ears and felt dizzy and disorientated as though she were being rocketed up into the sky on a spinning carousel.

A tremendous feeling of pressure, as though something were literally about to explode, filled her brain.

Chapter Twenty-Nine

Within seconds the treatment room had ceased to exist for Leoni – as if it had been blasted into tiny splinters and blown away in the slipstream of her fantastic ascent. Her own body, Doctors Monbiot and Shapira, UC Irvine, North America and all the other ingredients of everyday reality were simply gone, and all she knew was the whirlwind of pure force that impelled her upwards in a seemingly endless, vertiginous rush.

Then, with no slowing of her rate of climb, an incredible seething mass of rich, deeply saturated colors, coiled into intricate knots like the bodies of a thousand serpents, rising into nested wave patterns and decorated with bright dots, exploded across her field of vision. The spectacle was vast, breathtaking, devastating. Writhing and pulsating with its own inner light, it filled her with an indescribable sense of menace. She couldn't shut out the colors or ignore them. They had invaded every corner of her consciousness and demanded her attention.

Then, suddenly . . . *WHOOSH*! It happened fast. One second Leoni was outside that terrifying wall of colors, mesmerized and threatened by it. The next second . . . *BAM*! She was projected through it into a glassy geometrical space. The space was dominated by a large cylindrical machine lit up like a Christmas tree by hundreds of green and yellow LEDs flashing on and off in coordinated sequences. It seemed to be part metal, part organic, and was surmounted by a brainlike central dome divided into hemispheres. Attached to it by a spiral tube was a funnel, resembling an old-fashioned phonograph, and at least a dozen waving tentacles – some wiry, some fleshy – of varying lengths and thicknesses. As ridiculous as a cheap prop in a low-budget sci-fi movie, the whole bizarre apparatus protruded up through the middle of the floor where it was tended by five pallid humanoids about the height and build of eight-year-olds. They wore colorful clothes – reds, yellows and greens – but had the wizened faces of ancient gnomes.

Although she felt afraid, and deeply disorientated, Leoni drifted closer – her previous experience of the out-of-body state helped her to negotiate this alien new reality – and as she approached them the little beings turned towards her. *They can see me*, she realized with a shock – for she had believed herself invisible in her aerial form.

Of course we can see you, came back a reply. The words were not spoken aloud, yet she heard them inside her mind.

They can see me, thought Leoni, *and* they're telepathic.

She framed a thought as a question: "Who are you?"

"We're the switchboard operators," one of the entities replied, again without speaking aloud. He gestured towards the machine. "We're here to put you through . . ."

"Put me through to who???"

At this the five humanoids looked at each other and made an elaborate dumbshow of puzzlement with their small hands turned palms upward and baffled expressions on their wrinkled faces. Finally one of them, a little taller than the others, stepped forward: "Not *who*," he said. "*Where.* We're here to transmit you. Please tell us where you would like to go."

"Whaddya mean? Like to Europe? Africa? Mexico? Are you some sort of travel agency?"

The taller being took another step towards her and now Leoni noticed that he was holding a long flexible wand made of some silver substance with the liquid sheen of mercury. "This is the first time you've used this technology?" he asked – but it was more of a statement.

"I have no idea what you're talking about."

"The technology that brought you here?" He gestured around the room and Leoni confirmed her first impression that its walls were made of clear glass – or some material resembling glass – set at freakish, impossible angles and joined overhead into a crystalline pyramidal ceiling. Beyond, on all sides, and beneath the transparent floor – very scary, this – she could see . . . nothing. Just pitch-black night, stretching forever in all directions. It was as though she were suspended in a shard of light over a bottomless pit of endless darkness.

Wanting to answer the question about technology, she summoned an image in her mind of her meat body lying on the bed back in the lab at UC Irvine, of the IV line in her arm, and of Dr. Monbiot pushing down the plunger in the hypodermic that had flushed the DMT into her system. At once the tall being extended his hand and touched the tip of his wand against the shoulder of Leoni's aerial body.

The effect was dramatic. Her feelings of disorientation and confusion were banished, a mood of calm settled over her, and her mental processes seemed to sharpen and clarify.

"I know where I want to go," she said, and the thought evoked an immediate burst of whirring and clicking from the machine. The little beings rushed to their stations at various points around it, and its tentacles reached out towards her aerial body and drew her down – she made no attempt to resist – until she was peering into the phonograph funnel.

Now that she was up close it seemed . . .

. . . Big enough to swallow her.

With no obvious transition Leoni found herself inside it and moving through it at amazing speed. Its walls and sides gyrated around her, becoming a blur, she had the sense of dropping downwards, and then – *WHAM*! *THWOCK*! – she was back in a body again, subject to gravity, and dumped on her ass beneath the twin suns, and amongst the familiar iridescent green flowers, of the land where everything is known.

She looked around but there were no monstrous man-eating trees in sight. Then she heard the electrifying voice of the Blue Angel: "I'm so glad you've found your way to this technology. Now we can really get some work done."

Leoni had tumbled out of the sky onto a steep slope leading up to a ridge, and the voice seemed to be coming from the other side of the ridge. She climbed the slope and, at the summit, found herself looking down at the Blue Angel seated on the hillside a few steps below. Dressed in a scarlet robe spun from some magnificent and unearthly material, the Angel was looking down at the distant rooftops of an immense circular city, surrounded by a high metallic wall, commanding the floor of a lush green valley – a futuristic city of pyramids and glass towers, canals and hanging gardens, jade obelisks and crystal ziggurats, but one that seemed devoid of life and movement.

Leoni had not forgotten the Angel's promise to show her "Jack," the mysterious source of all her pain. But as she scrambled down to her side she asked instead: "You mean I can get to you whenever I want to with DMT? Is that the technology you're talking about? Is that what makes the veil between worlds thin?"

"Yes – a molecular technology, older than the stars. The machine elves seeded it in many worlds to effect transit and linked it to hyper-dimensional switchboards they control."

"I went through one of those switchboards. I think I met the machine elves."

"They like to play games, but many in the transit process are distracted by them and the switchboards don't always send you where you want to go . . . Much time is wasted. Much confusion caused . . ." In the Angel's hands there had appeared a small device, a little like a laptop computer. She flicked up the screen, revealing a control panel, pointed to the city and turned a dial: "Do you like it like this?" she asked.

To Leoni's astonishment the sky above the rooftops began to change color as the dial was turned. It had started off blue but now strobed through green, yellow and magenta before returning to blue and beginning the cycle again. The effect was mesmerizing. "Yes," she said, "I like it very much." She had a strong intuition that the flickering colors were reprogramming her brain, but she didn't mind. Then the Blue Angel reached over, plunged a long silver needle deep into her left temple and used the needle as a catheter to implant a thin filament of crystal.

The operation was fast, shocking and intrusive.

"Why did you do that?" Leoni yelled as the needle was withdrawn, "I trusted you."

"I haven't broken your trust. I've made some adjustments to simplify your transits in future. When you next use the technology it will take you where I want you to go without the delay of passing through a switchboard . . ."

"You've made some adjustments to what? My meat body is back on a hospital bed in UC Irvine. I don't even understand what sort of body – or brain – I have here . . . And what do you mean about taking *me* where *you* want me to go?"

"Don't you remember, Leoni, when we last spoke? I told you I have plans for you. I have a purpose for you to fulfill . . ."

"There you go again. *You're* going to transit *me*, wherever *you* want, to fulfill *your* purpose. But you haven't even told me what this purpose is or asked me if I want to fulfill it for you. Don't you need my permission? Or do you get to do whatever you like because you're an angel?" Leoni hesitated: "That *is* what you are, right?"

"Gods, angels, spirits, demons – we have many names."

"There's more than one of you?"

"We are legion. But this is talk for another time. I have work for you now."

Leoni could feel herself getting annoyed: "You still haven't asked my permission to involve me in any of this . . . work."

"I do not need to ask your permission."

"Ha!" Leoni was amazed at her own boldness: "You bet your ass you do!"

The Angel smiled: "You misunderstand me. I do not mean to disrespect your sovereignty. It's true I have *chosen* you for this work – and I did that without your consent. But the nature of the task is such that it would be pointless for you to undertake it unless you accede to it wholeheartedly."

Leoni was trying to figure out exactly what this meant. "So your plans don't involve forcing me to do anything?"

"I could not do so even if I wished to. You are my choice for this task. But if you do not accept then I will choose another."

"What made you choose me?" Leoni asked.

"You are human, you are female and you live in the twenty-first century. These were all essential prerequisites."

"Hey, I've got news for you! Women hold up half the sky. There are about four billion of us. What makes me different?"

"You were abandoned at birth. Your first five years were spent in an orphanage . . ."

"Nobody wanted me . . ."

"But at last you were adopted . . ."

"I'd given up hope. Longing to have a mother and father, seeing the other kids go off to happy homes – it all hurt too much. Just after I was five my dreams came true. For the next three years I thought I was in heaven. Then I found out I'd been adopted by the parents from hell."

"An apt metaphor. And this, finally, is why I have chosen you. You were adopted to serve as an offering to Jack, and Jack is my enemy."

"An offering?" Leoni repeated the words, feeling dazed. "I don't think I understand."

"Every moment of your life after your adoption was mapped out as a sacrifice to Jack. He delights in the destruction of human potential and the undoing of innocence. Your demolition was your parents' gift to him."

"But why? Why would they do that?"

"He demands such a sacrifice of all his followers. Some are ordered to kill a child, amidst blood and fear, in some abominable way. Others are required to inflict bewildering mental and physical tortures first, sometimes extended over periods of years. This was what happened to you."

"So that means my parents are Jack's followers?"

"Yes. And there are others like them everywhere – bad people he has spoken to in dreams, good people he has corrupted and subverted. A secret cult has begun to form and its members worship him as their god. Already they number thousands. They occupy positions of power and wealth in their nations, and every one of them has offered a child like you to Jack."

The words sounded true and at the same time made no sense. "I don't even know who Jack is," Leoni said.

"Do you *want* to know?" the Angel asked.

"Of course I want to know!"

In the lap of her scarlet robes the Angel still held the little device with its fold-up screen and control panel. Now she turned a second dial – not the one she'd used to adjust the sky – and the screen burst into life with a kaleidoscopic display of rotating patterns and colors. "Look into the screen," she commanded, "and I will show you Jack."

Leoni had to obey. The patterns within the screen opened up into a rushing, churning vortex of sound and light and she felt her consciousness fly out of her body into the maelstrom. Once more she had the sense of passing through a tunnel – *Alice down the rabbit hole*, she thought – and then *WHOOMF*! she was back in a place that felt like Planet Earth, under a single sun, standing close to a huge crowd of naked, brutish, pale-skinned men armed with crude but lethal-looking weapons of stone, wood and bone.

At first Leoni feared they might be able to see her – perhaps in the same way that the machine elves had seen her? – but it soon became obvious she was as invisible to these weird nudists as she had been to her parents when she'd approached them in the out-of-body state.

Increasing in confidence, she slipped unnoticed into the crowd, taking time to scrutinize the wild appearance of the men. Almost all of them were blondes with shaggy shoulder-length hair, electric-blue eyes, and teeth filed to sharp points. They were lean and muscular, built like prize-fighters, and their bodies were criss-crossed with scars. Slung across their backs, almost like an item of uniform, each of them carried three short spears and a peculiar wooden baton, about two feet long, with a handle of antler at one end and a sort of spur or hook, also of antler, attached to the other end.

Who were these people? Some kind of Caucasian survivalist cult from hell? Many wore bones through their noses and necklaces of what looked like human teeth – and that was a sight you didn't see often, even in LA. All had crazed expressions, their blue eyes blazing, peering upward with rapt intent, and she sensed about them a tremendous and terrifying power.

That was when Leoni began to realize just how big the crowd really was and that she was in the midst of *thousands* of men gathered in disciplined ranks in a great circle around the perimeter of a low hill. They were staring at a squat shelter built on its summit, open on all sides but roofed at a height of about seven feet with a grid of narrow wooden slats. Then they all shouted at once – a deafening, guttural, stomach-churning yell – as a young man appeared in front of the shelter and stood with his hands outstretched to receive their salute.

What sort of person could command the approbation of an army such as this?

Enjoying the freedom of her invisible aerial body, Leoni soared up to the summit to find out.

Chapter Thirty

Tied fast to stakes ten paces apart, Rill and Hond faced one another in the center of the woodland clearing. Rill was slumped forward against his bonds, silent now, his entrails spilling out in bloody coils from his stomach cavity, while the savage who had disemboweled him was striding towards Hond armed with a long flint knife.

Ria felt a lightning-bolt of energy jolt down her right arm as she let fly with the first of the five quartz hunting stones Merina had given her.

The deadly little egg was balanced and streamlined to perfection, but still it was a tricky throw because the furious crowd of naked braves continued to dance around the captives and their executioner. There were only two or three paces between each of the cavorting, rushing men and Ria's shot, taken on the run, had to pass through one of these fast-shifting gaps and strike down a moving target over a distance of a hundred paces.

The whirl of the dance obscured her view, but she heard a satisfying double *clunk*! – something like the sound of an axe biting into a tree trunk – as the missile bounced into the advancing brave's naked ankles. Still five paces away from Hond, he tumbled and fell head over heels. In the process she was pleased to see he had impaled his left hand with the flint knife he held in his right.

He didn't cry out, and an instant later, with an athletic bound, he was standing again – this time locking his gaze onto Ria with such force that she felt it like a blow to the face.

He was a fearsome giant of a man, bigger even than the biggest of the Uglies. Enormous knots of muscle stood out on his broad shoulders and narrow waist, and a huge penis and hairy testicles dangled between his thighs.

Ria wasn't afraid.

As she hurtled across the sunlit clearing towards him – eighty paces, seventy, sixty – what she felt was rage and remorse.

Above all, remorse.

For she could not escape the conclusion that the terrible events unfolding around her were her fault. Her brothers must have come out in search of her when she'd failed to return the night before. They were superb trackers and had followed her trail as far as this forest.

What they couldn't have known was that a band of ferocious killers, who'd just discovered the bodies of four of their scouts, awaited them there.

And now poor Rill was dead.

At fifty paces, as though responding to a silent signal, all the dancing warriors stopped in their tracks and turned in unison to glare at her.

Ria skidded to a halt too. She'd lost the advantage of surprise and would throw better from a standstill than on the run.

Her brother's murderer raised his transfixed hand in her direction and withdrew the blade. There was a spurt of his own blood and the unmistakable rasp of flint grinding against wet bone. He straightened, showing no weakness, and intensified his weird stare at Ria. At this distance she could see his eyes. In stark contrast to his pale gore-smeared skin, they were a startling and disconcerting bright blue.

He shook his shaggy hair, tilted back his head and began to laugh. A moment later the other twenty members of his gang joined in, opening their mouths wide and baring their pointed teeth. They all had the same mad blue eyes and the sound they made was like a pack of cave hyenas squabbling over a rotting carcass.

Summoning up all her concentration and strength, Ria threw her second stone. She could see from the surprise on her adversary's face that he hadn't expected this – least of all from her left hand – and she watched the missile connect hard with the side of his skull just behind the temple. His raucous laughter was cut off, his eyes rolled up in their sockets, and he stumbled, dropped to his knees and slumped forward on his face in the grass.

That was when spears the size of small trees began flying through the air from all directions, thudding into the naked bodies of the Illimani. There was a great roar and the spears were followed by a throng of Uglies, the entire escort of fifty braves who had accompanied Ria from Secret Place, wielding their clunky stone axes and hulking wooden clubs.

Pandemonium broke out amidst the Illimani, suddenly outnumbered more than two to one. Men fell, were knocked aside, hacked down. None of them ran. They fought as a pack, like wolves, with stunning ferocity. But for a brief interval no one was paying any attention to Ria who was soon straddling the hairy body of the Illimani giant she had felled.

He was conscious but dazed.

Ria stooped, wrenched his flint knife from his grasp, rolled him onto his back, and scythed off his cock and balls. As he struggled to his feet, jetting blood and bellowing in horror, she slit open his stomach from crotch to breastbone and stuffed his severed genitals into his gaping mouth. "That's for Rill," she screamed.

She darted forward and cut the ropes shackling Hond to the stout wooden stake.

The marks of torture were everywhere on his body. "Can you fight, brother?" she asked.

Hond dodged a spear thrust from an Illimani brave who leapt out at them from the melee, snatched the weapon from its owner, reversed it and brought the man down with a jab through the eye. "I can fight," he said.

Ria tightened her grip on the long flint knife and stood back to back with Hond as three more warriors converged on them.

Chapter Thirty-One

The summit of the little hill was flattened into a platform about thirty feet across, and what was going on there was much more complicated than it had looked from the ground.

The most striking part of it was the naked young man standing with his hands outstretched as though to receive an offering from the massed ranks of armed men below. Up close he was beautiful – not just good-looking but *beautiful* – in a way that managed to be both strong and effeminate, mysterious and tempting, wistful and joyous, dangerous and intoxicating, all at the same time.

Leoni had been too busy with sex and drugs to bust her butt at art school, dropping out before the end of her first semester, but she knew what she liked and Botticelli's famous painting *The Birth of Venus* was one of her all-time favorites. The guy on the platform looked enough like Venus to be the goddess's brother. His body was lean and hard, covered with knots of finely-sculpted muscle, but he had the same red-gold hair, cascading below his waist, the same long, sensitive features, the same alabaster skin, the same Cupid's-bow lips. His eyes were wide and luminous, but they were not gentle and introspective like those of the Venus, nor neon-blue like the eyes of the roaring army of men raising their voices in adoration from the foot of the hill. They were a strange mixture of green and amber, like the tawny eyes of an African lion, with smoky tendrils of a darker hue, perhaps purple, radiating out from pitch-black pupils.

His age was hard to guess. Was he twenty? Twenty-five? Maybe closer to thirty? He had about him an air of invincible confidence and experience that contrasted with his otherwise youthful appearance. *This is how an immortal might look*, she thought. *Maybe even a god.*

Indeed, the wild men massed at the foot of the hill were responding to him *exactly* as if they were venerating and praising a god. And, although their frenzied roars were meaningless to her, Leoni could hear two syllables repeated over and over with an ecstatic emphasis and realized they must be shouting his name:

"SUL . . . PA!"
"SUL . . . PA!"
"SUL . . . PA!"

More faintly, she also heard something else – gut-wrenching sounds of sobbing and high-pitched screams – arising from the other side of the low wood-framed shelter that Sulpa was standing in front of. She took to the air and saw a group of children being marched at spearpoint across the hilltop behind the shelter. There were three boys and three girls, none of them older than twelve, some who she thought were as young as seven. They were dirty and bloody, covered in cuts and bruises, and as naked as their brutal captors who kicked and punched them as they stumbled along.

The wretched column halted at the base of the shelter. Then the guards lifted ladders from the ground and forced the children to climb about seven feet onto the flat grill of narrow wooden slats forming the roof. There, sobbing and shivering with fear, they were made to lie face down and, one by one, their wrists and ankles were tied tight to the slats. The last of the boys, a little bigger than the others, put up a fight, squirming, punching and biting as they attempted to tie him. A lucky kick from his heel struck one of the guards full in the face and knocked him tumbling off the roof but the others subdued the struggling boy with a rain of blows so harsh they must have broken his nose and his jaw.

Leoni wanted to protect these damaged kids, with their bashed bleeding faces squashed down into the gaps between the roofing slats. She flew around them, searching for some way to set them free, but she could do nothing in her invisible aerial body.

There came another roar from the crowd at the foot of the hill and she saw Sulpa had picked up a sword and was holding it above his head. It was pure inky black from pommel to tip and had a narrow leaf-shaped blade that bore the dull glint of smoked glass.

Sulpa pivoted to look at the four guards who were standing just behind him, two on either side of the shelter, and his gaze rested on the one who had fallen from the roof. He said something to him in a guttural, incomprehensible tongue and the guard stepped forward and knelt at his feet.

Sulpa's manner was very gentle, even kind. He rested his hand on the guard's head and ruffled his unkempt hair, ran a concerned finger down his cheek and helped him to stand again. But next, without any change of demeanor, he gripped the sword double-handed, swung it in a lightning-fast figure of eight, and lopped off both of the man's arms at the shoulder joints. Blood splashed in all directions and the severed limbs thudded to the ground.

A roar of appreciation rose up from the crowd and Sulpa stepped back to inspect his handiwork and savor his victim's shrieks of agony. Then, with a sly look stealing over his beautiful features, he swung the sword again and hacked off the man's left leg at the hip, bringing him crashing down. As he writhed and squealed a final sword stroke amputated his right leg, also at the hip.

By now Sulpa's lean, hard body was spattered with so much blood that he looked like a demon from hell as he stepped over the shuddering torso of the butchered man and advanced into the shelter, holding the dripping black sword.

Above him the six children tied face down on the roof slats screamed in abject terror.

The roof was low, just a foot above Sulpa's head. Positioning himself beneath the sacrificial victims – for that was what Leoni now recognized the unfortunate children to be – he stabbed upward. His sword passed through a gap between two slats and into a girl's chest, impaling her with such force that its point emerged between her scrawny shoulder blades and protruded a foot beyond. She gave a single pitiful wail of distress. Sulpa twisted the weapon half a turn, opening a huge wound, and withdrew it, releasing a bright torrent of blood.

"*SUL . . . PA*!" bayed the army of spectators, as though all their thousands of voices were funneled through one gigantic throat:

"*SUL . . . PA*!"
"*SUL . . . PA*!"
"*SUL . . . PA*!"

Invisible witness to these events, Leoni felt she had become trapped inside a nightmare where the horror just grew and grew. Sulpa was standing under the gushing faucet of human blood. It pumped out from the girl's ruptured heart in a spurting stream, splashing onto his face and into his open mouth as he tilted his head back to receive it. In seconds his whole body was daubed crimson, his long hair was drenched, and his tawny eyes glared out from behind curtains of gore.

That was when he began to run back and forth inside the shelter, stabbing up through the roof and slicing the sword's blade along the gaps between the slats, hacking the five other children to pieces. As their blood too began to pour down in sheets into the shelter Sulpa capered and bathed in it until he was entirely red.

Red from head to foot.

A being of blood.

At last he slumped down onto his haunches in a deep puddle of blood, his mouth gaped, and he seemed to fall asleep.

Leoni threw herself upwards into the sky and looked down on the hellish scene – the roaring army gathered around the foot of the little hill, the bloodstained shelter, the children's slaughtered bodies . . .

"SUL . . . PA!"
"SUL . . . PA!"
"SUL . . . PA!"

The Blue Angel had said she would show her Jack.

Could Sulpa be Jack?

As she began to consider this possibility, Leoni discovered she was no longer alone in her out-of-body state.

Rising from the butchered corpses on the roof below her she saw the aerial forms of the six children. Like her they were transparent and insubstantial but otherwise looked much as they had in life. Although they seemed confused and uncertain, they soon began experimental maneuvers, like butterflies on their first flight, and she guessed they were experiencing the initial euphoria and liberation of being out of body.

The murdered guard too had made the transition from life to death and hovered above his own scattered and mutilated remains. He was attempting to gather up his amputated limbs – a task that was impossible in aerial form – and seemed oblivious to all other things.

Leoni's only concern was the children. They had left their bodies, as she had done, but for them there could be no going back. Before she returned to her own body, which she knew must be soon, she wanted to help them. After all, she had experience of weird OBE worlds. At the very least she could pass some of that on.

So far the kids hadn't seen her, but she was about to go and try to be a friend to them when something else happened.

Sulpa was out of his body too.

Chapter Thirty-Two

From the moment she castrated the giant, Ria felt the sharp flint knife come to life in her hand like a baleful supernatural being, as though it possessed its own insatiable will for blood. Gripping its handle of smooth mammoth ivory, aching for revenge, she stood back to back with Hond.

Two of the three men bearing down on them were armed with stabbing spears. They launched a wild assault on Hond, who blocked and deflected their first thrusts. As they wheeled and turned, maneuvering for advantage, jabbing and parrying, Ria was engaged in combat by the third brave. He was a stocky, perspiring youth, fast despite his bulk, and slippery as an eel. He muttered strange words while lashing out at her with a heavy wooden mace that had spikes and razors of obsidian embedded in its bulbous head.

It was hard to get inside the reach of the larger, heavier weapon, but Ria weaved and dived, dodging his blows, goading her assailant with quick cuts and stabs. At last he grew so frenzied he lost control and rushed her with his teeth bared and a thick foam of spittle flying from his lips. He smashed the mace down but she was already diving forward between his legs, slashing the big artery in his inner thigh with the edge of her blade. As he stumbled, spraying bright blood, she rose up behind him and thrust the knifepoint deep into his back, bringing him crashing to the ground.

Out of the corner of her eye she saw that Hond, who she'd lost in the blur of the action, was being pressed hard by the two Illimani spearmen. Then – *Clunk*! *Thwock*! – Grondin appeared out of nowhere with a stone axe hafted to a long wooden handle and chopped them both down where they stood.

Hond at once squared up to fight Grondin, but Ria rushed to separate them. "Trust me," she yelled at her brother. "These guys are our friends. I'll explain . . . if we live."

The epicenter of the battle had shifted away from them and Ria had space to draw breath and take stock of what was happening.

The sheer numbers of the Uglies – fifty of them against just twenty Illimani – made their victory certain, and no more than eight of the foe were still standing. But they were ruthless and practiced fighters while many of the Uglies were still weakened by their instinctive horror at the act of taking human life. Some, like Grondin, appeared to have mastered this inhibition, perhaps through recent experience of combat with Clan braves, but others could not do so and the price they paid was death.

One of the Illimani, a man with a face of wizened evil, was surrounded. But instead of spearing him on the spot the Uglies relented when he dropped to his knees in surrender. Ria was already reaching for a stone from her pouch as he scooped up a hatchet from the ground and cut his way through them, slaughtering three in the blink of an eye. "Not so fast!" she yelled as he ploughed onwards towards the edge of the clearing where other survivors of the Illimani war party were regrouping. She was taking aim when Trenko and Krisko, the gentle-mannered buck-toothed twins, barred the fleeing brave's way.

In a heartbeat Krisko was dead, his head half hacked from his shoulders by the Illimani's tomahawk, Trenko staggered back spouting blood from a jagged wound in his chest, and Ria let fly with the third of the five throwing stones Merina had given her. The heavy little quartz egg tore soundlessly through the air and then – *CLUNK*! – it caved-in the back of the Illimani's skull, bringing him down.

There was no time to worry about Trenko – he might live or die – just as there was no time to mourn poor murdered Rill. All that could come later. For now the only thing that mattered to Ria was that none of the Illimani must be allowed to leave the field alive.

With exceptional discipline and martial skill the last six had fought their way towards one another – the man she'd just felled would have been the seventh – and regrouped into a tight mass, bristling with spears and blades, formed in the shape of an arrowhead. At the tip of the formation, urging the others towards the shelter of the forest, was a huge bald brute swinging the largest axe Ria had ever seen. Two Uglies confronted him and he cut them down – *WHACK*! *WHACK*! Two more took their place – *WHACK*! *WHACK*!

"Hey, Grondin!" Ria sent out her thought-voice as she ran towards them. "Have your boys stand off a few paces and get some spears into those bastards right now!" Then she drew back her arm and threw her fourth stone at the Illimani axeman. It hit him between the eyes, knocking him head over heels, and at the same instant Brindle limped forward and finished the man off with a rain of powerful blows.

"That's the way, Brindle!" Ria shouted in out-loud speech. "No mercy! Kill them all."

She had meant to encourage him – this newfound killer instinct was exactly what was needed – but Brindle only looked back at her with sad and haunted eyes. "Old world has come to an end," his thought-voice pulsed inside her head. "Uglies must be murderers now."

Spears were raining in on the Illimani. They started to go down. It seemed impossible that any of them could survive. Yet, with a burst of speed, one, who had lost his weapon in the fighting, somehow broke free.

He was young, slim and fast. Unusually, his hair was dark but he had the same staring blue eyes as every other Illimani and, like the others, his body was criss-crossed with scars.

He dodged a few half-hearted attempts to catch him and fled into the trees.

"Let him go!" commanded Brindle's thought-voice. "Enough killing today!"

But Ria wasn't about to let anyone go, and it wasn't just a matter of revenge. If there was a larger force nearby she couldn't risk the possibility that even a single survivor might escape to alert them.

She ran alone into the forest in hot pursuit.

Chapter Thirty-Three

Three different things were happening at once.

First, the transfiguration of Sulpa. While his human form slumbered in a pool of blood, his aerial form issued forth from his open mouth as a writhing worm of smoke, shot through with glints of fire. The worm thickened into a helix, turbulent and flowing like a river in flood, the helix transformed itself into a man with the head of an alligator, and the man grew in an instant to giant size, twenty feet tall, towering above the place of sacrifice. Since neither the three remaining guards on the hilltop nor the army down below reacted to any of this, Leoni reasoned the monster must be invisible in the physical realm, just as she was. She had started to take her own invisibility for granted, confident of remaining undetected, safe from physical attack. But hideous new possibilities now loomed with Sulpa out of body too.

Could he see her?

Of course he could. The same way she could see him. He'd not noticed her yet only because she was out of his line of sight, hovering like a bird above and behind him in the sky.

Could he harm her?

Leoni felt equally sure of the answer to this. In all worlds, at all times, and in all forms, Sulpa could – and certainly would – harm her. She should fly away, high and far and fast, and not delay a single second.

But she was aware of another much more complex instinct. This was a strange feeling of compassion . . . and of *responsibility*. A feeling that she was somehow *required* to assist the spirits of the murdered children to pass on to the next phase of their existence. That this was her duty. She hesitated. The monster's attention was focused on the kids as they explored the out-of-body state with innocent self-absorption. They were so into this new thing, so energized by the sudden sense of freedom, that they didn't know he had followed them beyond death or in what awful form he now reared over them. Obviously sacrificing their bodies wasn't enough for him. Obviously he was here to demand more. For some bizarre, inexplicable reason the greedy fuck wanted to kill them again, this time in the aerial realm.

Simultaneous with all this, a shimmering circle of brilliant white light unfurled in the sky. Leoni recognized it as the mouth of the same sort of revolving tunnel she had entered during her near-death experience, and saw the children's transparent aerial forms were already being drawn up towards it. Sulpa saw the tunnel too and threw himself between it and his victims, blocking their escape.

The third thing that was happening concerned Leoni's grip on this strange, fast-moving reality she found herself in. Everything was beginning to fade and dim and she sensed herself being tugged back into her body. The scene before her – the tunnel, Sulpa, the spirits of the children – went completely blank, as though someone had switched off a TV set.

For a moment she was marooned in absolute darkness with no reference points, until – *CLICK*! – the horror was back, advanced a few frames, and Sulpa was stuffing one of the kids into his alligator face, eating him up, swallowing him whole. The spirits of the other five cowered before him, waiting their turn.

Leoni got mad and dropped from the sky like a stone.

She didn't give herself time to think and barreled into Sulpa at what felt like a hundred miles an hour. This was nothing like her earlier fruitless attempts to intervene in the physical world. Instead of passing through him, and perhaps distracting him for a moment – the most she'd hoped for – she was surprised by the hard jolt of a collision with his aerial body followed by a massive shock that dazed her and sent her spinning and somersaulting through the air. The monster, too, was caught off balance. He was dragging a second wraith into his gaping maw when the shock seemed to hit him and he stumbled. His spell over the four remaining children was broken and they scattered, flying towards the tunnel of light like moths towards a flame.

Sulpa was after them in a flash and again Leoni diverted him, streaking across his path, getting in the way. He caught another child and held on to her by the throat, but the last three had now reached the tunnel and passed inside. For a moment they remained visible, looking back with unreadable expressions, but soon they were drawn deeper into the light and disappeared.

That left Leoni alone, out of her body, with a twenty-foot-tall alligator-headed man. He kept one sly appraising eye turned towards her as he crammed the soul of the girl he held feet first into his mouth and gulped her down. Then the whole scene transformed itself into a gigantic firework display, the sky was filled by walls and nets and waterfalls of glowing color, and Leoni knew with absolute certainty that the DMT that had brought her here was wearing off.

"You're Jack," she said to Sulpa through the fireworks. She didn't speak the words out loud but framed them as a thought.

"What if I am?" The thought came back like an ice pick piercing her brain.

"YOU'RE JACK, YOU SON OF A BITCH," yelled Leoni as she soared up into the sky. For a moment she could imagine she had become a master of out-of-body flight, capable of outstripping any pursuer. But when she looked back over her shoulder she saw Sulpa right behind her.

For a second time everything went blank and Leoni found herself hurtling through absolute darkness. Then powerful hands closed around her throat, plucking her out of full flight, threatening to tear her head from her shoulders. There was the sense of a screen flicking on again. As light flooded back she discovered she had been carried to some realm between worlds – no earth below, no sky above – and that Sulpa was holding her up towards his gaping jaws which were filled with rows of jagged teeth like steel saw-blades.

Of his beautiful earthly features only the tawny feral eyes were recognizable in his new reptilian head, and these gazed at her with hunger.

Chapter Thirty-Four

The forest was flooded with mellow afternoon light filtered by the green canopy as Ria forced her way through the thick undergrowth of ferns and thorns in pursuit of the fleeing Illimani brave. He was never more than thirty paces ahead of her, leaping over obstacles, ducking under branches, tearing through clinging briars that snatched and bloodied his pale skin. Twice she drew back her arm to throw but each time he dodged into cover and she couldn't take the shot.

Then he was just gone.

No longer crashing through the trees, but . . . disappeared.

Ria's momentum carried her into a small glade, twenty paces across, where she slowed to a halt. She moved to the middle of the little clearing and spun on her heels as the unarmed brave burst out of the undergrowth, charging towards her, his arms and legs pumping, murder in his eyes. Ria released her last quartz hunting stone with a sideways backhanded throw. It seemed to shimmer as it flew through the air. Then – *CLUNK*! – it struck the Illimani square on the brow. For a moment he tottered, glaring at her, unwilling to accept the inevitable, before he crashed face down.

Ria was on him at once. She straddled his lean naked body, planted her left hand firmly in his thick black hair, and lifted up his head from the ground. In her right hand she held the flint knife, long as her forearm, glinting dully in the sun. She stooped, placed the edge of the blade against the brave's exposed throat and drew a line of blood. She could feel the coarse texture of his hair between her fingers, hear his hoarse, ragged breathing, smell his rank body odor, see the quiver of returning consciousness around his eyelids.

"DON'T DO IT!" Brindle's thought-voice filled her head. "RIA, DON'T DO IT! No more killing please. I begging you." She looked around and saw her friend running towards her out of the trees. Right beside him was Oplimar, the little fat Ugly with the bushy red beard. Behind them came Grondin and, last of all, Hond.

Ria stayed her hand but felt a wave of fury welling up inside her. When her own beloved Rill was dead and cold why was Brindle still being so fucking merciful? Why should even a single Illimani be allowed to live and breathe?

"Because he human like you, like me," Brindle answered. "Battle over now. All his war band dead. Don't have to kill him."

Still keeping a strong grip on her stunned captive's hair, Ria wrestled him over onto his back and knelt by his shoulder, her blade raised high. His blue eyes fluttered open and he gazed up at her, for a moment obviously not remembering where he was. But, when he saw the knife, blank unafraid acceptance crossed his face.

"For Rill," yelled Ria and stabbed down at his heart.

The blow didn't reach its target. Brindle's hands – strong and hard – gripped her wrist and pried the dagger from her fingers. Grondin and Oplimar pinned down the Illimani youth and bound his arms behind his back.

Now the fighting was over, and the explanations had to begin, Ria found she couldn't face Hond. She jumped to her feet and bolted out of the little glade, back in the direction of the battlefield.

There were corpses everywhere, scattered across the wide clearing. Blood painted the grass in great stripes and swathes in the late-afternoon sunlight and an Illimani head, with wide-open eyes, lay in her path. She directed a kick at it as she rushed past, sending it rolling and tumbling away. To her right a little huddle of Uglies gathered arm in arm, offering up their strange healing chant. She slowed and peered through the scrum to see Trenko on the ground. Another brave supported Trenko's shoulders, laying his big hands across the deep hatchet wound in his chest, pouring blue light into the torn mass of flesh, fat and muscle. But Ria had already passed by, her attention focused on her dead brother Rill, slumping forward against the ropes that bound him to the thick stake in the midst of the clearing, his abdomen split open and his entrails coiled around his feet.

She ran towards him and embraced his limp and lifeless body, all the while calling his name. Half out of her senses, she scooped up his guts and pushed them back into his stomach cavity, smearing herself from head to foot in his blood. She cut him free of his bonds, lowered him to the ground, and sat weeping at his side.

When she looked up she found Hond standing over her, his green eyes also brimming with tears. This was shocking as she'd never seen him cry before, even after the death of their parents. She got to her feet, her muscles turning to water, and fell into his arms. "It's my fault they murdered Rill," she whispered. "All my fault. If I'd come home yesterday you wouldn't have had to search for me and he'd still be alive."

"Don't punish yourself with such thoughts," Hond replied. He coughed – it was a wet sound, and for the first time Ria saw he had been wounded. A blade had passed through his side in the heat of the battle and now, when he breathed – and he did so with difficulty – flecks of blood appeared around his mouth. His voice was shaking with pain and exhaustion: "We've lost our brother – no power can bring him back – but you mustn't blame yourself. If we hadn't fought these wolves today" – he gestured with disgust at the slain Illimani who lay all around – "we would have had to fight them tomorrow and good men would still have died." He slumped in her arms and almost fell but struggled to speak: "The Uglies. How do you know them? Are we safe with them?"

"We're safe, Hond. They're my friends. You saw that in the battle . . ."

"They saved our lives." He was racked by a fit of bloody coughing. "Some died for us. Why?"

"I'll tell you everything. But not now." Her fear and desperation mounting, Ria looked around for Brindle, couldn't see him and sent out her thought-voice: "*Hond's dying, Brindle. I need your help. I need the magic the Uglies can do. I need you to sing him better.*"

"What's that?" Hond asked, almost as though he'd heard her.

"Nothing. It's – I can't explain right now – it's the way I speak to the Uglies."

"Speak to the Uglies? How can you speak to the Uglies? They can't even make words. I don't know why they fought for us in the battle but I don't trust them. I've never trusted them. Let's make a run for it now, while none of them are looking."

"We can't make a run for it, Hond! You need healing for your wound or you're going to die."

He disagreed: "It's not that bad. I'm not going to die! I can make it back to camp, see the medicine man, get fixed up." He staggered again. This time Ria wasn't able to support his weight and they sank together to the ground only a few paces away from Rill. "Who are those bastards we fought?" Hond rasped. "Are they demons or men?"

"They are called the Illimani. They bleed like men, they smell like men and I think they are men. But their leader is truly a demon and he commands thousands of them. They're here to wipe us out."

"How do you know this?"

"The Uglies told me."

As she answered, Brindle's thought-voice was back inside her head: "*Please tell brother don't be afraid. Don't be angry. We ready to try healing now.*" Looking up, Ria saw that a ring of Uglies had gathered round. One of them was Trenko! She felt a surge of hope.

Hond was at once belligerent. "What's happening?" he muttered. Ignoring Ria's protests, coughing more blood, he struggled to his feet.

Chapter Thirty-Five

Leoni had grown used to the idea that her transparent, diaphanous aerial body was not subject to physical laws and could not be seen, harmed or detained by physical beings. But now she knew she was not invulnerable in this form and *could* be seen, harmed and detained by other non-physical entities. This was why Sulpa had been able to follow her on her flight to the sky, had succeeded in fastening his hands like a vice around her throat, and was now transporting her towards his chainsaw teeth while maintaining a repulsive, appraising, leeringly sexual eye contact with her.

Despite the alligator face, the look in the monster's eyes was familiar. Leoni's father had given her just such a knowing look each time he had forced himself into her bed.

(*"It's what Jack wanted."*)

A howl of fury burst out of her and she fought Sulpa's grip, twisting and turning. Then something else new and utterly unexpected happened. Her transparent aerial body began to change. She felt hair sprouting, teeth and claws growing, the rumble of a roar rising in her chest, and in a rapid blur of motion, spitting and hissing, she underwent a spectacular metamorphosis into the savage form of a mountain lion. Unimaginable strength flooded through her, taking Sulpa by surprise. She lashed out at him with a paw, clawing his left eye out of its socket, and broke free of his stranglehold.

No tunnel of light had brought them here between worlds where they floated twenty feet apart like two astronauts in a vacuum – nothing above them, nothing below them, nothing beside them, absolutely nothing at all in this realm of air except Leoni the Lioness and Sulpa the Alligator-Man.

He put his human hand to his dangling eye and reinserted it into the gaping socket. "You have injured me," he said. The words, which were not spoken out loud, took shape inside her head like shards of ice.

"I haven't even started!" she spat. "You're Jack and you ruined my life."

"Ah!" he exclaimed with mock dismay. "A hero seeking revenge!" His good eye glared at her – the other had turned opaque, like the white of a poached egg. "But you have me at a disadvantage . . . I have ruined so many lives. Please do refresh my memory."

Before Leoni could unload a lifetime of hatred the scene before her shivered, returned with full force, and blinked off again into complete darkness. She felt a vast force at work, pulling her away. Far away. The next thing she knew – *WHOOSH*! *WHAM*! – she exploded back through a torrent of colors and dropped down into her body in the treatment room at UC Irvine.

Gasping for breath, she opened her eyes, sat up and looked around, half expecting that Sulpa had followed her even here. Instead she found Doctors Monbiot and Shapira standing on either side of her, staring at her as though they had seen a ghost.

Which, in a sense, they had.

Leoni couldn't bear looking at the three wiry black hairs growing out of Dr. Shapira's chin. They were hideous. But when she focused on Monbiot his lipless face and small circular spectacles proved to be equally disconcerting.

Fixing her gaze somewhere between the two of them she asked: "How long was I out?"

Monbiot checked his digital stopwatch: "Almost exactly fourteen minutes."

"*Fourteen minutes*?" Leoni couldn't believe it: "I feel like I've been away for fourteen *hours*."

"With DMT it's not unusual to experience expansion of time," Shapira cut in. "Sometimes you might believe yourself to be trapped in those realms for months or even years before you return. But in reality it's rare for more than twenty minutes to pass from the beginning to the end of the trip." She loomed over Leoni and, in quick succession, put a stethoscope to her chest, took her blood pressure, examined her tongue and shone a bright little light into her eyes. Finally she announced: "You're OK."

"Is there any reason why I *shouldn't* be OK?"

"We were a little concerned," the older woman explained. It was obvious she was making an effort to sound more friendly. "Your heart rate went way up. At one point you appeared to be choking . . ."

"And you started to make these sounds," Monbiot added, "like a mountain lion. Quite unsettling to hear . . ."

"Unsettling?" Leoni laughed. "I guess I was making those sounds because I turned into a mountain lion near the end of my trip. I fought a monster. He was twenty feet tall with a human body and the head of an alligator. Now is that weird or what?"

"Not so weird as it may seem," said Shapira. "Many of our volunteers have encountered such creatures, or even experienced transforming into them. They're known technically as *therianthropes.*" Leoni showed her unfamiliarity with the word and Shapira immediately added: "From the Greek *therion*, meaning 'wild beast,' and *anthropos*, meaning 'man.' They're a common motif in the phenomenology of deeply altered states of consciousness. The same goes for animal transformations – like your mountain-lion experience – where the subject believes herself to have turned into some sort of animal. In tribal and hunter-gatherer societies shamans use hallucinogenic plants to reach what they describe as the 'spirit world.' They say they frequently take on the forms of animals when they make such journeys and sometimes they may fight with other shamans or even demons – who will also likely be in the form of animals or therianthropes."

In the next half-hour, Leoni fulfilled her contractual obligations as an enrolled volunteer in John Bannerman's research program by giving Monbiot and Shapira a blow-by-blow account – which they recorded – of the "phenomenology" of her DMT experience.

"Everyone uses that phenomenon word," she protested. "I don't like it. It all felt very real to me."

"We're not saying it *isn't* real," soothed Monbiot. "In fact we're not making any judgement about its reality status. We just want you to tell us what you saw in as much detail as possible. That way we can compare it with the reports of other volunteers and flag up any common features."

So Leoni told them about the machine elves and the Blue Angel, and she told them about Sulpa, and what she had seen him do.

But she made no mention of the connection with Jack.

Because Jack was her private business.

When she left the treatment room her heart fell to see that another young woman was sitting outside in the corridor on a hard plastic chair waiting her turn. Although Leoni had been briefly introduced to all the volunteers on the afternoon of her arrival she'd made a point of not socializing with any of them and, two days later, she couldn't remember this girl's name. She was tall and heavily built – verging on obese – with an angular face, prominent chin, and big round cornflower-blue eyes set very close to the bridge of a long, pinched nose. Her mousy brown hair was cut in a layered pageboy. Not a good look.

Leoni was still feeling militantly antisocial so she mumbled a greeting, the absolute minimum basic decency required, and shuffled by with her eyes averted. What she was thinking was – *Please, universe, let this person not want to have a conversation with me.* But the other woman didn't even respond to her. At first Leoni was relieved her wish had been so easily granted, but after taking a few more steps she began to get a creepy feeling that something was wrong. She swung round.

And screamed.

Somehow, without making any sound, the young woman had sneaked up on her and now stood just inches away with her face thrust forward. For a beat there was silence. Then she hissed: "Jack's here."

Chapter Thirty-Six

"Tell your brother please stay still," Brindle's thought-voice counseled. Then, before she had time to stand, Ria felt a surge of something – some energy, some power – crackling around them like summer lightning, and Hond slumped down again beside her. "Don't let them touch me," he growled.

"Sorry. Have to touch," said Brindle. *"Otherwise can't heal."*

Ria's heart was pounding. "THEY'RE HERE TO HEAL YOU," she yelled at Hond, her voice cracking with stress and frustration. "There isn't time to explain this. I love you and you just have to believe me. They've got to touch you to make it work, and you have to stay still!"

"Heal me?" Hond scoffed. A big bubble of blood formed and burst on his lips. "They're Uglies! What do they know?"

Brindle dropped to his haunches, looked Hond straight in the eyes, and placed his hands over the entry and exit wounds in the human's side. Hond struggled but Ria held him fast. "They have a healing gift," she whispered. "It's amazing. I've seen what they can do."

"It's mumbo-jumbo," Hond protested, but it was obvious he was weakening fast. He let Brindle's hands stay on his wounds and put up no further objection when the circle of Uglies linked arms and began to chant in a low steady monotone. At last he lay back with his head in Ria's lap and closed his eyes, his breath rasping.

Slowly the chanting rose in intensity, the air around them grew charged, and Ria again became aware of the presence of some uncanny power. The Uglies were the source of it. She looked down at her beautiful, broken brother – he seemed to have fallen into a deep sleep – and watched, daring to hope, as the web of fine blue light wove itself around him, cocooning him from head to toe. Streams of the same substance poured into his wounded side from Brindle's hands, and his weight in her lap was lifted as his body floated free of the ground.

Was she imagining, or had some color returned to his face? Had his breathing become easier? Were there fewer new droplets of blood beading his lips? *What's happening*? – she threw a thought-question at Brindle – *Is he getting better*? Her friend gave no reply.

It was a long while before the circle of Uglies broke apart. When they did the blue light that had webbed Hond's body seeped away and he lay still and silent. At first Ria feared that his breathing must have stopped. But when she put her ear to his chest she could sense its minute rise and fall, rise and fall. There were no more of the horrible rasping and bubbling sounds.

Brindle stood up, reached out his big hands and helped Ria to her feet.

"Is my brother going to live?" she asked.

"Don't know," he pulsed back.

"What do you mean, you don't *know*?" Ria was suddenly shaking with fear. "You made Trenko better. I saw it happen. You can make Hond better too."

"Cases different. No vital organs of Trenko destroyed. But wound of Hond goes through lung. Lot of bleeding inside. Very hard for Uglies to make better."

Ria could feel tears welling up. "So does that mean he's going to die? Am I going to lose *both* my brothers today?"

"Hope not, Ria. We sang the healing song and magic entered Hond's body. We took his pain away. Eased breathing. Sent him sleep. Tomorrow we will know if we stopped bleeding."

"But I think you have, Brindle! I think you have! Look!" Ria stooped and gently touched her brother's lips. "No more blood."

"It's good sign. Tomorrow we will know."

"I believe you've saved him," Ria insisted.

"Tomorrow we will know," said Brindle again. "Better for Hond if we don't move him, but don't have any choice." He looked around the battlefield and scanned the surrounding forest. "We already been here too long." He returned Ria's flint knife to her, being careful to hand it over hilt first.

The danger was that other Illimani forces might be somewhere nearby. That was why Ria took the tough decision to leave Rill where he lay on the battlefield. No burial for him, nor for any of the fallen. She could only concern herself with the living now.

From the war party of fifty Uglies who had set out with Ria only thirty-seven remained alive. Six of these could not walk and a further fourteen walking wounded, including Trenko, were needed to carry them back to the safety of Secret Place. Of the seventeen able-bodied fighters still at his disposal Brindle sent twelve more, under Grondin, to bring in the outlying Ugly communities.

That left five to accompany Ria and Hond to the Clan camp on the Snake River. Ria already knew the names of three of this reduced escort – Brindle himself, Oplimar, and the gangling broken-nosed brave called Brigley who'd been one of the first to welcome her outside the Cave of Visions. The other two she remembered from the battlefield for showing none of the squeamishness over taking human life that had doomed so many of their fallen comrades. One was a pink-eyed albino in early middle age. He looked strong, with short, thick legs and a long, massive upper body covered in bulging muscles. He introduced himself as Porto. The second was much younger, lean and very slight by Ugly standards, but in the battle he'd fought hard and fast. "I am Jergat," he told Ria, "and you are good fighter too." He held out a skin-wrapped bundle to her. "You will need these again," he said. The bundle was heavy. With her heart beating faster she opened it and found her five quartz throwing stones nestling within. "Brindle told me to collect for you after fighting," Jergat explained. "That my job from now on."

Another thing that Brindle did was insist on keeping the captured Illimani with them, rather than sending him with Grondin's larger group. Keeping the weird bastard alive *at all* seemed like an unnecessary luxury to Ria, but Brindle was stubborn: "Wrong to kill if don't have to."

"That sounds wonderful," said Ria. She was tired of this side of the Uglies. "But think about what it means."

"You thinking it means he must be watched all the time, we must hustle to guard him, make sure he doesn't knife us in back or run off to get other Illimani to attack us."

"Right! So can we please just kill him now?"

The prisoner's expression was steady, almost insulting. Ria allowed her hatred to show. "Hey, you!" she yelled, switching to out-loud speech. "What's your name, you piece of shit?" But of course he didn't speak her language.

She crossed the few paces to where he was standing in the middle of the battlefield, guarded by Oplimar and Brigley, his hands tied behind his back. He was a full head taller than her, with a long mane of thick dark hair, pale skin and fine regular features. She took him to be no older than eighteen. His teeth hadn't been filed and, were it not for his startling blue eyes, he could have passed for a good-looking youth of the Clan.

She prodded his chest and repeated: "WHAT'S YOUR NAME, YOU PIECE OF SHIT?" When there was no response she tapped her own chest, pointed at herself and said: "RIA." Then she pointed back at him, and gave him a questioning look. He still didn't get it, so she pointed at herself again: "Ria," she said. "My . . . name . . . is . . . Ria." Then she pointed back at him: "What . . . is . . . your . . . name?" Suddenly his face lit up: "DRIFF!" he barked.

"Good." Ria leaned closer: "So here's how it is, Driff." Even though he couldn't understand a word, she figured he'd get her tone. "Give me the slightest excuse and I'm going to gut you without mercy. OK? Got that? You ignorant barbarian." She was holding the flint knife, not exactly menacing him with it, when Brindle laid his hand on her arm. *"That enough, Ria. Please try to think like this – we very lucky have this Illimani. He can teach us lot about his people. Help us defeat them."*

It was late afternoon – shadows lengthening, the air beginning to cool – when they left the battlefield. Hond was still deeply unconscious but the Uglies lashed together a stretcher for him and took turns to be his bearers, conscripting Driff to the task as well. Whenever the prisoner was relieved from stretcher duty Ria noticed that Brindle made a point of walking with him and that the two seemed to have struck up some rudimentary form of communication.

In this way they kept moving through the long summer evening, the last daylight leached from the sky, and night fell around them. The moon had not yet risen and the darkness became almost absolute. They did not pause for rest but it was hard to sustain a fast pace and Ria guessed it would be morning before they reached the Clan camp.

If they managed not to stumble on another Illimani war band first . . .

She marched beside the stretcher, fingers touching her brother's shoulder, from time to time smoothing his hair back from his brow. Although he was hot, and his skin damp, she never doubted he would recover if she could get him home.

As they walked she watched the big three-quarter moon rise slowly in the east, flooding the sky with light. It climbed higher and she began to recognize valleys and hills she'd hunted in before. The distance was far – they would still have to march the whole night – but now at least she could take the lead and pick out the best route.

Following a deer path, she guided the Uglies through a forest of ancient gnarled oaks and brought them out by the side of a little lake with still, dark waters that reflected the dazzling moon. They skirted the lake, climbed a steep hill and descended into a narrow winding valley where the hunting for deer and rabbits was good.

As they began the trek along the valley floor a cloud scudded across the moon and Ria sensed more than saw the sudden wild rush of an ambush. Her first thought was the Illimani and the flint knife was in her hand, stabbing and slashing, piercing flesh and striking bone, before she realized their attackers were Clan braves. She saw Hond spilled from his stretcher, Brindle clubbing a man to the ground, Brigley and Jergat back to back fending off a ring of assailants, and Oplimar wrestling with Grigo's father Murgh. But the surprise and speed of the attack, and the overwhelming numbers of the Clan, meant it was all over in moments. Something hard smashed against the side of Ria's head, stunning her. As she dropped to her knees she saw Porto go down, and Driff, unnoticed by anyone else, slipping away like a phantom. A second savage blow smacked into the back of her skull, bright lights exploded behind her eyes, and she fell on her face.

The last thing she remembered before losing consciousness was rough hands at work, trussing her with ropes, and the hated sound of Grigo's voice: "I told you I'd kill you the next time I saw you," he smirked.

Chapter Thirty-Seven

The young woman's cornflower-blue eyes were open wide and a smell of raw sewage wafted out of her mouth, as she and Leoni stood face to face in the long corridor lined with plastic chairs outside the DMT treatment room. *Uggh*! Leoni retreated and averted her nose to avoid breathing more of the toxic halitosis, but the woman followed and crowded her against the wall.

"What do you want?" Leoni yelled.

"I want to FUCK you," the woman growled. Her voice had become deep and resonant, like a man's. "Then I want to skin you ALIVE. After that I'm going to eat you right off the BONE." She snapped her teeth together: "Think you can stop me?"

One word was going through Leoni's mind and that word was . . . (*possessed*).

This crazy bitch was possessed.

By Jack.

Leoni turned to run, but the woman was all over her, fat and heavy, smearing her with slobbering, fetid kisses, forcing her squirming tongue into her mouth, groping her breasts.

Leoni got mad. She grabbed hold of her attacker's hair, banged her head against the wall and brought her knee up into her stomach. "Fuck you," she shrieked. "Fuck you if you're Jack. Fuck you whatever you are. Just stay the fuck out of my life."

The woman kept on coming. Her expression blank, she locked her pudgy hands around Leoni's neck and began to throttle her. Leoni fought back but her eyes were starting to glaze over when she saw Monbiot and Shapira burst out of the treatment room and charge to the rescue. *Useless fucks*! Far from breaking the woman's stranglehold their ineffectual tug-of-war only seemed to encourage her to tighten her grip. Thrusting her face forward again she planted more slobbering kisses on Leoni's mouth and whispered in her ear: "*You stole SOULS from me. Nobody gets away with that.*"

Leoni's head was spinning, and she'd started to black out, when she saw a lanky long-haired figure looming up – the guy from UC Berkeley who'd kept on trying to talk to her over the last couple of days. He shouldered Monbiot and Shapira out of the way, got hold of the woman's hands and did something to them that made her screech with pain and let go. Then, despite her great bulk, he swung her round – it looked like a dance move but there was another yelp of pain – and threw her face down on the floor. As she struggled to get back up he put her into an armlock and immobilized her.

"Hey, Becky," he said. "Chill, babes. This isn't you . . ."

But the woman wasn't listening. Her pale blue eyes were fixed on Leoni with hideous intent and dawning recognition. "I remember you," she snarled. "We've met before!" She slobbered and drooled yellow spit: "Oh, this is going to be so much fun." Her eyes rolled and she began to howl like a wolf.

In the previous days, despite his attempts to talk to her, Leoni hadn't paid any attention to the guy from Berkeley. His British accent – but with odd American notes and undertones – was the only interesting thing about him. Otherwise she'd assessed him as a tall, annoying, badly dressed nobody.

But the way he'd handled crazy Becky called for a rethink.

His sun-bleached blonde hair was unkempt and almost shoulder-length. He looked like he hadn't shaved for a week and he was wearing torn and repeatedly patched baggy trousers, flip-flops and a much faded, stained and stretched Burning Man T-shirt. Obviously he didn't care about his appearance, but once you got past first impressions he was quite cute in a beach-bum sort of way.

He'd just introduced himself as Matthew Aubrey (sounding plummy, awkward and English as he shook her hand) and now sat opposite her across a little metal table in Starbucks in Newport Beach.

As volunteers in the DMT project they'd signed an agreement not to leave campus during the trials, but after Becky, still raving, had been straitjacketed and admitted to the psychiatric wing of UC Irvine Hospital, they'd both wanted out for a while.

They hadn't talked at all during the fifteen-minute cab ride. Leoni had sat far over on her side of the back seat, brooding about Sulpa and Jack. She knew that somehow, in showing her the former, the Blue Angel had also revealed the latter.

What was even more chilling was the way her visionary battle with Sulpa had followed her into the physical realm in the form of Becky. And the way, at the last, that Jack had looked out at her through Becky's eyes and recognized her.

The same Jack, without a doubt, who had sent her adoptive father to her bed.

The same Jack who'd wrecked her life so casually that he seemed to have forgotten all about her until the Blue Angel had arranged for their paths to cross again.

The same Jack who was also, somehow, Sulpa, and bathed in the blood of murdered children.

The same Jack who now had further plans for her.

("*This is going to be so much fun*!")

Leoni shuddered and took a sip from her latte. Across the table Matthew was watching her. Their eyes met, and he said in a rush: "It wasn't an accident, you know."

"What wasn't an accident?"

"It wasn't an accident that I showed up to stop Becky strangling you."

Leoni sat forward: "I don't mind whether it was an accident or not. I'm just grateful to you for being there." She thought of the big woman's putrid tongue in her mouth and shuddered again. "If you hadn't stopped her something really bad was going to happen to me."

"I think she would have killed you," Matthew said with conviction. "That's why I was sent to protect you from her."

Leoni's heart skipped a beat, but she tried to look nonchalant: "Oh, really?" she said, "Sent by whom?"

Matthew shrugged and shuffled his big feet under the table: "If I tell you you're going to think I'm insane."

"Try me," laughed Leoni. "After what I've been through in the last few days I have a very high tolerance for insanity."

"OK." He took a big gulp from his bottle of water and lowered his voice: "I did something stupid."

Leoni raised an eyebrow: "Yes?"

"I wasn't scheduled for any DMT sessions today, but I had a really amazing one yesterday. I mean, utterly extraordinary. And I wanted to try to revisit it . . ."

"So . . ."

"So the thing is . . . I brought this little private stash of DMT with me when I joined the project. Not the kind Bannerman gives us by injection, but the kind you smoke. And this morning I suddenly thought – why don't I smoke some? So I got out my stash and fired up my pipe . . ."

"But that's totally against the rules!" Leoni exclaimed.

"I know. Bannerman would be pissed. But if I hadn't done it I wouldn't have been there to stop Becky."

Leoni looked puzzled and Matt continued: "I've smoked DMT before, but this time it was different. I didn't go shooting up into the stratosphere. There were none of the usual crazy colors. After three or four big tokes I felt dizzy and lay down on my bed." He paused, took another gulp of water: "Even though I'd closed my eyes I could see light pouring through the window – and I quite liked it. I felt drawn to it. Then this amazing woman came in on the light. I can't describe how she did it. One minute there was just me in the room. The next minute she was there. I reached out to touch her but my hands passed right through her. I said: 'You're not real, are you?' And she said 'Yes, Matthew, I am.' So I said: 'OK. What do you want?' And she said: 'Get down to the lab right away. Someone needs your help.' Believe me, I didn't feel like arguing. She was six feet tall and had blue skin."

Chapter Thirty-Eight

Ria had no idea how long she'd been unconscious. Now she was alert again, and her eyes were back in focus. But because she was lying on her stomach, with her wrists and ankles roped tightly together behind her back and her spine bent into an excruciating arch, she couldn't do anything except take it from Grigo. "You bitch," he shouted, raining blows down on her ribs and thighs with a thick wooden staff. "You messed up my face."

So Brindle's father had been right. Only Duma and Vik were dead. Treacherous Grigo, Sulpa's special friend,

("*You don't know him as well as I do,*")

was still very much alive.

Ria felt pleased that at least she really had messed him up. Even in the dark, lit only by the guttering flames of brushwood torches, with her own face crushed sideways against the spiky marsh grass of the valley floor, she couldn't miss Grigo's brow, split from his hairline to the bridge of his nose, or the big gaps she'd knocked in his front teeth.

Then – *THUMP*! – the heavy staff cracked hard against a rib and, despite her best efforts at self-control, she groaned.

As she had known it would, this sign of weakness only goaded Grigo on to greater efforts. Somehow he drove the tip of his staff under Ria's body and into her sternum, winding her and leaving her gasping for breath. Then she watched out of the corner of her eye as he moved around, searching for a good angle, and finally struck down at her face. "Should have married me, Ria," he taunted, "instead of screwing an Ugly."

She could sense that a second blow was coming, one that would break some important part of her head, when Grigo was intercepted by Vulp and Bahat, two older men she knew well who had both been good friends of her father. "Not like this," Bahat roared, hammering a punch into Grigo's chest. "It's not what we agreed."

"She's to get a proper trial," exploded Vulp as he grabbed Grigo from behind, pinned his arms, and dragged him kicking and screaming out of reach of Ria. "No harm comes to her before that."

Vulp and Bahat had both passed forty summers but remained important figures in the Clan and could still pull their weight in the hunt. Vulp had the shoulder-length white hair and venerable beard of an elder but a lean, strong physique. His left eye was gray and his right eye was brown. Bahat, swarthy and brooding, was known for his bad temper. Although not tall, he was broad and heavy with a livid crescent-shaped scar originating on the right side of his head above his ear, curving across his cheekbone and disappearing into his grizzled beard. Despite his reputation for ferocity, Ria remembered him best for trading funny stories with her father around their family hearth, and the way his eyes – now glowering and serious – used to twinkle with delight just before he delivered the punchline.

Bahat stooped and cut the rope tying Ria's ankles to her wrists but left in place the other ropes that still bound her wrists together behind her back and trussed her ankles. As he straightened, Murgh bustled up. He was a short, bow-legged, self-important man with a thick, powerful upper body and huge, rather sinister hands. "What's going on here?" he demanded.

"We're stopping your son from killing the prisoner," said Vulp.

"Many feel she *should* be killed now." Murgh made it sound like a reasonable proposition. He had a big, lumpy, florid face, a bruiser's nose, small darting eyes like a jackdaw's, and a ring of gray hair around his head that encircled a large shiny bald patch. "She and the Uglies murdered Duma and Vik," he continued in the same tone. "We all know they did it. So what's the point of a trial?"

Ria gasped, stunned at this unexpected turn. She and the Uglies had killed Duma and Vik?

"It was the Illimani," she croaked, but her voice was weak from the repeated blows and a tumult of shouts drowned her out.

"We don't know *anything* for sure yet," Bahat roared at Murgh. "We have the bodies of Duma and Vik, without their heads, a very terrible thing. Grigo has made allegations about how this happened. Many believe him. That's why we're all here. But Ria's side of the story MUST also be heard . . ."

"WE DON'T NEED TO HEAR HER SIDE OF THE STORY," someone else screeched, in outrage. "It's obvious she's guilty. We just caught her with the Uglies."

Paying a price of searing pain in her ribs, Ria rolled onto her side and struggled to sit up. She *knew* who had killed Duma and Vik, and it hadn't been her and the Uglies. So why had Grigo invented this story, pinning the blame on them? Was he acting from spite – calling out the braves, hunting her down – just to get back at her? Or was Sulpa using him to play some much bigger game?

Ria was also desperate to know what had become of Hond and the Uglies. She pulsed out a thought-question "*Brindle. Where are you? Tell me you're alive!*" But there was no reply and no sense of any connection with Brigley, Oplimar, Porto or Jergat either.

Meanwhile the argument continued to expand around her. The outraged screech had come from Vik's father Chard, tears dripping from his eyes, his features contorted with hate, who now stood shoulder to shoulder with Murgh. Then Duma's father Kimp joined them. "She's guilty," he said. "Let's kill her now."

Vulp and Bahat were solid guys. They might have been old but they didn't back down. Ria had to give them credit for that as she listened to the furious shouting match, piecing the story together as best she could.

Early that morning, Grigo had come running into camp covered in blood. He'd told how he, Duma and Vik had been out the day before on the hunt in a remote valley where they'd stumbled across Ria naked behind a tree having sex with a young Ugly male with a gimpy leg. Because such behavior was an affront to Clan morals they took the couple prisoner but were attacked by a huge gang of Uglies who murdered Duma and Vik, on Ria's instructions, and would have murdered Grigo as well had he not escaped. He claimed the Uglies had made off with the heads of the two murdered boys, obviously intending to use them in a cannibal feast, and Ria had left with them, not as their prisoner but of her own free will. Grigo also claimed some of the Ugly braves had pursued him but he had led them on a chase for most of the previous day and night before losing them and getting back to the safety of the camp.

This was the incendiary story he and his father had used to recruit a posse of a hundred men to hunt down Ria and the Uglies. With Hond and Rill already out of camp searching for her there were few who were prepared to argue against the idea. Nonetheless, her family was well respected so Vulp, Bahat and many others only agreed to join on condition she was captured alive and brought back for a fair trial before the assembly of elders.

Now Ligar and Bont, friends and age-mates of Hond, stepped forward to stand beside Vulp and Bahat.

Bont was a big bear of a man with a tangled mass of shaggy brown hair hanging down almost to his waist. He was thought by some to be slow-witted but he was good in a fight so nobody messed with him. Ligar, small and delicate with fine, sensitive features, was a deadly accurate shot with the vicious hunting bow presently slung over his shoulder. He was clever and funny, able to make a fool out of anyone in an argument. "Your story's full of shit," he told Grigo. "If Ria ran off with the Uglies like you say then how come she was heading back towards camp when we found her? If the Uglies killed Duma and Vik then how come they were carrying Hond on a stretcher and caring for him? I'm not saying you're lying, Grigo, but if you want to lynch this girl" – he nodded at Ria – "without a proper trial then you're going to have to get past me to do it."

"That goes for me too," said Bont. He'd been slouching but now stood up to his full height, towering over Grigo, and balled his huge hands into fists.

Watching the whole drama unfold from where she was sitting Ria was under no illusions. Her life hung in the balance. But little by little her protectors prevailed, winning more and more of the braves over to their point of view, and Murgh's lynch mob – reduced to a hard core of less than twenty – was forced to back down.

Grigo, spitting with fury, had to be restrained: "You'll burn in the morning," he yelled at her.

"Murdering bitch!" screamed Chard.

Somehow Duma's father Kimp got past Bont's guard and drove a kick into Ria's bruised rib. Then Bont hit him once and he dropped. "Anybody else want to argue about this?" the big man asked.

But there were no takers.

As Chard and Murgh helped Kimp away, muttering in indignation, the column began to form up for the march back to camp. Bont leaned down, cut the shackles on Ria's ankles and helped her to her feet. She was stiff and pain gnawed at her side.

"Can't you free my wrists as well?" she complained.

"You're still a prisoner," he said gruffly.

A terrible question was preying on Ria's mind but she was afraid of what the answer might be. "Where's Hond?" she blurted out.

"He's being taken back to camp with some of our guys who got injured when we grabbed you. He needs the medicine man."

"What about the Uglies?"

Bont gave Ria a weird look: "You mean *your* Uglies?"

"Yes, *my* Uglies. What's happened to them?"

"We killed one in the fight. We're using the other four as stretcher-bearers for Hond and the injured." Bont cleared his throat and spat. "Uglies! Don't know how you can stand to be around them. They make me sick." He gave a hollow laugh: "Anyway, they're all to be burned to death in the morning."

Chapter Thirty-Nine

"I call her the Blue Angel," Leoni whispered. She stood up and walked over to the bar where she scrounged several sheets of paper and a marker pen. Returning to the table she sat down again opposite Matt and began to sketch. "Here," she said after a moment, thrusting the drawing forward, "is this what your blue-skinned woman looks like?"

Matt whistled with surprise: "That's her! You've met her as well!"

"I've met her more than once. We go back a long way."

"So does that mean you think she's real?"

Leoni dodged the question: "What do you think?" she asked.

Matt shuffled his feet some more under the table: "She's got to be real. Or something so close to real it makes no difference. You've seen her. I've seen her. She sent me to stop Becky killing you. It would be pretty tough for a hallucination to do all that."

Leoni remembered something relevant: "Dr. Bannerman told me other people have seen her too."

"Other people on the DMT program?"

"Two on the program. But I think he said the others were also cases of his. I guess people who had near-death experiences. You know he's an ER doctor, right?"

Matt nodded.

"That's how I met him," Leoni continued. "I overdosed and died and he brought me back. While I was out I had a near-death experience and the Blue Angel was in it . . ."

"But this wasn't the only time you met her?"

"No. She used to come to me in dreams when I was a kid. And my DMT trip this morning took me right to her."

Without exactly intending to, Leoni began to pour out her life story to Matt – her abandonment as a newborn babe, her years in the orphanage, her adoption by the Watts family, a period of security and apparent love, and then the brutal rapes by her adoptive father with her adoptive mother's collusion – all, it seemed, at the behest of someone or something called Jack. She spoke of her near-death experience and subsequent encounters on ketamine – and finally this morning on DMT – with the Blue Angel. She described the land where everything is known, the bizarre animals and plants of that realm, the two suns hanging in its sky, the sticky green flowers underfoot.

When she paused for a moment, Matt leaned back in his chair, stretched, and put his hands behind his head: "Well," he said with a smile. "I started out worrying you'd think I was insane . . ."

"But now it's the other way round? You think it's me who's crazy?"

"I don't think you're crazy at all."

"Then wait till you hear this," Leoni said. And she went on to speak of the part the Blue Angel had played in showing her Sulpa, and what she'd seen him do, and how she was sure that it was Sulpa, also known as Jack, who had somehow followed her back from the trip and possessed Becky.

At one point Matt stopped her and had her draw examples of the flint knives, axes, and spears tipped with stone and bone points that she'd seen in the hands of thousands of Sulpa's naked followers. He also asked for a sketch of Sulpa's strange black sword and whistled when she described its glassy sheen. "Has to be obsidian," he muttered. "Very interesting . . ."

"What's so interesting about obsidian?"

"It's a kind of volcanic glass. There're only a few places on Earth where you can find single pieces big enough to make a weapon like this."

"We don't even know that what I saw happened on Earth."

"Oh, I think it did, don't you? Those were *men* you saw around Sulpa. Those were *human* children he murdered. There was one sun in the sky – right? There were no hybrid animals and trees, like you described in the land where everything is known. There was grass growing on the ground, not green flowers . . ."

"That's all true. It totally felt like I was on Earth. The only thing I couldn't figure out was *where*. I mean, I watch Discovery Channel, but where do you find a tribe of naked white men performing human sacrifice? I've never heard of that."

"Maybe *where* isn't the right question," Matt objected. "Maybe we should be asking *when* instead."

Leoni frowned and echoed him: "*When?*"

"Yes. When." He drained the last of his water. "Maybe what the Blue Angel did when she had you look in that screen was send you back in time."

"How could that be possible?"

"I don't claim to know. I'm just saying maybe that's what happened."

"But why? What makes you think that?"

Matt pointed to one of the sketches she'd just done for him. "Do you know what you've drawn here?" he asked her. It was one of the wooden batons, hooked at the end, that Sulpa's minions had carried slung across their backs.

"No idea," said Leoni. "First time I saw these things was around Sulpa. All his men had them."

"They're called *atlatls.* They were the nuclear weaponry of the Stone Age. Any tribe with this technology gained a huge advantage over their competitors."

"Why?" Leoni examined her sketch again: "It doesn't look useful for anything."

Matt had a glint in his eye. "It's a weapon for war and for hunting. It works by lengthening the throwing arm of a man with a spear. The extra leverage makes the spear travel faster and further. Look" – he pointed out the hooklike contraption Leoni had drawn – "the butt of the spear notches in here." He stood up and demonstrated the throw: "A flick of the wrist at the end and you can kill an animal or a man up to eight hundred feet away."

"So are you saying because I saw these atl-things that *proves* I went back in time?"

"No. Not quite. Different cultures and peoples throughout history have independently invented the atlatl. But the one you drew has a very distinctive design. Unmistakable. It turns up in archaeological sites across France and Spain around twenty-four thousand years ago. There's evidence it was brought from much further east – from the Balkans, in fact."

"How do you know all this?" Leoni asked.

"I'm taking a couple of courses in prehistoric archaeology at Berkeley. We learned about the Kazgarians last semester. That's the name we give to the people who brought the atlatl into Western Europe – we don't know what they called themselves." Matt leafed through Leoni's sketches again: "You're a pretty good artist, aren't you?"

"I flunked art school," she said – all his academic brilliance made her feel small – "but I guess I can draw."

"Great. So let's get back to the project, go online and check out the knives and axe heads you drew. That obsidian sword as well. You can tell a lot about when and where stone weapons were made just from how they look."

In the cab returning to Irvine Leoni asked: "You're English – so how come you're studying at Berkeley?"

"I drift around a bit, take courses here and there if they interest me. I wanted to know more about prehistoric archaeology and Berkeley seemed like a good place to do it."

"So you're a sort of perpetual student?"

Matt laughed: "Yes. You could say that. 'Matthew Aubrey, Perpetual Student.' Quite an accolade."

Looking at his ragged, patched clothes – despite his posh accent Matt obviously didn't have two cents to rub together – Leoni speculated that he must have enrolled in the DMT project for the miserly fee Bannerman was paying the volunteers. The cash, plus a month's free room and board out of term-time, would, she realized, be worth a lot to a guy who bummed around colleges like this.

The cab pulled off onto California Avenue and headed down towards the UC Irvine Research Park. They turned right onto Bison Avenue and saw at once that something ominous was going on at the two-story building where the DMT project was housed. Half a dozen black Ford Explorers with smoked-glass windows were parked outside and there were tough-looking men with short haircuts and dark suits everywhere.

Leoni quickly leaned forward, quelled the tremor rising in her throat, and told the driver: "Go straight ahead to the next junction, and take a left there."

"But this is the address you gave me, madam," he objected, waving a hand at the research building and slowing almost to a halt.

"No," Leoni insisted, "this isn't the place." She sharpened her tone: "Straight ahead, please, and left at the junction."

The driver, a lean elderly Armenian, sighed but put his foot back on the gas. The cab picked up speed and Leoni slumped deeper into her seat as a group of the men outside the research building swiveled towards them.

Chapter Forty

The taxi driver cast a furtive glance at Leoni in the rear-view mirror as she slumped lower in the back seat and flopped over sideways to avoid being seen. Matt took over the directions. "If you could turn left here," he told the driver in his imposing British accent, "then our building's third on the left." Leoni stayed low in her seat as the car made the turn, but she felt Matt's hand urging her upright. *"It's OK,"* he whispered in her ear. *"You weren't seen."* She looked back over her shoulder. The DMT project was already out of view and no one was following them.

Moments later they came to a halt in front of another of the white-painted, two-story buildings scattered across the green lawns of the research park. Matt paid the driver with some grubby bills extracted from the depths of one of his many pockets, ushered Leoni out, and led her towards the building as the cab pulled away. "I don't feel good about that cabbie," he said as they walked. "He knew we stopped him dropping us off at the project because of all the heavies outside. They look official, we look like fugitives, so he's probably trying to decide if he should go right back and report us to them now." He paused: "Your parents have got to be behind this, right?"

Leoni grimaced: "Yes. Count Dracula and his undead bride."

"But those men. All those suits. Like a uniform. And I'm pretty sure some of them had guns under their jackets. Maybe FBI or something?" Matt was peering around. They'd entered a corridor that ran all the way through the building to a rear exit at the far side. He took her hand: "Come on, let's get out of here."

They half ran, half walked, to the rear of the building, and once they were in the open again Matt continued to set a fast pace. Across more green lawns, dotted with mature trees, they caught occasional glimpses in the distance of the building housing the DMT project. It was too far away to make out what was happening but they could still see several men standing on guard outside.

Leoni nodded her head in their direction: "I don't think they're FBI agents," she said. My dad's not *that* well connected. But he's got the money to hire any muscle he wants – so I'm guessing maybe some sort of private security firm? Whatever. They're obviously here to grab me."

"Yes," Matt agreed. "I would say so." She was about to object to his cheerful tone when he produced a cellphone, pressed a speed-dial button, and became brusque as he arranged for a cab to meet them in fifteen minutes at the junction of Bison Road and the San Joaquin Hills Toll Road. He gave an address in a seedy district of South Los Angeles as their destination and confirmed payment would be made in cash.

"That's quite a ride," whistled Leoni when he hung up. "Might work out more than a hundred bucks, maybe a hundred and fifty. You want to check you've got that much cash on you? Because I sure as hell don't." She was turning out the pockets of her jeans while she talked and counted $187 and change. "Oh, I lie. I'm richer than I thought. How about you?"

Matt rummaged and found five crumpled bills. Three of them, Leoni was surprised to see, were hundreds. "We have enough cash," he said.

They walked in silence, avoiding exposure in the open whenever possible, darting from tree to tree. Eventually Leoni asked: "What are we going to do when we get there?"

"Get where?"

"South LA, East Century Boulevard in the eight hundred block. The address you gave to the cab company."

"We're going to walk some more, then take another cab."

Leoni must have shown her puzzlement.

"That way our trail stops after the first cab," Matt explained. "We need to make certain your parents and their heavies can't follow us."

They had reached the last building at the edge of the research park. Unlike the others, its large windows were shuttered and it appeared to be closed and deserted. There were no students or staff to be seen anywhere around and the building had an isolated, run-down feel. They fell into a guarded silence as they walked alongside it and, for the next minute, there was only the rhythmic sound of their footsteps crunching over the gravel path.

That was why they didn't hear the approach of the two men in dark suits who stepped out and confronted them at the corner of the building.

Both men were big – in very different ways.

One had the squat functional build of a circus strongman. He might have been of Turkish origin – or from some other place in the Middle East where people were swarthy and thickset, with large muscles. His black hair had been shaved to a stubble over the dome of his skull and his right hand clutched a chunky automatic pistol pointed at Leoni's stomach.

The other guy was tall, at least six-three, with a broad chest and narrow, muscular waist – the ultimate Abercrombie & Fitch uber-model. His blonde hair was cropped into a high and tight military cut above handsome peasant-boy features, and he held a pistol too.

"You got them covered?" the Turk asked.

"Of course." Abercrombie nodded, waving his gun from side to side.

The Turk stuffed his own weapon into his belt and pulled a cell-phone from his jacket pocket. He looked from the screen to Leoni a couple of times. "Little Miss Watts," he announced, "you can run and you can hide, but we have you now."

"What about him?" Abercrombie indicated Matt, who, to Leoni's dismay, was cowering in fear.

"He's seen too much," said the Turk. "I'm going to kill him." His gun was out of his belt again and he was screwing a silencer onto the barrel.

"You mean now?" asked Abercrombie.

"Yeah, sure. Why not? There's no witnesses for miles and the clean-up boys are right here to deal with the body. Couldn't be better." The Turk's face broke into a broad smile. "Tell you what. I want to recreate that scene from 'Nam. You know – the one where the Vietnamese officer shoots a prisoner in the head at point-blank range?" He giggled: "You got video on your phone?"

"Sure have," said Abercrombie.

"OK, then video this."

And with that the Turk strode over to Matt, thrusting the pistol barrel at his temple.

But Matt was already on the move. Shedding his submissive body language in an instant, he swayed his head, avoiding the thrust, and the Turk stumbled forward. Matt closed both his hands around the gun, somehow rolled the Turk's big strong fingers tighter around the weapon's grip, and kept the hold as he pirouetted away from him, snapping his wrist with an audible *POP*!

Now Matt had the pistol. He swept its barrel up and locked the sights on a point between Abercrombie's eyes while the Turk turned pale and slumped to his knees, staring at the bloody spike of bone sticking out of his forearm.

"Put your gun down," Matt yelled at Abercrombie. He thumbed back the hammer of the weapon. "You have just one second not to get shot."

Leoni could see how much Abercrombie didn't like this sudden reversal of roles but he obeyed at once.

"No sudden movements," Matt said. "I want you to slide the gun over here with your foot. I don't want you to kick it. Just slide it over to the young lady."

With a sullen glare Abercrombie nudged the gun across the lawn and Leoni picked it up. She didn't know how to use it but tried to look menacing as she pointed it at the Turk.

Matt hadn't finished with Abercrombie. "Take your shoes and clothes off," he ordered. "And you," he told the Turk. "Shoes and clothes off right away."

"I can't," the Turk complained. "You've broken my fucking arm . . ."

Matt stepped in on him and crashed the butt of the gun down on the top of his head, eliciting a howl of pain. "Shoes and clothes off right away," he repeated, "or I'll break your other arm."

The less clothes they had on, Leoni noticed, the more cooperative the men became. By the time they'd removed their underpants there was no fight left in them.

Now Matt produced a pocket knife and handed it to her: "We're going to tie them up. Cut their shirts into strips. Make gags and blindfolds as well."

Matt made the two men lie face down and when Leoni had finished cutting up their shirts he blindfolded and gagged them, then trussed and bound them with the strips of cloth. He concealed their guns in the pockets of his baggy trousers and hurled their shoes and clothes up onto the roof of the deserted building.

"Come on," he said and led Leoni away.

Chapter Forty-One

Bont's remark plunged Ria into turmoil but she was careful not to show it. "Burned to death?" she said. "That's horrible. Why?"

The big man shrugged and scratched his head: "I'm not sure. It's a new idea of Murgh's. Set an example to other Uglies, I think. Teach them not to trespass."

"My guys weren't trespassing," Ria protested. "They were helping to bring Hond back to camp – you saw that!"

But Bont held up his hand to stop her: "Not my problem," he said. "You'll be in front of the assembly of elders in the morning. Explain it to them."

Ria nodded: "Count on it, Bont, I will." She looked around, trying to seem casual. "You said you killed one of the Uglies tonight. Which one?"

He shrugged again: "How should I know? They all look the same."

"Then show me the body."

Bont gave her a suspicious glance: "You really *do* care about them, don't you?" he said. "You're making me wonder if maybe what Grigo said is true after all."

"That I took an Ugly lover? That I had them murder Duma and Vik? That's complete shit, Bont, and you know it. I thought that's why you stood up for me just now . . ."

His friend Ligar interrupted: "We stood up for you because of Hond . . ."

"And out of respect for your father's memory," said Vulp.

"And because you deserve a fair trial," added Bahat. "We're going to make sure you get one."

"I'm grateful to you," Ria said, lowering her eyes.

She knew that other braves had also spoken out against Murgh's plan to lynch her, but she had no doubt that it was to these four – Bont and Ligar, Vulp and Bahat – that she really owed her reprieve.

They would be Ria's guards, marching beside her for what was left of the night, until they reached camp in the morning.

She would try to make them her allies.

To footslog a hundred men at night through rough country and keep everyone together was no easy task but the Clan had been warlike for as long as anyone could remember and the braves Murgh had recruited organized themselves into disciplined ranks for the march back to camp. Having been ambushed by them, Ria felt not so much anger as a perverse sense of pride at how formidable, cunning, and ruthless her people could be. If she could get them thinking straight, they would make redoubtable foes for the Illimani.

Ligar and Bont were in the rank in front of her, roughly in the middle of the column, while Vulp and Bahat marched on either side of her. At first Ria said nothing. Just kept her head down, gritted her teeth against her many aches and pains, and waited for the right moment. But her opening didn't come until they climbed out of the valley and began a long, hard trek across a huge expanse of moonlit moorland. Then Bahat turned his grizzled head to her and said: "I've known you since you were born. You're a good girl – adventurous, perhaps, but you have a good heart. I don't believe a word Grigo said about you, so what adventure brought you together with the Uglies?"

His voice was kindly, reminding Ria of her childhood. She was just about to tell him the whole story when she noticed Grigo. He had fallen back from his place beside his father at the front of the column and somehow infiltrated himself into the rank behind her from where she sensed him listening in and giving her the evil eye.

She whirled round to glare at him: "Why are you spying on me, Grigo? Afraid I'm going to expose your shitty little plot?"

"What plot?" he blustered. "The only plot here is the one you're in with the Uglies . . ."

Ria laughed: "I know about you and the Illimani," she said. "I know what you're doing for Sulpa. I know why you had Duma and Vik killed. It's all going to come out at the trial."

She was bluffing, goading Grigo to test his reaction. Now he launched himself at her and tried to lock his arm around her neck, but Bont was on him in an instant and sent him tumbling with a series of tremendous cuffs about the ears. "Fuck off, Grigo," he said, wagging a massive finger. "You'll get your chance in the morning. Nobody harms the prisoner until then."

Ria looked out for Grigo after that. But he was nowhere to be seen – was he even still with the column? – as the rest of the night passed and she answered Bahat's question with the simple truth of what had happened to her in the last two days. She took her time describing every detail she could remember. Bahat listened, saying nothing, but sometimes nodding his head, and she saw that Vulp, Ligar, Bont and others round about were listening to her too.

She didn't feel her most important task was to persuade them that she was innocent of the ludicrous charges Grigo had brought against her, or even to implicate Grigo himself. That could wait until tomorrow. What mattered was that it was the Illimani, not the Uglies, who had killed Duma and Vik and it was the huge threat posed by the Illimani she wanted to impress on her Clansmen. So she told them about the battles she and the Uglies had fought with the outlanders in the past two days. How Rill had been killed. How Hond had been injured. How the Uglies had saved them at the cost of many dead. She described the Illimani, the way they looked, the way they fought, what a terrible enemy they were, and why she was certain the Clan would soon have to face them in their thousands.

Vulp questioned her closely. To be sure, she'd fought a war band of savage marauders. He was prepared to accept that. But why did she think there were more of them?

Ria figured he wasn't ready for explanations involving the spirit world and the ghost of an Ugly's deceased father. What she told him instead, not hesitating over the lie, was that a group of Ugly hunters had spotted the main Illimani force and estimated it to number more than five thousand men.

"Where is this force?" demanded Bahat, in a tone of complete disbelief. Five thousand fighting men was a staggering figure, a larger number by far than the Clan or any of the neighboring tribes could muster.

"Just a few days' march from us," Ria improvised. "The Uglies know the place. If we befriend them instead of burning them they can lead our scouts there . . ."

"Befriend the Uglies?" said Ligar. "I hope you're not serious . . ."

"Totally serious. We've got to stop seeing them as subhumans and start seeing them as allies. We're going to need all the help we can get . . ."

"But they smell so bad. They can't speak. They're stupid. Even if what you're saying is true, can't we have other allies? I think I would rather befriend bears or rhinos, or even large rocks."

"This isn't a joke, Ligar. They have . . . powers."

"Powers?" He looked skeptical. "What powers?"

Ria told him about the Uglies' remarkable ability to heal.

"But if they can heal," Ligar objected, "why didn't they heal Hond?"

"They did!" Ria exclaimed. "He was dying. They brought him back but they had to make him sleep for the healing to work." She looked up. Dawn was breaking and they were very close to camp. "He'll have recovered by now," she said. "You'll see."

The Clan were an abundant people, numbering more than two thousand. But it was only during the summer moons, from solstice to equinox, when vast herds of reindeer migrated through the region, that all the scattered hunting bands came together in the great camp beside the Snake River. With the equinox still almost a moon away the whole population of the Clan was therefore present to witness Ria brought in a prisoner in the midst of the column of braves.

She realized in a wash of emotion how tired and beaten-up and hungry she was feeling, and how bedraggled and done-in she must look.

She was sure Grigo would be close to enjoy her humiliation but he wasn't beside his father at the front of the column and there was enough daylight to see he wasn't anywhere amongst the ranks. It seemed all the more likely he'd slipped away during the night. But where? To do what? The only certainty, Ria thought, was that no good would come of it.

Their route took them past the ragged lean-tos and hide-covered bivouacs clustered round the southern edge of the camp where the forest ended and the cleared land began. A toddler ran into their path but was snatched up by his mother, then Ria was spotted by a crone named Garanit, famous for her shrill vindictive gossip, who cried out: "Murderer! Murderer! Murderer!"

It was nearly full daylight when they reached the camp's muddy thoroughfare, lined on both sides by wattle huts from which people poured to join in the chant: "Murderer! Murderer!" Murderer!" Someone shouted that Ria was a witch; other voices muttered about burning.

Her heart was pounding. Had everyone gone mad? And where had Murgh got this horrible new idea about burning people to death? Was he – spirits forbid it! – planning to burn *her* to death?

Up ahead was the lookout tower built of gigantic logs roped ingeniously together. No lookouts had been posted this morning but as she approached the looming structure Ria saw that dozens of children had climbed to its first level. Grigo's younger brother, an eight-year-old tearaway named Karst, was amongst them. When she passed beneath him he spat a fat glob of mucus into her hair.

There was still no sign of Grigo himself.

Two hundred paces north of the tower, in the heart of the camp, was the meeting ground, an open expanse of hard-packed earth three hundred paces from side to side, where the assembly of elders held their deliberations in public. The whole area was enclosed by a circle of huge logs, each one three times Ria's height, set upright at intervals into post holes.

It took her only an instant to grasp the essentials of the scene before her.

Brindle wasn't the Ugly who'd been killed during the ambush. That must have been poor Brigley – because Brindle was alive, tied to a stake at the center of the circle with Porto, Jergat and Oplimar, surrounded by an enormous pile of fresh-chopped wood and dry kindling. Yet another of Grigo's relatives, this time his tiresome uncle Grine, stood close by, holding a smoking brand, ready to set the bonfire ablaze. At a safe distance behind him, on the ceremonial stools of mammoth ivory they used only when judging a trial, sat all five of the elders. They had arranged themselves in their customary semicircle. Rotas, the most senior, was perched in the middle, flanked to his left by Torga and Otri and to his right by Krant and Ezida. Behind them stood the massed council of braves.

"*Help us, Ria.*" Brindle's thought-voice, absent this whole night, rang out again inside her head. He sounded lost and bewildered. "*Afraid to die by fire. Begging you, please ask Clan give mercy. Kill us quick . . .*"

Chapter Forty-Two

Leoni breathed a sigh of relief when they reached the rendezvous and found the cab already waiting with its engine idling. They ducked into its back seat and soon turned north onto the I-405. "Where did you learn to fight like that?" she whispered to Matt. "You made mincemeat of those two guys."

He looked embarrassed: "I did five years of military service in Iraq and Afghanistan. Late teens, early twenties. Before . . . well . . ." He seemed to hesitate: "It was before certain things changed in my life."

Leoni had a strong intuition that now was not the time to press Matt on what had changed in his life. The rush-hour traffic was heavy and as it swallowed them up in its safe anonymity she edged closer to him, rested her head on his shoulder and let her eyes droop closed. As she drifted into sleep she decided that she very much liked the fresh-washed smell of his hair and the lean, muscular feel of his body. Was there just the slightest tremor of a turn-on here? Too early to decide.

She had a strange dream. She was following a narrow trail along the floor of a pine forest on a sunny afternoon. Although beams of golden light lanced down through the thick canopy of branches and leaves, the trail was overgrown, faint and difficult to see, and at last faded out. She turned, but the trees had closed up behind her like water behind the keel of a boat. With mounting panic she began to search, first in one direction, then another, running and stumbling, sometimes finding a hint of a path only to lose it again moments later. The great trees rose up all round her, oppressing her, seeming to box her in, and no matter how fast she ran she kept coming back to the same place.

Just when things were getting really freaky a girl stepped from behind a massive pine and stood in front of her. Even in the dream she felt the physical shock of recognition. It was the girl with nut-brown skin and chestnut hair she'd seen on her ketamine trip – the girl she'd warned about the tree-birds. She smiled and took Leoni's hand. "Don't be afraid," she said. "Together we will find the way."

A tremendous warmth suffused Leoni's heart – was this what it felt like to know the love of a sister? – and she woke up with a jolt.

No forests here. And no sister.

It was late afternoon and they were in Los Angeles. The cab was rolling along a potholed street lined with broken-down homes and abandoned shacks. Groups of tough-looking youths loitered on corners, giving off a hostile vibe, and three police cars shot past, sirens wailing, lights flashing. "Welcome to South Central," said Matt with a grin.

Moments later they were standing by the side of the road. They waited until the cab had disappeared from sight, then Matt led the way to the right down a cross street and took a left at the end. After about fifteen minutes of apparently aimless walking, with very little conversation, he hailed another cab and gave an address in Venice Beach, where the procedure was repeated. It was not until they were in their fifth cab, heading for West Hollywood, that he finally seemed to relax. "I got Bannerman on the phone earlier when you were asleep," he said. "I thought it would be a good idea to meet up with him and see where we go from here."

"This is Bannerman's house?" Leoni was surprised twenty minutes later as they pulled into the long sweeping driveway of a spectacular Italianate villa. "I didn't realize he was this loaded."

Matt shook his head. "It isn't Bannerman's place. It's just where we're meeting. The house belongs to his funder."

The huge mansion appeared to be deserted except for Bannerman and his partner David who were already installed at one end of the refectory table in the kitchen. Matt found wine and beer in the refrigerator, pizzas were ordered in and by nine p.m. they were ready to talk.

Before sharing his news, which he said was all bad, Bannerman insisted on hearing a full account of Leoni's DMT experience, jotting notes on a yellow legal pad as she talked and questioning her at several points. When she described the way the Blue Angel had operated on her temple, implanting a filament of crystal, he looked puzzled: "You were on an out-of-body journey with DMT, so I'm confused about what she operated on."

"It's hard to explain. I have to leave my body to travel to the land where everything is known – that's what she calls her realm. But when I get there I find myself back in a body again. That was the body she operated on."

Bannerman made a lengthy note: "And did she tell you the purpose of the operation?"

"Yes, absolutely. She said she did it to make DMT more efficient at taking me where she wants me to go."

"Remarkable," Bannerman muttered.

Leoni described the second part of the trip – the brutal men, the Stone Age weapons, the human sacrifices, the encounter with Sulpa, the apparent connection between Sulpa and an entity called Jack whose shadow had hung over her since childhood, and how it was Sulpa/Jack who had possessed Becky.

Bannerman's manner became reproving: "You didn't say anything to me about Jack before."

"There're other things I haven't told you yet," Leoni admitted. "Private things between me and my parents that tie in to all this."

Bannerman sighed: "Well, I guess you'll tell me when you're ready."

The news Bannerman had for them was every bit as bad as he'd hinted.

Following Becky's attack on Leoni in the morning, Shapira had canceled the rest of that day's DMT sessions. She was convinced that Becky's spectacular psychotic breakdown had been triggered by the drug, and who was to say that other volunteers might not also be on the verge of equally pyrotechnic freak-outs? As a responsible clinician, she'd insisted, she couldn't possibly allow trials to continue after such an incident and of course she'd felt obliged to report Becky's case to the Head of the UC Irvine School of Medicine. Within an hour the DMT project had been officially suspended.

Then had come the afternoon raid that Matt and Leoni had narrowly avoided. The agents had flashed IDs from the Drug Enforcement Agency but had looked and behaved like thugs. Shapira and Monbiot had been so terrorized, fearing a scandal over Becky, that they'd allowed the project to be searched from top to bottom and surrendered their case notes.

Finally, a few hours ago, the UCLA Med Center had also suspended Bannerman from duty and minutes afterwards he'd received an e-mail from the California State Medical Board informing him he was under investigation for possible ethics breaches. "It looks like your parents have pulled some powerful strings to bog me down fighting for my job and defending my professional reputation," he told Leoni. "I guess they figure that way they'll stop me working with you."

Panic welled in her chest. There was so much further she needed to go with this. "So what do you plan to do?" she asked.

"I get stubborn when people try to bully me," said Bannerman. "I'm passionate about my research so I want to carry on working with you. You have the potential to be a very special subject and I think we've stumbled on something . . . well . . ." He hesitated: "Honestly, I think we've stumbled on something quite extraordinary. I'm a scientist, I do my best to stay objective, rational, grounded. But this phenomenon of the Blue Angel, the way she keeps appearing to more people, the special connection you seem to have with her. And now this Jack stuff. All that has me beat. I can't explain it with science. Not yet, anyway. Maybe it really is something supernatural. I'm open to that. Or maybe it isn't. But having my life demolished by your parents hasn't made me stop wanting to find out . . ." He seemed to look for the right words: "How about yourself? After all this, do you still want to find out?"

Leoni didn't hesitate: "I still want to find out. A million percent."

"Good," said Bannerman. "That's what I'd hoped." He rubbed his hands together, suddenly cheerful: "Now, what do you know about the Vine of the Dead?"

Chapter Forty-Three

"*I won't let them kill you,*" Ria pulsed to Brindle.

"How can you stop them?" Brindle's thought-voice was heavy. "They are so many."

"Trust me, Brindle. Don't be afraid. I'll get us out of this."

Executions were always popular and once inside the circle of great wooden pillars most of the braves who'd escorted her thus far melted into the huge crowd, already more than a thousand strong, pouring into the meeting ground. With only Vulp, Bahat, Ligar and Bont remaining at her side, while Murgh, Kimp and Chard cleared the way ahead, Ria was marched the last hundred paces through the throng to stand before the assembly of elders. Her eyes sought out Hond, convinced she would find him fully recovered and ready to speak for her, but he was not behind the elders in the ranks of the council of braves, or anywhere to be seen in the multitudes pressing in around them.

Instead Grigo appeared, forcing his way to the front of the crowd. He was flushed – perhaps he'd been running – and Ria found something strange about his manner. Was it excitement? Conceit? Triumph? If so, why was fear part of it as well? She couldn't be sure. He flashed a quick, nervous glance over his shoulder as he hurried to join his father.

As the most senior of Ria's accusers, Murgh had to make the initial address. He looked, Ria thought, faintly deranged, as though the presence of so many people had gone to his head, but his sinister, bullying tactics hadn't changed and now he actually *shouted* at the elders: "EXCELLENCIES," his tone was hostile and sarcastic, "VENERABLE LORDS. A great night's work has been done." At this he turned and gestured at Brindle, Porto, Jergat and Oplimar. "We have captured the dangerous gang of Uglies who murdered two of our boys and we have brought them here as promised" – he was shouting again – "TO FACE DEATH BY BURNING in the presence of the entire Clan." Murgh drew himself up to his full, not very impressive height and swiveled his neck until his stare fell on Ria: "We also bring this WITCH before you for judgement. She was caught in a forbidden act, COPULATING with an Ugly" – cries of outrage from the crowd. "She ordered the Uglies to murder Duma and Vik" – gasps of horror and revulsion. "For these crimes we demand that the witch Ria BE BURNED TO DEATH WITHOUT MERCY on the same pyre as the Uglies!"

There was a sudden buzz of controversy, and heated arguments broke out, the crowd dividing, Ria judged, roughly equally between those in favor of burning her and those vehemently opposed. She could understand why Murgh and Grigo had wanted her lynched when she was first captured. She had support here she could turn against them.

Finally Rotas, the highest-ranking elder, called for silence. Long, lean and angular, with joints that clicked and creaked when he walked, he was reputed to have passed eighty summers and to have been a great warrior in his youth. He had a full head of silver hair and a thick gray beard but also a certain mischievous expression that made him seem far younger than his years. Now he leaned forward on his ivory stool and Ria's confidence grew as he proceeded to reprimand Murgh in a slow, clear, emphatic voice, as though he were talking to a child: "We have *not* established that the prisoner is a witch. We have *not* established that the murder of Duma and Vik was the work of these Uglies, or any Uglies, or whether Ria ordered it or not. We have *not* established that Ria had sex with an Ugly male. We are here to prove or refute these charges. Show me your evidence."

"He has no evidence!" Ria exploded. Her bruised rib ached. Her hands, still bound tight behind her back on Murgh's orders, were numb. But she tossed her head, flicked her hair around her shoulders, and fixed the elders with a level gaze: "Everything he said about me is a lie, and I'm going to prove it."

"Nonsense!" snorted Murgh. He reached for Grigo, whose shifty eyes were darting from side to side, shoved him forward, and again addressed the elders. "Here is our evidence. My eldest son. A youth of irreproachable good name. He saw it all WITH HIS OWN EYES. He saw the witch copulating with the beast. He saw the murders. Didn't you, Grigo? SPEAK, boy!"

"Wait!"

The interruption was from Torga, nicknamed the "Vulture" because of his enormous hooked nose, bald head and wattled neck. He had vacated his stool next to Rotas and was hobbling towards Ria. "Turn around, girl," he said to her. When she obeyed he clicked his tongue and asked Murgh sharply: "Why is she tied?"

"Because she's a prisoner," Murgh snapped back. "Because she's a traitor to the Clan. Because she's a murderer. How do you expect us to arrest a bitch like this?"

"We expect you to do whatever is necessary. But it is a sacred thing from the long-ago that no man or woman of the Clan is to come before the elders tied at hand or foot. This girl's hands are tied . . ."

"She throws stones. She's said to be deadly . . ."

"A meaningless objection since there are no stones here" – Torga indicated the flattened earth of the meeting ground. "Please release her from her bonds."

"With respect, venerable ones, I prefer not to," sneered Murgh.

Now Rotas too was on his feet, his joints grinding in protest: "She must stand trial a free woman," he growled. "It is the law." Pulling a dagger from his belt, he beckoned Ria towards him, ignoring further protests from Murgh, and cut her loose. "Child," the elder observed, "you are covered in blood. How did that come about?"

Ria stretched out her cramped hands, finding to her astonishment that she was on the verge of tears – which she held back. "Yesterday I fought a battle," she whispered.

Rotas leaned closer: "Speak up. I am a little deaf . . ."

"Yesterday I fought a battle and was covered in the blood of my enemies. Not these poor Uglies" – Ria pointed towards the stake – "but terrible, fearsome and cruel outlanders never seen before in our valleys. GRIGO IS THEIR FRIEND," she shouted. "Ask him about the Illimani! Ask him about Sulpa!!"

"These are just diversionary tactics," scoffed Murgh. "There are no outlanders. The only battle she's been in was with us when we captured her last night. She cut up a few of our boys. That's where the blood came from – and from herself – not from some make-believe enemy . . ."

"Where's Hond?" Ria screamed. "He fought the Illimani too. He'll back me up . . ."

Murgh nodded as though he'd been expecting this, and beckoned to one of his followers standing at the edge of the crowd. The man came over and they exchanged whispered words. When the man retreated Murgh turned to Ria, a smug and gluttonous smile on his face. "I regret to inform you," he said, smirking, "that your brother died of his injuries during the night. On the journey. It was too much for him."

"Oh, you piece of shit!" Ria shrieked. "You murdering piece of shit!"

Murgh turned at once to the elders: "I request that the prisoner be silenced while we present our case to your excellencies."

"That is the correct procedure," admitted Rotas. He turned to Ria: "Be silent, girl. I will demand the same of your accusers when your time comes to speak."

Ria wasn't listening because Brindle was thought-talking in her head. "*Murgh lying*," he said. "*I carried Hond's stretcher. He did not die . . .*"

As Rotas and Torga returned to their stools, Grigo began to give his evidence and Ria pulsed to Brindle: "Are you certain Hond's alive?"

"Alive when reached camp. Not just alive. Getting better. Healing worked . . ."

Ria was doubtful: "That doesn't mean much. They could have killed him since then . . ."

"He still alive, Ria. I know it."

She was desperate to believe him: "So why are they saying he's dead?"

"Don't know. Maybe they *think* he dead?"

While she thought-talked with Brindle, Ria's attention had drifted from Grigo who was marching up and down in front of the elders with his chest puffed out, holding forth in a booming voice. He was describing his idyllic hunt in the far valleys with his good mates Duma and Vik, and when he reached the episode of their accidental discovery of Ria having sex with an Ugly he glared at the miserable captives tied to the stake and wagged an accusing finger at Brindle: "That one with the withered leg!" There was a sigh from Murgh's faction in the crowd. "He had his cock in her up to the root." Grigo pointed again and performed an obscene mime of sexual intercourse. "But when we tried to arrest them more Uglies came and Ria told them to kill us. They got Duma and Vik" – he bared his broken teeth at the elders – "but I fought my way out."

For a count of twenty there was silence. Then Krant, the wrinkled, pot-bellied elder seated to the right of Rotas, cleared his throat. "How do we know any of this is true?" he asked.

At first Grigo didn't seem to realize that the question was for him.

"How do we know you're telling the truth?" Krant repeated. His voice was quavering and petulant. "Isn't this whole thing just your word against Ria's?"

"But Ria was *caught* with the Uglies," protested Murgh. "That proves Grigo's story."

"I say it proves no such thing." It was the elder named Ezida, tiny and humpbacked, with eyes as bright as a bird's.

"Well, it does prove she was with the Uglies," added Otri, "but that by itself proves nothing else."

"For the rest it is Ria's word against Grigo's," confirmed Rotas. "Now I would like to hear the girl."

Ria was beginning to understand what was happening. Beneath the immediate crisis was the deeper issue of the leadership of the Clan which, by long tradition, was vested in the assembly of elders. Murgh and his group made no secret of their disrespect for tradition and their view that the assembly should be dissolved and its powers taken over by the council of braves, which they dominated.

Murgh was an opportunist. He'd obviously expected that his side would gain, though Ria couldn't immediately see how, from the spectacle of hunting her down, lynching her if he'd had his way, and then burning the Uglies in the meeting ground in front of the whole Clan. Things had started to go wrong when Bahat and the others had stood up to him and stopped the lynching. And now it had come to a trial after all, rather than just the persecution of a group of helpless subhumans, the elders sensed an opportunity to fight back, perhaps even to humiliate their arch-enemy in public.

Ria looked at her four friends roped together to the stake in the midst of the unlit bonfire. "*I'm going to win this thing,*" she told them. "*I won't let them burn you. I'm going to make them set you free.*" Then she turned back to Rotas and to out-loud speech: "I can prove Grigo's lying," she said.

"How so, my child?" The elder leaned forward again to hear her better.

"He said that the Ugly had sex with me." Despite herself she blushed. "But I've never had sex with anyone in my life. I'm a virgin."

A cornered look slithered into Grigo's eyes, and Ria felt a little thrill of triumph. When he'd been describing the sex scene with such relish the brainless thug had obviously forgotten – but now equally obviously remembered – that there were certain old women of the Clan who were infallible experts in the matter of a girl's virginity. "Lying bitch," he yelled. "That Ugly was screwing your brains out." But it was all bluster, and he knew it.

She was just about to call in the midwives to witness she was intact when she caught a flicker of movement out of the corner of her eye. It was Murgh signaling to his brother Grine who was still lurking at the rear of the bonfire.

Grine blew on the head of the brand he was carrying, until it sparked and flamed. Then he stooped to thrust it into the kindling.

Chapter Forty-Four

Bannerman said a word that Leoni didn't immediately recognize. It sounded something like "Ayawaska."

"What's that?" she asked. "Never heard of it."

"Aya-hwaska," Bannerman pronounced the strange word carefully, "spelled a-y-a-h-u-a-s-c-a. From the Quechua language of the Incas, *aya* meaning 'dead,' *huasca* meaning 'vine.' Thus the Vine of the Dead or the Vine of Souls. It's a foul-tasting witch's brew of two different plants that shamans in the Amazon cook up when they want to leave their bodies and travel to the spirit world."

"The Blue Angel wants me to use DMT," Leoni said. "That's why she operated on me . . ."

But Bannerman seemed to ignore her. "As I was saying, Ayahuasca is a mixture of two plants. One is the vine itself. I can tell you more about that later if you want to know about it. It's extremely interesting. But it's the second one that's really responsible for getting shamans to the spirit world. Its botanical name is *Psycotria viridis* – they call it *chacruna* in the Amazon – and its leaves contain DMT in a pharmacologically pure form. That's the Ayahuasca brew – the vine and the hallucinogenic leaf both boiled together with water. In most of South America it's still legal to drink it. In fact, its use is protected under laws of religious freedom. So here's my thought." He fixed Leoni with his spaniel gaze. "How about—"

Horrified, she held up her hand to silence him. "Please tell me you're *not* suggesting I go to the Amazon and actually drink this – what did you call it? – this witch's brew?"

"You got it!" said Bannerman.

Ever since she could remember, Leoni had been afraid of jungles. Insects from hell. Venomous reptiles. Exotic diseases. She didn't want to know about them. Nevertheless, as she listened to Bannerman's proposal to get her to the biggest jungle in the world, she had to admit that it made a weird and unexpected kind of sense. There was no way they were going to be able to continue with any kind of legal DMT research in the United States, and breaking the law would pose huge additional risks for Bannerman's career. But Ayahuasca was basically DMT and the fact that it was legal in the Amazon meant that he could carry on supervising and analysing her sessions there much as he would have done if the project had continued at Irvine. It would be an unorthodox way to gather data but at least he'd be on the right side of the law.

Another advantage was that it would be easy to arrange.

Bannerman had a colleague in Peru, an American anthropologist named Mary Ruck who for five years had been doing fieldwork amongst the *mestizos* – people of mixed indigenous and Spanish descent, often living in extreme poverty, who make up the majority of the inhabitants of the modern Amazon. Mary's special interest was the use of Ayahuasca by *mestizo* shamans, a subject on which she had become a great expert. But she herself also sometimes arranged Ayahuasca sessions for visiting academics at a jungle lodge she had established on the banks of the Amazon, twenty miles upriver from the city of Iquitos. If Mary could be persuaded to make it available to them it would offer a discreet, controlled setting in which Leoni could be given Ayahuasca under the guidance of an experienced shaman.

"So what do you think?" Bannerman asked.

"I think yes," Leoni replied at once. The Amazon was a hideous prospect but she was willing to go there if it got her back to the Blue Angel. "The only condition is that Matt comes as well."

Bannerman looked at Matt and appeared to be asking him a silent question.

"It's OK," Matt told him.

Leoni felt confused. "What's OK?"

"To tell you something you don't know yet," Bannerman said. "Matt's a bit more than just a volunteer on the DMT project. Actually he funded the whole thing."

Leoni's confusion deepened. Matt was Bannerman's *funder*? How could that possibly be? "But you're broke," she protested.

David laughed and Leoni turned on him: "What's so funny?"

"The idea of Matt being in any way broke," David replied. He dropped his voice to a conspiratorial whisper: "He's low-profile, *but he's loaded.*"

"Loaded" could mean anything but Leoni also remembered Bannerman saying his funder was a "very rich guy." So did Matt have millions? Hundreds of millions? Billions?

"I feel deceived," she told him.

"I didn't deceive you," Matt protested. "If you made judgements about me because of how I look that's your problem, but I never claimed to be broke."

Leoni thought about it. "I guess you didn't," she admitted after a moment. She grinned: "So how rich are you?"

Matt winced. "Look, I have some money. It's no big deal and I *really* don't want to talk about it. But I'm excited about taking this research to the Amazon and I'm honored you asked me to come along."

"Oh, shit." A sudden thought struck Leoni. "I don't have my passport. This is bad . . ."

But David was already waving her to calm down. "Don't worry," he said. "When I did the legal work to get you out of Mountain Ridge I made sure that Sansom gave us all your documents back." He pulled a large envelope out of his briefcase. "Your passport's right here."

David couldn't leave his one-man law office at such short notice and remained in Los Angeles, but Leoni, Matt and Bannerman caught the six a.m. flight from LAX to Peru.

On the journey Leoni told Bannerman everything she'd already told Matt about her childhood: the rapes she'd suffered, the mysterious connection between Jack and her adoptive parents, and the long-term interest the Blue Angel appeared to have taken in her life.

Gritty-eyed from lack of sleep, they landed in Lima and connected from there to the Amazonian city of Iquitos on a creaking LAN Peru Airbus. After they crossed the Andes – jagged white peaks under a clear blue sky – it was just jungle, jungle, jungle in all directions, as far as the eye could see, until the plane began to lose height. It went into a long turn, the pilot made an announcement in Spanish and English, and Leoni had her first look at the wide muddy swirl of the great River Amazon. It made her feel sick. She could only imagine what sort of creatures, large and small, with and without teeth, lay in wait beneath those waters.

The plane banked again and an implausible landscape came into view. On the west bank of the Amazon, at a bend where the river seemed miles wide and looped around a pair of islands, the primal jungle gave way without warning to a city. Maybe she'd been taking too many drugs but just for a moment, as she sat poised in the sky looking down at it all, she could have imagined that the buildings, square and blocky, painted in pastel shades, with glittering tin roofs, weren't even made by human hands but were some sinister new growth that the forest itself had brought forth.

The plane was coming in for its final approach. Leoni leaned over Matt and peered out of the window. From this new angle she could see a clear reflection of Iquitos in the waters of the Amazon. It was almost as though there was a city above and a city below the river. Two different cities in two different worlds.

She shivered. Which one would she end up in?

Chapter Forty-Five

There was a commotion near Grine, shouts and exclamations, a ripple of movement, and Hond burst forth from the crowd, naked from the waist up, his thick brown curls disheveled, his body streaked with fresh blood. He brandished a stabbing spear tipped with a heavy flint spike and at once plunged it into Grine's shoulder, bearing him down and pinning him squealing to the ground. Without interrupting the single continuous flow of his attack he stepped in on the fallen man, kicked down hard into his face with his heel, stooped to retrieve the brand – it had fallen only a hand's breadth short of the pyre – and threw it far into the crowd.

Grine was still conscious, whimpering and flapping like a harpooned fish. Hond stamped on his face again, this time silencing him, jerked the spear out of his body, and loped towards Murgh holding the dripping weapon at the ready. Murgh had been caught off guard and seemed frozen with shock. Now he grabbed Ria's arm, almost jerking it from its socket, and pulled her in front of him, while Melam, a thickset warrior of his faction, charged at Hond, swinging a battleaxe. As the two men closed Melam bellowed, raised his axe and brought it whistling down on Hond's head. Ria held her breath but Hond sidestepped the blow and tripped Melam with an outstretched foot as the other man hurtled past him, bringing him down with a crash that shook the ground.

More braves rushed forward to protect Murgh, blocking Hond's approach and jabbing at him with spears. But then Bont roared "Enough!" and in three paces he and Ligar were at Hond's side. Bont held no weapon, but this would not be the first time he had killed men with his bare hands. Smaller and quicker on his feet, Ligar had unslung his bow and strung an arrow.

There was an instant of silence as the two groups squared off. They were so intent on one another that none of them saw Rotas rise from his stool. Then he stepped between them. "Stop!" he shouted, a thunderous look on his face. "Stop now. I command it. Lower your weapons."

Murgh's braves weren't ready to obey. One of them lashed at Hond with a dagger only to be felled by a single prodigious blow to the side of the head from Bont's fist. In the same moment, wriggling like an eel, Ria broke free of Murgh's grasp and dashed away from him, allowing Ligar to aim an arrow at his heart.

The morning air, filled with tension and pent-up hatred, seemed to seethe and boil. "STOP THIS, I SAY!" Rotas ordered again. "Step back. Lower your weapons." Murgh looked at the arrow nocked against the string and at the fully stretched bow. Ria could see his mind working – Ligar had never been known to miss a shot, let alone at such close range. She wasn't surprised when Murgh signaled his men to stand down.

At once Ria ran to Hond and embraced him: "Brother, you live! I knew it!" Her hands went to the place in his side where the Illimani blade had pierced him but there was no longer any puncture wound between his ribs, not even a scar, only a livid black-and-blue bruise, spreading across his chest. "You were right," he said, kissing the top of her head. "The Uglies are our friends. They healed me with their magic. They brought me back to life."

Bont was shouting at Murgh: "You told us Hond died during the night. What was that about?"

"A simple mistake," the older man replied.

"Mistake, my ass!" Hond exclaimed with a bitter laugh. Giving Ria a parting squeeze of encouragement, he looked Murgh in the eye: "You shitball. You ordered my murder."

"I don't know what you're talking about," Murgh spluttered.

"Lisin, Imdug, Baba and Uras." Hond named four men well known as Murgh's bully boys. "They're the ones you sent to kill me." He pointed to the smears of blood drying on his body: "I killed them instead."

"What's this about?" snapped Rotas. "Why is Clan blood being spilled?"

Hond indicated the elders' ceremonial ivory stools: "First tell me why my sister is on trial." He turned and pointed at the bonfire. "And why you're planning to burn those Uglies."

The five elders whispered to one another and Rotas reeled off a summary of Grigo's accusations.

"It's all lies," Hond said when he was finished. "Ria is innocent. The Uglies are innocent. A savage people called the Illimani killed Duma and Vik, they killed my brother Rill, and the Uglies fought beside us against them. Many of them died for us. They should be welcomed as heroes here in our camp, not treated as enemies. So long as I live, I swear to you, I will never see them burned!"

Murgh tried to regain the initiative by stepping in on Hond and crowding him. "IT'S YOU WHO'S LYING," he shouted, spraying spit. "It's obvious. You'd do anything to protect your sister."

"There's a way we can settle this," Hond snapped back. And with a wolfish grin he backhanded the older man across the face.

Hond meant single combat. The ancient answer to all disputes.

In a trial, legal arguments might drag on forever, but when one brave called another a liar, and neither would back down, it was the view of the Clan that a fight to the death would determine the truth. Ria knew that by striking Murgh in such an insulting way, in the presence of so large a crowd, Hond had made it impossible for him to refuse the challenge.

Murgh called Grigo and whispered in his ear. Grigo whispered back.

Rotas loomed over them. "You've been challenged, Murgh," he said. "What is your reply?"

Murgh and Grigo both turned to stare towards the southeast, over the heads of the crowd, as though distracted by something happening outside the meeting ground. Then their eyes met and Ria saw a strange expression pass from one to the other. Finally Murgh shrugged: "I accept the challenge, of course."

Such duels were governed by a code of honor. No weapons used: only bare hands and feet. No mercy sought or given. Loser dies. Winner takes all.

"State your terms," said Rotas.

"The Uglies burn with Ria beside them," spat Murgh, wiping blood from his mouth.

"The Uglies and Ria go free," said Hond. He pointed at Grigo: "And after I kill your father I'm going to kill you."

There were no more formalities. To a great roar of excitement from the crowd, the combatants faced off.

Ria felt confident of the outcome; she had absolute faith in her brother's fighting skills. Hond was lean and hard, head and shoulders taller than his opponent, powerfully muscled and of prime fighting age, while Murgh was twenty years his senior, squat, with bandy legs. But then she saw that Murgh's short legs gave him a natural wrestler's stance, his upper body was enormously muscular and strong, and his arms, culminating in massive hands, were unnaturally long – more than compensating for Hond's greater height.

Murgh dived low and tackled Hond's legs. As his momentum carried them both to the ground he locked his huge hands around the younger man's throat. Hond punched him about the head, brought his knee into his stomach and got on top of him. But it made no difference. Murgh just clung on to his throat, keeping him at arm's length and squeezing the life out of him.

Hond's struggles weakened, his face turned purple and his eyes bulged.

Chapter Forty-Six

Iquitos was dirty and poor but Leoni didn't care. She felt liberated here. Suddenly out of danger. Thousands of miles away from her parents and their minions, their tame lunatic asylums and their hired thugs . . .

(*And from Jack*).

On the morning after their arrival, while Bannerman met with his anthropologist friend Mary to finalize their arrangements for the research, Leoni and Matt explored the quaint, faded city that seemed as hot and humid as a sauna bath. Everywhere there were flyblown and neglected buildings – paint peeling off, mildew rotting the walls – which had once been ornate and opulent.

They stopped for lunch in a crowded noisy snack bar off the Plaza de Armas but Matt ordered only fruit. "Are you some kind of fruitarian?" Leoni asked.

He said he wasn't. It was just that according to some studies he'd read it was a good idea to follow a pure and simple, mainly vegetarian diet prior to an Ayahuasca session – and their first session at Mary Ruck's lodge in the jungle was scheduled for tomorrow evening.

Leoni canceled the order she'd just placed for a large hamburger with bacon and cheese and substituted fresh fruit. She then had a long and inconclusive conversation with Matt about the nature of reality and the problem of parallel universes which left her feeling useless and stupid. He had a lot to say on the physics of the subject that she just didn't get at all. The guy was very smart and she was afraid he would conclude she wasn't on his intellectual level.

Perhaps this was why he showed no sign of any romantic interest in her. Maybe she just bored him stiff?

The other thing he wouldn't do was talk about himself. During the morning he'd resisted every attempt by Leoni to get him to spill the beans about his fortune or to provide details of his own life.

By mid-afternoon the heat and humidity became insufferable and they returned to the hotel to siesta in their separate rooms.

Leoni tried and failed to doze off.

She had a nagging presentiment at the back of her mind that there was something she was supposed to do and around five p.m. she ventured out alone in a garish three-wheeler taxi to revisit Belem, the city's main street market. She couldn't quite say why she felt drawn there. She just knew she had to go.

Although the temperature was more comfortable now, there was less produce on display and the crowds were much thinner than when she'd explored the market with Matt in the heat of the morning. But as she walked up and down the narrow cloth-shaded alleys between the stalls, breathing in ripe smells of fish and pineapples, splashing through shallow pools of water where buckets had been sloshed, Leoni saw that the Pasaje Paquito, the quarter of the market devoted to medicines derived from plants, was still buzzing.

Here every stall exhibited colorful bundles of aromatic roots, leaves and herbs in large plastic buckets. There were sheaves of thick mapacho cigarettes rolled with wild Amazonian tobacco so strong it was believed to have the power to ward off evil spirits. And there were literally thousands of hand-labeled bottled extracts touted as remedies for AIDS, constipation, diabetes, flatulence, impotence, infertility, business failure, malign spells cast by sorcerers, and any number of other conditions real and imaginary.

Leoni did not feel at all threatened or endangered by Iquitos. The people were naive, curious and kindly and even the gentle doe-eyed children who had begun to follow her everywhere, plaintively asking for small sums of money, were not an annoyance.

Her favorite was eleven-year-old Ramon, small and tough, a *mestizo* with red-brown skin, missing front teeth, a bent nose, and the roguish grin of a jungle elf. Since her arrival the evening before, when he had first attached himself to her, she had contrived to hand him close to twenty dollars in small bills and to buy him and his friends three huge meals of hamburgers and fries. She'd seen him sprinting after her when she left the hostel in the taxi a little earlier and wasn't surprised when he appeared at her side in the Pasaje Paquito, hardly out of breath, having run the intervening mile through the town.

"Give me one dollar," he said at once, and turned his huge gap-toothed smile on her.

She aimed a mock blow at him: "It's always money, money, money with you, isn't it, Ramon?" she protested. "If I had no money, I don't think you'd run ten feet to see me."

He grinned again and repeated his demand: "Give me one dollar, lady. No mother. No father. Very hungry."

Leoni began to haggle with a stallholder over the price of a love potion – she had half a mind to try it out on Matt – when something tugged at her attention.

Literally *tugged.*

It felt very personal and intrusive, like fingers digging into her mind. She turned in the direction of the pull and her eyes fell on a striking figure standing in a shop doorway – a man, tall and strongly built, wearing an elegant white tropical suit.

She squinted. At first he seemed to be youthful but his face was partly in shadow and at second glance she saw he might be closer to forty than twenty. She caught a glimpse of hooded dark eyes, sallow skin, high cheekbones, a wispy beard, and black hair that hung down lank and straight over his shoulders. He held Leoni's gaze for a long moment and again she felt that strange, intimate *tug* within her consciousness. Then he turned his back on her and vanished inside the shop.

"Who was that?" she asked Ramon, who was still tagging along beside her, waiting for a dollar.

"Who, missus?" An evasive look crossed the little boy's face and was gone in a fraction of a second, but Leoni saw it.

"That man, the one in the white suit." She pointed at the empty shop doorway. "You *saw* him, Ramon! Don't pretend you didn't! He was just standing there, looking at me. What's his name?"

But Ramon clammed up. He seemed afraid. He had seen no one, he said. And when Leoni marched over to the shop it was empty, its shelves stripped of produce. A back door, leading to another of the market's many alleys, was swinging open.

What was going on? Where had the mysterious stranger disappeared to? And how had he got inside her head like that?

Suddenly she felt it was imperative to find him – that he, indeed, was the reason she had been summoned back to the market this afternoon.

A grim certainty descended on her that if she left here without speaking with him something vital would be lost.

Leoni was still peering out of the back door of the shop. In one direction the alley led to town, in the other to the riverside. On instinct, she ran towards the river.

The market was closing around her now, stallholders packing up to go home as evening fell, hundreds of small boats loading passengers and produce. She dodged around three snarling dogs fighting over scraps, splashed through a foul-smelling puddle and caught a glimpse of the man's white suit in the gloaming just ahead.

"Hey, you," she called out after him. "Mister. Wait a minute."

He never deviated or looked back but just plunged ahead, leading her deeper and deeper into the warren of mean slums lining the riverbank to the south of the wharves and the market.

Daylight was leaching rapidly from the sky, a sinister velvet tone settling over everything, and the warm air, moist and rank, was filled with the sound of night insects.

Leoni shuddered, no longer sure what had impelled her to follow a complete stranger into a slum.

In the middle of the *Amazon.*

The last rays of the sun picked out the fabric of his white suit amongst the shadows in a narrow alley between tin-roofed shanties. And as though in response to her attention she felt again that strange demanding *tug* within her mind.

At the end of the alley was a narrow wooden pier, no more than four feet wide, built on stilts like many of the shanties and extending fifty feet out over the waters of the Amazon. There was just enough light for Leoni to see the man she'd been following. He was standing about halfway along the pier, looking down at the water.

She felt a small hand grasp her own and jumped with shock, suppressing her yelp of fear when she saw it was Ramon. His eyes looked big as saucers. "Better come away, missus," he whispered. "That man not good."

Leoni looked along the pier again but the darkness was now complete and she could no longer see the man in the white suit.

There was a soft *splash.*

Had he dived?

She squinted into the darkness but it was as though he had never been there.

Later, as she returned to the hotel, an inner voice prompted her to mention none of this to Matt and Bannerman.

They were her friends but there was no reason why they had to know every foolish thing she did.

Chapter Forty-Seven

Ria was at war with herself. Every instinct of love and family loyalty commanded her to break the age-old code of single combat and attack Murgh, but honor held her back.

Honor! What was honor when Hond's life was at stake?

Yet still she could not intervene.

For if she did the code was unbending on what must happen next. The fight would be stopped, Murgh would be declared the victor, his terms – "*The Uglies burn with Ria beside them*" – would be enacted at once, and Hond's life would be his to take by any manner of execution he chose.

So one way or the other, whether or not she stopped Murgh strangling Hond now, it was certain they were all going to die. She'd just resigned herself to the obvious conclusion – *might as well die honorably* – when Brindle's thought-voice rang out inside her head: "Fight not over yet, Ria!"

And her brother returned from the dead.

He was still on top of Murgh, and Murgh was still throttling him at arm's length, but now, with a violent effort, choking and spluttering, Hond found his feet and jerked himself upright, pulling the other man after him. For an instant Murgh's two-handed grip on his throat was loosened and Ria heard Hond draw in a huge, shuddering breath. Then he used his greater height to punch downwards hard and fast, a chopping right-hand blow that crashed into the side of Murgh's jaw and continued down between his arms in a single fluid swirl. At the end of it Hond dropped his shoulder, as though he were reaching for the ground, then reversed his direction, smashed his elbow back into Murgh's face, and, at last, tore free of his stranglehold.

Neither man immediately resumed the attack. Hond was gulping in air. Murgh's nose looked broken and was spouting blood. For a count of twenty they circled one another.

Ria feared Murgh might still have some fight left in him but was relieved to see there was none. His one strategy had been to get his hands round Hond's throat and strangle him to death right at the beginning. But that had failed and now he just looked old and out of ideas.

They circled again. Hond was recovering his strength and when Murgh lunged at him he slipped aside, kicked him as he shot past and sent him stumbling.

Hond waited, looking calm, breathing deep and steady, until Murgh turned and squared up to him. Then he advanced on the older man and drove three merciless, bone-shattering jabs into the pulpy mess of his nose.

Murgh sat down with a thump, obviously dazed, and Hond kicked the side of his head, knocking him onto his back. Taking his time, he knelt over him, pinned his shoulders, and began to punch down hard into the bloody center of his face. This time he didn't stop but just kept on punching until Murgh's features became unrecognizable and Ria lost count of the number of blows.

It was what the code of single combat demanded – that one man, unaided, kill another with his bare hands.

Yet as he watched his father being beaten to death it seemed that Grigo's self-control broke and he rushed towards Hond, with a guttural howl. Braves stepped forward to bar his way but he was fast-footed and dodged them all. Too late Ria saw the long Illimani knife glinting in his hand – the knife that had killed Rill; the knife she had seized in battle and that Grigo must have taken from her in the ambush. Before she could cross ten paces to stop him he had plunged it with such force into the center of Hond's back that it passed through his body and out of his chest.

A collective gasp of outrage rose from the elders and rippled out across the huge crowd as Grigo pushed Hond's limp body aside, slung Murgh over his shoulder and strode away with him.

Ria saw Murgh was not dead.

As he was carried off he opened one eye, filled with hate, and glared at her through a mask of blood.

Ria dropped to her knees beside her brother, cradling his head, willing him to survive, forgetful of all else. But she knew at once there was no hope for him.

Hond was gone. He had been taken from her and then returned, only to be snatched away from her forever. The breath had left his body. Not even the magic of the Uglies could save him now.

Ria raised her face to heaven to proclaim her anguish but no tears would come. Instead she was cold and clear in her grief, wide awake, as though she had dived into a mountain stream. Laying Hond back on the ground, she stood up and signaled Bont and Bahat: "Grab Grigo and Murgh before they get away. They broke the code. I want them dead."

She was already hastening to the bonfire to free the Uglies when she saw that Grigo's uncle Grine, his shoulder bloody where Hond had speared him, hadn't given up the fight yet. He was rallying braves from Murgh's faction and now four of them rushed to intercept Bont and Bahat while others, shouting their defiance, formed a protective ring around Grigo and Murgh.

The elders had seemed frozen with shock during these events, unable to react fast enough to exert their authority. But silence fell across the meeting ground when Rotas at last rose from his stool and adopted the ritual posture – arms crossed high over his chest – that signaled he was about to pass judgement. "The settlement of disputes by single combat is ruled by an ancient and binding code," he intoned. "By the cowardly murder of Hond, Grigo has dishonored the code and there can be only one judgement. HOND IS THE VICTOR AND ALL HIS TERMS MUST BE ENACTED. Ria and the Uglies go free. The lives of Murgh and Grigo are forfeit to Ria."

"Fuck your forfeit," yelled Murgh. "We're walking out of here. Try and stop us!"

Despite the beating he'd received he was on his feet again, standing beside his son in the midst of their growing group of defenders – a phalanx that had already swollen to thirty strong. He looked confident, like he knew a secret no one else did, and was hurrying away unopposed when one of the peculiar short spears of the Illimani whistled down out of nowhere, falling almost vertically, punched a hole in the top of his skull, tore through his brain, split his palate, skewered his tongue and his lower jaw, burst out in a splash of meat and blood below his chin and embedded itself in the earth between his feet.

"WAIT FOR THE FIRE!" Grigo screamed over the heads of the

crowd, seeming to appeal to someone far away. "YOU'RE SUPPOSED TO WAIT TILL WE START THE FIRE."

But the air was already filled with a menacing whirr, and a flight of the same short spears hafted to jagged flint points arched overhead and fell upon the meeting ground, killing men, women, children, braves and elders until the dead and injured lay heaped everywhere.

At once the sky darkened again and a second volley came in.

Ria took a spear through the muscle of her thigh; painful, but not crippling. She pulled it free and balanced it in her hand. Ligar and Vulp suffered flesh wounds but could still fight. Amongst the elders Torba and Otri were killed, Krant was speared through the foot, but Rotas and Ezida survived uninjured.

Almost the entire population of the Clan had scrambled to pack into the meeting ground to witness Ria's trial but now, after two volleys from an unseen enemy, the bloodied survivors scattered, shrieking and screaming, fleeing the next avalanche of spears.

All except Kimp and Chard, the fathers of Duma and Vik. Ignoring the danger from above, they were climbing the huge pile of firewood heaped up to burn the Uglies. They had axes in their hands and murder in their eyes.

Chapter Forty-Eight

Leoni stepped outside the thatched *maloca*, the longhouse that formed the central ceremonial space of Mary Ruck's jungle lodge, staggered three paces and dry-retched until she poured with sweat and gasped for breath. She had never needed to barf so badly but her stomach wouldn't let go and the spasm seemed to continue forever. Then the vile taste of the Ayahuasca she'd drunk an hour earlier rose up in her throat, her guts cramped and she vomited. It was embarrassing that the others had to hear the weird yodeling sounds she made, but she didn't care too much. It was just such a relief to hurl. Finally she straightened, lurched two more paces across the clearing, wiped her mouth with the back of her hand, and looked up at the vast Amazonian sky.

Amongst a few scattered clouds the stars glittered and the half-moon rode high, bathing the surrounding jungle in fairy light, outlining each leaf and bough with silver tracery. Heady fragrances filled the air – rot, orchids, the breath of the river – and Leoni was alert to the shrieks and whirrs of nocturnal birds and insects, to the soft flap of bats' wings, and to distant bumps and crashes that could have been branches falling or large animals pushing their way through undergrowth.

She coughed and spat. *Yecch*! By comparison with Ayahuasca, pure DMT by intravenous infusion was an absolute breeze. They stuck the needle in your arm, pressed down the plunger and *WHOOSH*, off you went to the other side of reality.

Ayahuasca was supposed to do that too, or so everyone kept saying. But for Leoni anyway one cup had produced absolutely no *WHOOSH*.

She stumbled back to the door of the *maloca* and poked her head inside. It was a simple rectangular room, maybe twenty feet long by twelve wide, and it was dark in there with just a single candle flickering on the shaman's table.

It occurred to her that, for all the hype, Ayahuasca should be like any other drug.

If you didn't have a big enough dose you wouldn't feel the effects.

Gut-wrenching though the thought was, she was going to have to drink a second cup.

On the twenty-mile boat ride from Iquitos to the lodge Bannerman had announced, since this was now private research, conducted legally outside the United States, that he intended to join their first Ayahuasca session this evening not as an observer but as a participant. "I need to see this kind of experience from the inside," he admitted.

Now, as she picked her way back across the crowded floor of the *maloca*, Leoni saw that Bannerman lay on his back on one of the thin mattresses they'd all been provided with, his eyes closed, his features composed, totally silent. In the very faint light cast by the candle she couldn't even be certain he was breathing but she suppressed an urge to check as she stepped past him.

She and Bannerman had been placed on one side of the *maloca*, on the shaman's left, with Bannerman closest to the shaman. Mary Ruck and Matt were on the other side, with Mary closest to the shaman.

The shaman was sitting cross-legged on the floor near the middle of the rear wall of the room with his little table in front of him and the two rows of mattresses arrayed on either side of him. Next to the flickering candle, in the middle of the table, was a bowl full of *mapacho* cigarettes, thick as rifle bullets. As well as an assortment of crystals and various small figures of wood and bone there was a bottle of *Agua Florida*, a cheap local cologne. Together with the tobacco, Mary had explained earlier, it was believed to clear dark energies from the room. There were also two *chacapas*, bundles of dried leaves bound together in such a way that when they were shaken they produced a rhythmic and hypnotic susurration.

For a short while during the first hour of the ceremony, the shaman had stood to sing eerie high-pitched songs called *icaros*, and had shaken the *chacapas*. But now he sat stock-still on the floor, his skin the color of shoe leather, his back straight, his black eyes sparkling in the candlelight. He was just a little guy – probably not more than five feet, Leoni guessed – but he had something about him, she couldn't quite put her finger on what, that made him seem bigger than that.

His name was Don Emmanuel Alvaro, and Mary had made a big deal about how lucky they were that he had agreed to "hold the space" at their ceremonies. He was eighty-six years old, not a *mestizo* but a full-blood Shipibo Indian who had been preparing Ayahuasca since the age of fourteen.

Well, great.

Except so far his brew had done nothing for Leoni.

No sooner had she asked for a second cup than Mary Ruck crawled forward over her mattress, where she'd been lying at Don Emmanuel's feet, and reminded Leoni that the shaman didn't speak a word of English. "It's a bit early to have a booster," she advised. "The brew can take a while to kick in. Maybe you should wait another hour?"

Leoni sat next to her and responded in a whisper, "I don't think so. This Aya just isn't hitting me, and I need it to hit me." She looked Mary up and down: "It doesn't look like it's hitting you, either."

"It is," Mary replied: "Believe me. But I've been drinking for ten years. After a while you learn how to walk in both worlds."

Despite her Anglo name, Bannerman's anthropologist friend claimed Native American descent on her mother's side and looked like a Spanish diva. She was in her late thirties, a sexy, tanned, full-figured woman with world-weary dark eyes and thick raven-black hair that cascaded over her shoulders. "The effects will come on soon enough," she said. "Be patient and you'll see. It's good not to be too eager with Ayahuasca."

But Leoni was adamant: "I need that second cup." She was counting on Mary's support. Nothing of her story had been held back and now the older woman wrapped her arms around her in a warm and deeply sympathetic embrace. Then she said a few words in Spanish to Don Emmanuel who gestured Leoni to come closer. As she did Matt got to his feet, hurried to the door and disappeared outside. A moment later Leoni heard the sound of vomiting.

Don Emmanuel was looking Leoni over, as though measuring her. When he was satisfied he reached out to his table, lifted the grubby plastic bottle containing the Ayahuasca brew – dark, almost black, with sinister red tones deep in its heart – shook it several times, and unscrewed the cap. There was a faint hiss and a reddish-brown froth rose up in the neck of the bottle and spilled over the top. Don Emmanuel allowed it to drip to the floor and poured what looked like three ounces of the brew, still slightly foaming, into a stained ceramic cup. He set the bottle back on the table and screwed down the cap again. Then he lit a *mapacho* cigarette from the candle, picked up the little cup and blew clouds of tobacco smoke into it while muttering words in a language Leoni did not recognize. Finally he passed the cup over to her, holding it with both hands, and indicated she should drink.

She took it from him and was hit at once by the indescribable smell of Ayahuasca. It caught in the back of her throat and made her gag. *Uggh*! She looked down and shuddered again at the red-black sheen of the thick syrupy liquid, wrinkled her nose, raised the cup to her lips and drank it in two gulps.

Argh! That taste! *Uggh*! *Yecch*! Somehow a thousand times worse than the first cup. A horrible gut-cramping amalgam of cheesy feet, raw sewage, jungle rot, sulphur, vinegar and chocolate that seared her esophagus on the way down and now lay in her stomach like battery acid.

Returning to her place, she noticed Matt had already finished purging and was back on his mattress, lying on his side looking at her. "She's incredible," he whispered groggily.

Leoni's ears pricked up: "Who's incredible?"

But Matt didn't seem to hear: "Her business is the planet," he slurred. "But she still finds time for us."

He closed his eyes and said no more.

Leoni lay flat on her back, gazing up into the darkness.

Surely visions must come after doubling the dose?

But how long would she have to wait? Half an hour? Forty-five minutes? She checked the time. They'd started the ceremony around nine in the evening and, somehow, now it was after eleven.

Her head and body felt heavy. She closed her eyes again and fell asleep only to be awoken by Don Emmanuel beating out a rhythm on his *chacapas*. Then he sang an *icaro* with such haunting notes and cadences that it brought her to tears. After that a melancholy mood settled upon Leoni like damp fog and she began to review episodes from her own life in an extremely self-critical and unsympathetic way.

In fact, the more she thought about it the more worthless and pointless her whole existence seemed. Sure, she'd had some tough breaks but it had been her choice to piss her life down the tubes all those years. She found herself dwelling on the countless small and not so small acts of meanness, the betrayals, the lies, and the utter superficiality that characterized her relationships with others.

She was overwhelmed by painful feelings of shame and regret.

Leoni looked at her watch and found that time had fled again. It was close to one in the morning, nearly two hours since she'd drunk her second dose. All around her the others lay silent, lost in worlds of their own, but she remained grounded in the here and now.

As she got to her feet a wave of giddiness and nausea washed over her but she fought it and picked her way around the table to Don Emmanuel. "Are you OK?" Mary whispered, becoming alert in an instant. Leoni sat down beside her: "You're going to think I'm crazy," she said "but I've decided to drink a third cup of the brew. You know why I have to do this. Please just back me up and ask the shaman to give it to me."

Once again the older woman embraced her. Then there was another whispered conversation in Spanish and at the end of it Don Emmanuel stood and lit a *mapacho.* Without explanation he gestured to Leoni to bend forward and began to puff smoke over her head and shoulders, enveloping her in its strong, sweet fragrance. Then he indicated she should stand and turn around while he blew more clouds of the smoke over her body and legs.

"Don't they use this to drive off evil spirits?" Leoni asked.

"Hush," said Mary. "It's better to stay quiet."

Resting the butt of the *mapacho* on a plate, where it continued to smolder, Don Emmanuel took up a *chacapa* rattle and shook it all around Leoni, making sweeping and brushing motions, singing *icaros* as he worked. When he was satisfied he told her to sit again, resumed his own position cross-legged on the floor, looked into her eyes and said a few words to her.

Mary translated: "He asks if any shaman is your enemy."

"I don't think so," said Leoni. "I don't know any other shamans."

More Spanish, then Mary shrugged. "Anyway, the diagnosis is that a shaman has put the evil eye on you. Don Emmanuel wants you to know you could be vulnerable to this guy when the Ayahuasca takes you. He says he'll try to protect you but this could be a tough trip. Are you sure you want to take the risk?"

Leoni thought about it. She knew the out-of-body state could be dangerous and she didn't doubt there were malevolent forces out there.

"I'm ready for the third cup," she said.

Chapter Forty-Nine

Ria ran full-tilt towards the bonfire as Kimp reached her friends. They were still tied to the stake and at his mercy. With a rock in her hand she would have had him cold. But the spear wasn't Ria's weapon – particularly this weird Illimani spear – and even as she threw it she knew she'd misjudged its balance. Instead of flying true, the heavy flint spike at the tip dragged the projectile down and it somersaulted, swiped Kimp across the face with its shaft, and clattered into the firewood at his feet. Showing his teeth in a bellow of hatred, he grabbed Brindle's hair, bent his head forward and raised his axe to decapitate him when a second spear, thrown with enormous force, shot in over Ria's shoulder. It was a Clan spear, not one of the foreign weapons. It smashed into the middle of Kimp's chest and bore him back, stone dead, away from Brindle.

Chard, a pace behind Kimp, had reached the Uglies. As he launched his assault, swinging his axe, an arrow took him in the left eye and burst out through the back of his skull.

Ria spun on her heels. The arrow had been fired by Ligar, who had already nocked another to the string and now gave her a look of mocking acknowledgement. She just had time to register that ancient Rotas had somehow made the powerful throw that had saved Brindle when the sky darkened and a third volley of the Illimani spears came in. She was hit again as a glancing flint point gouged a deep gash across her shoulder. Krant and Ezida died in the same moment. Bont took a spear in his back but tugged it out. Bahat was unhurt. On top of the bonfire the albino brave Porto was hit but Brindle, Jergat and Oplimar were left unscathed.

Because the spears were closely targeted on the meeting ground, from which so many survivors of the first two volleys had fled, there was less immediate carnage, but Ria was clambering the stacked firewood of the bonfire and saw that hundreds already lay dead roundabout.

At last she reached the Uglies, snatched up Chard's axe and used its blade to cut her friends free from the stake.

Porto had been disemboweled by one of the terrible falling spears. He was alive but it was obvious he was in unbearable pain and dying. As Ria cut the ropes supporting him he collapsed, uttering huge, heart-rending screams, his mind sending out waves of sadness and fear. Beside him there was horror in Brindle's eyes. Jergat looked half-dead with thirst and exhaustion. Only stocky little Oplimar seemed to be fully in command of himself and she heard his thought-voice loud and clear: "*Illimani going to come after their spears, Ria. We got to get out of here right now!*"

"*What about Porto?*" she was about to ask when Brindle shook himself out of his slump, took Chard's axe from her hand and with a single swift blow put Porto out of his misery. Ria felt only relief that there hadn't been an argument over what was the right thing to do. She looked to the sky. The fourth volley couldn't be long in coming.

But instead there was only an eerie silence from the direction of their attackers, punctuated by groans and cries rising up from the injured and the dying all around them.

Where were the Illimani?

While the ominous lull continued Ria hurried Brindle, Jergat and Oplimar down from the pyre and led them over to Rotas, Bont, Bahat, Ligar and Vulp. "You know these Uglies are my friends," she told her Clansmen, "and I ask you to accept them as your allies. They stood by me and Hond yesterday when we fought the terrible enemies who attack us now. They'll stand by you today." Bont looked as though he'd been asked to eat shit and Ria saw him exchange a stubborn bigoted glance with Ligar. "Don't even think about it," she warned. "None of us are going to get out of here alive unless we all work together."

"Many questions must be answered," said Rotas. Ria's heart sank, then rose when he added: "But there will be time for them later. Meanwhile it is a most intelligent idea to join forces with the Uglies to combat a common enemy." He glared at Bont and Ligar: "Do you accept this?" Bont seemed about to object but Ligar spoke up: "Ask questions later, Bont." After some urgent whispering, they both nodded their agreement. "And you?" Rotas directed his gaze at Bahat and Vulp. "I accept," said Bahat. "I too," said Vulp.

The elder's gray eyes turned on Ria: "Since you have fought this enemy before, my child, what do you suggest we do now?"

The Illimani spears had come in from deep in the forest beyond the southeast quadrant of the camp, arching up into the sky and raining down death from above. They'd been able to get such range, Ria guessed, because of the spear-throwers she'd already seen in action. But how had they known – for they clearly must have since they had concentrated their attack here – that the entire population of the Clan would be gathered in the meeting ground this morning?

The answer was unavoidable. Grigo and Murgh must have told them. Grigo with his boasts about Sulpa. Murgh with his hunger for power. This was what they'd hoped to gain from the spectacle they'd so carefully prepared in the meeting ground – the Clan all in one place, ripe for slaughter.

But why?

Despite Murgh's struggle with the elders, why would even he have an interest in the total annihilation of his own people?

Or had he thought the whole thing was going to work out differently? Just a shift of power from the elders to him, enforced by the Illimani?

If that had been his plan, then the Illimani hadn't waited for the agreed signal – the burning of the bonfire – hadn't given their collaborators a chance to get clear, hadn't cared whether they lived or died amidst the general massacre. And it wasn't over yet.

For what sort of shocking close assault must follow now the devastating spear volleys that had so badly unmanned and scattered the Clan seemed to have stopped?

Ria knelt by Hond's body, rested her hand in his hair for a moment, and withdrew the long flint knife that Grigo had plunged through his back and into his heart.

The Illimani knife that had killed both her brothers.

She took it up, used her neckerchief to clean the blade, folded the bloodied weaving carefully into a pocket of her jerkin and thrust the knife into her belt. Then without a backward glance she led the way towards the lookout tower two hundred paces south of the meeting ground.

* * *

Enclosed within its circle of huge wooden posts, the meeting ground lay at the center of the camp and the camp lay at the edge of a great forest nestling in a bend of the treacherous Snake River. The waters in which Ria's mother and father had drowned ran fast and deep, imposing a formidable natural barrier to the north and west, making the camp as good as impregnable from those directions. But now the river had become a trap. Because of it, survivors escaping the meeting ground and gathering up their families could only run towards the south and east – precisely the directions from which the Illimani spears had come.

From the vantage point of the tower Ria and her companions – only Rotas and Jergat had been too infirm to climb – began to track the surging tide of the fleeing crowd. Hundreds of frenzied and panicking men, women and children were spreading through the southern quarters of the camp. The fastest had almost reached the shelter of the forest when the front ranks abruptly turned back – even from this distance their abject terror was visible – and collided with those behind who in turn stampeded amidst oaths and screams.

It was at this moment of mayhem that the savage horde of the Illimani, thousands strong, naked, screaming their bloodlust, burst forth from the trees all around the camp's southern perimeter. They fell upon the disordered, terrorized, fleeing Clan with axe and knife, spear and club. Some of the fugitives slipped through their advance and fled into the forest. Some – a few – stood and fought before being brought down. But most fell to the ground in abject surrender where they were butchered like animals.

Most, but not all.

It was clear, despite their ferocity, that the Illimani were sparing the children.

Chapter Fifty

If the second cup was a thousand times worse than the first, the third cup was a thousand times worse again. Although she pinched her nostrils to block the smell, Leoni still gagged and choked as she gulped down the loathsome brew, grimaced as the thick liquid coated her tongue and teeth, and shivered with revulsion as the aftertaste hit her.

She tottered to her mattress, lay on her back, flung her arms and legs out, stared into the darkness once more and discovered everything was different. Her system couldn't have absorbed the third cup yet, so this storm of colors and weirdness exploding inside her head, these gushing fountains of light and energy she was immersed in, must be the delayed effects of the first two doses.

Coming on faster and stronger than anything she'd ever experienced before.

As the power of the drug overwhelmed her, Leoni surged out of her body, rose into the roof space of the *maloca* and looked down at the little group on the floor. Then she heard the Blue Angel's voice, speaking inside her head. The words seemed filled with enchantment: "Find me by the river. I await you."

Leoni needed no second summons but as she floated higher she saw Don Emmanuel looking right at her, his eyes bright with alarm. Was her aerial body visible to him? For some reason she felt a harsh twinge of guilt as she fled out through the thatched roof and into the night sky.

She saw at once she had not arrived in some weird parallel world but was still on planet Earth, in the Amazon rainforest, twenty miles south of Iquitos. She was directly above the *maloca* and the huddle of outbuildings of Mary Ruck's jungle lodge. The moon still rode high and every bush and tree, every leaf and flower, was lit by an inner fire and writhed sinuously, each one seemingly self-willed.

As she'd learned to expect when she traveled out of body, Leoni could still see her own hands and arms, legs and feet, but she had become so insubstantial she could pass through solid objects. The trees were no barrier to her. Nevertheless, she preferred to follow the same narrow path, leading back to the river, that she and her friends had used many hours earlier when they'd arrived here from Iquitos in Mary's motorboat and walked up to the *maloca.*

Except tonight nothing was quite the same. The floor of the path was aglow with scintillating light patterns, like the luminous trails of sea worms, and immense many-hued serpents with ivory teeth and ruby eyes were draped over the branches above.

Leoni mastered her terror. Both Mary and Don Emmanuel had warned her that she would see such serpents under the influence of Ayahuasca, and had reassured her they were benign creatures of vision that would not harm her.

Even so, she felt a twinge of fear and a glimmering recognition of the utter strangeness of her situation.

She sensed the vastness of the jungle, the presence of unknown creatures deep within, thick undergrowth pressing close all around her, and began to glide faster towards the river, the great sweep of which she could now see glinting through the ancient trees, wide as houses, tall as skyscrapers, that grew all the way down to the water's edge.

The path brought Leoni out by the jetty where Mary's boat was moored.

But the jetty transformed itself before she reached it from a thing of wood and nails into a living serpent, fifty feet long, its hulking, spade-shaped head thrust far out from the bank. Regardless of what she'd been told about these creatures, there was no way she would have stepped out onto its broad back, with scales like planks, if the Blue Angel hadn't been there already, waiting for her. Her back was turned, her scarlet robe swept out behind her, her long black hair shone in the brilliant light of the moon which made everything seem like day. She said nothing, but stood still as a statue at the end of the jetty, looking out over the earthy brown depths of the colossal river.

Leoni was nervous as she approached. Why would the Angel not look at her?

Then, with a lurch of horror, she saw the figure at the end of the jetty turn and begin to undergo a terrifying transformation. Her hair lost its satin sheen and became shorter and coarser, streaked with gray, her skin roughened and morphed from blue to jaundiced, her beautiful face lengthened and thickened, a wispy beard sprouted, her body became strongly masculine, and her robe shimmered through all the colors of the rainbow and took shape again as a white suit.

Leoni flew back and upward but was alarmed to discover that something held her down. She struggled and fought, only getting herself more tightly enmeshed so that she could hardly move at all. She suffered a moment of utter panic. How was this happening to her aerial body?

At first glance she couldn't see what held her but as she looked closer thin filaments of red light appeared, so faint they were almost invisible, woven into a supple lattice.

She was caught like a fish in a net.

Chapter Fifty-One

So overwhelming were the numbers of the Illimani, so ferocious, deadly and unexpected their onslaught, that the massacre of the Clan was accomplished with stunning speed. And even as the last adults were dispatched, Ria saw from her vantage point on the lookout tower that hundreds of children had been rounded up. They were subdued with shouts and cruel blows, their hands were tied behind their backs, and they were roped together tightly at the neck.

Vulp, Bahat and Bont all had close kin out there – including, in Bont's case, two young children. "What are they doing with the kids?" the big man said now, his voice hoarse. The spear wound in his lower back was still bleeding, spattering his legs with gore, but he seemed oblivious.

"At least they're not killing them," choked Vulp. Ria could see he was wrestling with his emotions. "They've killed everyone else."

"Not everyone," Ligar said, offering hope. "Some made it into the forest . . ."

Bont wasn't listening: "We have to save the kids. Right now. If you're not going to help me I'll do it myself."

"*He imagines he army,*" Brindle spoke up inside Ria's head. "*Can fight any enemy. But if don't fix his back he going to bleed to death pretty soon.*"

Ria surveyed the zone of slaughter around the outskirts of the camp. It was far enough, close to a thousand paces, for her little group on the tower not to be noticed so long as they kept their heads down, but there was no way this could continue. At any moment a patrol might be sent out from the main force to take possession of the meeting ground – the tower was an obvious strategic target – and then they would certainly be caught.

They couldn't escape. To the south the way to the forest was blocked by the Illimani horde. To the north the Snake River lay in their path.

"Of course we're going to help you," Ria told Bont. She looked around at her Clansmen – it was clear they were all of one mind – and led the way down the system of narrow ladders that connected the different levels of the tower. Bont descended above her, a continuous drip, drip, drip of blood falling from his back. Ligar, Vulp, Bahat and the Uglies followed.

Rotas was waiting at the base of the tower but there was no sign of Jergat. "I didn't see where he went," the elder said. "Seemed like he was unconscious. He might even have been dead. I looked away for a moment. When I looked back he was gone."

Ria exchanged a thought with Brindle – she sensed no concern from him for Jergat – and told Rotas of the coming of the Illimani and the terrible events they'd witnessed from the tower moments earlier. "We're going to save the children," she said.

"But that is suicide!" Rotas protested. "If our attackers truly number thousands we can do nothing. We'll be killed the moment we show our faces."

"We'll be killed anyway," grunted Bont. "There's nowhere to run to. I'm going in after my kids."

"I'm with Bont," Ria said.

Rotas thought about it: "It seems there is no other choice," he agreed at last.

Jergat reappeared, coming from the meeting ground. He looked energized, completely recovered from the ordeal of the bonfire. He held forth a deerskin pouch to Ria. It had a familiar heaviness: "*I found your hunting stones,*" he told her. "*Our Lady of the Forest showed me where to look . . .*"

"The blue woman?"

"*Waked me up when I was sleeping,*" said Jergat. "*Told me, hey you, Jergat. You got a job to do, remember? You're supposed to collect Ria's stones.*" Jergat's thought-talk was accompanied by images of the bewitching woman with long black hair and deep blue skin whom Ria had seen when she'd journeyed with the Little Teachers, whose power had saved her from the terrible river of the spirit world, and who had spoken to her of tests. Then the imagery changed and she saw the body of the brave who had taken the pouch and stones from her during the ambush the night before – one of Murgh's trusted men, struck down on the meeting ground, like his master, by an Illimani spear.

A roar of anger erupted behind her and she turned to see Bont strike

Brindle in the face with his huge right fist. "Touch me again and you're dead," he yelled.

"*What's this, Brindle*?" Ria pulsed.

"*Told you, Bont need healing or he die*," Brindle replied. His cheek was split and swollen. "*Tried to put hands on him to heal but he don't like*."

Ria turned to Bont. He was pale with loss of blood but he still had his fists bunched. His dark eyes, small in such a large face, glared out with suspicion. But just when he looked his most threatening, like a rhino at bay, his feet slipped from under him, his knees buckled and he collapsed in a heap.

He had not lost consciousness. "Listen, Bont," Ria told him. "The Uglies have healing powers. Give them a chance and they'll heal you now." He half sat up and uttered some incoherent words. "*THERE'S NO TIME FOR THIS*," she yelled and eased him onto his stomach, exposing the deep, oozing wound in his lower back. Brindle, Oplimar and Jergat stepped forward, kneeled, linked arms in a circle over Bont, and began their hooting chant . . .

"What's going on here?" It was Vulp who interrupted. "How do we know they aren't just going to kill him?"

"You have my word," said Ria.

"You have my word too," said Ligar. His bow was half drawn. "Heal my friend," he told the Uglies, "or be certain I'll kill you."

Brindle ignored the threat and placed his palm over the bubbling puncture in Bont's back. "*Spear went deep*," his thought-voice warned Ria after a heartbeat "*Maybe not enough of us to make magic work*." But almost at once blue light began to emanate from his fingers and poured into the big man's body, suffusing the area around the injury with a phantasmal glow. Its brightness grew until it became dazzling. Bont's body vibrated, then lifted and floated, still face down, a full handspan above the ground.

Vulp stumbled back with an oath, raising his arm as though to protect himself from a physical threat, Bahat made the sign of the evil eye, Ligar drew his bow to full stretch and took aim at Brindle's head. Only Rotas remained calm. With much creaking of joints, he dropped to his knees to pass his hands beneath Bont and satisfy himself there was nothing supporting him. "Extraordinary," he said after a moment. "I have heard of such things, from the long-ago, but never believed they were true."

The chanting of the Uglies reached a crescendo and ceased. Bont's body descended to the ground. He'd remained conscious throughout and rolled over and sat up, rubbing his head.

"*Stopped bleeding*," Brindle pulsed to Ria. "*Gave him energy. Put magic in his body. Wound will heal*."

"*Can he run*?" Ria asked. "*Can he fight*?"

But Bont himself answered by struggling to his feet and an instant later Ria understood what had alerted him. The meeting ground was surrounded by a zone of tightly packed wattle huts arranged around criss-crossing thoroughfares. Where the huts and streets came to an end, less than a hundred paces south of the tower, a dozen heavily armed Illimani braves burst out into the open and ran towards them, screaming guttural war cries. They were smeared from head to foot in blood. Some had freshly severed human heads dangling from leather waistbands, some had male genitals strung as gruesome necklaces and tied in their hair, one was even wearing another man's skin. Now all had their eyes fixed on the little group of Clan and Uglies beneath the tower.

After the mass flight from the meeting ground, discarded weapons lay everywhere. As Ria pulled the first quartz hunting stone from her deerskin pouch she saw Bont snatch up a big double-headed axe. He weighed it in his hands, swung it in a great sweeping arc, and then, with a roar, charged the advancing Ilimani.

Chapter Fifty-Two

The man in the white suit grinned at Leoni, opening a mouth crowded with jagged inward-turned teeth.

She wanted to be as far away from him as possible, but flight wasn't an option. The web of red light that he'd flung around her aerial body held her fast and now, with hauling motions of his hands, he dragged her towards him as though drawing in a net. His hooded eyes glittered as he spoke to her: "I am making this magic," he boasted. "It is very strong, yes?" Another vigorous heave brought her face to face with him: "See! You cannot resist me!" And with that he pulled tight the net's drawstrings, crammed them into his mouth and plunged into the river, towing her behind him.

Except it wasn't the muddy waters of the Amazon they'd entered but some gloppy, transparent, mucilaginous goo, like a torrent of thick snot. And her captor was no longer a man but had transformed into a monstrous white shark.

Leoni felt herself starting to freak out. It was entirely possible, if this continued, that she was just going to totally *lose* it. It had happened to her before on an acid trip that went sour. And this thing she was in the midst of now – this capture, this *abduction* – was already far more freaky than that, and horribly immanent and convincing. She had to keep reminding herself that she was out of body and that if anything real was happening to her at all – even now she couldn't be certain – then it wasn't happening to the physical Leoni. It was the non-physical part of herself, released by Ayahuasca, that had been spirited away.

It had occurred to her that her abductor could be Sulpa in one of his many guises. But she didn't think the beautiful monster she had seen, reveling in the blood of children, would have felt the need to boast about his powers in the way that this creature did.

With a massive effort of will Leoni controlled her panic and peered into the thick flood swirling round her. It had grown from a river into an ocean and the whole mass glowed with luminous particles. Below, the huge white shark swam straight down, his massive tail sweeping from side to side, drawing her along behind in her net of light, plunging into a seemingly bottomless abyss.

Leoni felt a renewed surge of fear but was distracted by the sudden arrival of a sleek dolphin. Improbably, it was pink. It materialized out of a cloud of bubbles, studied her for a moment with a large, quizzical, almond-shaped eye, and darted away as quickly as it had come. She just had time to wonder, *What was that about*? when a serpent bigger than a nuclear submarine reared up out of the depths below. It was bearded, like a Ming dragon, its head was surmounted by long plumes of feathers, a ruby the size of a small car was set into its brow, its eyes glittered amethyst and its teeth were quartz daggers. Its jaws yawned wide to reveal a churning whirlpool in its gullet.

The shark dragged Leoni straight down through the gaping mouth. They were spun and wheeled by the heaving vortex and rocketed into a sinuous light-filled tunnel, wide as a house, its walls patterned with grids of glowing jewels.

Leoni realized she had passed through similar contraptions on her journeys to the land where everything is known. Despite their high strangeness, and many superficial differences, these swirling tunnels and tubes and shafts of light seemed to be part of some sort of system, utterly beyond her understanding, that offered transit from realm to realm, from world to world, from the present to the past – if Matt was right about Sulpa – and even from the state of being alive to the state of being dead.

With a final rapid gyration she was spilled out onto a cold stone floor beside her captor who had already morphed back into his human form. The tunnel spun closed behind them and vanished, as though it had never existed, leaving no obvious return route. Simultaneously, Leoni discovered she was in a body again, dressed in simple clothing – much as she always found herself in the land where everything is known.

But was she back in that realm now? There was no way of knowing because they were in a bare geometrical room. Dimly lit at floor level from some unseen source, but with no windows, it felt cavernous – the size of a cathedral at least – and its immense walls, crafted from massive blocks of red granite, vanished into the darkness above.

She struggled to her feet. *Shit*! The net that had trapped her aerial body was gone but now there was a chain round her neck, attached to a thick leather leash in her captor's hand. He shook it, rattling the links, making her cough and choke.

"I tricked you very good," he bragged, "very fine! I, Don Apolinar, did this with my magic and you could not resist." He twitched the leash again: "What you say about that?"

Leoni gripped the chain with both hands and jerked it back hard. "You're an asshole," she hissed as he struggled for balance. "That's what I say." She let go of the chain so that she could point the index finger of her right hand at him. She didn't know why she felt she should do this, but as she made the gesture a surge of energy poured through her, Don Apolinar's eyes widened and he staggered as though punched by an invisible fist.

He dropped the leash and backed off several paces. "So," he said, "you have the force." She stepped towards him and he retreated; another step towards him, another retreat. He was still speaking: "But you don't know how to use it!"

He extended his free hand, flexed the fingers and closed them into a fist. At once Leoni lost all power of movement and fell sprawling on the granite flagstones. She could neither resist nor speak, yet remained fully conscious as Don Apolinar stooped down beside her and thrust his fingers deep into her brain.

Chapter Fifty-Three

The distance between the two groups was down to sixty paces and the Illimani were closing fast when Bont began his charge. Twelve against nine, but Ria intended to shorten those odds. Wincing at a fresh surge of pain from her bruised rib, she picked the brave wearing another man's skin, empty hands and feet flapping at his wrists and ankles, and smashed his head with her first stone. *Vermin*! Who the fuck did these people think they were? She palmed a second stone, targeted a warrior with a necklace of dangling penises, and broke his nose in an explosion of blood. He fell to his knees, clutching his face.

A shadow appeared beside her as she reached for more stones and she saw Ligar draw his bow and fire an arrow into a man's eye. Right away he drew and fired again, a belly shot that dropped a tough-looking brave screaming. His third arrow transfixed a brave's naked chest, protruding a span beyond his back. Then Bont was amongst them, his double-headed axe snaking out with incredible power as he smashed his way through the survivors, hacking off one man's head with a single blow, opening a huge fountaining wound in another's side, backhanding the blade into the next man's face, chopping the legs out from under another.

Screaming defiant war cries, the last three mounted a desperate attack, swarming the Clansman, pressing him hard, getting inside the reach of the axe. While Ligar was darting back and forth, searching for an angle, hesitating to shoot into the melee for fear of hitting his friend, Ria let fly with a third stone, bringing down another man. That left two, both big guys, one wearing penises in his hair, the other with a severed head tied to his waistband, grappling with Bont.

But Bont seemed energized after his healing. With a roar of fury and a tremendous explosion of raw strength he flung both attackers back, swung his axe double-handed and hammered its blade into one man's chest. The second circled, jabbing with a long knife, but Bont slapped it aside with the flat of the axe, stepped in on him and brought the blade down with such force onto the top of his skull that the blow split open his head from crown to chin, scattering brain tissue and teeth.

As the brave crashed to the ground at his feet Bont gave a great bellow of triumph, raised the dripping axe high in the air, shook it, looked around eagerly and shouted: "WHO NEXT?"

At once his question was answered. A blood-spattered Illimani, mightily built, with rippling muscles and armed with an axe bigger than Bont's, stepped out from a narrow alley and swaggered into the middle of the camp's main thoroughfare about two hundred paces to the south. He was bald but, as though to compensate, four severed heads of Clansmen and Clanswomen, dripping gore, were suspended by their hair from his leather waistband, their open eyes glaring. The massive warrior shouted something at Bont in the jarring, grinding gutturals of the Illimani tongue, loosened his waistband letting the heads thud to the ground, raised his own axe, and began to march forward, confident and threatening. As he walked, another brave stepped forth from the side streets, and another, and another.

Ria saw they were a second scouting party, this time numbering close to forty. They marched forward in a tight mass and stopped a hundred paces away, spreading themselves out across the thoroughfare in two wide ranks.

Ligar fired an arrow, taking a warrior in the throat. Ria palmed her last two hunting stones and began to jog towards the Illimani. At eighty paces she hurled her first stone. It struck the bald brave on the dome of his forehead and bounced off with a loud *clunk*. He stood looking stupid, then his eyes rolled up in his head, the axe dropped from his fingers, and he fell senseless.

Ria was still running as more arrows from Ligar's bow hissed past her. Two more men crumpled. A third, pierced through the eye, shrieked and clawed at his face, stumbled out of the line and fell. At forty paces, Ria brained another with her last stone. Realizing how far ahead of her companions she had run, she stopped just twenty paces from the waiting Illimani and pulled the long flint knife from her belt.

With a thud of running feet, Bont appeared beside her, his axe held loosely in his huge hands. Ligar was right behind him but a glance showed Ria he was out of arrows. He laid his bow down and pulled a dagger from his belt.

Then Brindle, Oplimar and Jergat pounded up. All had armed themselves with discarded weapons. Jergat had picked up one of the short Illimani throwing spears that lay scattered about and taken a jagged-edged knife from a brave Bont had killed. Oplimar held a big war axe in his right hand and a smaller wicked-looking hatchet in his left. Brindle wielded a heavy wooden club studded with shards of razor-edged flint.

Next Vulp pushed himself into the line, his mane of long white hair hanging to his shoulders, a dagger in each hand. Bahat was with him, swarthy and bearded, swinging an axe.

Last came Rotas. His movements were stiff and dignified, but he held a heavy Clan spear tipped with a long leaf-shaped blade pointed at the Illimani phalanx.

For a frozen instant the two groups, still more than thirty against nine, eyed one another in complete silence across the narrow strip of trampled ground that separated them. Then, in the distance, from the edge of the camp where the captured children were held, a great collective chant began to rise up from the mass of the Illimani force, thousands upon thousands of rough, snarling, brutish voices all calling out in unison. And what they were saying was:

"SUL . . . PA!"
"SUL . . . PA!"
"SUL . . . PA!"

The sound of that name, uttered like this, was spine-chilling. The Illimani braves seemed to cock their ears and listen. A blank look settled like snow over all their faces and, with a scream, they launched themselves at Ria and her companions.

Chapter Fifty-Four

This body that Leoni was in – occupying, inhabiting, maybe even possessing – was in many ways very much like a regular body, with all the normal functions. But you could do things to it that your meat body back on planet Earth couldn't handle.

For example, what was being done to her right now as she lay paralyzed on the hard stone floor of the shadowy granite chamber.

Kneeling by her shoulder, Don Apolinar was shoving his thick stubby fingers through various parts of her skull. He was moving them around inside her brain. The pain and feelings of violation were horrible. Yet she felt detached from the ordeal. It was a bit like being raped: you went numb; you blotted it out and survived.

"You cannot hide it," he said after a moment. "I with my magic will find it."

She just had time to think *Hide what? Find what?* when he placed his hands over her ears and plunged all his fingers and both thumbs into her head in a great explosion of pain.

"Tell me where it is," he hissed.

"Use your magic, douchebag! I don't even know what you're talking about."

He seemed to consider, a look of greed and violent machismo crossing his face. All his fingers were still inside her head, past the second knuckle. "Treasure!" he barked. "In your brain she buried it."

The thick fingers probed deeper and in a flash Leoni understood.

He meant the filament of crystal the Blue Angel had implanted in her left temple!

For some reason he wanted it. He called it treasure. Maybe this was the reason he'd grabbed her in the first place.

She was already fighting to suppress her memories of the surprise operation the Angel had performed on her when Don Apolinar grunted with delight and she knew he had read her mind. "See how easily you surrender to me," he boasted. "Like a child. You have the force yet I overwhelm you." His hand shot towards her temple and hovered over the exact spot where the crystal was buried. A finger went in. A thumb. "Oh, I am so clever," he crowed. "This is *my* magic, *mine*, that has found the treasure!"

He lunged, seemed to catch hold of something, grunted with satisfaction and pulled hard. Leoni screamed – the pain was unimaginable – and Don Apolinar giggled. "Yes! Yes!" – he sounded like he was having an orgasm – "I will take it now!"

She stared into his eyes, dark as smoked mirrors. In this paralyzed state there was nothing she could do to prevent him from ripping the crystal thread out of her brain and she felt sure he would kill her when he did. But as he tightened his grip something distracted him. He faltered, tilted his head to one side and seemed to listen.

Leoni could hear it too – the sacred melody of an *icaro*, muffled and indistinct. She felt Don Apolinar's grip loosen again. Leaving her prone and helpless on the floor, he removed his fingers from her brain and surged to his feet just as the granite wall of the great chamber split open and a small tawny eagle hurtled through the gap, so fast it was a blur. It flew straight at Don Apolinar, forcing him to dive, raked his face with its talons as it passed, and landed beside Leoni. She felt a reassuring hand on her shoulder and watched, stunned, as the eagle completed its transformation into a man.

Don Emmanuel! Of course!

As suddenly as it had set in, her paralysis left her. She struggled to her feet, tearing off and throwing down the choke chain and leash that still hung around her neck.

The two men were circling, their eyes locked, and a dangerous energy crackled between them.

Don Emmanuel gestured to Leoni to stay back and she moved to obey, keeping him between herself and Don Apolinar. Although she guessed the bodies both men inhabited were like her own – avatars with capacities their bodies on Earth did not possess – she couldn't help but feel the inequality of the contest. It wasn't that one was old and small while the other was tall and in his prime. Such attributes meant little in these realms of endless transformation. Rather, she sensed a spectacular difference of power, a difference of *force*, between the older and the younger man. Hovering like a miasma about Don Apolinar was a capacity for malice, an appetite for cruelty and a lust for evil that Don Emmanuel could not match.

Both men began to shapeshift as they circled, one form merging into another in dizzying succession. Don Apolinar became a bear, a wolf, a lion, Don Emmanuel became a stag, a boa constrictor, a cayman. Too fast for the eye to follow, their shifts and changes cycled through countless different forms until suddenly they clashed in a blur of transformation. Roaring and bellowing, Don Apolinar became a tiger biting down on the neck of Don Emmanuel as a buffalo who transformed into a porcupine to break free and back into a buffalo to throw the tiger over his head. But the tiger was already changing into a great serpent that wrapped its coils around the buffalo which became a mouse that escaped and transformed into a snarling dog.

Darting around the edge of the circle, Leoni needed no second bidding to keep as far away as possible from all the various manifestations of Don Apolinar. Don Emmanuel had returned to the eagle form in which he had entered the chamber, but as he swooped and slashed she could see his strength was failing. Don Apolinar's avatar had become a massive white jaguar, radiant with violent energy. He leapt, paws outstretched, and grappled with Don Emmanuel in flight. His claws raked a wing, spraying blood and feathers, there was a brittle crunch of broken bones and the eagle was smashed to the floor.

At once both men reverted to human form and Don Apolinar stood wide-legged in triumph, straddling the little Shipibo shaman who lay sprawled on his back, blood pumping from his chest and shoulder. His left arm was half torn from his body and grotesquely broken in three places. His eyes were wide and glassy.

"Foolish little healer," sneered Don Apolinar. "Your magic weak, my magic strong." He stooped: "I think I kill you now, yes? Maybe cut out your heart?"

Leoni watched in a daze as Don Apolinar drew a long thin knife from a pocket of his white suit.

Chapter Fifty-Five

A club glanced off Ria's shoulder, numbing her left arm, but she kept her balance, ducked under her attacker's guard, drove her knife into his belly and twisted the blade as she drew it out. Two more braves were bearing down on her, their crazed blue eyes burning. She dodged between them, stabbed one, opened the other's throat. She could see Brindle was in trouble, pressed hard by three Illimani braves. But he wasn't asking for help. Nobody was. Bahat had fallen already. Ligar too . . . Ria fended off a spear, a blade sliced her arm, something heavy bashed into the side of her head and suddenly – it was as though a mountain had fallen on her – she was smashed to the ground amongst a forest of pale, hairy Illimani legs. She surged up again, stabbing blindly, but more huge blows knocked her back down and she tumbled, it seemed forever, into darkness.

As consciousness seeped back Ria found a powerful grip fastened in her hair, dragging her body bumping and jolting over the ground. Her head pounded and her ears rang where she'd been clubbed. She blinked because her eyes were full of blood. Somehow she got a hand to her face, cleared her vision. A tall young Illimani was dragging her towards the meeting ground, tugging so hard on her hair that her scalp was about to tear free of her skull. She could see her flint knife tucked into his waistband beside a bouncing severed head, a cluster of penises and other grotesque trophies.

As the brave hauled her between two of the huge wooden posts that encircled the meeting ground she reached up her hands, seized his thick forearm, plunged her nails deep into his flesh, and threw all her weight against him. He stumbled in surprise, loosening his grip on her hair, and she was on him at once. With a howl she snatched her knife from his waistband and stabbed him in the groin, sawing the blade upwards before jerking it free. He fell screaming beneath her and she felt mad joy stirring in her heart. Where was the next Illimani to kill? Then a big knuckly fist struck her full in the face and she was flat on her back on the ground again, unable to resist as her knife was wrested from her grasp, ears ringing, flashing lights dancing before her eyes.

Ria peered up, blinking through more blood, feeling dizzy and sick, and saw Grigo, flanked by Illimani braves, standing over her holding the knife.

She was still too dazed to fight back as he stooped and cut her leggings away from her hips, leaving her naked from the waist down. "You're part of my prize," he explained, as he shoved her knife into his belt. "Lord Sulpa gave you to me." His face darkened: "But I guess you don't get what that means." He leaned closer, dribbling spit, grabbed her hair and forced her onto her face, thrusting a knee between her thighs. "It means I finally get to fuck you, you BITCH. After that I'm going to burn you with your friends."

Turning her head, Ria saw, with a leap of hope, that her companions were not dead. They were being herded together close to the bonfire at the center of the meeting ground. Brindle was bleeding heavily from a head wound and Bont was carrying him like a child in his massive arms. Bahat was on the ground in a pool of blood. He moved, so he was alive. But he looked done for. Ligar was also hurt. Vulp, Rotas, Oplimar and Jergat were in better shape but all had taken savage beatings.

Grigo clamped his right hand onto the back of Ria's neck. She could feel him squirming on top of her, his knee jammed up tightly between her buttocks, as he tried to unbelt his leggings. But it seemed he needed two hands for that and he let go of her neck again. She didn't know why she found it funny but suddenly she was laughing and shrieking her defiance: "What's the matter, Grigo? Can't you find your prick?"

She raised her head.

A ring of Illimani braves, naked but for the weapons they carried and the ever-present spear-throwers slung across their backs, had gathered round to shout what sounded like encouragement to Grigo in their harsh, growly language. He grunted, punched the back of her head, and finally tugged down his belt and leggings with both hands, exposing a pale, floppy penis. "Look at that!" Ria cackled through waves of giddiness and nausea. "You can't even get it up" – and her laughter spread to the five braves encircling them, driving Grigo into a frenzy.

WHACK! His fist smashed into the back of her head again and she crumpled. Her face was turned to the side when she hit the ground and her eyes were open. Grigo was preoccupied with his limp, stinking cock – Ria could actually smell it from this close – and the Illimani were having too much fun watching, so she alone saw Driff, naked as the rest of his tribe, loping towards them with a tomahawk in each hand. He strode right through the ring of braves and, before anyone took notice, stepped in on Grigo, chopped one of the hatchets deep into his face and kicked him away from Ria as he tugged the blade clear.

At first the Illimani didn't react – as though betrayal by one of their own was impossible even to contemplate. Driff charged them, his face pale, and in a heartbeat three of them went down, screaming and spouting blood. Two more surged forward to take their place but also fell under his hatchets. By then he'd lost the advantage of surprise and more braves converged on him from the larger group guarding the prisoners beside the bonfire. A spear pierced his side, a club glanced off his head and it seemed he must be overwhelmed.

Half naked, beaten and bloody, but momentarily forgotten, Ria rolled to her feet, ignoring savage jolts of pain, and retrieved her knife from Grigo's belt. Then she darted into the melee to stab one of Driff's attackers in the back, thrusting the long blade deep between his ribs, withdrawing it and slicing open a second man's throat. As a howling scrum of close combat surrounded her she weaved and dived and killed again. She'd been lucky so far but she knew she only had moments left to live – Driff too: what madness had inspired him to try to rescue her? – when out of the corner of her eye she saw another long line of charging braves bearing down on them.

She cackled – why did the Illimani need reinforcements? – and shook her head to clear the blood from her eyes. Only then did she register that the new attackers were not more of the outlanders but Uglies, led by Grondin. His mission had been to bring the populations of the outlying camps into Secret Place and he must have worked fast, or encountered them already on the way, because he now commanded a powerful force of braves – perhaps as many as a hundred. Less than thirty of the Illimani scouting party still stood after the furious fighting of the past moments and they were soon killed.

"*Brindle, speak to me.*" Ria sent out her thought-voice as she ran towards the little group of her companions. But she saw that her friend was unconscious, his eyes rolled up in his head, blood dripping from a huge gash in his skull. She tried again: "Speak to me, Brindle," and again there was no reply. "He gone very deep, Ria," Oplimar told her. "Maybe don't come back."

"You can bring him back," Ria said. "You can heal him . . ."

Suddenly Grondin was amongst them, his massive figure towering over all, his thought-voice full of authority: "No time for healing now." He gestured towards the southern sector of the camp where the mass of the Illimani force were still gathered. Faint screams carried on the breeze and the menacing chant went up again – "*SULPA*! *SULPA*! *SULPA*!" – followed by great howls and roars of approval.

"It is worse than we feared," Grondin said now. "There are more than seven thousand of these devils. They are here in our valleys to kill us all. Driff told us their plans."

"But what's in it for Driff? I don't understand why he's helping us" – Ria glanced over at the young Illimani. She could see he was racked with pain but that he refused to cry out, or to acknowledge her attention, as two of the Uglies pulled the spear from his side.

"Brindle made rope with him, changed his heart, helped him start to thought-talk. After Clan captured you he found us, told us what happened, brought us here to rescue you."

"Can *you* thought-talk with him?"

"A little. Enough to understand. Takes time."

"Can I trust him?"

Grondin turned his huge head towards Ria and his eyes were intelligent and quizzical: "He saved you. Why would you not trust?" Then he strode away to see to his own injured braves. "Prepare your people. We must go from this place."

"But go where? Go how?" Ria sent her thought-voice after the big Ugly warrior. "We're boxed in by the Illimani. The river's at our back. There's nowhere to escape to."

"We will use river," Grondin said. "How you think we got here?"

Chapter Fifty-Six

If Don Emmanuel's avatar in this world was killed, if his heart was cut out, what would happen to his body and his consciousness back on Earth? Leoni felt sure it must be bad and knew what was required of her; if she had this "force," whatever it was, then she had to use it to help him.

Don Apolinar was still stooping over the little shaman's battered body, but now he swiveled and glared at her, reading her mind. "Be still!" his voice cracked out. "I imprison you!" The effect was instantaneous. This time Leoni stayed on her feet but she found that she was again paralyzed, as though set in plaster. Don Apolinar sneered and walked over to her, waving his knife: "I will take the treasure from your head," he promised. "I will cause you very much pain. Your body in this world will die. Your spirit will be driven into the Between and you will never get out."

Leoni couldn't speak – her mouth was frozen shut – as he turned his back again, stalked across the floor to where Don Emmanuel lay broken and crouched beside him, positioning himself so she had a clear view. "First I kill your stupid little healer," he said. He raised the knife for her to see. "Take his heart; take his magic."

Leoni could feel her anger charging up, like a weapon inside her. Don Apolinar's sadistic murderous conceit made her want to destroy him and now, as he gripped the knife in both hands, the tip pointing down, and held it poised over Don Emmanuel's skinny chest, her temper exploded and her body seemed to expand, smashing loose from the paralysis that had gripped her. Don Apolinar had no time to react as she raised her right hand, pointed her index finger at him and wished him dead.

She hadn't believed it would work a second time, so she was astounded when something jagged and fiery, like a bolt of lightning, flew out from her and struck Don Apolinar in the chest. It knocked him away from Don

Emmanuel's side and sent him tumbling, with a gasp of surprise, to the floor. She could see no visible wound but to her satisfaction Apolinar looked dazed and had let go of the knife.

Fast as thought, Leoni raised her left hand and pointed her finger at the dropped weapon, summoning it. As though she held a powerful magnet it began to slide towards her across the floor, and as it neared her it rose into the air. She gripped the hilt.

That was when she knew she would kill Apolinar, if she could.

But he was already back on his feet. He flicked his hand in Leoni's direction and a menacing cloud of little black objects flew at her, buzzing. She dodged to her left and they shot past, but immediately swung round and homed in on her again. She was desperate to evade them, zigzagging around the room, slapping them away with her hands, but they were all over her within seconds like a hundred bees.

Only they weren't bees. Close up she saw they were tiny machines with moving metal jaws. As they settled on her they burrowed into her flesh and she fell to her knees, screaming in agony.

Don Apolinar stood over her. "I am very powerful," he boasted, "very clever. My magic is very strong, yes?" He beckoned: "Come to me, beauties," and the little black machines took flight out of Leoni's skin, drawing another scream from her and leaving her covered in oozing spots of blood. Apolinar flicked his hand again, this time towards Don Emmanuel, and the swarm boiled out towards the unconscious shaman, pouring in streams through his nose and open mouth until his whole body writhed and convulsed as though he were being devoured from within.

Don Apolinar flexed his fingers. "I think I take your treasure now," he told her.

"No!" Leoni yelled. His ego was so big he'd obviously forgotten she still had his knife. As he crouched to plunge his fingers into her brain she stabbed upwards at the crotch of his white suit. The point slid deep into his groin and stopped with a jolt.

If she'd done that to someone on Earth he would have died, but Don Apolinar didn't die. Leoni twisted the blade, wanting to inflict as much damage as possible, but he just kept coming, his fingers scrabbling at her head. "The treasure," he was muttering "I must have it! I must have it!" He sounded like a drug addict, hot for his next fix.

Still on her knees, Leoni shoved the knife up into his body again, trying to force him away from her. Yet there was no blood and he seemed unhurt: "Stupid!" he spat as he got a firm grip on her neck with his left hand and brought the finger and thumb of his right hand down like pincers towards her temple. "I am maestro. You cannot kill me in this world."

"That is true," said another voice. "But *I* can."

Apolinar froze and Leoni saw him look up. She followed his gaze. Rearing over them was a giant anaconda with amethyst scales, its massive head swaying from side to side and its eyes, vertical dark slits in amber, glowing with an inner fire.

"My Lady of the Forest!" gasped Apolinar. He wasn't swaggering now. "On my life, I did not know!"

The huge serpent swayed again, a rapid series of oscillations, and began a beautiful and spectacular metamorphosis into human form. It took only seconds for her to become recognizable as the Blue Angel.

She strode forward and struck the cowering Apolinar twice about the face, knocking him onto his back. Then she clapped her hands and he was lifted, struggling and blustering, into the air. Finally she drew back her arms and thrust them out in front of her. His body was thrown hard and fast across the echoing chamber. It smashed into the massive granite wall with a solid *crunch* and thudded to the floor.

Leoni's first thoughts were for Don Emmanuel. She ran to his side but his body was limp and still, his eyes open and vacant. "Is he dead?" she asked the Blue Angel.

"He lives no more in this realm. His spirit has entered the Between. His Earth body lies in a deep sleep."

"Can he come back . . . from this Between?"

"If he is skillful he can navigate the Between and reawaken in his Earth body."

"What about him?" Leoni pointed to the slumped form of Don Apolinar. "Can he come back too?"

"He has the skill. He will come back."

"What is he?"

"He is human, a *nasty* little Amazonian sorcerer who has embraced evil and walks the dark path. He was powerful enough to detect the transit device I placed in your head. Quite a treasure for one such as him. You know the rest. He lay in wait for you, seized your spirit and carried you to his torture chamber on this world." She looked around: "You would have died here – and you do not have the skills yet to navigate the Between – if I hadn't reached you in time."

"He disguised himself as you. That's why I let him get close to me."

"He has never seen me in this form. If he had he would not have risked my wrath. He plucked the image from your mind and used it to win your confidence."

"So he knew you only as the serpent?"

"Yes. As Sachamama. The Lady of the Forest. The spirit of the Ayahuasca vine. But I have many forms and names . . ." She sighed and took Leoni's hand. Her grip was firm and dry. "Come," she said. "I have much to tell you."

Chapter Fifty-Seven

When Ria told Ligar what Grondin had said the injured bowman responded with a bitter laugh: "Use the Snake? They must be mad." Lying on his left side, wincing at the pain of the deep stab wound in his right buttock, he was simply stating the obvious. Of course the Snake *could* be crossed – less than half a day's march to the east there was a stretch where it ran shallow over huge beds of stones and the far bank was easy to attain. In order to prevent surprise attacks from the north, however, the Clan's summer camp had been situated where the Snake ran so fast and wide and deep it was almost impossible to swim. As the drowning of Ria's parents seven years before had proved, the river here was deadly.

But no deadlier than the Illimani. Ria had decided to go for Grondin's plan, whatever it involved. Better to take any chance in those wild glacial waters than face an evil death at the hands of seven thousand savages.

Who might be upon them at any moment.

Ria's rib still ached from the beating she'd taken, she had a pounding head, a shallow spear wound to her right thigh and a gashed shoulder. But all fear had left her and she was energized by her hatred of the Illimani. If they came on now she would fight them to the death. If she escaped she would return to take bloody revenge for what they had done to the Clan today.

She considered her friends. How much fight did they have in them?

Jergat was able-bodied. He'd gone to search the battlefield for Ria's throwing stones. Vulp had climbed the lookout tower to keep watch on the main Illimani force as Grondin and his braves prepared the wounded for travel. Bont sat slumped in misery, eaten up with fear for the fate of his children. He'd accepted they couldn't be rescued, but Ria wasn't sure what he'd do next. A suicidal attack on the Illimani horde was by no means out of the question.

Ria touched Bont's shoulder: "If you let them kill you, my friend, your children will be lost for sure. There will be no one to fight for them." He pushed her hand aside. "So you must live to fight these Illimani another day." She was surprised by the tremor in her own voice. "We must all do that."

Ria turned her attention back to Ligar. He wasn't going to able to walk unaided but would heal if they escaped. She moved on to Brindle. He'd been struck with an axe and a wide strip of flesh had torn loose from his scalp, exposing his skull. He was still unconscious but the thick white bone did not seem to have been penetrated. She helped Oplimar to bandage his head and bind him to an improvised stretcher.

Bahat lay groaning, paralyzed, covered in his own blood, his body almost cut in half by a cruel wound that had severed his spine. There was no way he was going to survive this and Ria had delayed coming to him while she decided what to do. Could she give her father's old friend the same mercy Brindle had shown to Porto?

She wasn't so sure but Rotas settled the matter for her. Cupping a hand under Bahat's grizzled head, the elder looked into his eyes, seeming to await some signal or affirmation, and then very gently slit his throat.

As Ria watched Bahat's lifeblood soaking into the earth and heard his last choking gasps, something changed in the distant shouting of the Illimani. The roars of approval had stopped. Now they were baying like wolves.

"THEY'RE COMING!" Vulp yelled as he hurtled down the steps of the lookout tower, his white hair flying. "THOUSANDS OF THEM."

Before she ran, Ria remembered Grigo.

Knife in hand, she hastened to where his body lay sprawled, his leggings around his ankles, and kicked him in the ribs with the toe of her moccasin.

As she'd suspected, he was still alive. With each labored breath little bubbles of blood frothed out of the hatchet wound that split his face from his right eye to his nose.

"Grigo," she hissed. "Wake up." She tugged off his leggings and put them on. They were too big but she belted them tight. Then she kicked him again – "Wake up, you piece of shit" – and his undamaged left eye fluttered open.

Good. He recognized her.

She stooped down, gathered his testicles, and gelded him with a single savage blow. She didn't take his penis because she didn't want him to bleed to death.

She hoped he'd live.

Relishing his screams, she threw his balls in his face and sprinted out of the meeting ground, soon catching up with the rearguard of Grondin's braves as they fled north towards the Snake.

The Illimani had begun their charge on the southeastern side of the camp, at least a thousand paces south of the lookout tower and the meeting ground, but Ria couldn't guess how much of a head start she still had after dealing with Grigo. She placed her foot badly and stumbled. A shock of pain jolted through her bruised and battered body, and an Ugly she'd never seen before, one of the newcomers Grondin had brought, reached out a strong hand to steady her as she ran.

Their retreat lay through the camp's once populous northwestern sector, lying between the meeting ground and the river. Rows of close-packed wattle shelters hid their pursuers but Ria knew from their excited shouts that they were closing in. She kept looking back over her shoulder, expecting new volleys of the terrible spears, but none appeared.

Had the Illimani spent all their projectiles on the meeting-ground massacre and not yet gathered them up?

Moments later Ria burst out through the last line of shelters and the river lay two hundred paces ahead.

But she couldn't make any sense of what she saw there. There were Uglies everywhere and it seemed that a herd of reindeer had crouched down on the riverbank and somehow been persuaded not to flee while wooden platforms, lashed together from clusters of straight branches about the length of a man and the thickness of Ria's arm, were placed on their backs. Each platform was supported by four reindeer. As she drew closer she saw the animals were legless and headless. But it wasn't until she got her hands on one of them that she discovered it was just an empty skin stitched together into a tightly closed bag and filled with air.

Ten Ugly braves picked up one of the platforms with its inflated reindeer-skins, jumped into the Snake with it and – *What magic was this*? – the contraption floated on the fast-flowing waters. "It is called a jaala" – Ria heard Grondin's thought-voice before she sensed him looming up behind her. "Uglies have known this magic since the long-ago."

The braves had already clambered up onto the jaala and now sat suspended on it, a hand's breadth above the water, carried along by the current at great speed towards the west – the direction of Secret Place. Two of them held long flat blades of wood which they jabbed into the river, not guiding the little vessel across to the other side but keeping it in the midstream instead. Suddenly Ria grasped what Grondin had meant about using the river. The Uglies weren't trying to cross it with the jaalas, they were going to use it to stage a spectacular escape and let its current carry them back towards their hideout.

She watched another group of braves enter the water, and another and another. "We have twelve jaalas," said Grondin as more continued to take to the water. "Enough for us all."

Ria glanced at the northern edge of the camp. The Illimani were almost upon them and Grondin was already working fast, lashing Brindle to the platform of the last remaining jaala. Then, in the same instant of shock, she and Grondin both registered that Jergat was nowhere to be seen – had not, in fact, been with them when they'd fled the meeting ground. "He went to find my throwing stones," Ria remembered. Grondin nodded, his head cocked to one side. "Alive," he said, his gaze turning inwards. "Running. Illimani right behind him. Coming to us."

Bont, Vulp and Rotas had drawn to one side on the riverbank and were hanging back, muttering to each other. Ria could understand why. None of them, including herself, had seen anything like a jaala in their lives before. Riding on water! The very idea made her head spin. But it was either that, and some hope of escape, or stay here and certainly die, so it was obvious what had to be done. "THERE'S NO TIME FOR THIS!" she yelled at her Clansmen. "Get on the fucking jaala *now*!"

There were no complaints – although Ligar refused to be tied down in the way that Brindle was, insisting, despite his injury, that he could fend for himself. Oplimar, Grondin, Bont, Vulp and Driff lifted the jaala into the water and held it there against the current to allow first Ligar and Rotas and then all the rest of them to board. The elder's feet were unsteady and he had to crawl on his hands and knees to his position at the back of the little craft.

Ria waited until last, scanning the line of shelters two hundred paces behind them, sending out her thought-voice – *We are here, Jergat, we are here.* She felt a huge wash of fear – his fear – rolling back at her and suddenly, like a wish come true, the lean, short-statured Ugly exploded into view from between the rows of huts, his hands full of salvaged items, and began to sprint towards the river. He raised his head and she saw utter terror in his eyes. Then a thousand Illimani burst forth behind him, screaming bestial war cries, their eyes wide, their teeth bared, their naked bodies painted with blood.

"It's going to be close," Ria told Grondin. She had one foot on the jaala, which was bucking and bumping against the current, and one foot on the bank. She was acutely aware of the moment, which seemed to extend forever, as Jergat thundered towards them. But the fastest Illimani braves were closing the distance behind him. Putting on a burst of speed one caught up and raised a stabbing spear above his head. "Behind you, Jergat!" Ria sent her thought-voice. "Dodge to your left." He reacted at once – the spear thrust missed him and the brave stumbled.

Now there were just ten paces to go. Ria gave the signal to launch the jaala, and at five paces Jergat threw himself into space and landed crouched on the platform amongst his companions as the little craft was wrenched away from the bank. For a moment it juddered and veered as though it might pitch them all into the river, but then returned to balance and began to skim along on its floats. Grondin and Oplimar took control of its direction, using flat wooden slabs like those she'd seen on the other jaalas.

Amongst the objects Jergat had salvaged from the battlefield were Ligar's bow and three arrows. "Give me those," the archer demanded. Mastering his pain, he sat upright, nocked an arrow and drew back the string.

Ria followed his eyeline and saw he'd taken aim at a young Illimani, naked as they all were, who stood amongst the swelling crowd of braves lining the edge of the riverbank. His body was lean and hard, red-gold hair fell in thick waves to below his waist, and he might have been very beautiful had he not been covered from head to foot in blood.

The current was sweeping the jaala away, increasing the range. Grimacing, Ligar drew back the string to its maximum extent and took the shot. Ria watched the arrow flying true, a sure kill, but at the last moment the young man sidestepped lightning fast, snatched the shaft from the air and snapped it between his hands.

Then they were out of arrow range, heading towards mid-river. Ria sensed a peculiar force of personality emanating from the beautiful blood-soaked Illimani, and she knew, with a sudden shiver of certainty, that he was Sulpa.

Weirdly, in that instant of recognition, it was as though he had also recognized her.

His eyes followed her, tracking the jaala as it was swept away. With lazy, almost careless movements he unslung a spear-thrower from his back and held out his hand. Ria's heart fell when she saw another brave reach over and pass him one of the short spears.

After that things happened very fast. There was a whirl of movement and the spear disappeared up into the sun and shot down again straight towards the jaala. Vulp didn't even see it coming. He was seated at the front, on the right side, above one of the inflated reindeer-skins. The flint spike took him through the spine, exited at his groin and plunged between his legs where it punched through the skin of the float, releasing the air it contained in a great hiss.

At once the jaala sagged lower in the water, nose down on the right, ceased its smooth forward movement and began to turn in dizzying circles.

From the warriors on the bank there came a growl of anticipation.

Chapter Fifty-Eight

For an instant, as she held on to the Blue Angel's hand, Leoni could imagine she had a mother who loved her, who put her first, whose presence was so reassuring she could vanquish all terrors, whose strength was so great no enemy could defeat her.

They moved to the middle of the immense granite chamber and a long silver wand appeared in the Angel's free hand. She touched its point to the flagstones and made Leoni turn slowly anticlockwise with her as she inscribed a circle around them both. Even before it was complete an unearthly glow had began to spill out from its rim and now the floor dropped away beneath them and they tumbled, as Leoni had guessed they must, into another of the familiar tunnels of light.

She had no sense of up or down. But she was out of body, flying with an angel! What could be cooler than that? Around them she could see the opaque glowing walls of the tunnel shooting by and she realized they were moving fast – much faster than she had ever done before – but she felt no fear.

Leoni was thinking, *This is where I want to go, this is who I want to see*, when the journey ended as suddenly as it had begun. They swirled through the last curves and turns of the tunnel, decelerated, and materialized in a high-ceilinged, spotlessly white circular room, fifty feet across. The room was bare of all furniture, but the floor was carpeted in thick white fleece. Panoramic windows provided an unbroken three-hundred-and-sixty-degree view over a futuristic cityscape very far below.

In a body again, clad once more in a simple smock, Leoni walked barefoot to the windows and gazed out at the two suns of the land where everything is known. She had recognized the city at once. It straddled the floor of a lush green valley. The Angel had shown her its towers, obelisks, ziggurats and canals just before sending her to Sulpa.

"I feel like I'm in a computer game," Leoni confided. "Sulpa, Jack, my childhood, my parents, you, Don Apolinar, these tunnels that run between different realms and worlds, monsters, demons . . . Is this where you finally tell me what's going on?"

"That is my intention." The Angel waved her hand and a row of the floor-to-ceiling windows slid back, giving access to a wide balcony beyond. "Come," she said. "Shall we talk outside?"

Two striped canvas deckchairs stood on the balcony. The Angel settled into one and indicated that Leoni should take the other and for a few moments they looked out, saying nothing, over the strangely empty and silent city that lay far below.

"What do you know about the problem of evil?" asked the Angel at last.

"I know evil when I see it," Leoni retorted. "It's come into my life. It used to come into my bed. I can put a face to evil and it's the face of my father."

"Yes. But how would you define this evil? What is it? What's it all about?"

"Evil takes an innocent child and violates her again and again, and afterwards tries to convince her she imagined the whole thing. Evil takes whatever's good and tries to turn it into shit. Evil takes whatever wants to fly and tries to tie it down. Evil takes whatever's beautiful and tries to make it hideous. Evil takes the truth and tries to make it look false. Evil can't abide love and tries to turn it into hate. That's what I know about evil."

"So would it be right to say that evil is a negative force that wants to make things less than they might be?"

"Yes. It's that. And it's doing bad, hurtful things to others intentionally. It's taking pleasure from their pain. And – oh, I don't know – so much else."

"A wide spectrum of horror and unpleasantness, in other words? Of kinds that are commonplace on Earth?"

"Yes, I guess so," Leoni conceded.

"Hence the so-called problem of evil. Human philosophers deploy the existence of evil as an argument against the existence of God – or, anyway, of an all-powerful and all-good God. You know, either God wants to abolish evil and can't, in which case he's impotent, or he can but doesn't want to, in which case he's evil himself."

"Neat contradiction."

"But an irrelevance, like much of what passes for thought amongst humans, because from no world is it possible to banish evil entirely and there exists no benign, all-powerful 'god' to do away with it. Rather, in all realms, from the most material to the most ethereal, spiritual powers and principalities are at work, and while some serve the good and seek to spread its light, others magnify evil and seek to become rulers of darkness."

"So it's a sort of contest . . ."

". . . Between spiritual goodness and spiritual wickedness, for the souls of all sentient beings. It has continued since the dimension of time took form. In many worlds good and evil coexist in roughly equal measure. In some worlds good is greatly in the ascendant, and in some worlds it is evil that prevails."

"And you're one of those who serves the good?" Leoni asked.

"Have you ever doubted it?"

"Never! You can be scary, but I've always known you're good through and through. Just like I know Jack is evil – whatever he calls himself. That's what you wanted me to understand, right, when you showed me Sulpa? That in some sort of schizo way he's also Jack? He was murdering children – butchering them with a black sword. It was horrendous."

"You had to see it so you would know the true nature of the creature we confront. The foul sacrifices Sulpa demands, the blood he drinks and bathes in, the fear and suffering he evokes, the joy his followers take in pain – all these things are consecrated to a terrible purpose."

"You know that he followed me back," Leoni interrupted. "He possessed the body of a young woman and when he spoke through her mouth he wasn't Sulpa any more. He was Jack. I'd have been dead on the floor if you hadn't sent Matt to save me."

"I regret it came so close. I had failed to anticipate how fast Sulpa's power has grown. Already he casts his spirit far ahead, contaminating and corrupting all in his path. The sacrament that will allow him to pass through in bodily form nears completion . . ."

"Pass through in bodily form – what do you mean?"

The Angel didn't seem to hear Leoni: "One final gigantic act of wickedness remains to be performed, one more colossal holocaust of the innocent, and all hope of stopping him will be lost." That unreadable expression – was it grief? – once again troubled the eerie beauty of her face, and she fell silent.

"If he can't be stopped," Leoni prompted, "if he . . . passes through in bodily form. What will he do?"

"He will wrench the last shoots of goodness from the Earth," the Angel replied, her voice so quiet it was almost a whisper. "It will become a hellworld, forever beyond salvation. I cannot allow that to happen, Leoni – but neither can I prevent it without your help."

Chapter Fifty-Nine

"You need *my* help?" Leoni was amazed the Blue Angel had suggested such a thing. "But you're a supernatural being. How could I possibly help you?"

"Look around," said the Angel. "What do you see?"

Their deckchairs were positioned a few feet back from heavy gold railings that guarded the edge of the balcony. Leoni stood and walked to the railings, placed her hands on the top bar, and gingerly peered over the edge.

"WOW!" she exclaimed.

She'd known they were high up from her first views through the windows of the white room behind them. But now she saw the room occupied the top of a dizzyingly tall cylindrical tower, mounted on the apex of a gigantic silver pyramid marking the geometrical center of the Angel's city. The pyramid's square base, as big as six Manhattan blocks, was encircled by a broad canal filled with glistening silver liquid. Arranged in concentric rings around it, separated by gardens and parklands, alternating with zones of elaborate and extravagant architecture, were four further huge canals, respectively of crimson, blue, green and gold, spanned by soaring bridges that hung in the air without visible support. The outermost canal was ringed by a wall of some beautiful copper-colored metal hundreds of feet high and dozens of feet thick.

Sensing a trick in the Angel's question, Leoni took her time looking around.

Scattered across all the architectural zones were stupendous ziggurats of white crystal arranged in groups of four around rectangular plazas, and giant chateaux of blue crystal embellished with Gothic spires and turrets. There were edifices that might have been cathedrals or temples or mosques of emerald and garnet surmounted by domes and needle-thin minarets capped with gold. There were immense arches and flying buttresses, forests of skyscrapers fashioned entirely from glass with no stone or metal visible, and wide elevated thoroughfares connecting all the zones. Most imposing of all were perhaps a hundred obelisks, each as tall as the Empire State Building, seemingly carved from single immense blocks of jade and positioned to form the outline of a giant five-pointed star encompassing the entire circular city.

As though responding to Leoni's attention the obelisks began to glow and discharge bright flashes of lightning straight up into the clear and cloudless sky.

"What do you see?" the Angel asked again.

"An incredible city! Obviously! I mean, this is utterly amazing! Like something out of *The Wizard of Oz.*" Leoni paused and looked around one more time. "So what's the catch? The way the obelisks reacted to me makes me feel it's not real. Is it some kind of unbelievably convincing projection? Is it – I don't know – just an illusion? Like a mirage or something?" She walked back to the deckchair and sat down: "Maybe this whole experience is just one big hallucination?" she muttered. "I took some weird drug, now I'm in the Emerald City."

The Blue Angel smiled and shook her head: "All of this is real." She made an expansive, proprietorial gesture. "But look." Suddenly the small device like a laptop computer that she had used to send Leoni to Sulpa had appeared in her hands and she flipped up its screen.

"WHOA!" Leoni objected. "I'm not doing any more transits until I get some answers."

"Don't worry. I only want to show you this." As before, the Angel turned a dial on the control panel beneath the screen. "Observe," she said, pointing to a distant complex of four white-crystal ziggurats. There was a shimmer in the air around them and they disappeared. "Or how about this?" offered the Angel. She turned the dial and the ziggurats were back but their crystal structure was now cobalt blue. "I can also do this." She turned the dial a third time and the ziggurats morphed into four huge glittering spheres that united into a single larger sphere and rose a hundred feet into the air, spinning rapidly.

Leoni was puzzled and a little annoyed: "Why did you say it was real? You couldn't do any of that if it was real." She leaned over and took a closer look at the instrument the Angel was holding. "It has to be a projection. You control it with your laptop-whatever-it-is gizmo like you did the color of the skies the last time I was here."

The Angel shook her head: "I know it looks that way, but that's not what's happening. Everything around us is real in every meaningful sense of that word. These pyramids and ziggurats and obelisks and towers are made of matter. So is the body you find yourself in. You know it doesn't suffer from the same constraints as your Earth-body but you also know it feels pain and you've probably guessed – rightly – that it can be killed . . .

"Like you killed Don Apolinar and he killed Don Emmanuel?"

"Yes. A bit like that. Although utterly different in all other respects, the fundamental structure of matter in the realm where Apolinar built his torture chamber is almost identical to its structure in this realm."

"Fundamental structure of matter? If you mean atoms and such then this is already way over my head."

"Atoms are child's play. I'm speaking of much deeper levels."

Leoni started to object again but the Angel quieted her with an upheld hand and continued: "Dear impatient one, this is not an examination. I don't expect you to master knowledge that the greatest human minds have yet to grasp. I simply wish to inform you that my powers to confront Sulpa on the Earth-plane are finite. I am constrained by certain immutable constants, certain limiting conditions of the Totality. Because of these I need your help."

"Totality, Angel? Immutable constants? You're losing me again."

"The Earth is a single planet in a single solar system amongst trillions of solar systems in one universe. This universe, in its turn, is a tiny speck within the Totality – the multiplicity of all possible universes, and all the possible worlds they contain, comprising the whole of reality. Matter is organized and coheres at many different levels, across all these numberless realms – from the lowest, most physical and embodied states to the highest, most ethereal and *dis*embodied states . . ."

Leoni pinched her own arm, stamped her foot on the balcony and tugged at the fabric of the deckchair. "Feels pretty solid to me," she said.

"Oh, it is. But the fundamental structure of all the wondrously organized matter of this realm lies close to the lowest level at which I can be effective on the physical plane. There are other worlds, where matter resonates at far lower and heavier frequencies, in which physical intervention becomes impossible even for me. The Earth is such a world."

"That helps to explain something I've never understood. You came to me in my dreams, you even comforted me, but you never tried to stop my dad from raping me."

A sorrowful expression crossed the Angel's face. "It was beyond my power to prevent him, Leoni. You have no idea how many others there have been – in greater need by far than you, in pain, in difficulty, in fear – whom I have also failed."

"So you're a bit like God in that contradiction you told me about? Good but powerless?"

"On the Earth plane, yes. Almost powerless."

"Almost – but not completely?"

"Sometimes," said the Angel, "I can perform miracles." She sounded wistful, not boastful.

"Miracles? Like in the Bible?"

"By definition they're exceptional phenomena that don't occur often – and this quite exactly describes all my attempts to intervene physically on the Earth plane. At rare intervals – when I work the magic – I'm able to step down and do something excellent. But with such unreliable access to physical power I can't use it to influence events on any significant scale in such a realm. I must reach out to people through their dreams and visions – as I have done with you – when I want to do that. In other words, I must work through human consciousness." She sighed: "And unfortunately that also raises huge problems . . ."

Leoni laughed, remembering the way she'd been before her near-death experience, the things she'd valued and enjoyed: "A lot of us live pretty much unconsciously," she said. "I did, for a long time."

"I would not say *un*conscious. I would say shackled, limited, tied down. You humans are spiritual beings in physical form who have fallen so deeply into the heavy material realm of Earth it has enchained your consciousness. You don't remember your true origins, or the purpose of your incarnation. You imagine that the infinitesimally small section of the Totality you are able to know through your limited physical senses, and through instruments devised to extend them, is all that there is or ever will be to know. You are easily convinced you are just your bodies and there is no such thing as the soul, or if you do believe that the soul exists then you often do so blindly, according to religious dogmas rather than personal inquiry. You must understand, therefore, how frustrating it is for me, as a being of intelligent, conscious, non-physical energy, to have to deal with you. Except for the occasional miracle I cannot manifest physically in your realm. I should be able to reach you easily at the level of consciousness, but humanity's imprisonment in matter is so complete that most of you block me out."

"You've reached *me*."

"There are back doors. Certain naturally occurring substances, certain spontaneous states of brain chemistry, certain techniques and practices available to all humans, unlock the prison and set the spirit free."

"Like the Ayahuasca I drank tonight?"

"Yes, or near-death experiences, or DMT, or psilocybe mushrooms, or the trance-dance of the Kalahari bushmen. When humans are in these extreme states of consciousness I can reach them, just the way I've reached you . . ."

"But why do you want to do that?" Leoni objected. "I don't understand. Why do you feel that you have to reach us at all? Why not just leave us imprisoned in matter and go somewhere more interesting?"

The Angel smiled: "I can journey where and when I will across the Totality, but no world interests me more than my beautiful, precious Earth, and there is no intelligent species I value more highly than my wonderful, beloved, paradoxical, lost human race."

"The Earth I can understand." An image of the planet, indigo as the Angel's skin, filled with light, floating in the darkness of space, had come unbidden into Leoni's mind: "It's pretty amazing . . . But the human race? What's so wonderful about us? We're mostly monsters, Angel. You must know that. We dream up endlessly clever and horrible ways to kill and hurt each other and rip each other off. We're murderers and rapists and liars and thieves. We're sick, cruel, evil-minded killers."

"Yes. All those things."

"And yet we're your 'beloved?'"

"What else would you be?" the Angel asked. "You're my children. My only children. I cannot stop loving you."

Chapter Sixty

The river was two bowshots wide where it rushed past the camp and it flowed faster than most men could run. Ria knew this because in happier times the youth of the Clan had sometimes amused themselves by racing the Snake – a game that involved throwing a branch into the current and charging along the bank after it. The terrain was rough, filled with humps and waterlogged hollows, and only the fleetest of foot could match the current's speed over distances of more than a thousand paces. Eventually even the best of them began to tire, but the river never did.

So Ria could see how the Uglies' plan might have worked – how, in fact, it was already working for those now far ahead of them, and would have worked for her and her companions on the last jaala if they hadn't waited for Jergat.

With a splash the front of the little vessel where the reindeer-skin float had been punctured lurched below the surface, sending an icy wave foaming over the wooden platform and soaking them all. Vulp was pinned by the spear that had killed him but the wave shoved his limp body sideways so his arms and head trailed in the water, acting as a further brake against the current and turning the jaala on an even more direct course towards the bank and the Illimani.

Brindle was still unconscious, strapped to the front of the platform on the left. Grondin and Oplimar struggled to influence the course of the jaala, plunging their wooden slabs into the river but to no effect. At the rear Bont sat brooding, his great war axe in his hand. Everyone else seemed dazed, scarcely acknowledging the prancing Illimani warriors on the bank. Their huge numbers, the terrible sounds they made, their joy in cruelty, their lust for blood, the hate and violence that seethed out of them – all these things had a stupefying intensity.

Ria could feel the weight of their malevolence like a physical assault but refused to give way. Gritting her teeth against the pain of her injuries, balancing against the bucking turns of the jaala, she edged forward through the spray to Vulp, got two hands on him and tried to push him free. But he wouldn't budge. She didn't see Driff moving to her aid, but suddenly he was beside her, reaching down into the skin of the punctured float to free the tip of the spear. It tore loose and they heaved Vulp into the current, his long white hair streaming out behind him as he sank.

The explosion of action seemed to break the evil spell that had fallen over them all. Relieved of Vulp's weight, the front right-hand side of the jaala bucked clear of the water for a moment before splashing down again and, as though waking from sleep, everyone came alive to their plight. "We need to move back," Grondin pulsed urgently to Ria. He was already untying Brindle from the frame. "Tell your people. Put weight on back, lift front up."

"Why?"

"Just do it or we all dead."

With Jergat's help, Grondin dragged Brindle to the rear and wedged him between Bont and Rotas. Oplimar and Ligar were already there and now Driff and Ria leapt to join them. The shift in weight raised the front right-hand side of the jaala out of the water a second time, much higher than before. It didn't crash back and suddenly the little craft was on a smooth course again, skipping along the surface of the river on three of its four floats.

They'd drifted close to shore while they'd careened out of control, but now Grondin and Oplimar steered them back out towards mid-river again.

Howls of disappointment rose up from their pursuers.

For the first time Ria allowed herself to hope. She was daydreaming of the bloody punishment she would inflict on the Illimani when the lashed branches forming the floor of the platform rolled beneath her, a rope snapped, a gap suddenly opened and she plunged up to her armpits in the freezing river. At once Oplimar's calloused hands shot out, caught her by her hair and the shoulder of her jerkin, and pulled her back up.

The bumping and jostling sent fresh surges of pain through her head and side and reopened the spear wound in her thigh, but there were more urgent concerns.

Ria saw now that the way the nine of them were riding the jaala would soon destroy it. She shivered with cold from the soaking she'd taken. To keep the front right-hand side out of the water they'd clustered towards the left and rear of the fragile craft, twisting it along its central axis. If another of the ropes binding the platform snapped then the whole thing would disintegrate.

Still shivering, Ria squinted over her shoulder. They'd nearly reached midstream. No more of the fearsome spears had been thrown – they must indeed have been left strewn, as yet uncollected, on the meeting ground. Most of the Illimani had dropped back and only a handful now kept pace with them along the bank.

There was time to risk a repair.

Ria and Grondin decided what needed to be done and had their companions rebalance themselves on the loose, unstable platform, allowing it to fall level. With no float to support it, the front right-hand side dived again, slowing the little craft's progress. As before it rotated instead of pursuing a straight course, and began to move back across the current towards the shore.

The punctured reindeer-skin float and the floor of the platform right above it had to go. Once these were removed there would be nothing left on that side for the current to drag under water. They set Bont to work on the problem, breaking the floor one branch at a time, very carefully and precisely so as not to hasten the disintegration of the whole jaala. Meanwhile Grondin and Oplimar drew rope from their shoulder packs and began to rebind the loose branches tightly.

They worked until their fingers bled, but the constant rotation and juddering wrenched knots apart as soon as they were tied and for too long they seemed to be making no progress.

Ria looked up at the bank and drew in her breath. Her attention had been so focused on the desperate struggle to save the jaala she hadn't noticed how close they'd drifted.

(*Too close.*)

The Illimani they'd outdistanced earlier were back with them, shouting and jeering, boiling out along the bank.

Ria's first fear was they might somehow have rearmed themselves with enough of their deadly spears to throw a volley. But instead she was astounded to see a dozen of the pursuing braves grip knives between their teeth, jump into the river and swim out into the current. Two of them . . . three . . . then a fourth were dragged under by the turbulent waters but the others were powerful swimmers – better than the best in the Clan – and began to gain on the crippled rotating jaala.

Ria felt Jergat at her side. He held out her five quartz hunting stones, wrapped in a bloodied cloth. She took them from him and placed them back in their deerskin pouch, keeping one in her right hand.

Then she stood up.

"You still have two arrows left?" she asked Ligar.

"Yes, but my bow's useless. The string's wet. I won't be able to shoot again until it dries."

The Illimani braves were closing in, swimming like otters; if all eight of them swarmed the jaala they'd tear it apart. Ria hated to lose the stones, but there was no other option. She had to start picking them off in the water.

One brave led the others by a couple of body lengths, his bright blue eyes fixed on her, his pale wet hair glistening around his head in ringlets. Ria knew it wasn't going to be an easy throw because of the erratic movements of the jaala and the pounding she'd taken, but she judged her moment and let fly. She gasped as new pain exploded in her side but the heavy little quartz egg slammed into the brave's skull and he sank from view.

The other seven would soon overhaul them. Accepting the agony it cost her, Ria threw again, skimming the stone low across the water, aiming for a swimmer coming in fast from the right. There was a wet *SMACK*! and a burst of blood exploded from his nose. His eyes rolled up in his head and he was gone.

Ria knew the power and effectiveness of her throws was improving. Getting stronger. Getting more accurate. Was it the magic that Merina had put into her arms? Or was it the stones themselves? *WHACK*! She made her third throw, sending another man to the bottom. *CRACK*! Her fourth shot hit its target just above the ear. Blood blossomed and the brave wallowed in the water, threw up his arms and sank.

Now Ria had just one stone, the last of her gifts from Merina. Her fingers caressed it as she drew back her arm and threw. There was a solid *CLUNK*! and a fifth man disappeared beneath the surface.

Only three of the swimmers remained, but they were almost upon the jaala and still Grondin, Oplimar and Bont worked feverishly. "Driff!" Ria yelled. But he'd already seen the danger and now he hurled his two tomahawks, one with his right hand, one with his left. The weapons cartwheeled as they flew across the water and their blades smacked – *CLUNK*! *CLUNK*! – into two of the bobbing heads.

Ria looked to the bank. It loomed terrifyingly close and the Illimani clustered there began to howl and stamp their feet. Simultaneously the last swimmer drew level, grabbing for a handhold, and Bont finished his work on the platform, swept up his axe and killed the man with a single blow.

Without the impediment of the punctured float the jaala leapt forward. Grondin and Oplimar tied the last knot to strengthen the framework and picked up the steering slabs again. Everyone repositioned themselves, distributing their weight around the now much smaller platform.

Ria snatched a glance. They were once more outstripping their pursuers on the bank. Better still, they were approaching the next big bend in the river, a stretch she knew well. The land inside the elbow of the bend was treacherous and swampy, full of pitfalls and massively overgrown with thorns, brambles and stands of tall willows. It wouldn't stop warriors like the Illimani but not even they were going to be able to get through those obstacles in a hurry.

She was starting to hope again when two more of the terrible short spears plummeted down on them out of the sky. One killed Rotas, entering between his shoulder blades and exiting through the center of his chest. The other passed under Bont's arm without causing injury but pierced and deflated the reindeer-skin float beneath him.

Now the break-up of the jaala became unstoppable. The individual branches in the floor of the platform rolled and separated, snapping their new ties, and everyone was dumped into the bitterly cold fast-flowing river.

Ria saw that Grondin was a poor swimmer. He didn't ask for help but he was having trouble keeping Brindle's head above water as well as his own. Then Bont surged towards them, somehow got his huge arms around them both, rolled on his back and used the long handle of his axe to draw them securely to him as he let the rushing current carry them. Ligar was also in difficulty but Jergat and Oplimar buoyed him up. Driff was swimming right by her side.

The freezing, foaming river had already begun to swirl them all into the start of the bend when Ria felt a peculiar prickling at the nape of her neck.

It wasn't the cold.

She turned in the water to look behind.

Chapter Sixty-One

Leoni was confused. "You mean the whole human race?"

"Yes," agreed the Angel. "That's right."

"But how can we be your children? There're billions of us."

"I didn't say I gave birth to you."

"You adopted us?"

"No, not that either."

"It's like a riddle. We're your children, but you didn't give birth to us and you didn't adopt us. So what did you do?"

"I created you," said the Angel. "I created all life on Earth."

"You're beginning to sound like God again."

The Angel laughed. "I already explained that no being exists across the whole of reality who is all-powerful and all-good like the god of the Christians."

"And I suppose I just have to take your word for it?"

"The effects of the medicine will wear off soon, Leoni, and you will return to the Earth-plane. There's much I still have to tell you, so for now, yes, it will be simpler if you just believe me when I say that the creative and destructive powers of the Totality, the authors of truth and lies, good and evil, are all beings like myself – intelligent, conscious, non-physical energy. Sometimes we've been called gods, even worshipped as such, but human notions of angels, spirits and demons are a better fit. We came into existence with the Totality but none of us have ever been able to discover with absolute certainty how or why we're here. We have powers but we are by no means all-powerful at all levels of reality."

"If you can create life then you're pretty powerful, Angel."

"Did I not tell you I perform miracles from time to time? Four billion years ago it was I who breathed the magic of spirit into the empty matter of Earth and wrote its code of life . . ."

"You're four billion years old?"

"Much older," the Angel said. The screen of her laptop device displayed a kaleidoscope of swirling colors and Leoni found herself gazing down from the depths of space onto a fiery, barren, empty and lifeless world.

Then, slowly at first but soon speeding up, the character and colors of the planet began to change. Oceans covered it, land masses emerged, and Leoni zoomed in to see that life, in fantastic variety and abundance, was everywhere.

She could still hear the Angel's voice: "After I manifested the first simple organisms, billions of years had to pass on the Earth-plane before creatures with sufficient intelligence to choose freely between good and evil could evolve. The first to do so was the human species."

Abruptly, Leoni found herself seated in a classroom behind a wooden desk, looking at a big flatscreen monitor on the wall. It was displaying a graphic of a large tree with little shrewlike animals in the lowest branches, various kinds of lemurs and monkeys higher up, apes above them, followed by a number of progressively more human-looking creatures. At the top, the tree divided into two final branches, beside each of which appeared a superbly rendered three-dimensional human figure. One, labeled NEANDERTHAL, was stocky, heavily muscled, virtually neckless, chinless, big-nosed, beetle-browed and very ugly in a coarse, apelike way. The other, labeled CRO-MAGNON, tall, slim and well-muscled, with handsome sculpted features and a daring, intelligent glint in his eye, was a good-looking modern human being.

"Two similar yet fundamentally different species of fully conscious humans evolved in parallel," the Angel commented. "Cro-Magnon is a name given by scholars to one – the anatomically modern humans who are your own direct ancestors. Though there were mystics and visionaries amongst them, many fell deeply into the physical plane and in time they forgot they were also beings of spirit. For them matter became everything. Evil angels mingled with them, and drew them towards wickedness . . ."

"Evil angels?" Leoni asked.

"Demons, if you prefer."

"Like Sulpa?"

"Yes. Sulpa is a demon, and one of my own kind, a being of intelligent, conscious, non-physical energy. But his purpose – his only purpose – is to magnify evil and send his malevolent presence out into all times and across all universes. The more pure and innocent the good he destroys, the more horror and pain he inflicts in the process, the more his own power grows. That is why he hungers for the Neanderthals."

"The Neanderthals? I saw a story about them on Discovery Channel. Aren't they supposed to have been stupid? And my kind of humans wiped them out?"

"It's true that the Neanderthals were less materially competent than the Cro-Magnons. In fact, they cared nothing for wealth and possessions. But they were highly evolved spiritual beings and they carried within them a quality of pure, innocent goodness that warmed the Totality. Their goodness was power, Leoni, raw cosmic power, but they used it only for healing, to communicate telepathically with one another, to live in harmony with the Earth, leaving almost no mark. Your species found them ugly, but beauty and truth shone forth from them like a beacon."

"I'm not surprised we wiped them out then," said Leoni. "We can't stand too much beauty and truth."

"Well, now we approach the heart of the matter," said the Angel. "Because it is not at all certain you *did* wipe them out. Your scholars only know that the last population of Neanderthals survived in Spain until twenty-four thousand years ago and then became extinct. But they don't know why this happened. They have no evidence. No observations. In such a case, where an event has not been observed, you may only speak of probabilities . . ."

"OK, so it's probable, not certain, we wiped them out."

"In which case it's also probable but not certain that they became extinct in some other way . . ."

Leoni shrugged: "I suppose so – but why is this important?"

The Angel's reply was baffling: "For the sake of every human alive today it is a matter of the utmost importance that the Neanderthals are *not* exterminated by Cro-Magnons twenty-four thousand years ago. In fact, the fate of the human race depends on it . . ."

Chapter Sixty-Two

They were being hunted by more Illimani swimmers, still a bowshot behind but closing fast. Ria squinted through the freezing spray. Just six of them. But they were all big men with flint daggers gripped between their teeth.

Beside her she heard a growl of anger as Driff saw them.

Bont had seen them, too. He was on his back, using the handle of his axe to hold Grondin and Brindle against him and keep their heads above water. Ligar, Jergat and Oplimar were struggling just to stay afloat.

Driff shook his soaking mane of black hair out of his eyes. There was a crazy intensity there that Ria had seen in other Illimani braves, and she didn't like it. But whatever Brindle had done to turn him against his own people, she hadn't seen him waver for a heartbeat since he'd saved her life on the meeting ground.

She looked back.

The pursuing swimmers were fast and determined. They'd already halved the distance. But behind them on the bank, the treacherous swamps, overgrown thickets and dense stands of trees that lay across the great bend of the Snake had slowed the Illimani horde almost to a halt. Yelling with frustration, many more of them, perhaps a hundred, now gripped weapons between their teeth and dived into the water.

Suddenly Ria saw Sulpa. His lean blood-drenched body and long red-gold hair were unmistakable. He sauntered to the bank, brought his hand up to shade his eyes, and seemed to be looking directly at her. Then his arm snaked lazily forward and he pointed his finger.

Ria glimpsed some fast-flying object coming her way. It seemed no bigger than an insect but it threw up a burst of steam when it entered the water beside her and smacked into her thigh with the force of an arrow, causing her to scream out in shock. The pain was sharp and agonizing, as though the projectile was tipped with fire, but when she put her hand down to explore she found no wound, only a lump under her flesh.

Sulpa pointed at her again. But before he could shoot her with another little dart she and her companions were swept round the curve of the Snake and shielded from him by a rank of tall willows growing close to the water's edge.

Ria heard Grondin's thought-voice. "We are saved." And an instant later she understood why.

The current was carrying them towards a barren little island in the middle of the river. There, out of sight of the Illimani, the other Ugly braves had beached their jaalas and stood with arms outstretched, some holding spear shafts, others coils of rope, waiting to rescue them from the water.

Ria was allowing herself to hope she might make it when one of the Illimani swimmers gripped her ankle. She just had time to take a gulp of air before her whole body was dragged beneath the surface.

She didn't panic. After their parents had drowned, Hond and Rill had taught her everything there was to know about swimming. She'd learned to hold her breath and swim underwater in ice-cold rock pools in the mountains. She prided herself on being able to stay down for the count of two hundred. So she kept her eyes open in the cold blur. Her attacker had a dagger in a sheath at his waist but didn't reach for it. He was still holding her ankle, jerking her under, and his free hand snaked out, scrabbling for her throat, leaving his flank vulnerable. Ria stabbed him hard and fast, driving the blade deep between his ribs. She heard his scream, muffled by the water, a cloud of bubbles burst from his mouth, and she was free.

Even before she could reach the surface and fill her lungs another Illimani swimmer was all over her, pale legs thrashing, hairy armpit in her face. He had a knife clamped between his teeth but, like the first man, he didn't use it and tried to grapple with her instead. Ria slashed her blade across his belly, releasing a huge wash of blood, and broke loose, surging upwards, desperate for breath, shaking her hair out of her eyes as she surfaced.

The four surviving Illimani were ignoring everyone else, converging on her, and Ria guessed why they weren't using their weapons. Sulpa wanted them to capture her and bring her back alive.

With her last reserves of strength she thrashed across the current towards the island. Brindle, Grondin and Bont had already been pulled ashore by the Uglies, and Ria saw Ligar, Oplimar and Jergat being helped from the water. She'd become separated from Driff in the struggle but he caught up with her now, just as the four Illimani reached her. One wrapped his arm around her head, another grabbed her thigh, another her hair, as Driff flailed into them, biting and pummeling. Then the river tumbled them all in a heap against the island where the Uglies were waiting. Ria and Driff were hauled to safety and the Illimani were hacked to death in the shallows.

There was a swirl of activity as the crews rearranged themselves amongst the remaining jaalas, and Ria was quickly back on one of the little vessels with her companions beside her. But the next wave of Illimani swimmers was almost upon them, and more than twenty splashed close enough to swarm the jaalas as they were launched. Ria reached over the side and stabbed one of the attackers in the eye as he tried to climb aboard. Another brave swam up and she slashed at him, screaming defiance, forcing him back. She saw Bont and Grondin laying about with their axes, cutting a way through, saw Uglies on the other jaalas doing the same, until at last the little fleet broke clear and surged into the mainstream, scudding over the surface.

Ria didn't look back; the men in the water couldn't match the speed of the jaalas.

She crawled across the floor of the raft to where Brindle lay, still unconscious, and rested the palm of her hand on his chest. His eyes were closed, his breathing was steady, and he did not seem to be in discomfort or pain. She confirmed again that the axe wound to his head, though bloody, had not penetrated his skull.

"He going to be OK," Grondin pulsed. "He sleep deep now. We heal at Secret Place."

Since she too was very tired, and there was nothing more to be done on the bucking craft as it shot along with the river, Ria stretched herself out on the deck next to Brindle. Almost at once Sulpa's image came into her mind, his lean body drenched in blood, pointing at her.

She reached down inside her leggings and touched her right thigh where his little dart had struck.

The hard lump under her skin throbbed and radiated heat.

Chapter Sixty-Three

"But that's ridiculous," Leoni protested. Her mind was reeling. "How can we make any difference to something so long ago in the past? Whatever happened happened and there's nothing we can do about it . . ."

The Angel smiled: "That's not quite how time works." She made some adjustments to the controls of her laptop device. "But once again you're just going to have to take my word for it."

"Take your word for what?" Leoni asked.

"That we may influence events at any point in Earth's history or prehistory providing the results we want to achieve aren't ruled out by existing evidence and observations."

The Angel had spoken formally, almost as though she were quoting from a legal document, but now she reverted to her normal tone: "In the case of the Neanderthals, history only has evidence they became extinct twenty-four thousand years ago, and this happened in Spain. But history does not tell us how or why they died out. We're therefore free to attempt to influence not the extinction itself – which is an observed historical event – but how and why it happened . . ."

"Yeah," said Leoni. "If we have a time machine."

"But we do." The screen of the Angel's laptop had sprung into life again, displaying its vortex of menacing colors. "Surely you guessed when I sent you to see Sulpa I was sending you back in time?"

"Not at first, no. It didn't even occur to me. Matt suggested it later when I drew pictures of the weapons Sulpa's people were carrying. But it doesn't make any sense to me."

"How do you think time works?" the Angel asked. She pointed to the screen: "Draw it for me with your finger."

Leoni reached out and traced a glowing green horizontal line from left to right across the middle of the screen. She scrawled PAST above the extreme left side of the line, PRESENT at the center, and FUTURE at the extreme right.

"Ah," said the Angel. "Time's arrow. For one event to cause another it must precede it."

"Well, obviously – duuh . . ."

"Or perhaps not so obvious. Perhaps, for example, time is more like this."

The Angel waved her hand, erasing Leoni's line, and touched the screen with her own index finger. Though continuous, the line she drew was not straight but looped and twisted and sprawled across all parts of the screen, making multiple meandering curves and turns, often winding back and recrossing its own path, here forming a spiral, there a cat's cradle, and there coiled into a tangled knot.

"Different things happen at different points along the line," the Angel explained, "and there are multiple causal interconnections running in all directions, so it's not, strictly speaking, inevitable that one thing must occur before another in order to influence it. That's how it seems to humans – almost all of you agree on it – because you're so deeply immersed in matter. But leave the body, step outside the flow of earthly time, and you see that everything is continuously unfolding at every point along the line . . ."

"And once you've stepped out you can step in again at any point you choose?"

"Or you can be sent in, as I sent you in," said the Angel, and she touched a tangled point on the line with the tip of her finger.

"But out of body, right? Like I was in the middle of all that Sulpa madness? It's not like the land where everything is known, or Don Apolinar's dungeon?"

"You have no physical avatar when I send you into the past this way" – the Angel touched the laptop again. "You are pure, non-physical consciousness. You are spirit."

Leoni felt her eyes drawn back to the meandering line on the screen – a brilliant luminous green trail, standing out against the background of deeper, darker, swirling colors. "Wherever time recurves, and passes close to its own course, such as here" – the Angel pointed to a place where two sections of the line ran in parallel for a short distance and appeared to touch. "Or where time crosses over itself, such as here" – she pointed to one of the many loops she had drawn. "And particularly where it becomes intricately raveled and intertwined such as here" – she indicated one of the most densely knotted areas of the line – "then special possibilities emerge both for good and for evil." The Angel turned her intense gaze on Leoni: "Connections form between the different epochs thus superimposed, and the lives and fates of certain individuals can become entangled . . ."

Leoni was staring into the screen again. The swirling colors had vanished. It was now as though she was looking down at the Earth through a trapdoor in the sky. What she saw was a group of little rafts, launching from an island in the midst of a wide fast-flowing river, surrounded by a crowd of swimmers.

She zoomed in. The people on the rafts were fighting the swimmers, hacking their way through them with axes. With a final mighty effort they broke free and the rafts were carried off by the current.

Leoni zoomed in again and found herself on one of the rafts. Most of the people on board were cut and bleeding. Some, with no necks, big chunky bodies and crude ungainly features, resembled the figure of the Neanderthal the Angel had shown her earlier. Others were humans like Leoni and, with a jolt of excitement, she recognized the mysterious girl she had warned about the tree-birds – the girl with nut-brown skin and chestnut hair who'd come to her in a dream and taken her hand and told her that together they could find their way out of a terrifying forest. She lay on the floor of the raft beside a club-footed Neanderthal with a head injury. She was injured, too. Her lean hard body was soaked from the river, and blood seeped from multiple flesh wounds. Her face was a mass of bruises but her eyes shone with the same bright intelligence Leoni remembered. There was no mistaking her.

"Her name is Ria," said the Angel. "She lives in the Stone Age, in what is now the northern part of Spain, by the banks of a glacial river that dried up millennia before you were born. She's a member of a tribe of Cro-Magnons who call themselves the Clan."

"And the other people with her?"

"Some are survivors of the Clan like herself. The rest are Neanderthals. Usually you would not see them join forces, but in Sulpa they face a common enemy."

Abruptly the river vanished from the screen and the meandering green line was back. The Angel pointed to a densely coiled and knotted section. "Though separated by twenty-four thousand years of linear time, your epoch intersects with Ria's epoch here" – her finger touched one of the points where the line crossed over itself and there was a flash of green. "Your life is in the twenty-first century, Ria's is in the Stone Age. But because there really is no present and no past everything in these two intersecting timelines actually unfolds simultaneously."

"So what you just showed me, the rafts and the river, this Ria girl – it was all happening twenty-four thousand years ago but also, in a weird way, right now?"

"In a weird way, yes."

The screen display changed again. The green line was gone and Leoni found herself looking down on the brutish naked ranks of Sulpa's pale-skinned bloodstained army.

"They belong to a Cro-Magnon tribe of eastern Europe who call themselves the Illimani," said the Angel. "Sulpa has possessed the body of one of their young warriors, killed their former king, shaped them into this instrument of evil, and led them on a mass migration across Europe, ending up in northern Spain. He has come there to torture and kill the last Neanderthals on Earth. But all the Cro-Magnon tribes who cross his path are also being annihilated, including Ria's people."

"She looked like she'd been in a fight . . ."

"She had been. A fight for her life. Barely an hour ago in her timeline the Clan were attacked. The adults were massacred – only a few dozen escaped, Ria amongst them. Hundreds of children were sacrificed to feed Sulpa's thirst for innocent blood."

"Why? What's the matter with this guy?"

"It is as I told you – the more pure the innocence he destroys, the more horror and pain he can inflict in the process, the more his own power grows."

"That's why he sacrifices children?"

"He drinks not only their blood but also their souls . . . He snuffs out their consciousness forever so they may never again take shape in new forms. He takes everything they were and are and could be and feeds it to the evil within him. It is the same hunger for pure souls, magnified a thousandfold, that draws him to the Neanderthals. Never before, across the whole of reality, has such goodness and innocence as theirs come into existence."

A flicker caught Leoni's eye and she glanced down at the screen.

The green timeline was back.

The Angel once again pointed to the place where the twenty-first century intersected with the Stone Age. "You will note," she said, "that the knot here is very dense and this intersection is also surrounded by other superimposed epochs . . ."

Leoni looked. She could see many points that would have been widely separated if the Angel had simply drawn a straight line across the screen, but that lay close together and frequently overlapped in this intertwined and knotted line.

"To grasp the danger," the Angel continued, "you must know something of what Sulpa is attempting to do."

"Didn't you say he wants to make himself more powerful by murdering good people?"

"That is simply a means to his larger objective." The Angel's beautiful voice had fallen almost to a whisper: "The goodness of the Neanderthals presents him with a special opportunity. If he succeeds in destroying them, as he intends, the psychic charge he draws from their life force will allow him to jump the ages and manifest in physical form in the twenty-first century as well."

"He already has!" Leoni objected. "Manifested physically, I mean. Isn't Jack just the name Sulpa goes by today?"

"It is. But Jack is not a fully formed physical being. Sulpa used the entanglement of the two timelines to send him forward into the age of technology as a dark and corrupting influence, something without solidity, intangible, more like an intelligent cloud than a man. But, with each new sacrifice he performs in the age of stone, his shadow in the twenty-first century grows stronger and more physical, and followers flock to him. All that remains is the mass murder of the last Neanderthals and Jack will become a fully materialized avatar. Then Sulpa will stand astride the intersecting timelines and begin to weave the doom of all that is good."

The Angel's finger touched the screen again: "Because time is so densely entangled in this region, many other epochs lie closely superimposed. Very soon he will be able to spread his tentacles through all of them. The balance of the Totality itself stands at risk."

"But if we stop him massacring the Neanderthals none of this happens, right?"

"None of it. Only in this way can he gain sufficient power for the full materialization of Jack."

"I don't ever want to see that day come," whispered Leoni.

“Then will you help me prevent the massacre? This is the adventure I have chosen you for.”

“Yes,” said Leoni with passion. “Yes, with all my heart. But how will we do it? You said you can’t intervene physically. You said I’m just spirit when I go into the past.”

“Ria stands between Sulpa and the Neanderthals and I have entangled your life with hers,” said the Angel. “You are sisters in time now. Together you will find the way.”

Leoni looked down at the screen. The swirling colors were back. They seemed to draw her in and she began to fall.

Part III

Chapter Sixty-Four

When Leoni fell through the colors of the laptop's screen she experienced a horrible moment of déjà vu. The last time she'd done this she'd been on her way to a terrifying encounter with Sulpa. Now she was in another one of those tunnels – swooping swirls and turns, long vertical drops. It seemed to go on forever. Then *WHOOMF*! She emerged from the transit out of body, invisible in the midst of thousands of Illimani warriors, on the bank of the same fast-flowing river where earlier the Angel had shown her Ria with her companions fleeing on rafts.

How much earlier?

Leoni saw the position of the sun had changed. Somehow morning had become afternoon and it seemed hours must have passed here while she'd gone through the transit. It was going to be hard to find Ria now.

She took to the air and hovered twenty feet above the jostling, agitated Illimani. In the thick of the crowd was a wide circle of clear space occupied by only one man. His back was turned to her, but she would recognize Sulpa from any angle. He looked like he'd been bathing in blood again – the evil fuck – and his hair was matted thick with it. He was also talking to himself, muttering very fast in some unknown language. It was scary, the way this babble kept pouring out of him.

Leoni was fascinated and terrified at the same time.

Would Sulpa somehow be able to detect her presence, even though she was out of body and he was not?

Even though this was all happening twenty-four thousand years ago?

She kept drifting closer until she was floating right over his head.

A dirty-gray sphere nestled in each of his hands, which he held out before him, palms up, fingers flexed, as though he were juggling. The spheres were about the size of tennis balls and had a filmy soap-bubble consistency, much like her own aerial body but opaque.

Leoni risked dropping lower. There was thick smoke swirling inside the spheres in which, from moment to moment, strange hints of shape and substance threatened to appear.

Was that a wing? Was that a talon? Was that a haunch?

Just a littler closer and . . .

Now she had it . . .

Seemingly formed out of the smoke itself, a hideous little beast with muscular hind legs, clawed feet and folded leathery wings crouched within each of the spheres. The pair seemed to be identical combinations of bat, pterodactyl and gargoyle. Their gaping mouths were filled with tiny needle-sharp fangs. Their eyes, the color of blood, were fixed adoringly on Sulpa.

Even if their master couldn't see her while he was in his physical body, Leoni was sure his creatures could.

She had already begun to back away when they burst forth from the spheres, flapping their wings, and flew to perch on Sulpa's shoulders. She saw them cock their heads as he whispered something to each of them. Then they leapt into the air and streaked towards the river.

Leoni knew with cold certainty they'd been sent after Ria. Keeping what she hoped was a safe distance behind them she followed.

The little monsters were flying very fast just above the midstream.

No problem. Leoni could do fast.

As she had discovered before, there was something exhilarating about being out of body, an amazing sense of freedom and boundless possibility that was almost . . . intoxicating. The feeling that you could do anything you turned your mind to. For an instant she thrust her consciousness thousands of feet into the sky and saw that the river ran through a fairy-tale domain of snow-capped mountains, steep green valleys, shining lakes and vast forests.

This was the land Ria called home.

Her sister in time.

Leoni swooped back to Sulpa's little gargoyles. They were so close to the surface of the river they seemed to be sniffing the water. She settled into position a hundred feet above and behind them but they never once looked round and flew on, covering mile after mile – perhaps as many as thirty miles, she guessed. Then, without warning, they veered to their left, crossed the riverbank and began to speed across open rising country towards a distant wall of mountains.

Leoni could see nothing that would explain why they had changed direction, yet they had swerved like heat-seeking missiles locked onto their target.

She guessed Ria and her companions must have dumped their rafts here for the river to carry away and begun to trek overland, believing they'd traveled far enough from the Illimani horde to make a safe escape. They'd been careful to leave no tracks but Sulpa's spies obviously had some other way to home in on them.

As she darted in pursuit Leoni felt a heavy responsibility. She had to help Ria somehow.

The air shivered in front of her and for a moment everything blurred, then swung back into focus.

She knew what it meant.

The Ayahuasca was wearing off. At any moment she was going to be returned to her own time and place.

She began to see the first signs – a smear of blood, a broken spear, part of a leather sandal, a pile of turds – that a large group of people had passed this way. How many had been on the rafts? Fifty? A hundred? She couldn't be sure but the further they got from Sulpa the less care they were taking to hide their tracks.

The trail led past a lake and up a steep mountainside. There was a forest here, sprawling across the slope of the mountain. The gargoyles dived eagerly amongst the trees and within seconds, still deep in the forest, had caught up with the stragglers.

They were Neanderthals, all males, dressed in skins and rough weavings. Many were bloodied with cuts and stab wounds. Some were badly injured. But Sulpa's creatures showed no interest in them. With increasing urgency and purpose, seeming more and more excited, they slalomed through the trees, shot across a broad clearing littered with corpses – had a battle been fought here? – and darted straight for a small figure being carried on an improvised stretcher in a mixed group of Neanderthals and humans.

Ria! She had been covered with wounds but fully conscious, her eyes bright and intelligent, when Leoni had glimpsed her earlier on the raft. Now she was unconscious, slumped in the stretcher, her deeply tanned skin a sickly shade of gray, her eyes ringed by huge dark circles. Most of her wounds had stopped bleeding but her leather leggings had been cut away over the outside of her right thigh to reveal an ominous dark swelling, like some frightful tumor breaking through her skin.

Leoni saw it was to this the gargoyles had been drawn.

Although it was obvious that neither the humans nor the Neanderthals could sense their presence, Sulpa's creatures had attached themselves to Ria's leg. Their leathery wings were folded and their snouty mouths were thrust directly into the tumor, making disgusting guzzling and slurping sounds. *Oh, gross!* They were in ecstasy. Their eyes had rolled up in their heads. Slurp. Suck. Suck. There was something in there they hungered for.

The air shivered again, everything turned midnight black and a vast cloud of fireworks exploded before Leoni's eyes. For an instant she could see nothing at all, seemed to be falling, seemed to be flying. The scene came back into focus just as Ria's stretcher-bearers stepped out of the belt of forest and back onto open mountainside, and the succubi unclamped their jaws from her leg and flew up into the sky.

Leoni was after them at once and by the time they leveled out at a hundred feet she was already far above them.

Ahead of Ria's little group a long line of Neanderthals trekked up the steep open grassland beyond the forest. They were stretched out in single file and the leaders were already close to the massive wall of cliffs, running for miles along the ridge-line of an interlinked chain of rugged mountains, that seemed to be their ultimate goal.

As Leoni watched she saw the lead group move aside a section of the thick undergrowth that lay at the base of the cliffs, revealing a hidden path.

She looked down. Sulpa's creatures had seen it too.

The air shivered and steadied, shivered again. Only seconds now, minutes at the most, and she would be out of here. Ria and her friends would never know Sulpa's spies had followed them and found their hiding place. Within a day he would bring his army here and slaughter them all.

Leoni was determined that must not happen. And there was a simple solution. All she had to do was kill the gargoyles.

It was tricky. Leoni was out of body, and the gargoyles were clearly some kind of aerial species too. But aerial bodies could be held, damaged, detained – the way Don Apolinar had trapped her in his net, the way she herself had fought Sulpa out of body. She remembered how it had been when she'd barreled into him – solid resistance and a massive shock, not fog passing through fog. If the same rules applied here then she might be able to do some damage to his loathsome little monsters.

She dropped very fast, aiming for a point between them, and grabbed their scaly necks as she shot past. There was an immediate slap of contact, reassuringly solid and real, and she dragged them, shrieking and flapping their wings, towards the ground, alighting close to Ria as she was carried by on her stretcher.

It was good . . . to be able to do something for her sister.

Leoni tightened her grip on the creatures' necks and felt them claw at her aerial body with their hind feet. Their wings hummed and vibrated with frantic energy, but they weren't going anywhere.

SMACK! Just like that she smashed their snouty heads together.

SMACK! A second time for good measure.

SMACK! *SMACK*! They didn't exactly have brains. Their skulls were full of smoke.

SMACK! *SMACK*! *SMACK*! *SMACK*!

Their aerial bodies were already disintegrating, evaporating, blowing away on the wind and soon Leoni was left holding nothing.

Another shiver of the air, very strong this time, before the image of the mountainside and the ragged column of fleeing Neanderthals came back into focus. As well as Ria, Leoni had counted only three other humans amongst the entire group, one also on a stretcher, the other two walking but with injuries.

She tried to imagine what events had led up to this moment, deep in prehistory, to which she was an invisible witness. Ria and her friends had made common cause with the Neanderthals to fight Sulpa. So much the Angel had told her. And Sulpa was in their land with his Illimani army to hunt down and kill those same Neanderthals – the last Neanderthals who would ever live on Earth – because he wanted to murder their goodness and innocence.

So there was something very special about this group of refugees fleeing up a mountainside in northern Spain. Something very precious and special. Something of great value that had to be protected.

She looked for Ria. The stretcher-bearers had already carried her hundreds of feet higher up the mountain towards the hidden path, and soon she would be safe.

Then a terrible thought struck Leoni. She had killed the little spies but whatever it was in that wound on Ria's leg that had led them to her was still there.

It had to be extracted now or Sulpa would send more spies after her to sniff her out wherever she hid.

Leoni darted forward. Somehow she had to warn the injured unconscious girl.

The air shivered again.

Chapter Sixty-Five

Ria's eyes snapped open and straight away she was fully conscious and aware of her surroundings. "Stop!" she tried to shout, surprised at the weakness of her voice. She switched to thought-talk: "Stop. Please."

Grondin was carrying the front of her stretcher. He looked around and sent her his thought-voice. "We have to get to Secret Place fast. Very dangerous to stop. Maybe followed."

"We must stop!" Ria pulsed. "Sulpa shot something into my leg."

"Not stop now. Many need healing. All wait to get to Secret Place."

"NO! You don't understand. Sulpa shot something into my leg. It's still there. If we take it into Secret Place it's going to lead him to us."

"How you know this? You been sleeping long time."

Before she answered, Ria raised her head and looked around. They were on the mountainside beneath the cliffs that guarded Secret Place – far too close. Up ahead some of the Uglies had already reached the entrance. The mad Illimani kid Driff was carrying the rear of her stretcher. Over there were Ligar and Brindle, also on stretchers, each carried by two big Ugly braves from Grondin's war party. Ria felt a lurch of concern to see that Brindle was still unconscious. Jergat and Oplimar were both walking, Bont, too, nursing his big axe as though it was a baby. There were cuts and bruises all over his body, but of the spear wound to his back, healed by the Uglies, there was almost no trace.

Mixing words and images Ria showed Grondin the amazing girl with golden hair who'd come to her in a dream just moments earlier. It was the same girl who'd warned her about the tree-birds in the spirit world, but now you could see through her as though she were made of water or air. She seemed hugely excited and alarmed. As before she shouted in a language that meant nothing to Ria. But this time her words were accompanied by fleeting images and emotions and a message came through with complete and awful clarity. Something lay concealed deep inside the swollen wound that Sulpa's little dart had made in her thigh. As long as it was there he would be able to find her. Then the girl disappeared and Ria woke up.

"Dreams not same as visions," said Grondin. "Cannot always believe them."

"I've seen this girl once before," Ria replied. "The Little Teachers brought her to me. I was in danger then and she gave me a true warning. That's why I believe her now."

Grondin stopped and he and Driff laid down her stretcher. Ria still couldn't get used to the Illimani's wild blue eyes or read the expression in them – but then, how could she ever hope to know what lay in the mind of a savage such as this? As other stragglers filed past them and continued to make their way up the mountain, Grondin crouched at her side, a small sharp flensing knife in his hand. Ria looked down at the weeping swelling on her thigh. "Cut it open," she said. "Let's find out what's in there."

The pain of Grondin's knife exploring the wound was unlike anything Ria had ever experienced before. Even though she had braced herself, her shrieks rose to the sky, sweat drenched her brow and a stream of terrible oaths poured from her mouth. Driff knelt beside her, holding her steady as Grondin cut and cut. Then something seemed to burst and a mass of pus and blood spewed out of the wound.

Grondin probed with his fingers. There was less pain now. "Nothing inside," he reported.

"No! There is! You have to cut deeper!"

"You crazy," said Grondin.

Dripping with sweat, shaking, dizzy, Ria shrugged off Driff's restraining grip, sat bolt upright, grabbed the big Ugly's jerkin and glared into his eyes: "You must cut deeper," she pulsed.

Grondin was reluctant. "Don't want hurt your leg. Maybe you become lame. There is nothing inside."

Ria gasped with frustration and snatched the flensing knife from his hands. "Then I'm doing it myself," she told him.

Grondin gently took the knife back. She could sense his conflicted feelings. "One more cut," he agreed.

As the knife went in Ria screamed again. "AHHHHHHHHHHHHHHHHH!!!" The pain was unbelievable, but just as she was sure she could bear no more the tip of the blade snagged on something deep within her flesh.

Something that *writhed.*

Grondin hunched forward, peered into the wound, probed again with the knife, grunted and suddenly twisted his wrist. There came a second writhing clench within her flesh, followed by a sharp tug and Ria gasped as another huge explosion of pain hit her.

She looked down.

Skewered on the tip of Grondin's knife, but alive and struggling, was the front end of a disgusting maggot or slug, slimy and black, long as a human tongue. It was anchored in Ria's flesh by its rear end, which she could see was swollen into a bulb and covered with little hooks. She watched, fascinated, as Grondin carefully pulled more of its body free, dragging the hooks loose one by one until, with a wet *plop*, the whole creature was out.

He placed it on a boulder that lay nearby and cut it in half.

But each half immediately took on a life of its own and there were two new slugs where one had been before.

Driff looked at them in horror. "Sulpa?" He seemed to be asking a question. In the chaos of the river escape, Ria realized, he probably hadn't seen his former master firing his little dart into her.

Despite her pain she limped over. "Yes . . . They're Sulpa's work."

The wriggling black slugs were at the edge of the rock now, leaving thick trails of bloodied slime. They couldn't be allowed to escape into the ground. But before Ria's bruised body could react Grondin stepped in ahead of her and pinched one of the loathsome little creatures in each hand, his big, hard fingers gripping them tight as they writhed and twisted. Ria sensed some sort of thought-talk taking place between Grondin and Driff but she couldn't catch it. Then Driff rushed back to the tree line and began to make a small fire where the canopy of leaves and branches would dissipate the smoke.

Grondin strode down to join him, with Ria hobbling after. She arrived in time to see them place both slugs into the heart of the fire, holding them in place with sticks. The creatures squirmed, and screams that sounded almost human burst out of them as their flesh bubbled and split. They began to expand, growing to the size of a man's hands, thrashing and flailing before exploding – *WHOOSH*! – in clouds of pungent sooty smoke that roiled up into the trees. The few remaining scraps of black flesh crackled and burned, and soon there was nothing left but flames and glowing embers.

Ria looked up into the canopy where the last of the smoke could still be seen melting away amongst the leaves. A feeling of unease came over her. Was this the end of the matter? Or would traces of Sulpa's creatures somehow remain for him to sniff out and follow? She shrugged. Either way there was nothing more she could do about it. As she turned back towards the mountainside a bout of dizziness shook her and darkness welled up behind her eyes. She collapsed in a heap, only faintly aware of Driff's strong arms catching her before she hit the ground.

Then came oblivion.

Chapter Sixty-Six

"Thank God." The voice was Bannerman's. "I think she's coming out of it."

Leoni was in her own body. She hadn't yet opened her eyes but she'd been conscious of her surroundings for a few moments. She was in a hot, shadowy room, on a bed, with a light sheet draped over her legs. She could hear a persistent fly buzzing and bumping into a windowpane. Bannerman and the person he'd just spoken to were both sitting by her bed and one of them – he had a dry, gentle, reassuring grip – was holding her hand.

She opened one eye.

Oh, good. It was Matt.

Leoni felt content for about half a second until her memories of Ria's world began to flood back.

Those wild mountains and moorlands.

And the dreadful threat of Sulpa and the Illimani.

Had she succeeded in warning her time-sister about the tracking device in her leg?

Or had she fucking failed?

She'd felt so pleased with herself for killing Sulpa's gremlins, but if she hadn't got that simple message through in her last frantic moments with Ria then it would all have been in vain.

She needed to go back. Right now!

Leoni opened her eyes and sat up, taking a great gulp of breath. Matt pulled his hand away as though scalded. Bannerman was on his feet so fast his chair crashed over: "Leoni!" He sounded relieved. "Are you OK?"

She blinked and looked around the room, getting her bearings. It was one of the outhouses near the *maloca* – a dorm with a dozen beds where they'd left their bags and changed into loose clothes just before last night's session. Her bed – she must have been carried to it unconscious – was closest to the door. The others were empty but had an untidy, slept-in look. Although the sun seemed to be shining outside there were thick drapes on the windows that filtered out much of the light.

"Are you all right?" Bannerman repeated.

Leoni could hear the stress in his voice. He probably thought she'd fried her brains taking too many of his weird drugs. "I don't know," she replied. "I've had a very strange night . . ."

"You went deep with the Ayahuasca. We couldn't wake you."

Leoni sat up in the bed and put her hand on Bannerman's arm: "I have to drink again," she whispered. "I have to drink right now. I was pulled back too soon from the place Aya took me to. Someone's in danger and I've got to help her . . ."

Bannerman held up his hand: "Slow down, Leoni. Take your time. Which place? Who's in danger?"

"It doesn't matter." Leoni realized she was close to shouting. "I'll explain later, OK? Right now I need to drink more Aya. I have to. You've got to help me."

Bannerman looked severe: "There's a problem with that."

The problem was Don Emmanuel. "He's not doing well," Matt said. "He woke this morning totally freaked out. I mean really gibbering."

"A most extreme and unexpected reaction for such an experienced practitioner," Bannerman was saying when Mary Ruck walked in. She saw Leoni and her face lit up in a smile. "Welcome back!" she whooped, darting to her side to embrace her. "You've had a long journey."

The news about Don Emmanuel had depressed Leoni and when Mary was through hugging her she asked about him. The older woman became grave: "Last night, soon after you drank your third cup, Don Emmanuel also drank again. Like you, he went very deep. My guess is he suffered . . . shall we say a psychic ordeal? This happens to shamans sometimes. When he snapped out of it a few hours ago he was . . . traumatized."

"Raving," Matt corrected.

Mary flashed him an irritated look: "Well, anyway, he's already much better. I just left him in the *maloca*. He's awake but he hasn't told us what happened yet."

"I know what happened to him," said Leoni. "I was held prisoner on another world" – you could say that kind of thing to this group of people and they'd understand. "He came to rescue me but the body he was in was killed . . ."

Mary's eyes had opened wide. "Killed?" she asked. "By what?"

"By the shaman who took me prisoner. Don Apolinar. They transformed into different kinds of animals. They fought each other. Don Emmanuel wasn't strong enough to beat him."

"Don Apolinar!" Mary whistled. "Shit!"

"You *know* him?"

"He's a *brujo* – a sorcerer. Everyone in Iquitos is afraid of him. But if they want to use black magic to murder a love rival or zombify an enemy he's the one they go to. Very bad guy."

Mary and Bannerman were both adamant, over Leoni's protestations, that they felt a duty to protect her and would not allow her to drink Ayahuasca again immediately. "A shaman has to control the ritual," Mary insisted. "You've seen the dangers now, and you know why it's a must. If Don Emmanuel recovers he can give you the brew tonight . . . Anyway," she added, "we all have important work to do before you drink again . . ."

Leoni had awoken just before three p.m. By six, after a frugal dinner, with the velvet darkness of a jungle evening closing in, the whole group was seated in a circle in the *maloca* to review the previous night's session. With the exception of Leoni's few remarks it was to be the first time any of the participants had heard anything about the others' experiences – for on Bannerman's insistence there had been no comparing of notes during the day. Don Emmanuel himself would not join in this "sharing" (as Mary called it). The little Shipibo shaman had quietly helped himself to a further cup of Ayahuasca and now lay still on his mattress in a corner of the room.

Matt spoke first, describing what he had seen and experienced under the influence of Ayahuasca. Bannerman was next, then Mary. Despite differences in the details of their accounts it was soon obvious to all of them that something extraordinary was going on.

Ayahuasca had swept Bannerman away "like a whirlwind." He was taken up into a heavenly realm and confronted by a majestic winged woman seated on a golden throne. She had indigo skin spangled with golden stars. "Protect Leoni," she told him.

Amidst endless jungle, at the foot of a towering capirona tree, Matt stood face to face with a cerulean jaguar who spoke to him in the voice of a woman. "Protect Leoni," she told him.

Mary was carried down through crystal caverns to the lair of Sachamama deep underground. A giant anaconda with amethyst scales reared before her: "Protect Leoni," she commanded.

In each case the encounter was loaded with powerful significance, and each of them emerged from the experience convinced they must do what had been asked of them – that in some profound sense it was their task, and their commitment, to protect Leoni through this extraordinary time.

But what did that mean?

It was Leoni's turn to speak of her night journey.

"So the bottom line," Matt summarized an hour later, "is there's this girl Ria twenty-four thousand years ago who's the only person in the world with the balls to stand up to Sulpa and stop him slaughtering the Neanderthals. This matters to us because if Sulpa gets his way with the Neanderthals he devours their primal goodness and transforms it into evil – which he then uses to complete his jump into the twenty-first century. Our secret weapons are Ria and Leoni. We also have a supernatural ally – the Blue Angel. She's the same being who's called 'Our Lady of the Forest' here in the Amazon and, as we all know, she has many other forms and identities as well. She's what the ancients would have called a goddess, I guess, and she's used her power to entangle Leoni with Ria in some sort of advanced, hard-to-understand quantum manner that potentially gives them the strength to defeat Sulpa. Since Our Lady of the Forest is also the spirit of the Ayahuasca vine it's not surprising she's used altered states of consciousness to bring them together. I'd say our task is to make certain Leoni can keep returning to Ria's time-frame – which means more Ayahuasca – and to protect her physically and spiritually while she's there."

Bannerman spoke next: "I don't claim to understand this transpersonal experience we've all just had, I don't understand how past and present can intersect, and I particularly don't understand how a so-called hallucination can give the same instructions to different people." He took a breath: "As a scientist I could dig into all this for years – as a matter of fact, I intend to do so – but whatever's happening here is extraordinary enough to justify setting the science aside for now." He locked eyes with Leoni: "Despite the difficult journey you obviously had last night, the proposal seems to be that you do more Aya sessions while the rest of us provide you with a safe space in which to explore . . . these experiences . . . I'm ready to go with that if it's truly what you want." He looked around the room. "I think we all are."

"It's absolutely what I want," said Leoni. "I can't explain it. How I feel about Ria. But I'm not going to let Sulpa get his hands on her if there's any way I can prevent it."

"My one concern . . ." Bannerman hesitated.

"Yes?"

"My one concern is the way the Aya hit you last night. I've studied the medical literature and generally the brew is safe. But a few individuals have had exceptional reactions. There have been deaths. A handful of people who were already mentally unstable became psychotic . . ."

"I don't believe it's going to kill me or drive me mad," Leoni said, cutting him short. "This is the first worthwhile thing I've ever done in my life and I'm not going to stop now."

From the corner of the room where Don Emmanuel lay came a loud groan. The little shaman sat up wrapped in a sheet and gabbled some sentences in Spanish.

Leoni became alert as she recognized her own name, followed by the names Apolinar and Jack.

Strange.

She didn't remember anybody mentioning Jack to Don Emmanuel.

Chapter Sixty-Seven

Little by little Ria's consciousness returned, as though she had dived deep into a pool of darkness and was now swimming up again – up, up, up towards the light. She could hear sounds of movement around her, shuffling footsteps, a fire crackling, and further off the grunts and bleats of a herd of red deer. She didn't need to open her eyes to know exactly where she was and she felt no fear when a small leathery hand touched her face and smoothed back her hair. The contact was gentle and compassionate, as though her own long-lost mother had returned to comfort her, and her stomach rumbled at the homely smells of rabbit roasting nearby.

A disturbing memory clamored for her attention – the golden-haired spirit girl who'd warned her of Sulpa's vile creature buried in her thigh. Her fingers strayed to the place where Grondin had cut deep with his flensing knife, but the ragged wound he'd made was mostly healed with no swelling and very little pain.

Then everything else came back to her in a rush. The ghastly deaths of Hond and Rill. The show trial. The treachery of Murgh and Grigo. The almost unbelievable massacre of the Clan. Everyone she knew and loved, slaughtered like animals by Sulpa's demonic army.

Could it be so? Could such a terrible thing really have happened?

Surely it must all prove to be some nightmare? Not the truth.

Surely not the truth.

She opened her eyes to find herself prone on a bed of soft skins. Ancient oaks towered overhead and sweet morning light diffused down to her through their leaves. Merina, the magic woman of the Uglies, was kneeling by her side, gazing at her with sadness: "The Clan is no more, Ria. This is something you must accept . . ."

Ria choked back a howl of anguish: "There are survivors. I will find them."

"If there are survivors we will help you find them," pulsed Merina, "and bring them to safety here."

Ria raised herself on one arm and turned sideways to face the magic woman. "Where's Brindle?" she asked, fearing the worst. "And my two Clansmen – Bont and Ligar? Are they OK? What about Jergat and Oplimar? And Driff, the Illimani kid? They were all injured in the fighting."

"All have been given healing," Merina reassured her. "All are well. They will come to us soon." Her brown eyes twinkled: "*You* needed much healing, Ria. While you slept. So many wounds on such a small body. But you have fought the Evil One! And lived to fight another day! Few can say that."

"I did nothing, Merina. It was Grondin turning up with a hundred braves who got us out of there."

"You did much! Grondin himself has told me. Brindle has spoken. Oplimar and Jergat, too. You are clever. You have courage in battle and keep a clear head. You are young but others look to you to lead them. Spirits chose you to fight the Evil One – that's what Brindle's father said."

"I don't believe I've been chosen by anybody."

"I was told to give the five throwing stones to you and you alone, Ria of the Clan. You *have* been chosen! This also you must accept."

"The stones are gone." For some reason Ria felt guilty as she admitted it, but she refused to hang her head. "All five of them."

Merina smiled: "Don't grieve their loss. I've heard how well you used them. Besides" – an image of the blue woman appeared in Ria's mind – "Our Lady of the Forest has other gifts for you. You must eat the Little Teachers tonight."

The hundred braves who had rescued Ria and her companions from the massacre were from the Uglies' outlying camps. Grondin had found them on the south side of the Snake, already on the march towards Secret Place. While the braves had fought the Illimani and escaped on the river, their females, children and elderly had completed the journey overland. The result was the population of the Ugly hideaway had more than doubled since Ria had last seen it two days before. But the floor of the vast Cave of Visions easily accommodated every member of the enlarged community.

Ria sat with Bont, Ligar, Driff, Jergat and Oplimar in places of honor next to Brindle and Grondin. As Merina had promised, all had received the healing magic of the Uglies and even the more severe injuries were mending well. Ligar, crippled by a spear thrust deep into the muscle of his buttock, was on his feet again and could even run. Brindle, knocked out in a dead coma by an axe blow to the head, was wide awake, animated and excited. Ria's aching rib no longer troubled her. Her other wounds, including the laceration of her thigh muscle where Grondin had cut out Sulpa's creature, had closed and healed and seemed to have been inflicted months before, not yesterday.

Despite all her sorrow Ria was happy to be reunited with Brindle and she too felt energized when she should have been paying the price of days of beatings and accumulated exhaustion. "Healing channels the life force," Brindle explained. "Of course it wakes you up."

After yesterday's fight against the Illimani, the events of the escape, and the miraculous healings they had witnessed and benefited from, Bont and Ligar were changed men. Everything they had ever been told or believed about the Uglies had been proved wrong, they admitted to Ria, and they found themselves not amongst cruel, stupid savages as they had feared but amongst kind-hearted and intelligent human creatures who had saved their lives and brought them to refuge here in this hidden place. When Ria asked the two Clansmen to join in tonight's vision quest they agreed, accepting her promise they would not come to harm from eating the mushrooms the Uglies called the Little Teachers.

Driff sat close to Ria, glowing like the others from the healing process. She knew Grondin and Brindle had both thought-talked with him, but so far she hadn't been able to do the same. Since he'd saved her from certain death she was more open to the idea of forgiving him for being an Illimani but she still wasn't sure she liked him at all. He was good-looking, fast on his feet, strong and well put together, and yesterday he'd fought . . .

(*like a demon*).

But he still had a long way to go before she could start thinking of him as a friend.

Soon Ria could feel the Little Teachers beginning to take effect.

She breathed in deep. She was ready for this.

A wave of giddiness struck her but she forced herself to her feet and found her way to the same patch of the rock wall, bone white and glistening, that had attracted her attention three nights earlier. Once again she stood before it and brought her eyes close to its shimmering reflections. Then the dizziness surged back. She crumpled in a heap to the floor and felt herself leave her body and pass through the rock into the tunnel of water and sky that lay beyond. She surrendered to the current and allowed it to sweep her out of the night of the cave and into the bright daylight of the spirit world with its familiar twin suns.

Ria had expected she would arrive again in the meadow of green flowers, but this time, although she was provided with the same body wearing the same strange clothing as before, the tunnel brought her out at a different location – high up on a hillside overlooking a broad valley. In the valley floor sat a camp like none she had ever imagined. A thousand times larger than the Clan's camp, it consisted of countless towering structures of wood and stone arranged in a perfect circle and surrounded by a vast stockade.

Standing with her head turned in profile a few paces lower down the hillside was the spirit woman with deep blue skin whom the Uglies called Our Lady of the Forest. She was awesomely beautiful and dressed in wondrous garments that shimmered and changed color with any slight movement she made. Her voice was rich and strong: "I can help you defeat Sulpa. He is my enemy as well as yours."

"You're a spirit," said Ria as she reached her side, positioning herself a little higher up the slope so their eyes were at the same level. "You look like a powerful one. Why don't you just defeat him yourself?"

"I cannot defeat him in your world."

"I heard that. My friend Brindle told me, but I didn't believe him."

"Nevertheless, it is true . . ."

"I should have known! The Uglies never lie about anything . . ." Ria paused and thought back. "Brindle said Sulpa is a demon."

"Amongst the very worst of demonkind."

"And that you had him chained up for a long time, but he escaped?"

"He fled into a human body where he is beyond our power. In that body, if he is not stopped, he will destroy your world."

"I'm going to stop him."

"I have confidence in that. It's why I chose you . . . and one other to fight alongside you. She is the first of three gifts I bring you today."

Out of nowhere the blue woman had conjured a peculiar square wooden frame, about two spans on each side, with what looked like a sheet of glistening water stretched tightly across it.

"Look here," she said. She held the frame up for inspection.

At first Ria saw nothing, was not even sure what she was expected to see, until slowly, in the shining surface, the face of the golden-haired girl began to appear.

"I know her," she whispered. She craned her neck to peek behind the frame. "She saved my life. Is she a spirit? Like you?"

"She is human. Like you. Her name is Leoni. She too fights Sulpa."

"Then why do I only see her in dreams and visions?"

"Because she is not yet born."

"I don't understand."

"She lives a thousand generations in the future . . ."

"I still don't understand . . ."

"It is not necessary to understand, only to act. You cannot defeat Sulpa now without Leoni's help, and Sulpa cannot be defeated in her time unless he is defeated now. Together you and she possess great strength that neither of you have yet imagined. Better you meet in dreams and visions than not meet at all."

"I feel like you're using us," said Ria. "Both of us. To fight your battles for you."

"Have I not already said as much? Sulpa is in human form, so of course it is humans who must fight him . . ."

Ria gave the blue woman a ferocious look: "I saw you with my parents. The last time I ate the Little Teachers. I saw you with my mother and father and they were alive even though I know they're dead. What was going on there?"

"There are realms in which your mother and father still live."

"Can I see them again?"

"Perhaps there will be a time for that."

"If it's only 'perhaps,' why did you even show them to me in the first place? Are you trying to drive me mad?"

"It was a test. The balance you draw between love and reason. I had to be sure I chose well when I chose you to fight Sulpa."

Ria was getting angry. Whatever made this being think she had the right to test her for anything? Or decide who or what she was to fight?

But then she remembered Hond and Rill and swallowed her pride. The truth was she did want to fight Sulpa. She wanted to destroy him. Any way it could be done. "You said you have three gifts for me today," she said.

The blue woman held up a glittering crystal, smaller than an acorn but with a thousand intricate facets. "This is my second gift," she said. She leaned forward, holding it between her thumb and forefinger. "Accept it and you will have the power to speak and understand all languages."

Ria thought about Driff. It would be good to know the Illimani tongue. She'd be able to get much more out of him that way to use against Sulpa.

And she thought of the neighboring human tribes in near and distant valleys – the Ree, the Jicaque, the Merell, the Dirker, the Naveen, the Sher, the Yona, the Spearjig, and many others whose names she could not bring to mind. She thought of the strandwalkers called the Aine who lived along the borders of the Great Sea, and of the fierce mountain folk called the Kosh who hunted mammoths in the tall ranges to the east. All these different peoples – isolated, scattered, mutually hostile, ignorant of one another's languages – would be in grave danger from Sulpa, and some had perhaps already suffered the same fate he had inflicted on the Clan. Ria did not doubt he intended to pick them off one by one and annihilate them all, and knew in a flash that her task was to unite them against him. This would be much easier if she spoke their languages.

"Only a fool would refuse such a gift," she said.

The spirit woman's right hand shot out, and with the speed of a striking snake she plunged the crystal deep into Ria's temple. "You have the gift of languages," she told her. "Use it well."

"Ahh!" Ria gasped. The pain was excruciating. She put her hand to her forehead but found no wound there.

"The pain will pass," said the woman. "Now look here, please. My third gift for you." She held up the frame. This time the water was not still but swirled in a spiral and Ria found herself first drawn into it, then falling through it.

Then it was night again and she was no longer in the blue woman's realm. The moon was nearly full, high in the sky, and she was flying, out of her body, over the mountains and valleys of her homeland.

She looked at her legs, arms, hands and realized that she could see through parts of herself to the ground far below – that she was as transparent as the night sky. Invisible! Weightless! Flying faster than any bird, without any flapping of wings, simply by directing herself here or there.

As she recovered from the initial surprise she paid more attention to where she was. Winding amidst dense forest, she recognized a deep, precipitous, rocky gorge through which, with much rush and noise, tumbled the foaming headwaters of the Snake River. This was the wild region, claimed by no single tribe, known as the Gate of Horn. It was a day's hard march upstream of the Clan camp and Ria had been here just a few months before on a hunting expedition with her brothers.

Movement caught her eye.

Ahead, scurrying across a wide clearing, casting long shadows in the bright moonlight she saw a group of people – twenty at least, maybe thirty.

Ria dived towards them, swooping so low she was skimming the treetops. There were men and women in the group. And children. Hope stirred as she began to recognize faces. These were survivors of Sulpa's massacre of the Clan! Then she was amongst them, excited, crying out, trying to embrace them, but they couldn't see or hear her.

They were obviously terrified. Running from the horror of the Illimani horde. Running for their lives in the dead of night. Many were wounded. All seemed exhausted. The kids and the elderly were falling further and further behind.

Disembodied and invisible, Ria let them stream past her.

Last of all, hundreds of paces behind everyone else, was a little family group, a mother and two small children. Perhaps it was because the hair had been singed entirely from one side of the mother's head, or because her eye was swollen closed, or because the little boy and girl were so battered and dirty, that Ria didn't recognize them at first.

Then it came to her. The mother was Sabeth, Bont's wife. And the two children were Nibo and Maura, his son and daughter.

An irresistible force drew Ria up into the sky.

Up amongst the stars.

A gaping hole opened at her feet and she tumbled through it into a whirling tunnel.

When she awoke in her own body on the floor of the Cave of Visions she knew exactly what she had to do.

Chapter Sixty-Eight

As Mary translated, occasionally stopping him to clarify a word or phrase, Don Emmanuel told them why, despite the terrors of the night before, he had drunk the brew again this evening.

First, he was an Ayahuasca shaman. If he was too afraid to drink then he would be obliged to abandon his calling – which he was not prepared to do. He needed to prove to himself he could master his fear.

Secondly, he wished to spy on Don Apolinar. With the help of the brew he had traveled out of body to the *brujo's* home in Iquitos. He was alert to the danger that Apolinar might sense his presence. But finding his enemy in the midst of a ritual to summon a spirit and oblivious to all other things, Emmanuel had made himself smaller than a fly and settled in to observe.

Apolinar sat in a high-backed wooden chair in a dimly lit room. He was alone, but positioned a few feet in front of him, set at an angle so that he could not see his own reflection, was an ornate full-length mirror with an antique scratched and stained surface. Apolinar was rapidly repeating the single word "JACK" in a low sibilant whisper while staring into this tilted mirror.

Slowly, Emmanuel said, he began to see what it was that the *brujo* had called.

An amorphous mass of darkness was welling up within the glass, seething, chaotic, stormy darkness shot through with glints of lightning. And as the mass swirled and turned, threatening to burst free from the confines of the mirror, an imperious voice boomed forth from it and demanded: "*¿PARA QUÉ ME HAS INVOCADO?*" ["FOR WHAT HAVE YOU SUMMONED ME?"]

"*Para alertarlo, Señor,*" stammered Apolinar. "*Se trata de esta muchacha.*" ["To warn you, Lord . . . There is a girl."] "With my magic I entered her mind and learned her thoughts. She seeks your destruction."

"Many seek my destruction." The voice was quieter now.

"This one is special. She has the force. And the Lady of the Forests protects her."

In the mirror the thundercloud seemed to heave and swell: "THE NAME OF THIS GIRL?"

"Her name is Leoni. Give me power and I will lead you to her."

The voice from the cloud fell to a hiss: "You have a knife, Don Apolinar?"

The *brujo* seemed puzzled by the question: "Yes . . . ?"

"Show me the knife."

Emmanuel described how, with a flourish, Apolinar pulled a thin long-bladed dagger from the pocket of his white suit . . .

"Good," said the voice. "Excellent. Now cut your throat, please . . ."

"My throat? But . . ."

"One deep slice from ear to ear."

Apolinar had struggled, but it was as though his body was not under his control. Very slowly, fighting against himself, he brought the knife up to his throat until the blade nicked his skin and a rivulet of blood ran over his shirt collar and down onto the shoulder of his white suit.

"From ear to ear, Don Apolinar. *Now,* please!"

Again the blade cut. Deeper this time. Blood flowed.

"But I can help you," the *brujo* sobbed. "I am your slave . . ."

"*Give me power and I will lead you to her,*" mimicked the voice from the mirror, then suddenly ramped up the volume "YOU DON'T BARGAIN WITH ME, SLAVE. YOU JUST DO WHAT I WANT."

"Yes, master! Yes! My word on it." The jacket of Apolinar's suit was streaked red, and fat drops of his blood dripped to the floor around the chair. "Whatever you require. I beg you, do not kill me. I and my magic are yours to command."

"Your magic? Ha! I DO NOT NEED YOUR CONJURING TRICKS. You are a WORM."

"Then let this worm take you to the girl, master . . . I know the jungle. I can be of service."

"Can a worm be of service?" The cloud in the mirror seemed to consider the matter and relent. "Perhaps so. Perhaps after all I can find a use . . . for a jungle worm."

The blade still cut into Apolinar's mangled throat but now, Emmanuel reported, the *brujo* was allowed to drop his hand to his side and let the knife fall. The cloud roiled and billowed within the mirror and the voice spoke again: "When my servants reach you tomorrow you will take them to the girl. They will know what to do with her."

Apolinar sat slumped in the chair, his breath coming in ragged gasps, and slowly, like a thick gas seeping away, the cloud began to recede – but then, with shocking speed, came boiling back again.

As he felt Jack's attention burn into him, and Apolinar's eyes swivel in his direction, Emmanuel fled.

He knew no more of what took place in that room.

Don Emmanuel had been told very little about Leoni's case but he could not be kept in the dark any longer. The connection between Jack and Sulpa, the role of the Blue Angel, whom he knew as "Our Lady of the Forest," the connection with Ria, Leoni's troubled life history, and the pressing, imperative need for her to continue to work with Ayahuasca were all explained to him.

"We're in grave danger," he said when Mary had interpreted everything. Jack and Apolinar both knew he had spied on their conversation and although Jack's "servants" might not arrive until tomorrow there was nothing to stop the *brujo* rounding up a gang of local thugs and bringing them here tonight by fast motorboat.

Iquitos was Apolinar's stronghold so there was no question of attempting to escape in that direction.

But there was an alternative.

Two hundred miles to the south along the Ucayali, one of the mighty tributaries of the Amazon, lay the homelands of the Shipibo, Don Emmanuel's own tribe. There were no roads in that region. No electricity or piped water. It was a land of small villages, some strung out in plain view along the banks of the river, others hidden away in isolated creeks and backwaters. They could take refuge there, Don Emmanuel promised, where no one could find them. The work with Ayahuasca could continue. He looked apologetically at Leoni. He regretted he had failed to protect her from Apolinar in the spirit world. The *brujo* was too powerful. But in the Shipibo heartland there were shamans far more powerful than he who walked the path of light and would come to the circle to strengthen their defenses. "Evil confronts us," Don Emmanuel said, "but it can be fought."

* * *

All the supplies they needed for the journey upriver were at the lodge – gasoline for the outboard motor, fresh water, food, medicine. There was a tight sense of urgency but loading and stowing everything still required two hours and it was after midnight when they pushed off from the jetty.

Heavy clouds filled the sky, obscuring the moon, and the warm darkness felt thick as a blanket to Leoni. As they turned south against the current she looked back to the north, the direction of Iquitos, and saw a light flash in the distance.

There it was again.

Matt had already spotted it. "It's a boat," he said. The light flashed a third time, glancing off the water. "A fast boat, coming this way."

Chapter Sixty-Nine

Nobody doubted the truth of the vision Ria had received as her third gift.

Survivors of the Clan, Bont's wife and children amongst them, had fled east into the forests of the wild hill country called the Gate of Horn. An attempt had to be made to rescue them.

The Gate was claimed by no single tribe and, by long convention, any could hunt there. The most direct way to reach it from Secret Place lay through the Clan's territory, but this would be a perilous route with the main Illimani force, thousands strong, in full control there. The alternative was to head further south before cutting back north and east again towards the Gate of Horn, and this meant passing through the lands of the Merell and the Naveen – tribes as hostile to the Clan as they were to each other. They were the least promising candidates for the army Ria intended to bring together to confront Sulpa's horde. But she had to start somewhere and there was no time to lose. Besides, it was a safe guess the Illimani would be boiling out in all directions, killing everyone they met, putting their marks of ownership on the land, so the main problem by any route was going to be avoiding them.

Ria had assumed, without question, that Brindle would join the expedition. They had been through so much together, and she counted on him. So it came as a blow when he told her, as they walked side by side out of the Cave of Visions, that he could not accompany her this time.

She was surprised how hurt she felt: "I suppose you've got more important things to do now you're king."

"No!" Brindle protested. "It's not that!" He projected a thought-image of the blue woman into Ria's mind. "There's a fourth gift," he explained. "Our Lady of the Forest gave three to you last night, but the fourth one she gave to me. That's why I must stay. She wants me to build it at once – right here at Secret Place. It's to help us fight Sulpa."

"I don't understand . . ."

For a moment Brindle looked exasperated. "The fourth gift is an idea," he said. "It's a picture Our Lady of the Forest put in my head." As he spoke he shared the image. It came through with enormous force and Ria gasped at the richly textured bird's-eye view he had sent her of three huge concentric circles of tall upright stones. "This is what I'm supposed to build," he said. "What do you make of it?"

Ria found she could move around Brindle's thought picture to examine it from different perspectives, and felt herself reacting as though it were really there. It was deeply strange. Even as an image it seemed to radiate a brooding and menacing power.

She counted an outer ring of thirty gray stones, all massive, some rising to twice the height of a man, and thick around the base where they were set solidly into the earth. Their shapes were irregular, rough, weather-beaten. They were patched with lichen like any natural rock. But their arrangement into a perfect circle a hundred paces across was obviously designed. A second circle, made up of twenty black stones – these ones about Ria's height – was placed inside the first. It was fifty paces across. At the center of the whole contraption was a third circle, twenty paces across, of eight gigantic, roughly conical white stones, each one almost four times the height of a man.

"It's beautiful," Ria said as the amazing thought-picture evaporated. "I've never seen anything like it. But how's it going to help us fight Sulpa?"

"It's a stone gateway . . ."

"Which means what?"

Brindle shrugged: "Our Lady didn't tell me that. She just told me to build it."

To Ria the whole mysterious task seemed impossible, beyond natural power. How could so many stones that big ever be found – let alone moved?

"Our Lady told me where to find them," said Brindle picking up her thoughts. "She told me how Uglies can lift them, how we can make them stand up. She told me where I must place them."

"Where?"

Brindle turned to indicate the entrance of the vast cavern behind them. "Inside the Cave of Visions," he said. "That's where they have to go."

* * *

Brindle wanted to send a war party of a hundred braves to escort Ria but she declined. "We need to stay out of sight," she said. "A hundred is way too many for that, but it's nowhere near enough if we get dragged into a pitched battle with a larger force."

Over Brindle's objections she insisted a small group was much safer and since she and her companions had forged a strong bond over the past days they were the ones who should go. "Give me Grondin," she said. "He's my rock. I need him with us, Jergat and Oplimar as well. I'll be taking Bont and Ligar, of course. Driff, too. That makes seven including me. We'll move fast, leave no trail, find the survivors and we'll all get back here alive."

"OK, Ria," said Brindle, "I know you always do things your way." He shrugged and changed the subject: "You accept Driff now?" he asked.

Ria thought about it: "I guess so. But I can't figure him out. What did you do to him? How did you get him to turn traitor on his own people?"

A look of mild annoyance flared in Brindle's eyes: "Driff is the first of the Illimani to do the right thing. That doesn't make him a traitor. Could be it makes him a hero. All I did was help him see the truth."

"Would be nice if more of them could be helped to see the truth. That many less for us to fight."

Brindle considered the proposition: "I made a rope with Driff, remember? He thought you were a crazy woman who would kill him for sure. I took his side, protected him from you. He saw I was his friend. From then on I could reach him. It won't be so easy to get close to other Illimani. If we can't get close to them we can't make a rope with them."

Feeling suddenly awkward, Ria embraced Brindle. "Make the stone circles," she said, "whatever they're for." She feigned a stern look. "I expect to see them complete when I get back."

After their night in the Cave of Visions, Bont and Ligar had both opened up to the thought-talk of the Uglies and begun to converse with them in a rudimentary way. Perhaps this enhanced level of communication was a natural effect of the Little Teachers – or perhaps it was because the blue woman had done exactly what she'd promised when she implanted the crystal – but Ria soon found herself exchanging images with Driff, then words and phrases. By the end of the first morning of the march they were thought-talking with increasing fluency, occasionally slipping into out-loud speech. And to the surprise of the others in the group, what they were speaking was *his* guttural alien language. Soon Ria stopped noticing how weird this was and began using her new gift to learn about the enemy.

Before Sulpa's coming, Driff told her, the Illimani were a nomadic, warlike, hunting people who saw all other humans as prey to be exploited by force or guile. They took what they wanted from them – women, supplies, slaves – and moved on. So it had been for as long as anyone could remember. Then in Driff's sixteenth summer, two years previously, Sulpa had appeared amongst them.

"You mean he just walked into your camp?" Ria asked.

"No, it wasn't like that."

It seemed an Illimani warrior called Beche, renowned for his physical beauty, was mortally wounded during a raid on another tribe. He was brought back to camp and died in the night. At dawn, as was the Illimani custom, his body was placed on a funeral pyre, but before the brands were lit he returned to life, his face still corpse-white, his eyes rolling, his muscles moving strangely beneath his skin and all his injuries miraculously healed.

"Beche exists no longer" he roared from the midst of the pyre. "You will call me Sulpa now."

Driff had witnessed these events, and what happened next.

Sulpa leapt down from the pyre. The color had returned to his features and he seemed like a new person entirely. A person remade. A person who looked like Beche, but was not Beche. A person filled with danger and power. He reached out into the air and by some magic a huge black knife appeared in his hand – an obsidian knife as long as a man's leg. He whirled it around his head, walked five paces to where the old king stood, and chopped him in half at the waist with a single blow. "I am your king now," he told the Illimani while the dying man's blood fountained around him. The king's three sons, who were mighty warriors, contested the claim but he killed them all in hand-to-hand combat and no one else cared to stand in his way.

Thereafter raids on other tribes stopped being about murder and mayhem with the purpose of securing women, slaves and supplies, and became exclusively about murder and mayhem. Killing, which before had been a means to an end, became an end in itself, and a new way of death was born for the Illimani. Without exception everyone who crossed their path, and everyone they could hunt down, was killed. Entire peoples were exterminated, wherever possible by means that were agonizing and long-drawn-out. Any Illimani who displeased Sulpa likewise suffered a slow painful execution. "He is the Eater of Souls," Driff explained. "He feeds on pain and death."

From the day he took over Beche's body Sulpa began to speak of the cause that would bring the Illimani into Ria's land.

He told them he was mobilizing them and would make them stronger than every other tribe because they had a sacred purpose to fulfill.

To them had fallen the honor, and the responsibility, of extinguishing the Light in the West.

He did not tell them what this Light in the West was but as the moons went by they all began to notice he was leading them ever westwards, towards the ice deserts and the vast unknown lands that lay beyond.

Before crossing the ice the Illimani numbered almost thirty thousand men, women and children, and when they reached the other side fully twenty thousand of them still lived. Of these, seven thousand were tough, battle-scarred braves. They fell like ravening beasts on the peaceful and unsuspecting valleys beyond, killed all their inhabitants, took the new lands for themselves, and settled their families there.

Sulpa sent scouts and spies ahead – the Light in the West was close now – and after three more moons had passed he led out his seven thousand braves and marched them towards Ria's homeland killing everyone in their path. Mass sacrifices of captured children were staged almost daily. Sulpa butchered the victims himself, with his long black knife, and drank their blood.

Ria gasped in horror, remembering how she had seen the Illimani sparing the children during the massacre of the Clan.

"Yes," said Driff, sharing the image, "that's what we . . ." He hesitated. "They . . ." He hung his head. "That's what we're trained to do. Children aren't to be killed on the battlefield. They're rounded up and brought to Sulpa for sacrifice."

"But why?" Ria asked. She was having trouble grasping the concept. How was it possible for anyone to be so depraved he would murder children and drink their blood?

"He is the Eater of Souls," Driff repeated, as though that explained everything. "He kills the innocent and the good to increase his power . . . That's why he brought us into your lands." He looked around at their Ugly companions – Grondin, Oplimar and Jergat. "He brought us here to kill them," he said, making sure she got his meaning clearly. "To kill *all* the Uglies. They're the Light in the West."

By mid-afternoon they were deep inside the territory of the Naveen, following the course of a mountain stream along the bottom of a stony valley, when they saw vultures and ravens circling up ahead.

A great many vultures and ravens.

This was more than just some rotting deer carcass.

And there was the smell of smoke in the air.

Like most people in these parts the Naveen were hunters, gatherers, fishermen and raiders who spent their lives migrating in bands of a few hundred between a series of transient camps. It was one of these that had been hit, just around the next turn of the valley – a huddle of conical tepees standing amongst trees on a narrow stretch of flood plain overlooking the stream.

Many of the tepees had been gutted by fire; those few that had not seemed isolated and out of place. Smoke still curled up into the air, but there was no sign of movement nor sound of human life anywhere – not a child's cry, not a lookout on the alert, not the chop-chop-chop of flint being knapped.

It seemed they approached a camp of the dead but only as they drew closer did they grasp the true extent of the horror.

Judging from the signs on the ground, and the injuries they had sustained, the Naveen who had been trapped here – somewhat less than two hundred of them – had surrendered and been disarmed without a struggle. All had multiple wounds but without exception these resulted from the peculiar way they had been put to death.

They had been nailed to the trees that grew throughout the camp by means of long, narrow flint spikes hammered through their hands and feet, ankles and wrists. They dangled from the lower branches like clumps of strange, bruised, rotting fruit and clung in contorted freakish poses to the thick upright trunks. The tallest tree was festooned with twenty of them, their mouths open in silent screams, their eyes already plucked out by ravens, their flesh rent by vultures. But not a single tree had been left innocent of the carnage. On three of them there were Naveen – two men and a woman – who still clung to life.

As even the Uglies admitted, the injuries these unfortunate people had suffered were beyond healing. None of them had any hope of survival, and withdrawing the flint spikes would cause insufferable pain. It was surely kinder to kill them now.

The two men, both unconscious, were quickly dispatched by Bont and Driff. The woman, nailed head down to a tree near the middle of the camp, one eye pecked out, one still intact, was the strongest of the three. She spoke in the Naveen language, repeating the same words over and over. By the third repetition Ria understood: "They have taken our children! Spirits help us. They have taken all our children."

It was true: there wasn't a single child amongst the dead here.

Ria questioned the woman. How many braves had attacked them? When did they attack? In which direction did they go? But she spoke no more sense. At last, with a reluctant grimace, Ria unsheathed her knife to put her out of her misery when a man's voice, hoarse and emotional, bellowed from beside a smoldering tepee: "Touch her and die." As Ligar nocked an arrow and drew his bow in a single fluid motion, and Bont unslung his war axe, a dozen Naveen hunters, seven with bows drawn, the rest brandishing spears and hatchets, strode towards them from all directions through the trees.

Chapter Seventy

Mary Ruck's boat was a twenty-footer, with two fixed benches towards the rear seating six passengers under a tarpaulin canopy and an open storage area in the bows. Mary was at the back, controlling the big Yamaha outboard motor. "I've got two hundred horses here," she said, and the boat leapt forward as she thumbed the throttle. "I think we can outrun them."

"That's a fast engine," commented Matt. He, Leoni and Bannerman were just in front of Mary, occupying the rearmost of the two benches. "But, with due respect, your boat's a tub and we don't know what the other guys have got. In fact, we don't even know who the other guys are. We *think* it's Don Apolinar but it could be someone else. Could be nothing to do with us at all."

Leoni looked back to the north again. The lights were definitely closer.

"So do you have a suggestion?" Mary shouted. She was barely audible above the sound of the outboard and the slap-slap-slap of the river racing by.

"Yes," Matt yelled. "Throttle back – get into the shelter of the bank NOW! Where it's overgrown with trees . . . Right here will do."

"Do it, Mary," Bannerman urged.

"We'll take cover," Matt continued. "Keep absolutely silent, show no lights. If they whiz past your jetty and carry on upriver we'll know they're not here for us. If they stop . . . well, it might be an interesting idea to let the current carry us down to them. I'd like to have a go at scuppering their boat while they're searching the lodge."

Mary had already throttled back and was turning towards the nearby bank. "Sounds dangerous," she muttered.

"But in my opinion less dangerous than leaving them behind us," said Matt. "Out on the open water we'll be sitting ducks if they've got guns."

The jungle grew thick here, gigantic ferns spreading like fans, huge trees looming into the darkness, sinuous mossy creepers hanging down. Mary cut the engine and let the boat's remaining momentum carry it beneath an immense palm that had toppled sideways over an undermined bank and lay part in and part out of the water. Standing in the bows, Don Emmanuel reached up and slung a rope around the palm's trunk, bringing them to a halt.

Behind the lights were much closer and with their own engine silent they could all hear the powerful throaty roar of the other boat.

They'd have caught us in five minutes, Leoni thought.

She guessed the jetty lay about quarter of a mile downstream and that the approaching boat must now be very close to it. She found herself praying for it to pass by but instead, with awful inevitability, she heard the engine note change and saw the lights veer towards the bank.

"OK," said Matt, "That settles it. Is everyone with me on this?"

There was no point in trying to escape upriver. Their engine would be heard as soon as they started it and they would be overhauled and caught. There were no other options that Leoni could think of. "I'm with you," she said.

"Me too," said Bannerman. "It's risky but so is anything else we could do."

Mary and Emmanuel conferred in Spanish and agreed. There was no alternative. "When you are cornered by a hungry jaguar," Emmanuel said, "it is best to attack it."

This was all going to be very tight, Leoni thought as the current whisked them downstream. Apolinar would suspect they had fled, since their own boat wasn't at the jetty. On the other hand that might be a trick – so he couldn't afford to leave the lodge unsearched. Even men in a hurry would take five minutes to get from the jetty to the lodge, perhaps another five to search it and find it empty, and five more to get back to the boat.

So Matt had about fifteen minutes to pull this off.

The cloud cover was thinning out. Not good. Then a gap opened and a shaft of moonlight speared through it, illuminating the jetty a few hundred feet ahead. The gap closed again just as fast but not before they all saw the big twin-engined speedboat moored at the jetty. Steering with two stubby oars, Emmanuel and Bannerman guided their own smaller vessel towards the bank and Matt slipped into the water.

Moments earlier Leoni had tried to persuade him to rethink. Couldn't this be done without swimming?

"No," Matt had said. "There's bound to be a guard on the speedboat. This is the only way to reach it without being heard."

Before leaving Iquitos, Leoni had borrowed Bannerman's laptop and run a series of Google searches about the Amazon. As a result she now knew that the great river and all its major tributaries seethed with monstrous creatures – hideous alligators called caymans that grew up to twenty feet long, anacondas like firehoses, piranhas and even bull sharks that had adapted to fresh water.

It was suicide to get in this river – she checked the luminous hands of her Rolex – and Matt had been in it for more than seven minutes.

Where the fuck was he?

She glanced at Bannerman and Mary, crouching on either side of her and peering into the darkness. There was enough light coming through the clouds now to see the expressions on their faces, and they looked worried. Emmanuel was in the bow; he'd roped the boat to an overhanging branch and stood ready to release it on Matt's signal.

Which still did not come.

Eight minutes . . .

Nine minutes . . .

Was he dead?

Eaten by one of those fucking caymans?

Captured or killed by whoever was guarding Apolinar's speedboat?

The searchers who had gone up to the lodge must return at any moment at which point, even if Matt was still alive, it would be too late for him to do anything. Leoni found she was counting the seconds, glaring into the darkness, whispering under her breath: "Come on, Matt! Come on! Come on!"

Chapter Seventy-One

The Naveen hunters looked wild-eyed and frantic, half mad with grief, fearful for their own safety yet spoiling for a fight. It was a wonder arrows hadn't started flying yet.

"Stay your hands, brothers," Ria called out in the Naveen tongue. "We are not your enemies." She knew the Uglies wouldn't rush to violence but she pulsed to Driff, Bont and Ligar to lower their weapons: "Don't start anything. I'm going to try to talk our way out of here."

Ria still held her long flint knife in her hand. She sheathed it now, gestured at the smoldering remains of the camp and at the trees festooned with bodies, then at her companions: "We are only seven," she told the Naveen. "We did not do this!" She indicated the woman nailed upside down, her one eye rolling, gasping her last breaths. "I sought to give this poor one mercy, for she is beyond saving."

The closest of the hunters, the same man who had challenged Ria moments before, dropped to his knees in front of the dying woman, his eyes level with hers, touched her face and began to murmur to her softly. "My love. Who has done this to you? Where are our children?" He reached to where her hands and wrists were nailed to the tree and his fingers fluttered over the bloodied heads of the cruel flint spikes. He looked up. Each of her legs was pinned from the knee to the foot with three big skewers that had smashed her shin bones and disjointed her ankles. The futility of any attempt to free her must have become obvious to him, and his body was racked and twisted with great sobs and groans. "REVENGE!" he shouted. "I SHALL HAVE REVENGE!" Then he unsheathed his knife and cut the woman's throat, kneeling silently by her while her lifeblood drained and the last of the light seeped out of the one eye the birds had spared.

The hunter was a tall broad-shouldered man of thirty summers or thereabouts. He had a heavy black beard, a fierce hooked nose, tawny eyes like a wolf, and tanned weather-beaten skin. Now he stood and turned on Ria: "You!" he hissed. "You speak our language. Who are you? What are you doing here? Why do you have Uglies with you?"

Ria looked around. The ring of Naveen hunters had closed tight. Some of the braves were young, nervous, lacking in experience, likely to be rash, and the seven archers were getting shaky holding their bows at full stretch. "Tell your men to unbend their bows," Ria said, "and then we'll talk. If they fire on us it'll come to a fight and everyone loses. There's been enough dying here today."

"If it comes to a fight we'll kill you all."

"You will. You have the numbers. But how many of your men are going to die doing it? That's the question. And what's the point? We're just like you. We've lost loved ones to the same evil enemy who struck you here. We should join forces against him. It's madness to fight each other."

The hunter's wolfish eyes stared at her for a ten count: "It seems this enemy has stolen our children away," he said. "Do you know why?"

"When your men put down their bows," answered Ria, "I'll tell you what we know."

The hunter's name was Aarkon. He wasn't the only one of his band to have dead relatives nailed to the trees; they all did. Nor was he the only one whose children, or younger brothers and sisters, had disappeared. So they were all desperate to understand what had happened. But as Ria told them of the massacre of the Clan by the Illimani horde, and of how Sulpa collected children for sacrifice, their faces darkened. "We have to get after them," said Aarkon grimly, "We have to try and save our kids."

"It was a large band that smashed this camp," Ria reminded him. "Must have been hundreds of them, and the whole Illimani force numbers more than seven thousand. What can twelve of you do?"

"We have to try . . ."

"Instead of throwing your lives away, join us," she urged. "We're going to build an army to fight them."

Aarkon cast his eye over Ria's motley gang of Uglies and humans. "An army to fight thousands?" His tone was close to mockery. "Led by a mere girl?"

Ria ignored him. "Yes. An army to fight thousands. Why not? We'll build it not just from one tribe but from many. Uglies. Humans. Naveen.

Clan. Merell. It doesn't matter. The only way we're going to win is to put old hatreds aside."

Before nightfall the two groups had separated, Aarkon and his men following the trail of the Illimani raiders, Ria and her companions continuing their journey towards the Gate of Horn. "If our plans work out we'll be back this way in two days," Ria told Aarkon. "If you change your mind and decide to join us – even if you just need a place of safe refuge – wait for us then."

The moon was close to full, providing more light than they needed for marching despite the rough terrain, and with the effects of the recent healings still coursing through their bodies they were filled with energy. Ria was between Bont and Ligar. Driff, Grondin, Jergat and Oplimar were in single file behind them.

"Where are you getting all these languages from?" Bont asked.

"What languages?" Ria's tone was innocent.

"You know, you're talking Illimani to Driff, you're talking Naveen to Aarkon. What's happening?" He wrinkled his brow. "Feels like witchcraft to me."

"If it's witchcraft I want some," Ligar exclaimed. "Imagine the opportunity to be charming in twenty languages."

"It's a gift," said Ria. She wasn't in the mood to discuss what had happened to her yet. "It's useful. That's all there is to it."

She fell back behind her Clansmen. Since the destruction of her people, she loved and valued Bont and Ligar all the more, but still they could be maddening.

For a long while they marched in silence through a landscape of rolling hills. Then they were over a ridge, with the moon setting behind them, and heading down the long slope of a valley.

Below they heard the high-pitched scream of a woman in terror.

Chapter Seventy-Two

Leoni saw Matt's signal – three brief flashes from the Maglite he'd carried with him in a waterproof pouch.

There it was again: flash, flash, flash.

Don Emmanuel slipped the mooring rope free of the branch and ran forward to join Bannerman at the oars. Within seconds, aided by the strong current, they had reached the jetty.

"Hi," said Matt. "What kept you?" He was still dripping with water, standing on the side of the speedboat with a canvas bag in his arms. He passed the bag over to Bannerman and jumped after it himself. "I think we'd better be going now," he said. They all heard gruff male voices and saw the blink of torches on the path from the lodge.

"But their boat," Leoni objected. "I thought you were going to *scupper* it."

"I have scuppered it."

"It doesn't look very scuppered to me."

"Trust me, it's not going anywhere."

There was a choking cough followed by an ear-splitting roar as Mary fired up the big outboard and pointed the riverboat out into the current. At almost the same moment the moon surged from behind a scudding cloudbank and lit up the whole scene bright as day.

Five big men, with Apolinar in the lead, were pounding towards them.

Shit! *Guns*!

Suddenly the Yamaha's two hundred horses felt way too few to Leoni. They seemed to dawdle by the jetty. For a moment it looked like Apolinar might make a leap for it but slowly the distance widened.

Bullets spattered into the water around them and some hit the boat, tearing into it like a jackhammer. But someone was firing *from* the boat as well! Leoni had her head down but risked a look and saw it was Matt, crouched at the back next to Mary, armed with an automatic rifle – where had that come from? – and spraying bullets at the shore. The firing from that direction ceased, the clouds blew across the moon again and the night's darkness swallowed them up.

Matt stopped firing. Mary was holding the outboard on full throttle.

Then, back at the jetty, someone flipped all the speedboat's spotlights on. Its twin engines burst into life and it shot out into the river.

"Is that what you call *scuppered*?" Leoni yelled at Matt.

He didn't reply. Just for a second he looked unsure of himself.

The speedboat was quick. It had already halved their lead and was tearing up behind them with all its lights ablaze. Leoni found herself cowering, anticipating the next hail of bullets, when the powerful thrum of the twin engines faltered and the pursuing vessel slowed and wallowed, its spotlights flickering first at the sky, then at the jungle, then back at the water, missing them by a hundred feet. *Hoo-ray,* Leoni started to whoop, but the cheer died in her throat as she heard the engines roar again. The speedboat steadied and surged forward under full power, then faltered a second time, notably lower in the water, its lights still not finding them. There were three loud bangs, the engines picked up, faltered a third time, and failed.

"Sorry," said Matt. "That took a little longer than I expected."

Gunfire erupted from the men on the other vessel but the current was sweeping them downstream, they didn't seem to be able to traverse their lights, and the bullets went wide in the darkness.

Leoni half stood to get a clearer view. With Mary keeping the riverboat on full throttle and heading upstream, the distance was widening fast.

"I'd say we're out of range," Matt announced. "Anyway, they've got other worries."

As he spoke the moon found a hole in the clouds and Leoni saw that Don Apolinar's boat was sinking. The men had clustered together at the prow, the only part still above water. One of them fired again before they all went under.

Leoni looked at Matt. "I see what you mean about scuppered," she admitted.

The automatic rifle was an AK-47, Matt said, adding without further explanation: "I took it off the guy who was guarding the speedboat."

Leoni pointed at the canvas bag: "What's in there?"

Matt lifted it and placed it in her lap. It was heavy and clunked when she set it down. She opened it and saw four curved ammunition clips for the AK-47 and two chunky pistols. "Hmm. Quite an arsenal."

"Well . . . I thought it might come in useful."

Mary was behind them, holding the outboard's throttle handle, no longer racing the engine but keeping up a steady, mile-eating pace. "You nearly got us killed back there, Matt," she complained.

Bannerman had been sitting on the bench beside Leoni, lost in his own thoughts, but now he spoke up: "I don't agree," he said. "It's just as likely Matt *saved* us all from getting killed. If he hadn't done this we'd still have men with guns after us in a much faster boat."

Mary seemed to think about it. "You're right," she said. She turned to Matt: "I'm sorry. That was . . . ungrateful of me. You were very brave. It's just this has all been so sudden. And now guns, you know? Boats being sunk. There's a good chance some of Don Apolinar's gang have drowned. It's all turned very heavy."

Several times through the night Matt and Bannerman relieved Mary at the outboard, and by dawn they were fifty miles further south on the Amazon's vast tributary, the Ucayali.

It was hard not to feel threatened here, Leoni thought, knowing what lay beneath the surface of the muddy waters, the caymans, the bull sharks, the piranhas, the giant anacondas – a seething underworld of monsters from which they were separated only by the flimsy hull of the boat.

They stopped at a riverside Shipibo village. The few dozen single-roomed homes were simple rectangular structures, raised two feet above the ground on stilts, with roofs of thatched banana leaf, but they were led by a crowd of giggling children directly to a larger communal *maloca.* It too had a raised floor, and its walls of coconut matting had been rolled up to admit cooling breezes from the river.

Everyone seemed to know Don Emmanuel and gathered round the visitors in a curious, friendly press. Leoni's thick blonde hair came in for particular attention and half the village wanted to shake her hand as though she was some sort of celebrity. A breakfast of roast river turtle and ducks' eggs, neither of which Leoni could bring herself to eat, was prepared for them, but she accepted a plate of bananas and a tin mug of hot sweet tea and felt much refreshed.

An hour later they were heading south again towards the Shipibo heartland through a vastness of trees and rivers, interminably branching and subdividing, a waterworld lost in an immensity. Yes, it was hard not to feel threatened here – and not only because of the monsters that lurked beneath the surface. The scale of everything was so grand – the miles-wide river, the endless sky, and the presence of nature so lush, so green and so abundant it took Leoni's breath away. But there was also a much smaller-scale, down-home simplicity about the countless hamlets and villages that lined both banks: miniature communities, sometimes of just a few families, all seemingly living in harmony with their environment, as at home in this world, Leoni thought, as she was amidst skyscrapers and traffic jams.

She fell asleep, lulled by the steady motion of the boat and the river slapping against its sides, until, without warning, she found herself sitting on the end of a dusty double bed in a shabbily furnished and dimly lit room. Could have been in a low-budget motel. She knew she was dreaming but it all seemed very real somehow.

There was an old-fashioned television set against the back wall. Gray static was fizzing across its screen.

And a voice came out of it.

A whisper.

"Kill yourself, Leoni," the voice urged. "Do it now."

"But I don't want to," she protested. "I want to live!"

The voice hissed and crackled: "It's too late for that. You must kill yourself. The sooner the better. It's the only way."

Leoni saw this was true. She didn't want to die but obviously there was no alternative. She knew it was absolutely inevitable. "How shall I do it?" she sobbed.

"Don't worry about that," whispered the voice. "I will guide you."

At once Leoni snapped wide awake, gasping and cursing, her heart pounding, engulfed by horror. Matt was beside her, holding on to her, something he'd been doing quite a bit since last night and to which she had no objections. Mary, Bannerman and Don Emmanuel all stared at her with expressions of concern as she shook her head to clear it. She looked around to get her bearings. While she'd slept they had at some point left the mainstream of the river and were now motoring very slowly along some side branch with steep muddy banks surmounted by thick overarching trees. There was less than an hour until sunset, somehow a whole day had passed and – SHIT! – there was another person on the boat, up front at the prow.

Leoni jumped in her seat: "Who's that?"

"He's Don Emmanuel's nephew," Matt reassured her. "His name is Don Esteban. We picked him up at his village an hour ago; you were still sleeping like the dead." He hesitated as she winced at the simile. "He's guiding us to the homestead of a big-time Shipibo shaman who hopefully will help us." He hesitated again: "Look, I don't want to worry you but you need to know this . . ."

"Need to know what?" Leoni demanded. She could sense the bad news coming her way.

"Less than two hours before we got there Esteban's village was visited by a fast boat full of *gringos.* Very bad guys. *Muy peligrosos.* They had *mestizo* guides with them and they were looking for us."

Chapter Seventy-Three

The woman started screaming again, shattering the night with a long-drawn-out series of shrieks and sobs. A man was yelling alongside her. His voice was hoarse and desperate, pleading and threatening at the same time, and although Ria was still too far away to make out what he was saying the tone of fear was unmistakable.

"Wait," she said. She stopped walking and everyone else slowed to a halt around her, Grondin and Driff to her left, Bont and Ligar with Oplimar and Jergat to her right. Another heart-rending scream rose out of the valley, reached a crescendo and died away into whimpers and moans. There came a burst of raucous male laughter – three, maybe four men. It wasn't a nice sound.

"We've got two choices," said Ria. "We can walk away from this or we can try to do something about it. I want to do something about it."

"It's none of our business." Bont sounded belligerent. "We already wasted the best part of half the day with the Naveen. It was you who told me Sabeth and the kids are still alive. I just want to get up to Gate of Horn and bring them back."

"I can understand that, Bont, but think. Suppose that woman being tortured down there *was* Sabeth? Suppose some folks came by who could help her? But suppose they said to themselves 'That's none of our business, we don't have the time,' and walked away? How would you feel about that?"

Bont screwed up his small eyes in discomfort: "I'd want to kill them . . ."

"Exactly! Which means you know it's wrong for us to walk away now."

Ria turned to the Uglies: "Walk or help?"

"We must help if we can," pulsed Grondin. "Evil is here now, in our valleys. We've got to fight it."

More screams and another burst of rasping laughter rose up from the floor of the valley. "If the laughers are Illimani," said Ligar quietly, "then I'm for killing them all. They sound like hyenas. Besides" – he unslung his bow and attached the string by touch while gazing intently down the valley – "I'm not one to turn my back on a woman in trouble."

Bont gave a great sigh of frustration: "OK, OK. I get the message. Let's go and rescue this unknown woman." He looked at Ria: "It's what I would want for my Sabeth," he admitted.

Still well lit by the big moon, the valley floor lay about five hundred paces below them. A stream wound through it and there were numerous stands of mixed trees and bushes.

It was from one of these, a copse no more than a hundred paces across, with just the faintest glow of a campfire visible near its center, that the terrible screams were coming.

Ria decided what to do and informed the others as they scrambled with her down the valley side. There would be no out-loud speech, only thought-talk. They would surround the copse, all enter it at the same moment, and converge on that fire. If they were outnumbered they would back off without engaging the enemy and the woman would be left to her fate. But if this was a fight they could win they would attack and try to save her.

It had seemed like a good plan from outside the copse. But once inside, Ria began to have doubts. Suppose this turned out to be nothing to do with the Illimani? Or suppose it was the opposite and there were dozens of them there? Suppose there were sentries? She was aware of the minds of all her companions as she made her way forward. "You won't let me down, will you?" she pulsed to the Uglies. "Give them no mercy this time."

"We will give them death," came the reply.

The woman's screams had begun again, much closer. The man, who had fallen silent, released a fresh volley of hoarse cries, and there were more guffaws of that hideous hyena laughter that Ria now recognized, with complete certainty, as the sound of the Illimani.

Her right hand went to the new deerskin pouch hanging at her side. Brindle had given it to her filled with five good throwing stones. She pulled two out. They couldn't match the beauty of her lost hunting stones but they would do the job.

Up ahead she caught the glow of the campfire flickering through the trees, shadows moving around it. There was a sickly smell of burning flesh in the air and the sounds kept getting louder. Screams. Snuffling. Slaps. What were they doing to that poor woman? And what was the man groaning and pleading about? Ria listened intently as she crept forward. He was speaking the language of the Merell. She understood the individual words but they were garbled and incoherent and she couldn't make sense of them.

Then the little group around the fire came into view.

With light from the bright moon and the flickering flames not much was left to the imagination.

A spit had been rigged up.

Impaled on it, roasting over the fire, was the sad, pathetic torso of a small boy.

An evil-looking Illimani was slowly rotating the spit. His narrow pinched face had been transformed to a grinning skull by warpaint. His penis was erect and his glittering eyes were eating up what was happening a few paces away where a naked young woman, her long willowy body smeared with blood, was being raped by two more Illimani braves. One of them was very tall, with huge muscular arms. He was pinning down her head and shoulders, fondling her breasts and half-stifling her screams with a hand clamped over her throat. The other man, thickset and covered in body hair, was penetrating her, forcing her legs apart as she struggled against him. He was pounding into her, uttering grunts of animal pleasure.

Ria could feel anger building in her chest like a storm, and her mind-contact with her companions told her they too were witnessing this and were ready. *Wait*! she pulsed.

She edged two steps closer. Could this be a trick? Could there be an ambush? Were other Illimani lurking to attack the moment they showed themselves?

But on the opposite side of the fire she saw only two more figures. One, wearing the Merell plaid, lay beaten and bloody on the ground. The second, a massively fat Illimani whose naked back and ass were covered in swirling tattoos, was shaking with laughter, leaning over the fallen man and offering him something.

Ria squinted.

The smoke from the fire was in the way. She moved a pace to the side and saw that the Illimani was holding a child's arm – no doubt the child whose torso roasted on the spit – and encouraging the fallen man to eat it. Then Ria understood everything. The man on the ground was the child's father, the woman being raped was his wife and the Illimani were playing a vicious game with them.

What was the deal? They'd stop raping her if he'd eat his own son?

That wouldn't do at all.

Chapter Seventy-Four

Kill yourself. The sooner the better.

That's what the voice had urged Leoni to do, and for a moment, in the dream, she'd accepted absolutely that she must.

Visions could be true. Leoni was past doubting it. They were a doorway into supernatural realms, where time and matter behaved differently. When she went through that door to pursue the mysteries that lay on the other side, she knew she was exposing herself to psychic attack – the way Sulpa had attacked her when she'd tried to stop him devouring the souls of the children he'd sacrificed, and the way Don Apolinar had abducted her.

Such risks came with the visionary territory. She accepted them every time she made the journey. But it was somehow much more disturbing to consider that a similar threat might just now have stalked her in a dream.

A macabre and horrible dream.

Surely it had been no more than that? Her subconscious working overtime, editing together bits and pieces from here and there? It made sense that the voice emanating from the static on the TV screen had been influenced by Don Emmanuel's account of Jack speaking out of a mirror. And the instruction to kill herself was likely connected to her alleged "suicide attempt" by OxyContin overdose.

Or so, at least, she fervently hoped.

The other really disturbing development, despite sinking Apolinar's boat the night before, was the shocking speed with which their pursuers had caught up with them again, missing them by just two hours at Don Esteban's village. Jack had said his "servants" were on the way, but to get there so fast they must have bypassed Iquitos and begun their search from the river town of Pucallpa in the Shipibo heartland.

It was almost impressive – how they got things done.

With a great effort of will Leoni shifted her attention back to the gloomy and constricted side branch of the Ucayali they'd entered while she slept.

Perhaps it was just the aftermath of her dream, but the sinuous way the river wound through the dense rainforest, frequently doubling back on itself, was bewildering and scary. It was only about twenty feet wide here but its labyrinthine course repeatedly branched, offering multiple alternative routes and Leoni realized if it were viewed from the air it would look like a path through a gigantic maze – with walls of trees a hundred feet high. God forbid she would ever be alone here because she would *never* find her way out. She was impressed by the way Don Emmanuel's nephew Esteban – a lean and wizened man of more than seventy – always knew which turn to take.

Late afternoon had become early evening. The sun was still in the sky but down here on the river, with the trees towering overhead, it was already growing dark. The night insects were out, looking for blood. As she slapped away a cloud of mosquitos, Leoni heard the distinctive call – a long falling liquid note, rising at the end to a percussive whoop – of the colorful yellow and black bird Matt had told her was called an oropendola. There was something so haunting and lonely about the sound that she found herself blinking back tears.

Matt was sitting behind her now, keeping the outboard bubbling over at low revs and the speed right down as he steered the course called out to him by Don Esteban in the bow. The river was narrowing, probably less than fifteen feet wide at this point, and there was a lot of jungle debris in the water. Soon they came to an entire tree that had fallen across both banks, like a bridge. They scraped beneath it after some industrious hacking away of branches by Don Esteban who had brought an axe and a machete for such eventualities.

A couple of miles ahead, with darkness almost upon them, Esteban signaled to Matt to take a left fork into an even narrower channel, not much wider than the boat itself. They followed it through a series of long serpentine loops until it spilled them into a broad lagoon dotted with huge water lilies.

The dome of the sky was a deep purple velvet, still touched in the west by the last glow of sunset, and the water was dead calm beneath them as they crossed the lagoon. Leoni loved the tremendous sense of openness and space it gave her, and gritted her teeth when they reached the other side. They forced a path through a thick tract of water lilies and entered another narrow winding channel with yet more forks and switchbacks. She looked over her shoulder at Matt. "Those men hunting us," she said, "I don't see how they're going to find us here." She wished she felt as confident as she was trying to sound. "This is totally the boondocks."

Matt nodded his agreement: "It would take a lot of local knowledge, which hopefully the other side don't have . . . do they, Mary?"

Mary Ruck bit her lower lip. "I'm not so sure of that. Even if he doesn't know the area himself Apolinar will certainly have connections here." She switched into Spanish to put a question to Don Emmanuel and translated his answer: "The Shipibo have their *brujos* too – men who will help Apolinar. But the shaman whose protection we seek is more powerful than all of them."

They came at last, in full darkness but with a good moon lighting their way, to a tiny homestead perched right at the end of a curving back-water creek. As they approached, Leoni saw only a single structure, a small simple *maloca*, thatched with banana leaf, perched on short stilts in a patch of earth no larger than a tennis court that had been cleared out of the dense jungle.

Halfway down the gently sloping bank leading to the creek, silhou-etted by reflected moonlight, a short hunched man waited, one hand raised in salutation. Matt cut the engine, letting the boat drift the last few feet, while friendly greetings were exchanged in the Shipibo language. It was obvious Esteban was welcome here but suddenly the man on shore seemed to understand Don Emmanuel was also in the boat. He gave a great shout of greeting and ran forward into the shal-lows to embrace him and help him disembark.

Leoni, Matt, Bannerman and Mary were not formally introduced to Don Leoncio Amparo, whose homestead this was, until he had ushered them into the *maloca*, lit several paraffin lanterns, and rolled the side-screens fully open for ventilation.

He was not a prepossessing physical specimen. Barefoot, wearing mud-spattered cotton trousers and a torn work-shirt, he was balding and ugly, with squashed froglike features, his nose almost flat against his face, bulging brown eyes, short thin legs, thick muscular arms, powerful shoulders and a hunched back. It was hard to guess his age – perhaps fifty? – but so much experience, strength and warmth overwrote his ugliness that he made a strong, immediate and positive impression on Leoni.

Speaking perfect English, he commented on the similarity of their names, both meaning "lion." He had a deep, rumbling, gravelly voice, with strangely formal New England undertones. When she complimented him on his mastery of the language he replied: "The Protestants taught me well."

"Protestants?"

"Missionaries." A hint of anger. "Americans. They've infested the whole of the Ucayali basin as though they have a personal feud against our culture. They persuade us our spirituality is evil and convince us with money and food – and education – to accept Christ."

"Sounds like they didn't convince *you*!"

"No." A wry smile: "I escaped them." He looked to Don Emmanuel: "I passed through a personal crisis. This great man accepted me as his pupil and I learned the path of the shaman from him. It turned out to be the right path for me."

In the background Mary had been giving Don Emmanuel the gist of the conversation in Spanish. Now Don Emmanuel made a remark and Mary translated it into English: "The pupil long ago surpassed his master." It seemed that immense discipline and determination, an intense focus of the will, and long periods spent alone in the jungle seeking visions with Ayahuasca had transformed Don Leoncio into an adept of the highest order. He claimed no special credit for his skills and spent nine months of each year traveling from village to village as an itinerant healer, accepting only food, shelter and peasant wages. For the other three months he retired to this homestead in the middle of nowhere and lived the life of a hermit. Only Don Esteban and one other close friend knew where to find him.

In the next hour a simple meal of fish and plantains was prepared and eaten. Leoni found it strange, but perhaps a matter of Shipibo etiquette, that at no point in the conversation was any explanation asked, or given, for their visit. *For fuck's sake*, she thought, *get to the point*! She was here for only one thing – to drink Ayahuasca with Don Leoncio and get back to Ria's side.

But she stopped herself from blurting this out and finally, after dinner,

Don Emmanuel drew Don Leoncio aside and they sat cross-legged near the rear of the small *maloca*, speaking in Shipibo. *At last*! Leoni thought. She couldn't understand what they were saying but she heard her own name mentioned several times and felt the conversation grow tense and serious. Don Emmanuel must be filling Leoncio in on everything that had happened.

She felt tired, as though she'd been awake for a week, and curled up in a hammock slung between two of the *maloca*'s support posts.

She heard the two men's voices droning in the background. Nearby Mary and Matt were also talking.

Leoni didn't plan to close her eyes but sleep overwhelmed her in seconds and returned her at once to the cheap motel room of her dream, sitting on the edge of the bed, watching the flickering television screen from which that horrible whispering, crackling voice still emanated. "*Kill yourself . . . Do it now. You know it's the right thing.*"

Though repulsed, she was again seized by a sense of the inevitability and rightness of this command and by a powerful compulsion to obey. "I am ready," she answered.

"Are others present? Do they observe you?"

"Yes."

"The jungle is near?"

"Yes. Very near."

There was a pause and the voice fell to a hiss that was almost lost amidst the static: "When those around you are asleep you will walk into the jungle. Go quietly, be certain you are not seen and DO NOT STOP . . ."

A hand touched Leoni's shoulder and she woke with a shock, baring her teeth in a silent snarl. Don Leoncio, Matt, Bannerman, Mary and Don Emmanuel were all gathered round her hammock, their faces set. Her whole body was soaked with sweat, her brow and hair slick with it. A sudden sob shook her and she sat up shaking. She knew she was breathing too fast, as though she'd been running for her life, but she couldn't stop herself sucking in more air in great heaving gulps.

Don Leoncio asked the others to step back. He produced and lit a big *mapacho* and began to chant a deeply strange and otherworldly *icaro* while at the same time blowing clouds of fragrant smoke over Leoni.

She felt a little calmer. Within half an hour she had composed herself and was ready to talk about what had happened.

It seemed that she had only slept for a very short while. However, in those few moments, said Don Leoncio, he became aware – "It is a sense I have cultivated" – that some negative entity was trying to exploit her vulnerable liminal state. "It is intelligent, this entity, but it is not human . . ."

"It's Jack," groaned Leoni, scrambling out of the hammock. "He's a fucking demon. He got to me in a dream. Convinced me I had to kill myself."

Don Leoncio chuckled: "A fucking demon, eh? No doubt the same one Emmanuel has been speaking of? In what form did he appear to you?"

"He has no appearance. Today he's just a shadow – didn't Don Emmanuel tell you? – not even a shape. He spoke to me out of the snow on a TV screen."

"What did he say? Try to remember exactly."

Leoni replayed the dream in her mind: "He kept telling me I had to kill myself. He asked me if other people were around. He asked if they were observing me. He even asked if the jungle was close."

Leoncio's face broke into a broad smile and he pounded his fist into the palm of his hand. "I thought so!" he exclaimed. "He doesn't know where you are."

"How sure are you of that?" Leoni asked. "He was right there in my dream."

"He lost contact with you when I woke you up. If his eye were on us now I'd feel it." The shaman's expression became more somber: "But let's not underestimate him. Even to track you in the dreamscape must have required enormous power . . ."

"Jack *is* powerful," said Leoni. "I know that already."

Leoncio hesitated: "So the question then becomes – I mean no offense – why is such a powerful demon interested in you at all? Doesn't he have, how do you put it, bigger fish to fry?"

"He's not interested in me. Not directly. But there's someone else, a girl, twenty-four thousand years ago, who I'm connected to . . . It's her he's really after."

It was not clear how much Leoncio had already learned from

Emmanuel but he seemed to want to hear the whole complicated story from Leoni herself. She compressed it into the shortest possible telling: what Jack had wanted from her childhood, the connection between Jack and Sulpa, her near-death experience and subsequent experiences with Ayahuasca and other substances, her encounters with the Blue Angel – Our Lady of the Forest – and her entanglement with Ria and the fate of the Neanderthals.

She was describing her last Ayahuasca journey and her desperate attempt to save Ria from Sulpa's spy creatures when Don Leoncio leapt to his feet and made a pantomime of slapping himself on the forehead. "Of course," he exclaimed, "I should have guessed sooner . . ."

Leoni gazed at him open mouthed.

"After such a long connection with you, the question we must ask ourselves is why Jack is suddenly going to such lengths to track you down? And why now?"

"My parents are part of his cult?" Leoni proposed. "Maybe he fears I'm going to expose what they did to me?"

Don Leoncio made a dismissive sound – "*Fauugh*! He wouldn't care. Think about it. It's something new, something unexpected, that he fears."

"My connection to Ria! The Blue Angel said we possess great strength together. She said we have to find it and use it."

"To destroy Sulpa . . ."

"Yes."

"And therefore Jack . . ."

"Yes."

"Then we have our answer. If you are willing, I believe we should attempt to take the battle to the enemy tonight . . ."

Chapter Seventy-Five

Ria threw her first stone with all her anger behind it. It smacked into the side of the rapist's head and he collapsed in mid-thrust. The brave who'd been helping him to hold the woman down surged to his feet but an arrow from Ligar's bow, fired from close range, pierced his heart before he could take a step. The Illimani who'd been turning the spit died snarling under Driff's hatchets. The brave with the tattoos had dropped the child's arm and snatched up a knife when Bont stepped out of the darkness swinging his war axe and chopped him to the ground with two huge blows.

"Well," said Ria in out-loud speech, "that was easy." She hadn't even thrown her second stone and the Uglies hadn't needed to kill anyone since the humans had done the job so efficiently.

"Sorry we're not as quick as you, Ria." It was Oplimar's thought-voice.

"Don't worry about it," she replied. "You're learning. We're learning too. We're all living in a new world."

She hastened to the side of the Merell woman and with Grondin's help pulled away the body of the man Ligar had shot. The brave she'd brained with her stone was still alive. His eyes flickered open and Ria unsheathed her knife to cut his throat. Then another idea came to her so she had the Uglies drag him to the base of a tree and bind his hands and feet.

He lay there, muscular, hairy, naked and tightly trussed. He'd regained full consciousness while he was being tied and now he glared murder at Ria.

"I'll be back," she promised him. Surprise crossed his face as she spoke in Illimani.

She turned to attend to the woman.

Bont was for pressing on immediately but Ria disagreed. The couple they'd saved had suffered savage beatings and would have to be given healing to have any hope of survival.

"I don't care whether they survive or not," said Bont, his face streaked with the blood of the brave he'd killed. "We saved them, OK? Now let's get the fuck out of here."

"Your problem is you're not thinking long-term," Ria replied, "and we have to think long-term – all of us – or we won't survive."

Bont rolled his eyes in frustration but Ria was adamant: "We need to make an alliance with the Merell," she said. "That's going to be easier if these two walk out of here in the morning and speak well of us to their tribe – which we've just given them every reason to do . . . Are you with me so far?"

There was no response from Bont.

Ria felt almost as though she were talking to a child: "But here's the problem. If we get out of here now, like you say, and leave them the way they are, then they definitely won't walk out of here in the morning. They'll die, in amongst these trees, and no one will ever know what we did for them . . ." She paused: "That wouldn't be very helpful to us, would it?"

Bont groaned: "I don't know what's helpful. I don't know what's not helpful. I just want to get Sabeth and the kids back. I can't think of anything else . . . It hurts my head."

Ria rested a sympathetic hand on the big man's arm. "I understand," she said, "and we *will* get them back. But first we need to let the Uglies heal these good people."

With so few Uglies to administer it, the healing took a very long time. Dawn light had flushed the sky before it was done. Both the man and the woman had been kicked and beaten half to death, the woman additionally had been brutally and repeatedly raped in the presence of her husband, and they had witnessed the Illimani murdering and roasting their child. Their minds had been damaged much more terribly than their bodies, Grondin explained, and such damage was not easy to heal.

The couple now sat by the ashes of the fire. Their son's pitiful corpse, wrapped in a deerskin, lay between them.

"Can they walk? Ria asked Grondin.

"Yes, if they have the will. We have healed their bodies."

Ria guessed the husband's age at forty summers, although it was hard to be sure. His nose and teeth had been broken by blows and one eye was swollen closed. His thick black hair, which curled down over broad shoulders, was shot through with streaks of gray.

His wife was much younger, sixteen or eighteen, close to Ria's own age. She was slender with long, long legs, now folded birdlike beneath her. Her pale skin was freckled and her dark red hair tumbled almost to her waist. Her face was so bruised and battered it was impossible to tell if she was beautiful. Her huge green eyes, still full of pain and terror, darted from side to side as though she expected at any moment to be attacked again.

Ria stepped over to her, took her hand and helped her to her feet. "Come," she said in the Merell language, "there's something you need to do."

She led the young woman around the fire to where the Illimani brave, scowling and struggling, lay bound tight amongst the forking exposed roots of an ancient tree. He had a big discolored bruise on the side of his head where Ria's throwing-stone had connected but otherwise was uninjured. Vibrations of violence, lust and threat rose from him like a bad smell. The Merell woman's hand, still clasped in Ria's own, trembled and grew slick. She sobbed, her whole body racked with pain and grief, and tears streamed down her face. This was hardly a sexual moment but the Illimani's fat penis stirred in his loins as he witnessed her misery. He began to bellow with laughter and barked in his barbaric language: "Shall I pleasure you some more, slut? Come here, suck my cock first." And he looked suggestively at his crotch.

Ria did not translate his words but spoke calmly in Merell. "This one has taken much from you," she told the shaking woman. "Now take something from him. It will not heal your pain but it may help."

Through her tears the Merell seemed confused. She didn't comment on Ria's ability to speak her language but asked: "What shall I take from him?"

"His manhood," Ria replied. She unsheathed her long flint knife and put it into the woman's hand.

It was a bad death.

The woman was not quick and when she was done her husband took up the knife and cut out the Illimani's still-beating heart.

"I don't like this," Grondin pulsed to Ria. "It's wrong to kill a bound prisoner."

"Even after what happened here last night?" Ria could never quite second-guess Ugly logic. "It's like you said, Grondin. The Illimani murdered her child. They raped her in front of her husband. Both she and he needed this revenge. Think of it as my contribution to their healing."

Ria led the couple away from the blood-spattered scene and sat down to question them at the edge of the little copse, looking out at the open grassland beyond.

The man said his name was Sebittu and claimed to be one of the seven Speakers of the Merell – a high position, if true. Despite the beating he'd taken, and the humiliations of the night, he carried himself with pride and the air of one used to power.

His young wife was called Tari. She had seemed a fragile, broken creature before she had mutilated the Ilimani, but now, with her bruises already responding to the magic of the Uglies, high spots of color had appeared on her cheeks and she held her head up.

Like the Naveen, the Merell were divided into nomadic bands, each a few hundred strong, whose tepees could be pitched almost anywhere and carried from camp to camp – to stay for a year or a moon or a day as the hunting allowed. There were seven bands, hence seven Speakers.

So much Ria knew from Clan lore about the Merell.

She asked Sebittu about his own band.

They were called the Fox, he replied, and they had numbered less than three hundred – men, women, children, young and old, all added together. Poor hunting had forced them to leave their last camp and seek out a new one.

Yesterday, on the march, they had been ambushed by an overwhelming force of strange and terrible barbarians who slaughtered their men and women, but rounded up and dragged off their children. Sebittu and Tari, carrying their own one-year-old son, had been amongst the few who had escaped the battlefield, but they'd been tracked and captured before the day was out. Ria had witnessed the rest. "We owe you our lives," Sebittu concluded. "Without your courage – you and your friends – we would be dead now."

When Sebittu fell silent Ria told him of the fate of her own Clan, and of the Naveen, and she spoke of the character of the Illimani and the demon named Sulpa who led them, and the horrible truth of what he did with captured children. "He's destroying us by picking us off one by one. We have to unite the tribes to bring him down."

Deep-set in his battered face, Sebittu's gray eyes seemed to weigh her up: "Who can unite the tribes?" he asked, as though the task were of the same order as flattening mountains or draining the sea.

"I can," Ria replied. After her encounter with the Naveen hunter Aarkon she knew she risked ridicule with such talk. But this was a time for risks. Besides, she'd shown what she could do: "I'm building an army to fight Sulpa, and there will be no tribes in it. Just people of these valleys united against the Evil One."

As she spoke a strange look, swiftly hidden, seemed to pass between Sebittu and Tari. "You are of the Clan," Sebittu said to Ria: "Who taught you to speak the Merell language so well?"

"No one taught me . . ."

"You speak the language of the Illimani also?"

Ria shrugged. "It's a gift I have. When I hear a language I can speak it."

"Quite a remarkable gift if I may say so. Some might call it a gift from the gods. Perhaps you will indeed unite the tribes."

Aware of Bont glowering in the background, Ria got to her feet: "I intend to try. It will be a good beginning if the Merell will join us."

"If any of us are left alive," Sebittu answered, without making any commitment, as he helped Tari to stand. "We're heading southeast. Last I knew the Lynx and Wolf bands were camped up that way. Our best hope is they haven't been hit yet . . ."

"What if they have?"

"Then we'll look for survivors. And you? Where do you go now?"

"The Gate of Horn." Again Ria noticed that strange, furtive glance pass between Sebittu and Tari. Were they mocking her? Let them. She didn't care: "I wish you good fortune finding your people," she said. "Join us or not, if they need a place of safety and shelter we can offer it. We'll be back this way tomorrow. Look for us on the trail."

Ria saw how Tari clung to Sebittu as they turned their feet to the southeast. Despite the healing, the willowy young woman walked with pain, her husband supporting her, so much unspoken between them.

Ria and her companions turned northeast towards the Gate of Horn, trekking in single file through rising country. It was already bright morning. None of them had slept and the Uglies were drained by the healing. Ligar knew the area well and took the lead, warning that a long day's march still lay ahead before they entered the unclaimed wilderness of the Gate. "So this time no stopping," growled Bont. "I'm going to find Sabeth and the kids tonight."

They carried dried meats and waterskins so they could eat and drink on the move, and soon they settled into a loping, far-striding hunter's pace that brought the jagged mountain peaks on the distant horizon steadily closer. The terrain was uncompromising and at one point the only viable route – cliffs on one side, treacherous marshes on the other – forced them across a wide expanse of bleak open moors. They were exposed to view should any Illimani scouts be in the vicinity and Ria huffed with relief when at last they entered the sanctuary of an immense forest.

The respite was short-lived. After hiking a few bowshots they came upon the body of an old man nailed by his feet to the branch of a tree so that he hung upside down over the track.

Chapter Seventy-Six

What Don Leoncio meant, it soon became clear, was that Leoni should drink Ayahuasca again at once and return to Ria's time to help her – "since it seems that is precisely what Our Lady of the Forest wants you to do and what the demon wants to stop you doing."

Bannerman objected that Leoni had just eaten a meal: "Isn't it better to wait until tomorrow and drink on an empty stomach?"

But Leoni was having none of it. "I'm ready to drink," she said to Don Leoncio. "My place is with Ria. I've been hoping you'd help me get back to her."

Within forty minutes of forcing down a single small cup of the bitter brew – so much faster than the first time – Leoni began to detect a change in the moonlit jungle.

At first it was no big deal when this corner of the sky, or that tree over there, or even the pillars of the *maloca* itself slowly flowed, dissolved and dispersed. But soon the process speeded up, affecting every part of the scene, until, after a few moments, she felt herself suspended in a bubble of light and could see only a blur of shifting colors all around her as though the pixels of reality were being reshuffled.

Patterns of light and sunshine, swirling and coalescing, turned night into day, where the vast trees of the equatorial Amazon had swayed a forest of lofty pines now stood, and the wood and thatch dwellings of Don Leoncio's homestead on the creek gave way to a glimpse of hell. By a stream in a clearing fifty large tepees had been reduced to their scorched conical wooden frames, the mutilated bodies of hundreds of men and women – mostly red-haired and pale-skinned, some naked, some wearing scraps of rough plaid – were heaped up in piles, and the ashes of a great bonfire were filled with charred human remains.

Although there had been no familiar tunnel of light to mark her transit, Leoni didn't need the confirmation of the crude flint weapons that lay scattered about, or the ghastly tortures inflicted on the victims before they died, to guess the Illimani had done this and that she'd returned to Ria's epoch. And although the Blue Angel had not appeared as she had before to send her on her way, Leoni knew she was at work somewhere unseen, manipulating time and space, and remembered what she'd said: "Ria stands between Sulpa and the Neanderthals and I have entangled your life with hers. You are sisters in time now. Together you will find the way."

The words were fixed in her memory but Leoni wasn't sure what she was supposed to do and didn't even know if her last attempt to help Ria had succeeded. Besides, was that all there was to it? Was all this time travel just about helping her sister out of tight fixes? Or had the Angel been speaking of something else when she said they possessed great strength together?

Invisible in the midst of the smoldering camp, Leoni felt panic seize hold of her. Had she failed, after all, to warn Ria of Sulpa's tracking device in her leg? Had it brought him and the Illimani straight to her? And was this scene of mass murder the result?

Almost at once Leoni's fears were laid to rest as she saw Ria approaching from amongst the trees with six companions. Though their lips weren't moving they seemed to be communicating and she could almost imagine she heard words in some strange language, faint as whispers carried on the wind.

Three of the group were Neanderthal males, more varied in appearance and stature than she had imagined. The other three were all human. One held a bow with a long flint-tipped arrow half drawn. He was in his twenties, slim, almost delicate, dressed much as the others in a leather jerkin and leggings and tough simple moccasins. The kid to Ria's left – black hair, wild blue eyes – looked a lot like an Illimani and gripped a hatchet in each hand. *Go figure*! To Ria's right was a shaggy-haired giant, almost twice her height and girth, armed with a lethal-looking double-headed stone axe. He had massive shoulders and eyes that glinted with uncompromising belligerence.

They were obviously a team, all seven of them, used to working together and watching each others' backs. They looked ready to defend themselves as they moved through the carnage of the clearing. The big guy had unslung his axe, Ria clutched a stone in her left hand and a flint knife in the right, and the Neanderthals all held weapons.

But Leoni could see no danger. The massacre hadn't happened today, maybe not even yesterday and she hoped the killers were long gone. With a nudge of will she sent her aerial body soaring above the forest and scanned the ground in all directions. There was no threat in the immediate vicinity of the camp. Further off, the huge pines grew too far apart to hide large numbers of men but there might still be the risk of an ambush from a smaller group.

She dropped down again to take another look at Ria. Her thigh, where Sulpa's tracking device had been, was hidden by her leggings but there was no swelling and she was lithe and balanced on her feet. Her lean, tough, sun-browned body had been ripped and torn by battle wounds when Leoni had last seen her but now every gouge and stab was fully healed, with only faint scars and bruises to mark their place.

It was just one more mystery amongst so many.

Close up, Leoni could still see the tomboy prettiness in Ria she'd noticed before, but what struck her about the other girl now – in fact, it took her breath away – was the wild and terrible beauty that shone from her face. There was sorrow there, mingled with pain. There was courage, determination, wisdom, experience, a cool, calculating intelligence – all far beyond her years. There was strength – strength of character, strength of will, strength of purpose. But above all there was an inner fire in Ria that burned bright, and something remorseless and unstoppable about her that the others in the band responded to – for it was obvious they all accepted her as their leader.

They were across the stream now and out of the clearing, following a well-beaten trail through the forest. Leoni hovered right in front of the group, gliding back as Ria moved forward. She didn't know why she did it – some impulse, some whim – but she reached out her diaphanous aerial hand and touched the other girl's shoulder. Ria halted in her tracks, as though she'd felt the contact, and looked at her.

Ria had magnificent eyes, wide and bright under long lashes, with hazel irises lit by flecks of gold and violet.

Resisting an overwhelming urge to shoot twenty feet into the sky, Leoni stayed where she was, wondering if she'd been seen.

Ria didn't move either. There was an intense eager expression on her face. Her companions too had stopped and their eyes were fixed on her. She reached out her hand and probed the air, then shook her head as though to clear it. As the look of recognition faded from her eyes she stepped right through Leoni and marched off along the trail without a backward glance.

So . . . not seen, then.

But sensed.

Definitely sensed.

It was a gift of their entanglement, Leoni was sure of that, a connection that seemed to break all the rules of aerial bodies in physical realms. Because of it, despite her fears, she had indeed got her warning through to Ria about Sulpa's tracking device.

(*"Together you and she possess great strength."*)

Leoni darted over the heads of the little group of humans and Neanderthals, leaving them behind as she hurtled along the trail through the forest. If she could communicate with Ria then she could scout for her, warn her of dangers in her path, keep her safe from ambush.

She could be useful.

She could help.

Leoni followed the trail to the edge of the forest but for all that way she saw no sign of danger and neither human, nor animal, nor bird, nor insect moved.

The open land ahead still had some tree cover, being dotted with little coppices, and rose in rolling undulating hummocks towards a ridge about two miles distant. Leoni sped up to it only to find more of the same landscape stretching in all directions.

Once again there was no danger in sight.

She flew a mile further.

Two miles.

Five miles.

Still nothing.

But when she crested the next ridge the Illimani were suddenly everywhere – a big force, perhaps five hundred of them, streaming up the side of a hollow where they'd been concealed from view. It was easy to identify the leaders – two monstrous warriors, tall and massive, swaggering in the middle of the front rank. They looked so similar they had to be twins. Their hair hung in filthy matted dreadlocks to their waists. What distinguished them from each other were their scary headdresses.

One of them wore the long curved horns of a bull, the other the toothy snarling skull of some giant species of bear.

Their line of march would take them straight to the forest through which Ria and her companions were trekking.

Leoni somersaulted in the air and streaked back to warn Ria.

Chapter Seventy-Seven

The body dangling from the tree was stiff, dead, faintly putrid and cold to the touch, which meant this had not happened today. If luck was still with them there was a good chance the Illimani who had done this had moved on in search of new victims.

On the other hand, it was also possible they were still here.

With Ligar in the lead – it was he who knew this track – Ria and her companions picked their way through the forest.

There were corpses everywhere, most stripped but some still wearing the distinctive plaid of the Merell. Not all of them were nailed to trees. Dozens had been impaled on long wooden stakes. Many others appeared to have been flayed alive. A few had been beaten to a pulp with stones and some had been roasted over slow fires at the side of the track. Everywhere, thick and cloying, the smell of death filled the air.

Ahead in a clearing, beside a bright stream, stood the remains of a large Merell camp. Utter destruction had been unleashed here. Fifty tepees had been reduced to scorched frames, hundreds of mutilated bodies were heaped up in piles, and the ashes of a great bonfire were filled with charred human bones.

They didn't stop to count the bodies but it looked like more than four hundred adults, men and women of all ages, had been killed. As usual the children of the camp were nowhere to be seen.

When at last Ria emerged from the forest with her companions, high sun had come and gone and vistas of rolling uplands lay ahead, dotted with little stands of trees and bathed in mellow afternoon light.

In this undulating terrain, just over that ridge-line, or on the other side of that hill, or hidden in that hollow, an entire army could lie in wait and you would not know until you came upon it. So perhaps the strong intuition to hide by which Ria now found herself seized was just her logical mind at work.

And yet . . .

It was almost as if a voice was whispering an urgent warning in her ear . . .

"*Hide now!*"

Although she had seen nothing she was certain it was the golden-haired girl whom the blue woman had called Leoni – her ally from the future, come to help her defeat Sulpa. She'd felt a presence in the forest but had convinced herself she'd imagined it. Now, with the hairs on the back of her neck crawling, she knew she had to act.

They were climbing towards a ridge up an open slope of rugged tussocky grass. Back below them and off to their right about a thousand paces away was a small coppice of gnarled and ancient oaks.

Ria pointed it out to her companions. "We need to hide in there," she told them. "Right now!"

Bont was surly: "No, Ria. I'm going on."

"If you go on you'll get us all killed. Something's coming." She bared her teeth at him. "Believe me, Bont," she hissed. "SOMETHING'S COMING!"

For a moment he blinked at her in astonishment. She was expecting a volcanic outburst of temper but instead he shrugged acceptance and then they were all running headlong downhill towards the coppice.

Ria was the last to reach the shelter of the trees.

As she turned and looked behind she saw a host of armed men, naked and shaggy, surging like a tide over the ridge and pouring down the slope behind them.

She dropped to her belly and wriggled deeper into the undergrowth, peering out through a tangle of brambles and ferns. The great oaks of the coppice towered above her, swaying gently in the afternoon breeze, their leaves rustling. All around she could sense the explosive tension and fear of her companions. If even one of the advancing braves had seen her in those last few heartbeats before she darted into cover then it was all over.

But their luck held.

Descending the long slope ten abreast, in disciplined ranks, the Illimani pouring over the ridge showed no interest in the coppice and pursued a course that would pass, at the closest point, about a hundred paces north of it. "*Forty-five, forty-six, forty-seven*" – Ria silently counted the ranks as they crested the ridge – "*forty-eight, forty-nine, fifty.*"

Fifty ranks of ten.

A column of five hundred men, like a vast millipede swarming across the land.

And with seven thousand Illimani at his disposal, it was quite possible that Sulpa had sent out a dozen death squads of this strength to roam the countryside in search of tribes like the Merell and the Naveen. Their natural subdivisions into small units made them easy targets for annihilation; very few of the bands, on their own, had sufficient numbers to challenge five hundred fierce and ruthless men.

Ria's gaze was drawn to the head of the column, now less than a bowshot away, and to two impressive braves who marched at the center of the front rank, naked as the Illimani always were and so alike they had to be twins. Both loomed over the others around them, and had big flushed meaty faces set into almost identical angry sneers. She guessed their age at thirty or perhaps thirty-five summers. Their massive upper bodies seemed as wide around as the biggest trees in the coppice, their legs and arms bulged with bands of muscle but, despite their bulk, both had the lithe, balanced, threatening walk of fighters. Their pale hair, braided into thick locks, hung down almost to their hips, both of them wore spectacular headdresses, one of aurochs horns, the other fashioned from the skull and jaws of a cave bear, and each carried a heavy axe with a double-headed obsidian blade.

"He who wears the aurochs horns is Martu," Driff's thought-voice spoke up in Ria's mind. She knew the name meant "bull." "He leads this five hundred, but Sulpa favors him. There is talk he will give him command of the whole army. The other one is his brother, Sakkan." This name meant "bear." "He is Sulpa's torturer. If the spirits hear my prayers my blades will take his head."

Ria looked to her left to where she could just see Driff's blue eyes glaring out of the underbrush. The thing about thought-talk was that it conveyed emotions as well as words and when he spoke of his desire to kill Sakkan she also felt the intensity of his hatred for the man.

Burning hatred.

Like a fire in his heart.

She glanced quickly at the oncoming Illimani, now very close, and back to Driff: "What happened?" she pulsed.

"Sulpa declared my mother and father traitors. Sakkan tortured them. I served as his assistant. In the end it was I who killed them."

Ria's eyes swung back to the solid phalanx of marching men. The thick soles of their bare feet thumped down on the earth with a sound like repeated blows. Their course had not changed and they would still miss the coppice, although perhaps by less than the hundred paces she had originally estimated. "May the spirits hear your prayers," she said softly to Driff. "But not now."

Sakkan had broken away from the column and was striding towards them.

Had the hulking Illimani heard their thought-talk? Surely not. He made no call for support and he wasn't behaving like a man who'd detected enemies. He paused in mid-stride, and a look of concentration crossed his face before he cocked a leg and released a series of thunderous farts.

Could it be he was just going to take a shit?

Ria knew she was well hidden. Driff, too. And although she had a clear mental picture of where everyone else was – Bont and Ligar to her right, Grondin, Oplimar and Jergat about ten paces behind her – she couldn't actually see any of them amongst the trees and thick undergrowth. Hopefully Sakkan wouldn't see them either. "Everybody stay absolutely still!" she pulsed. "Not a word, not a breath, or we're dead."

"We can kill him," suggested Driff.

"That would be incredibly stupid. Think about it. If he doesn't go back to the column how long will it be before all five hundred of them are in here after us?"

Sakkan had reached the edge of the coppice and the column was already streaming by, fifty paces away. He stepped past the first trees. His right foot, large and dirty, came down within a hand's breadth of Ria's face. Then he was past her and into the little patch of clear space between her and the Uglies that they'd all avoided when they'd concealed themselves.

With a sigh of satisfaction he chopped his axe into the ground, squatted down, planting one massive hand on each knee, and farted again – a high-pitched, strangulated squeal, ludicrous coming from such a huge man. Ria bit back a giggle that rose in her throat and glanced sideways to Driff, just discerning his outline as a shadow close to the ground.

A shadow with raging blue eyes, a hatchet gripped tight in each hand, rising to a crouch.

Chapter Seventy-Eight

"No, Driff!" Ria pulsed. "No! You'll kill us all."

Through the open channel of thought-talk she could feel the restless energy of his body, see the red haze of madness fogging his mind. "No!" she pulsed again – and this time she sent it out like a lash. "Get down, Driff! Right now!"

She saw him hesitate, felt resignation wash over him together with another more complicated emotion she couldn't name, and watched as he lowered himself silently back to the ground.

Sakkan was straining and grunting and hadn't noticed anything. His hairy ass bobbed up and down over the spiky grass. He groaned, two more squeaky farts followed and suddenly he was launched on a massive, noisy, stinking shit that splattered out of him in a rush. He grunted and strained again. Two more bursts of loose turds followed, then he was done. He snatched up a handful of leaves and dry grass from the ground, cleaned himself, shouldered his axe and strode away.

For what felt like a very long time no one moved. Then Ligar emerged from a bush just an arm's length from the pile of excrement. He was holding his nose and glaring with disgust in the direction Sakkan had departed. "That man feeds on rotten meat," he said.

With the Illimani gone, and the first faint hints of the oncoming evening already touching the afternoon air, Ria and her companions resumed their trek towards the Gate of Horn. Bont was sullen and morose, infuriated by the continuing delays. Ligar walked with the Uglies. Once again Ria found herself beside Driff. "So it wasn't just Brindle," she said, "who got you to come over to us. Sulpa and Sakkan made you torture and kill your own mother and father. That's enough reason for anybody to change sides."

"Sulpa was my god. I admired Sakkan. I was happy I had killed mother and father for them! Until the day you captured me I never questioned what I'd done. Then Brindle got inside my head. Showed me right and wrong. He showed me how they'd USED me. Sulpa, Sakkan, Martu, all of them. That's how they do it. They make you dive into evil so deep you can't get out and then you're theirs forever . . ."

He paused, set his wild blue eyes on her: "I want to tell you about my vision, when we ate the Little Teachers."

Ria nodded: "Please, yes. Tell me."

"I was shown everyone I have killed," Driff said. He rubbed his forehead with the long, strong fingers of his left hand: "All the innocent dead. I did not remember there were so many. They came to me one by one, Ria. They reproached me . . ."

She had to be honest: "You *did* take their lives."

"They told me they'll wait for me when I die." He shivered: "They'll make me pay for every death." He put his hand gently on her arm. "How can I satisfy the dead?" he asked her.

"Save the living," she answered at once. "Help us kill Sulpa. Your ghosts will move on."

Ria felt relieved when Driff withdrew his hand. She hoped very much he wasn't forming a romantic attachment to her. She wasn't in the mood for that kind of thing at all.

As the late afternoon wore on into the long summer's evening, the landscapes through which they trekked became ever more rugged and boulder-strewn, criss-crossed with plunging ravines, and heavily overgrown with gorse and brambles. They came to a thunderous waterfall on the upper Snake, where rainbows played within the cascade, and followed the course of the great river eastward into a narrow valley. All they had to do now was continue to follow it upstream towards its headwaters until they reached the steep gorge in the Gate of Horn that Ria had seen in her vision. There they would begin the search for Bont's family and the other survivors of the Clan.

They hadn't gone far before a roe deer burst from a thicket in front of them and Ria killed it with a single stone. They field dressed it on the spot, Grondin slung it over his shoulders and they were on their way again.

With the sun still in the sky they continued to make good time despite the rough and increasingly mountainous terrain. But as darkness settled around them, with moonrise still a long way off, they were forced to slow their pace. First Oplimar, then Bont, cursing and tumbling, suffered painful falls. Neither broke a leg but Ria shuddered at how easily either one might have done so.

Nor was this their only consideration. All of them were exhausted, not just from two days on the march with no sleep, sustained only by nuts, berries and tough strips of dried meat, but from the days and nights of fighting and running they had endured before that.

Ria called a halt and for once Bont, limping from his fall, did not object.

They were following a clear broad track rising through trees. The river was forty paces to their right. A hundred paces to their left a rocky outcrop loomed against the darkness. They found shelter there, under an overhanging ledge where the light of a fire would not be seen, and sat with their stomachs rumbling while the deer roasted. It was not a large animal, but to Ria, at the end of that hard day, it was a mouth-watering feast.

Before they had reduced it to its bones, heavy clouds closed in overhead and a drenching rain began to fall. The ledge kept them dry and the fire was warm despite the sudden chill that came with the downpour. With a sigh of frustration, mingled with relief, Ria accepted there was nothing to be done but the one thing they all needed to do most.

Jergat took the first watch while the others slept. Ligar would replace him, then it would be Ria's turn. If the clouds cleared enough to show the moon everyone was to be wakened and they'd get on the move again.

It seemed only heartbeats later when Ria felt Ligar's hand jog her shoulder. As she sat up with a start, he held a warning finger to his lips. "*Listen,*" he pulsed.

The fire was out. Heavy drops of water still fell from the rim of the ledge but the rain had stopped. The moon glimmered through scudding clouds and tendrils of damp mist clung to the ground.

In the distance, approaching down the track from the direction of the Gate of Horn, Ria heard gruff male voices raised in anger.

They were speaking Illimani.

"How many?" she pulsed.

Ligar's thought-voice was uncertain: "Hard to say. Five? Maybe six?" He fingered his bow: "Shall we take them?"

Ria listened to the voices again. She counted more of them than Ligar had – at least eight, possibly ten. They were locked in a heated argument, getting closer, but she still couldn't make out individual words.

She didn't like it. There was hardly time to set an ambush, they really didn't know how many they would be up against, and wasn't it more important to get the Clan's survivors back than risk everything by picking a fight in the dark? "No," she said. "We'll let them pass."

There came another burst of coarse shouting, much closer now, and a chorus of children's voices arose, crying out in fear and despair.

Ria surged to her feet with a stone in each hand.

Some of those terrified children were pleading for mercy in the language of the Clan.

"Wake the others," Ria pulsed to Ligar. "I'm going to find out what we're dealing with here. Remember we have thought-talk and wait – *wait*! – for my command." She was already running, swift and soundless, towards the track, darting from tree to tree. Moonlight came and went with the clouds, now bright, now dark again. Faint and pale in the east, still no more than the softest blush brushing the sky, she could sense the approach of dawn.

An immense pine had fallen here in some recent storm. Wrenched free out of a gaping crater in the earth, its huge branching root mass offered plentiful cover and a good vantage point. Returning her two throwing stones to their pouch, Ria climbed and burrowed in amongst the roots where they overhung the track.

The Illimani whose quarrel had alerted Ligar appeared out of the trees less than a hundred paces away. There were four braves in the front rank. Right behind came thirty, maybe forty children, some weeping and protesting, others glum and silent, herded into a pale formless pack. Four more Illimani flanked them, two on each side. Finally there was a rearguard, also of four.

The braves were still making a lot of noise, shouting their argument back and forth, and Ria already had the gist of it. They'd captured the children yesterday. Standing orders required they take them to Sulpa for sacrifice but many in the group resented the diversion and wanted to kill them right away.

"They're slowing us down too much," one barked. "There are battles to fight."

"We serve Sulpa," another reminded him.

"We'll serve him better by finding the Light in the West than climbing down mountains in the dark with a bunch of sniveling kids."

"Anyway, they're *our* captives. Sulpa doesn't even know we've got them. We can do what we like with them."

Ria had heard enough. "*To me*!" she pulsed to her companions as she unsheathed her knife. "*To me*! *We have twelve to kill.*" And with the words she sent a clear mental image of where she was and what she saw. "*Bont, Ligar. Get up ahead to take out the leaders. Grondin, Oplimar, Jergat – the rearguard is yours. No mercy. NO MERCY*! *Driff, take their right flank; the left is mine.*"

The Illimani front rank and the foremost of the children were already passing beneath her perch. The moonlight strengthened as the clouds continued to clear, and with a pang of recognition Ria spotted Bont's seven-year-old son Nibo and his five-year-old daughter Maura.

It could only mean one thing.

This little Illimani war band had been into the Gate of Horn, found the Clan survivors she'd seen in her vision, and massacred the adults. Bont's Sabeth was certainly dead.

Abruptly a brave at the front called a halt. He was a short, stocky man, older than most of Sulpa's toughs, with a wild shock of gray hair and a snoutlike snub nose. "Very well, lads," he growled, raising his voice to be heard by those at the rear. "I'm sick of you all complaining. Here's as good a place as any to get rid of these snot-nosed kids." He drew a knife and turned on the children with an evil grin: "Might as well have a bit of fun while we're at it, eh?"

Ria looked down. Directly beneath her, one of the two guards on the left flank roared with satisfaction and unslung his axe. The children wailed.

"*Ready*?" Ria pulsed to her companions.

Instantly a resounding "*YES*" came back.

"*Then hit them*! *Hit them now*!"

Chapter Seventy-Nine

Flying out of her body, far from her own time and place, Leoni felt elated when she saw Ria had understood her warning and had run with her companions into the shelter of a little wood. Elation was replaced by turmoil when the big warrior she thought of as Bear Skull marched into the same wood to take a shit, but he unloaded and marched out again without noticing anything.

Leoni flew over Bear Skull's head to his regiment, already half a mile away, and watched the five hundred men streaming down the long slope into the huge forest from which Ria had so recently emerged. They marched in a disciplined mass and looked unbeatable. Yet they were only a fraction of the much larger army she'd seen gathered round Sulpa by the river when he'd destroyed Ria's Clan.

Where were all the rest?

Leoni hurled herself upwards, thousands of feet into the sky.

In all directions, near and far, rose ominous pillars of smoke, and in the distance, like ants swarming, she could just make out another long column of marching men. Who could doubt the Illimani were everywhere, in huge numbers, killing everyone they could find?

When the last of Bear Skull's regiment had disappeared into the forest, Ria emerged from her hiding place with her companions and Leoni watched them scrambling up the slope in the opposite direction. Ahead, beyond the ridge, lay the tough, wild country out of which the Illimani had marched – a landscape filled with hummocks and deep hollows but tending ever upwards, criss-crossed by streams and dotted with small forests, the terrain growing steeper and more savage mile after mile. In the far distance it merged into the foothills of a range of jagged snow-capped mountains.

The only sure thing was that there would be more Illimani in there somewhere.

Leoni was already darting forward to search them out for Ria when a tunnel of light, unexpected and unwelcome, swirling and pulsing, blinked open in the sky beside her. An enormous force was already drawing her in. She struggled against it but couldn't fight it and her last glimpse, looking back and down at the vanishing landscape of the past, was of Ria walking resolute and unafraid into danger.

Leoni felt her consciousness plunging back into the warm breathing mass of her meat body, unstoppable as a diver entering the water from the high board. *No*! *Too soon*! *Too soon*! A wave of fear, regret and pain washed over her. Deserting Ria now, leaving her unprotected in that deadly wilderness, felt like a terrible betrayal.

But then Leoni began choking and coughing, all her senses alert.

A speedboat was approaching, the snarling industrial roar of its outboard tearing the quiet night air of the jungle to shreds.

Leoni was still seated upright on the little bench she'd used for the session. Leoncio was standing beside her with one hand between her shoulder blades, the other holding a glowing censer releasing clouds of astringent smoke into her nostrils. She coughed and spluttered again. This was what had brought her back! As her head cleared of the residual giddiness and disorientation of the journey Leoncio whisked the censer away and helped her to her feet.

The sound of the speedboat's engine was closer. "We have to run," said Leoncio. "Into the jungle! Mary has your backpack . . ."

"But why? What?"

"Your demon has found us. He's more powerful than I guessed. His people are here. We're leaving immediately."

Bannerman was on his knees on the floor of the *maloca*, reorganizing his knapsack. He'd thrown out most of the clothing, a towel, books, a pair of shoes, and was stuffing in a flashlight, a compass, a Swiss Army knife, a lightweight raincoat, and multiple packages and tubes of medicines from a box that had traveled with them in the boat. Mary had a row of 32-ounce Nalgenes lined up and was filling them with purified water from one of the big plastic barrels they'd brought from the lodge. Don Esteban was packing dried fish, strips of beef jerky, and bunches of plantains into a shoulder bag. Matt was just a shadow down by the creek where the moon, now low in the sky, picked out the metallic glint of the AK-47.

Suddenly he came charging back. "There's more than one boat," he announced. "Could be two. Maybe even three . . . We're out of time." The beams of spotlights became visible, juddering and shaking, cutting through the night, and Leoni understood that their pursuers were already on the creek, coming in fast along the other side of the last switchback.

Mary had finished with the water bottles, handing two to each of them. Leoncio led the way, Matt took up the rear, and with Bannerman still fumbling with his knapsack they fled into the jungle.

Stumbling, almost losing her balance, Leoni still found the presence of mind to check the luminous hands of her Rolex as she ran. It was just after three a.m. Less than three hours of darkness remained, and the moon was still bright. Way too bright. Back at the creek the macho roar of the speedboats' engines fell silent. She heard men shouting – there were so many – and saw their flashlight beams lancing through the trees.

Leoncio was up ahead, leading the way, but if there was a trail Leoni couldn't see it. She was wearing denim jeans and a pair of good walking boots which kept the worst of the undergrowth from tearing her legs and feet to shreds, but her short-sleeved cotton shirt did nothing to protect her upper body and arms which were soon covered in painful scrapes and scratches.

Then she ran into something solid, smacking her forehead very hard, and fell with a stifled scream into a heap of brushwood teeming with biting insects which swarmed into her hair and clothes. Bannerman, who'd been right behind her, rushed to her side, whispering soothing words: "Hush, Leoni, hush, I'm here. Don't be afraid." He took her hand, supported her back and was hauling her to her feet when gunfire broke out from the direction of the creek.

Suddenly – horror – bullets were whipping and buzzing through the trees all around them. Leoni screamed again as something plucked at her arm, Bannerman grunted, an awful sound, and slumped forward against her, a dead weight bearing her down.

Chapter Eighty

Ria slithered out of the knot of upended roots she'd hidden in, fell onto the guard's back, wrapped her thighs around his waist for purchase and sliced her blade through the big artery in his neck. With a fountain of blood gushing up from him he dropped his axe, staggered and crashed to the ground. She crouched over his heaving body, looking left and right.

There'd been two guards on this flank. Where was the second one? Distracted by screaming stampeding kids Ria caught his sudden charge out of the corner of her eye and avoided a wild spear thrust. She palmed a stone, threw herself sideways in a somersault, and ducked into the shadows beside the track.

She heard shouts and blows from the front and rear of the column, and a chorus of screams, but there was nothing to be done about that. The brave with the spear lunged at her, panting and cursing as she squirmed and wriggled away from him. She dived into thick bushes, feeling thorns tear her skin, twisted her body to escape another vicious lunge, forced her way ahead and burst out the other side. Right behind her the Illimani had become tangled in the briars and his forward rush had stopped. He struggled and freed himself but by then Ria was thirty paces away behind a tree, and ready.

The moon gave her a good look at the shaggy, murderous savage. He stopped twenty paces from her, charged at a bush and thrust his spear into it. He glared and charged again, spearing another bush. But it was obvious he'd lost her and he turned back, suddenly wary, towards the track where the sounds of fighting had now died away. Ria heard Driff's thought-voice, and Grondin's, inside in her head, both filled with concern, trying to locate her. "*I live,*" she pulsed and stepped from behind the tree.

"Hey, shitface," she said softly in Illimani.

The brave whirled and she saw him register the flint knife she held, glinting in the moonlight. He seemed to realize for the first time that he confronted a girl, bared his filed teeth in a scornful sneer, and charged.

As she hurled her stone left-handed to strike him between the eyes a cloud blew across the moon. She heard a heavy *clunk* but knew she'd missed the kill when the roaring Illimani smashed into her in the sudden darkness, knocked her to the ground with his full weight and crashed down on top of her in a tangle of knees, hard muscle and bad smells. Ria felt the shaft of his spear trapped under her body – *good*! – but the brave was all over her, thrusting at her like a lover. He got his powerful hands round her throat, bore down on her windpipe and lifted his upper body to increase his leverage. His fingers tightened but she'd held on to the knife and as the moon reappeared she stabbed the long blade into his hot, sweaty armpit, found the soft unprotected spot there and pushed upward so hard the point erupted through the top of his shoulder. He screeched and spat blood but didn't let go and when she twisted the knife and jerked it out to stab him again he took his left hand off her throat and grabbed her wrist. He continued to strangle her with his right hand, his big thumb grinding into her larynx, so Ria didn't much mind the indignity of being rescued when Driff came flying out of the darkness and killed him.

Everyone had played their parts, it seemed, and all twelve of the Illimani were dead. But were more following? Did more lie in their path? When she and her companions had numbered only seven, Ria reflected, they could move fast and hide in an instant. Now, with close to forty children to bring back to Secret Place, they would be slow, unwieldy and very easy to see.

As Ria walked back to the scene of the ambush with Driff she saw Bont clutching his little son Nibo and his daughter Maura in great bear-hugs of joy, whooping and cheering with relief. Through the openness of thought-talk, she shared the deep pain and distress he struggled hard to hide at the certain news that Sabeth was gone.

Past Bont, the other children they'd saved were still milling on the track. With a few exceptions, they had the look of a pathetic panic-stricken herd. None had more than eleven summers, half had yet to reach seven, most were bruised and battered from multiple falls after the forced night-march, and several were close to collapse. All had seen their elders murdered. Some were so browbeaten and brutalized they cowered at the slightest movement. Some wept and called out for dead parents. Others were wide-eyed, shocked and silent.

Including Nibo and Maura, only eight were of the Clan. The other twenty-eight were from various local and some more distant tribes – mostly the Merell and the Naveen, but also a smattering from the Ree, the Jicaque, the Spearjig, and even the Kosh. Ria moved amongst them in the rising dawn light, speaking to them in their own languages, ruffling this one's hair, resting a cheering hand on that one's shoulder, even drawing hesitant smiles from a few.

All told much the same story: a narrow escape from Illimani raiders deep in their homelands, followed by terrified flight, mostly in small family groups, to what they'd thought was the safety of the Gate of Horn. There, one by one, they'd been hunted down – the adults slaughtered and the children rounded up for sacrifice – by the war party of a dozen braves that Ria and her companions had just destroyed.

Had they seen anything, Ria asked, to make them suspect other Illimani war parties had been in the area and might be heading this way? None of them could answer. They did not know. But many looked back with fear in the direction from which they had come.

Ria's first instinct was to run.

Now.

But it was obvious the children were too tired, hungry and confused for that. They wouldn't get far on the long march to Secret Place unless she got some food and some courage into them. It was a gamble but Ria ordered the whole group off the track, away from the splayed bodies of the Illimani and into the rocky outcrop where she and her companions had spent the night. With full daylight coming on fast, a new fire was lit and a good breakfast made of the supplies of fresh meat – rabbit, wildfowl and a side of hog – that the Illimani had been forcing the children to carry for them.

Although they had seen the Uglies fight to save them from the Illimani, most of the kids were suspicious of these strange-looking creatures who featured so often as ogres and monsters in scare stories told by their parents. But Ria summoned Jergat and Oplimar into their midst and soon the whole group began to calm down. There was something kindly and sympathetic about Oplimar that transcended language, and his bushy red beard, wrinkled leathery features and twinkling eyes gave him a comical air. Jergat, lean and slight for an Ugly, had an innocent sense of fun. He sat on the ground amongst a group of the smaller children and allowed them to prod and poke at him and pull his matted hair. It wasn't long before he had a little Naveen boy and a girl of the Spearjig on his shoulders.

While they ate, and the Uglies provided gentle healing to the most damaged, Ria studied the few children who stood out, who didn't look defeated, who still had some fight in them. She settled on four who she thought would serve her purpose. This was to marshal and organize the others and keep them moving through at least the two days – quite possibly three – that it would take them to reach Secret Place. Such a trek would have been difficult for the younger children at any time. But now they had Illimani war parties to contend with as well – including at least one entire troop of five hundred under the leadership of Martu and Sakkan, roaming these parts looking for trouble.

Darza, a boy of nine, was of the Clan. Ria had not known his family well but she remembered him as a plucky little brat always getting into fights with older children who tormented him on account of a livid birthmark covering the entire left side of his face. He was small-boned and quite delicate, with a calm, serious manner. He didn't seem in the least bit afraid.

Then there was the Naveen boy Entu, aged ten but as heavily built as a teenager. His domed head had recently been shaved, no doubt to clear lice, giving him a strange stubbly appearance, but his strength would be an asset and she'd seen he was gentle with the younger children.

Birsing, a tall fierce-faced eleven-year-old of the Merell, had the thick red hair, green eyes and pale freckled skin typical of her people. Right after the fight she'd spoken in a rush in a high, clear voice, saying something Ria hadn't been able to understand very well. Something baffling about a prophecy. Then she'd clammed up tight and said no more. Her green eyes stared out with hostility and rage at everyone. Ria liked the look of her.

Finally there was Panalan of the Kosh, another eleven-year-old. He was lean and dark, with an intense unblinking gaze, and the only one of the children who had joined in the fighting against their captors. He'd been at the back of the column where the Uglies had attacked and Grondin told her how he'd piled in to support them, tangling the legs of one of the rearguard and helping to bring him down.

To each Ria gave command over eight other children. "You're my generals," she told them. "If you can keep this rabble in some sort of order we might get out of here alive."

* * *

The morning air was fresh following the rain, but by high sun the heat had become intense. The younger children, no matter how chivvied they were by Darza, Entu, Birsing and Panalan, or how amused by Jergat's continuing antics, were slowing down. Some looked on the verge of collapse again. When they reached the waterfall they'd passed yesterday, which threw up a cooling spray, Ria ordered a halt and they found shade under trees for a short rest. There was no alternative if half her new protégés were not to die of exhaustion.

Stops were needed with increasing frequency after that, and although it was downhill all the way, retracing the route of the day before, progress was slow. Ria sent Ligar and Jergat to scout ahead for dangers and in the mid-afternoon she fell in beside the Kosh boy Panalan. "Tell me about mammoths," she said.

He wrinkled his face: "They are very large, they move in herds, their meat tastes good. What else is there to say?"

"What happens when a mammoth fights a man?"

"The man dies."

"But how does he die? How does the mammoth kill him?"

"Have you *truly* never seen a mammoth?" asked Panalan. He sounded amazed.

"No, never." The almost mythical creatures had not ranged as far west as the Clan hunting grounds for as long as anyone could remember.

"They're as tall as two men and as heavy as twenty," Panalan explained. "So when they want to kill someone they can just stamp on them, or sit on them, or spear them with their tusks . . ."

"Tusks? That's what ivory comes from, right?"

"They're the mammoth's teeth but grown extremely long" – he spread his arms wide – "longer than this. They stick out of the front of his mouth, one on either side, and he uses them for digging and fighting."

"But you of the Kosh, you hunt these creatures, yes? And trade their skins and meat and . . . tusks?"

"We've learned their ways. We know how to kill them . . ."

"Could you catch one for me, if I asked you to? Without killing it?"

"We could trap one in a pit. But what use would it be to you alive?"

Ria didn't answer.

In the distance she saw Ligar and Jergat returning at a run.

Chapter Eighty-One

A pungent burst of hot thick fluid drenched Leoni's face and hair as they fell, and kept on pumping as Bannerman slumped on top of her. *Blood*! *It had to be blood*!

Leoni screamed and turned her head, spitting and gagging as her mouth and eyes filled with stinking glop. She fought to free herself, was dimly aware of the sounds of gunfire, which seemed to be all around her, heard footsteps charging down on her, thought she must die.

It was Matt. Silent, moving fast, he hauled Bannerman off her, thrust him aside, wrapped his left arm around Leoni and lifted her to her feet. The AK-47 was in his right hand, firing short rapid bursts back towards the creek. The muzzle flashes lit up the night and in the horrible yellowish on-off strobe effect, like riding a ghost train, she caught a glimpse of Bannerman's slumped body and saw the jagged splinters of white bone and gouts of blood and brain matter where half his head had been blown away.

As the horror of the scene consumed her, two shadowy figures burst out of the trees and charged towards them. A burst from the AK-47 sent one of them tumbling but then the gun snicked and seemed to jam and the second man was on top of them. Matt had let go of Leoni to grapple with him and there was a bellow followed by an agonized scream – *Not Matt, please let it not be Matt.* The attacker fell, there was a rush behind them and Matt whirled, the long blade of a hunting knife gleaming in his hand, to face the new threat.

But it was Leoncio, not an enemy. "Quick," hissed the shaman and he turned, gesturing for them to follow. When Leoni tried to drop to her knees beside Bannerman, Matt jerked her upright and growled: "Nothing to be done for him." Then they were running deeper into the jungle, snaking through the trees, the darkness thickening.

There were insects crawling over Leoni's body, in her hair too, some biting her, and the soup of Bannerman's blood was congealing in a sticky mass on her face and throat, dribbling between her breasts and down onto her belly under her clothes. But she hardly registered the discomfort now, her heart thumping, her breath coming in ragged gasps, all her senses alert to the sounds of the pursuit.

A lot of men – *How many? Twenty, thirty?* – were still crashing through the undergrowth behind them, flashlight beams stabbing the night, rough, excited voices calling back and forth to one another, and Leoni felt the oppression of the jungle hemming her in all around. More gunfire came in a long burst, followed by sporadic individual shots and distant muzzle flashes. A few bullets whipped by very close but all the rest went wide.

Leoncio kept up a steady, loping pace, Leoni behind him. Once more she couldn't see a trail – creepers and thorns grabbed at her legs and she felt Matt's hand on her arm, steadying her. "Down," hissed Leoncio, dropping flat to the jungle floor and worming his way forward. Matt and Leoni followed. "In here," the shaman whispered. He squeezed through a gap between low-lying branches and tangled vines, and led them to a narrow sloping muddy watercourse into which they all slithered downwards, helter-skelter in the darkness.

At the bottom of the gully, after a bruising, soaking, jarring slide, Leoni and Leoncio landed in a heap right at Mary's feet where she was waiting in the shadows with Esteban and Emmanuel. Matt was behind them, still clutching the AK-47.

There could be no talking but as Leoni staggered upright she wrapped her arms around Mary and whispered the awful news quietly into her ear: "I'm sorry. John's dead. They shot him. He was trying to save me. It's all my fault."

With a raw stifled moan the other woman shoved her away.

Had they escaped their pursuers at the watercourse?

The sounds of the chase were growing faint and distant, turning at a tangent from them, but Leoncio wasn't satisfied. "If they have a good tracker they could be back on our trail in minutes," he hissed. "We have to move fast – no talking, just follow me."

"Where are we going?" Leoni asked.

"A long way," Leoncio whispered. "A village I know. We'll be safe there. You'll be able to drink Ayahuasca. Good Ayahuasca. We'll get you back to your Ria again . . ."

They walked in single file, about five feet apart. Leoncio was once again in the lead, setting a fast pace, followed by Mary, Esteban, Emmanuel and Leoni, with Matt taking up the rear. He had unjammed and reloaded the AK-47, and both the handguns that he'd stolen from Apolinar's boat were stuffed into his belt.

Somewhere during their headlong escape Leoni had lost her Rolex, and with it all track of time, but soon enough she saw daylight filling the sky from the east. Troops of red howler monkeys were already swinging through the canopy overhead, welcoming the dawn with grating roars and groans, and the high-pitched *rrrk, rrrrk, rrrrk, rrk* calls of huge-billed toucans reverberated from the treetops.

Down on the jungle floor, although it was still quite dark, Leoni could now see enough to avoid the major hazards, which was good, but she also saw the thick matted bloodstains that hadn't been washed out of her jeans and shirt in the watercourse. Up till now there'd been so much else going on it had been easy to avoid thinking of poor dead John Bannerman, but recognizing his blood all over her brought back the whole horror of what had happened.

Leoni braced herself as memories of their encounters during the past week flashed through her mind. He'd saved her life twice. Once in the emergency room, and once again right here tonight – except this time he'd taken bullets that otherwise would certainly have killed her.

Leoncio pushed ahead and the light brightened into full morning.

How much time had passed without them taking a stop? An hour? Two? Three? It was hard to be sure, but suddenly the sun was above the trees and even though the dense green canopy diffused its rays into a soft emerald glow, the heat and humidity of the day soon became almost unbearable.

Leoni had been taking frequent sips from one of her big water bottles but was now horrified to find she had only a few ounces left. What was she going to do when the other one was empty as well? Drink from the Amazon, presumably, and get amoebas in her guts.

She turned her attention to her feet, which hurt, and her legs, which felt weak and wobbly. She had a beating headache and her whole body was covered with scratches and cuts inflicted by the jungle. In contrast Don Emmanuel in his eighties, Don Esteban in his seventies and Don Leoncio in his fifties seemed to float along the almost invisible trail, expending no effort, somehow avoiding all contact with the vines, thorns and random debris that lined their path.

Gritting her teeth, Leoni forced herself to keep up with them, trying to imitate their easy, fluid gait, when she heard a sound from back along their trail that did not belong to the jungle.

Don Leoncio held up a hand, a finger to his lips for silence, and everyone stopped.

There it was again.

Hunting dogs, baying.

Chapter Eighty-Two

The news brought by Ligar and Jergat was good. There were people ahead on their path. A lot of people. But they weren't Illimani. They were Merell and they were led by Sebittu and Tari, the couple whose lives they'd saved the day before. "They're talking about a prophecy," said Ligar.

Ria grimaced. "One of the kids mentioned something like that as well. Any idea what it's about?"

"Haven't a clue," said Ligar in out-loud speech. He leaned close and whispered: "To be honest, it looks like they've all gone mad."

Late in the afternoon, with the setting sun shining almost directly into their eyes, they came over a ridge. A few bowshots downslope lay the great forest into which Martu and Sakkan had disappeared yesterday with their five hundred Illimani. Now an even larger number of Merell – perhaps a thousand of them – began to swarm out of it. As the distance shortened, Ria saw that many were armed and that a disciplined body of archers stood to the front of the huge crowd. They came to a halt twenty paces from her and Sebittu made his way through the archers until he stood at their forefront. Ria stepped forward also – it seemed the right thing to do – and they faced each other across a few paces of open ground.

There was silence for a heartbeat. Then all the rescued Merell children, including Birsing whom Ria had put in charge, bolted for the Merell ranks where they were scooped up and embraced by sobbing, delighted relatives. Birsing, Ria noticed, found nobody waiting for her and wandered, looking from face to face, until Sebittu's wife Tari came to her.

"I've gathered the survivors of four bands," Sebittu told Ria. "There wasn't another Speaker amongst them so I have command. Yesterday you offered me a place of safety for the Merell. Is that offer still open now you see our numbers?"

"Of course it's still open. Just follow us. We'll take you there."

"There is another matter we must settle first," said Sebittu. He signaled to Tari who brought Birsing forward: "Speak, girl. Tell us your story."

Birsing's fierce green eyes glared up at the adults: "When the savages destroyed our camp my mother and I sought sanctuary in the Gate of Horn. My brother Jengo was with us."

Her tone was cold and flat.

"We found others there fleeing the same savages, but more savages had followed. They killed all the grown-ups – Jengo too, though he wasn't fourteen summers. The rest of us they took prisoner. They made us march at night but we were too much trouble so they decided to kill us."

Her face lit up and she turned her green gaze directly on Ria: "Then Ria of the Clan came out of the sky with six brave warriors." She waved in the direction of Bont, Ligar, Driff, Grondin, Oplimar and Jergat. "Ha! You should have seen them fight. They killed all the savages and saved our lives."

Birsing stepped forward two more paces and stood right in front of Ria, looking up at her with burning eyes: "You're the girl from the prophecy," she said. "I knew it when you saved us. When you came from the sky. I saw the way you killed that guard. So fast it was beautiful. I want to learn to do that." She reached out, took Ria's hand and kissed it – an action that evoked a sigh from the crowd. Then she returned to Tari's side.

"The girl from what prophecy?" Ria asked.

"Birsing voices what we all believe," said Sebittu.

Ria gave him a blank, uncomprehending look.

"Forgive me," he said. "You speak our language so well it's easy to forget you don't know our traditions. There is a prophecy of Our Lady of the Forest – passed down to us from the long-ago . . ."

Our Lady of the Forest. The name by which the blue woman was known amongst the Uglies! Were the Merell too part of the web she was spinning backwards and forwards in time?

"At first I couldn't be sure the prophecy spoke of you," Sebittu continued. "But there's no longer any doubt." His voice ringing, he began to recite:

"In the time of darkness will appear the Harbinger of the Light. She will fight against the Evil One for the future of the world. By these signs you shall recognize her . . ."

Starting as a whisper of a few isolated voices, quickly taken up by others, and soon intoned by hundreds, the rest of the Merell joined in the recitation, the words growing louder and stronger with each new revelation until they reached a crescendo:

"She will come from the east, out of the Gate of Horn, a protector of children. Great courage will be hers, and great cunning in battle. All the tongues of the world will be at her command. She is the one who will unite the tribes . . ."

How or when the blue woman had planted this prophecy in the Merell's past Ria didn't know or care. All that mattered was to use it to her advantage.

Things were moving fast.

Sebittu dropped to one knee before her: "The Evil One has come into our valleys," he said, "and his name is Sulpa. His forces have destroyed our camps, raped our women, stolen our children, so it cannot be an accident you appear now, out of the east, a protector of children . . ."

Ria looked around. All the rest of the Merell were down on their knees as well.

"There can be no doubting the prophecy," said Sebittu. "Our Lady of the Forest has chosen you to fight the Evil One. You have already offered a place of safety for my people, and I have accepted. Now I offer you in return my Merell archers at your command until Sulpa is destroyed. What do you say?"

"I say yes."

What other answer could there be?

Chapter Eighty-Three

Don Leoncio and the others had been moving too fast for Leoni even before they heard the dogs. Now they doubled their pace to a run. She couldn't sustain it and after only a few moments she was bent over by the side of the trail, gasping for breath, sweat drenching her filthy clothes.

Matt stooped, put his shoulder into her waist and the next thing she knew he had picked her up in a fireman's lift and was jogging through the jungle with her to where Leoncio and the others waited just up ahead. Then they were all off again at a run: "I'll carry you as long as I can," Matt panted. "Get your breath back – you'll need it."

Being shouldered like a sack of potatoes and bumped up and down with every footstep was uncomfortable but beat running for a while. It gave Leoni a chance to listen to the dogs. She thought there were four of them. Two were still quite far back, two others were closer and moving fast.

Five minutes passed, Matt set her down, and Leoni put everything she had into keeping going and not being a burden. But it was no good. Her body was soft and weak, she was still reeling from the effects of last night's Ayahuasca trip, and the sound of those dogs was turning her bowels to jelly.

Mary looked done in, too. Don Emmanuel's normally nut-brown skin was gray and slick with sweat. Even Matt was showing signs of strain. The heat and humidity were unbelievable – it was like running in a sauna bath – and Leoni's heart was kicking. "I have to stop," she gasped, doubling forward. "Can't . . . can't . . . I can't . . ."

Without a word, hardly breaking his stride, Matt swept her up again.

He ran with her for what seemed a long time. *Strong as an ox,* she thought, but the dogs were still gaining on them. Finally, with a grunt of exhaustion, he swung her down to her feet, stepped to one side and cocked the AK-47, pointing it back along the trail.

Gasping for breath, everyone else stopped and turned. But when

Leoncio saw what was happening he hurried to Matt and laid his hand on the gun. "This is just dogs," he hissed. "Let's not tell the hunters our position before we need to." He drew a machete from his belt, and in the same instant a brown muscular streak, some sort of pit bull/mastiff cocktail, snarling and spraying saliva, launched itself at him from the undergrowth and clamped its teeth onto his arm, bearing him to the ground.

Matt dived after the animal, thrust his knife right up its anus and twisted the blade. The brute yelped and let go of Leoncio who smashed his machete into its neck just as the second dog burst from the jungle. Still crouched low, Matt shouldered aside its leap for his throat and plunged his knife to the hilt between its ribs. It dropped to the ground, all the life gone out of it.

Don Leoncio's arm was cut and bleeding, Mary was white as a sheet. Don Emmanuel looked close to collapse and was being tended by Esteban.

Leoni figured the first two dogs had been let loose for whatever mischief they could do – and they'd done enough – but back down the trail the second two were still baying, choking against the leash, and she could now also hear the distant excited shouts of the hunters.

Because surrender wasn't going to be an option with Jack involved, and they were all going to die, she wanted to apologize to Mary: "I'm sorry you got dragged into this," she said.

The older woman surprised her. "It's not your fault. We're all adults here. I'm sorry I reacted the way I did when you told me about John." She stepped closer and embraced Leoni: "This whole thing. It's an amazing experience. I wouldn't miss it for the world."

Still nobody had moved. "Come on!" said Leoncio. "This way!" And he plunged off the faint trail they'd been following and led them straight into dense jungle, hacking through the clinging vines and thorns.

"The river's about five hundred feet over there," he explained.

"The river?" Leoni didn't see why that was useful.

"Tributary of the Ucayali. If we can get across it we'll be safe."

"How do we get across it?"

"Swim."

Behind, the dogs bayed.

* * *

Five hundred feet is a long way in virgin jungle and just as they reached the river's high bank, overgrown with palms, a tremendous hue and cry from their pursuers told Leoni the bodies of the dogs must have been found. There was an instant of delay and then the hunt surged towards the river. Crouching down, facing back the way they had come, Matt seemed to have been waiting for this. He fired a long burst from the AK-47, ejected the empty clip, locked a new one into place and fired again. "In the water," yelled Leoncio, barely audible above the rapid rattle of the assault rifle. "Ditch your packs. Hold on to each other."

Leoni looked down at the muddy swirling river, wide as a football field, undercutting the bank fifteen feet below. *Monsters,* she thought. *It's full of monsters. I can't get in there.* She saw Esteban and Emmanuel jump and realized bullets were flying out towards her from the jungle. There was a whiz and a slap. She felt heat part her hair and a gush of blood poured down into her eyes from her scalp. She put up her hand, fearing that her brains had been blown out, like Bannerman's, but found instead a shallow bleeding groove running diagonally across the top of her skull. With a yelp she dumped her pack, grabbed Mary's hand and they jumped together from the bank, hitting the water with a tremendous splash.

At once the current swept them out towards the midstream where Esteban was keeping Don Emmanuel afloat. A few seconds behind, Don Leoncio hit the water and swam to join them. Matt was the last. Still standing on the bank, he fired a final long burst back into the jungle, threw down the AK-47 and his pack, and jumped in.

A second later a huge tawny mastiff with jaws like a steel trap came flying off the bank, hit the water and swam after him, fast as an otter, gaining on him. Leoni was still holding on to Mary's hand and the two of them were treading water, watching hypnotized and aghast, but just before the dog got its teeth into Matt he rolled, pulling a pistol out of his belt, and – *Bam*! *Bam*! – shot the animal twice in the head.

As it sank beneath the surface without even a yelp there was a muffled scream. Mary's hand was torn from Leoni's grasp, and there was a tremendous agitation in the water. Turning in horror, Leoni saw the older woman had been seized in the jaws of a massive black cayman. It shook her from side to side the way a terrier shakes a rat.

Chapter Eighty-Four

Of the thousand Merell who came out of the forest with Sebittu, most were either too old, too young or had been too badly wounded in previous skirmishes with the Illimani to be any use if it came to a fight. Still, Ria counted a hundred and eighty-seven able-bodied braves amongst them – a credible force. All were armed with the usual assortment of spears, clubs, maces, axes, hatchets and knives, but the real prize was that a hundred and nine of them also carried powerful hunting bows and quivers full of arrows.

It wasn't enough to beat Martu and Sakkan – nowhere near enough – but Ria hoped the presence of so many archers might at least make the Illimani think twice before attacking. She put Ligar in charge of them and gave Bont command of the other seventy-eight. Communication was going to be difficult, perhaps dangerously so, but for the vital decisions she needed people who'd fought by her side before. Besides, Ligar already knew a little Merell, and there were Merell in both groups who could speak enough of the Clan language to pass orders on. The arrangement would have to work.

Then there were the women. Again, there were many who were injured, ancient or infirm, but with Tari assisting her Ria selected close to two hundred who were able-bodied and had them stand to one side. Being Merell, all of them were already armed with some weapon or other. Their job now, Ria told them, was to be the last line of defense for the children and the elderly. She placed Tari in charge of them.

With half of his men and ten of Ligar's archers Bont would march at the head of the column with Sebittu, Driff and Ria. Grondin, Oplimar and Jergat volunteered for the rearguard. Ria assigned the rest of Bont's men, along with ten more archers, to join them there and divided the remaining archers under Ligar's command to protect the flanks. The column could close up or spread out, depending on the terrain, but this would be the general disposition. Relays of the fastest runners were sent out ahead to scout the route for danger and unforeseen obstacles.

Ria decided to keep the rescued children together and to preserve the command structure she'd established on the mountain. Birsing, Entu, Panalan and Darza remained in charge and the first task she gave them was to ensure everyone had a weapon – even if it was only a sharp-edged rock or an improvised club. They were to form an organized core within the larger mass of non-combatants at the center of the column, and unlike the others, who would be no help, Ria told them she expected them to fight back if they were attacked: "Fight for your lives. You've seen what the Illimani do when they win."

"Is it true," Birsing asked, "that their leader drinks the blood of captured children?"

Word was getting round. "Yes," Ria admitted, "it's true."

Birsing shuddered: "But you're going to stop him, aren't you? That's what the prophecy says."

Ria smiled: "Of course we'll stop him." She could see Birsing believed her, but inside she was filled with doubts and the weight of her new responsibilities weighed her down. Everything in her life was moving and changing so fast that it was hard to remember who and what she'd been just a few days before. Now she was to be a hero to every little girl and boy, some of them only a few years younger than herself, and she had the hopes and expectations of a whole tribe focused on her.

She would march them through the night, without stopping. That way there would be less risk of encountering the Illimani. And she would march them all the next day. If the spirits were with her she would get them back to Secret Place safely sometime after nightfall tomorrow.

The return journey through the great forest began before the last light of the long summer evening had left the sky, but when full night arrived, with moonrise still a long way off, the darkness grew thick as blood. This was a Merell forest and scouts who knew it well guided the column through the trees, but still the going was slow and difficult.

Ria was at the front with Sebittu at her side and with Bont, Driff, Grondin, Oplimar and Jergat all nearby. Sebittu had been talking at length about the Merell's worship of their goddess, the Lady of the Forest, and about the prophecy she had given in the long-ago that Ria fulfilled. It had been passed down by word of mouth from generation to generation – every Merell learned it in childhood – and it now emerged there were other verses which further strengthened the connection. One, which described Ria exactly, said that the Harbinger would be "an unwed girl of sixteen summers." Another predicted she would be "an orphan, born of the Clan." And a third stated that Uglies would fight beside humans in the army of the Harbinger of the Light – so the presence of Grondin, Oplimar and Jergat had been taken by all the Merell as further confirmation of the truth of the prophecy.

It was all very strange, Ria had to admit, yet this was how the blue woman worked – not directly but in roundabout ways, manipulating others to fight Sulpa on her behalf and finding them means and allies. She hadn't told the Merell yet about her own encounters with the Lady of the Forest. It would have seemed boastful, when they were already acclaiming her as the subject of the prophecy, to hold up her hand and say, "Yes, I've met your goddess. She gave me my gift of languages."

Probably they all took that for granted already anyway.

As the slow passage through the forest wore on, and the moon rose to light their way, a new phenomenon became apparent. Groups of ragged refugees, mostly women and children but some with braves amongst them, appeared through the trees, following the column, crying out for protection and in some cases for food. They came from many different tribes, though none of them were Clan, and all told the same story of Illimani attacks on their camps, of bloody massacres and spectacular cruelties, and of their own desperate escapes.

Ria refused nobody, not even a Naveen hunter with shifty eyes and wearing ragged skins who gave her a bad feeling the moment she saw him. The column kept growing with the constant stream of new arrivals and Ria could sense Grondin was troubled. "The spirits gave Secret Place to the Uglies to keep us safe from your kind of people," he pulsed as another large group was assimilated. "Now we're taking more than a thousand of you inside . . ."

This had all been discussed with Brindle before they set out and the policy had been agreed. Despite the appalling risk it posed to the Uglies, all people of whatever tribe who were fleeing the Illimani would be welcomed. Nothing had changed, but Ria understood how scary it must be for Grondin to see for real the flood of refugees their generosity was about to bring into their sanctuary. "Who's to say they won't just kill us all when they outnumber us?" Grondin now asked.

"*I* say that," Ria pulsed. "I say it a hundred times. I will rule these people until Sulpa is defeated and they will respect and honor the Uglies."

Gray dawn light was already filtering through thin clouds and mist lay chest-high across the ground as the column passed in silence through the foul-smelling charnel house of the Merell camp by the stream.

Soon afterwards they emerged from the forest onto the bleak open moors beyond, and the full numbers of the refugees who had joined them became clear – around another four hundred, Ria estimated, amongst them approximately sixty braves whom she assigned to Bont's advance party and the rearguard. After being hunted and harried for days it seemed everyone was eager to be part of the great and strong counterforce building before their eyes, and there were no challenges to Ria's authority.

But at mid-morning more than a hundred Naveen braves, who had somehow evaded detection by the scouts, appeared over the crest of a hill on a collision course with the column. Although they kept their bows slung across their shoulders they held their spears forward and approached at a threatening run.

Ligar had his archers stand by but instructed them to keep their bows unbent unless the Naveen fired first. "We want these people for allies," Ria said. "Let's be friendly."

The Naveen commander didn't carry a bow, but was armed with three spears gathered in a bundle in his huge left hand. He was tall and powerful, a thick, muscular slab of a man, as big as Bont or Grondin. He had high cheekbones, a massive jaw, a hooked nose and fierce slanted eyes. From the lines in his face Ria guessed his age at close to forty summers but he was agile and fast on his feet. His most striking feature was his skull, which was shaved bald except for a topknot of black hair gathered into a pigtail that hung down between his shoulders.

He drew up his men in ranks twenty wide right in the path of the column and everyone came to an abrupt halt. "You are welcome in the land of the Naveen," he said to Sebittu, speaking fluent Merell. "I am Balaan." He looked along the column with its ragged ranks of refugees now spreading out to right and left, and nodded his head. "Our valleys too have been invaded," he continued, "but some of us are ready to fight back." He indicated his men. "If I add my force to yours we'll be powerful. My price is joint command."

"That's not for me to offer," said Sebittu at once. He turned and looked at Ria.

"I heard there was a bitch in charge here," Balaan exclaimed in a tone of disgust.

Trying to hide himself amongst the braves behind Balaan, Ria recognized the shifty-eyed hunter whom she'd noticed the night before. He was another of those Naveen who spoke good Merell – in fact, the two languages were closely related. Obviously he'd only stayed long enough to estimate the column's strength and gather what tittle-tattle he could before fleeing to report to his master.

"What a fucking waste of effort," Ria spat, pointing out the spy. She spun towards Balaan: "You could have stopped us any time," she yelled, "and asked me anything you wanted to know and I would have told you. You can still do that. We all face the same enemy."

The Naveen commander studied her in silence for what felt like a count of thirty. His eyes, hard as flints, roamed her body. "I don't work with bitches," he said at last.

He turned to Sebittu: "So, joint command – yes? You and me? But the bitch goes back where she belongs with the women and kids, otherwise no deal."

Ria took another step forward. "I'm in command here," she told Balaan. "No one else. Call me a bitch again and you'll have to fight me."

Chapter Eighty-Five

Bam! *Bam*! *Bam*! *Bam*! – Matt fired at point-blank range into the cayman's monstrous armored body but it seemed unaffected. Its heavy tail churned the muddy water into a wild foam, caught Leoni a glancing blow along her left side and shoved her under, choking and swallowing the river. She resurfaced screaming, and saw the creature's jaws were clenched across Mary's waist, its snaggle teeth locked into her like meat hooks. There was blood but Mary was still alive, still struggling, her face contorted with terror, and – *Bam*! *Bam*! *Bam*! – Matt was still firing. The cayman's tail threshed the water like an iron flail and it shook its head from side to side with great violence. Leoni saw Mary's poor body flipped around, her arms and legs flapping scarecrow-limp. Suddenly the monster barrel-rolled twice amidst a tremendous surge of waves and spume, and Mary was torn almost in half in an instant, blood spewing out of her in a dark mass, her guts fouling the water. Leoni got an awful glimpse of her friend's dead eyes, frozen wide open in her last moment of horror. Then the creature carried her beneath the surface and she was gone in a swirl of blood.

Leoni's first thought was of self-preservation.

With so much blood around she had to get out of this fucking river before another cayman surged from the murky depths or she was stripped to the bone by a school of piranhas. She could feel hysteria and uncontrollable panic building and began to thrash towards the bank, kicking and splashing, her skin crawling.

"NO, LEONI!" Matt yelled after her. "WRONG SIDE!" He jerked so hard on her ankle that he pulled her head under. She surfaced at once, spluttering and screaming, and he grabbed her by the shoulders and steadied her just as they heard the *clack clack clack clack* of automatic rifle fire and the *zing*! *bzz*! *splash*! *splat*! of a swarm of bullets smacking into the water all around them.

She looked back. At the point on the bank where they themselves had entered the river – now three hundred feet behind them, thanks to the speed of the current – their pursuers had burst out of the jungle. There were maybe a dozen, some with *gringo* fair hair visible even at this distance, but none showed any inclination to jump in and there was no way for them to continue the pursuit along the overgrown bank, so they just kept shooting.

"DIVE!" Matt yelled. "DIVE!" He took her hand: "HOLD YOUR BREATH AND DIVE!" A bullet plucked at Leoni's ear, she felt Matt dragging her under and she dived – *Screw the piranhas* – swimming blind, suddenly not caring any more.

They surfaced and dived again.

The next time they surfaced Leoni saw Don Leoncio just ahead but there was no sign of Esteban and Emmanuel. "AGAIN," Matt yelled.

She held her breath and dived and when they came up for air the firing had stopped. The men back on the bank were just dots now as the river swept Leoni and Matt round a wide curve and carried them out of sight.

They dragged themselves out of the water onto a short stretch of sandy beach a few hundred feet beyond the bend, on the opposite side of the river from their pursuers. Leoncio had got out just ahead of them.

Leoni looked for Esteban and Emmanuel.

"They didn't make it," said Matt. "Hit by a burst of fire from the bank. At least it was quick for them, not like poor Mary."

"I'm beginning to feel like the fucking Angel of Death," sobbed Leoni. "Everyone I touch gets killed." She squinted at Matt and Leoncio through her tears "You sure you guys want to stick around?"

Leoncio's voice was grave: "To play a part in a great cosmic struggle, perhaps even to speed the victory of the Light – what more could any true shaman ask? Besides, we've all lost good friends fighting this darkness. It would dishonor their sacrifice to give up now."

"I've never been more certain of anything in my life," said Matt. "I pledged to protect you."

Neither man had been hit. Leoni had a piece the size of a dime missing from her right ear, a burning groove across the top of her skull, and a row of aching bruises down her side from her shoulder to her hip, but she knew how fortunate she was to be alive.

Matt wrapped his arms around her for a moment, saying nothing, and she took strength from him.

Then they resumed the march.

Leoni's thoughts turned to Ria. She'd left her in danger, trekking into wild country infested with Illimani patrols. What had happened to her since then? A night and a day had passed here. How much time had passed in Ria's world and how had she used it? Was she even still alive? Or had she been caught and slaughtered by Sulpa's army?

Ignoring the throbbing pain of her cuts and bruises, Leoni stepped out faster. The only way she was going to be able to answer such questions, the only way she was going to be able to do anything more for Ria, was to get to the village Leoncio had spoken of and drink Ayahuasca again.

They had no packs and therefore no supplies, no bottled water – pretty much nothing except two pistols, one of them still fully loaded, stuffed in Matt's belt, two knives, a machete, and a leather bag of Leoncio's containing certain bottled potions and other objects he had somehow held on to through all the craziness.

There was one piece of good news, he said. Now at least they were on the right side of the river – for they would have had to cross it anyway further along their route – and the going would be easier here because the trees were much taller and grew wider apart.

"Do you even know where we are?" Leoni asked him, looking around at the riotous profusion of green palms and soaring hardwoods that stretched away as far as the eye could see in all directions. Again there was a kind of emerald half-light down here, a blissful, diffused shade rather than the glaring sun that had beaten down on them when they were in the river. But it was also humid off the scale, and Leoni knew that within minutes she'd be pouring with sweat.

Leoncio reassured her he visited these forests often to hunt and gather medicinal plants, and that the loss of their packs should be viewed as an inconvenience, not a fatal blow. There were numerous streams where they would be able to drink and cool themselves, and he could provide food for them from wild plants and roots they'd find along their way. "I lived three years here as a wild man," he said without elaborating further, "so I think we will survive until we reach the village."

"Which will take how long?" Leoni asked.

"About another thirty hours," said Don Leoncio.

Leoni was stunned: "*Thirty* hours?"

"Yes. Perhaps a little more, perhaps a little less."

The rain began shortly before nightfall, diffusing through the canopy into a constant dripping shower of fat drops. Leoncio helped Matt and Leoni to improvise personal shelters of palm leaves on frames of branches which they set up close to the trunk of a large tree, but Leoni was uncomfortable from the outset. The shelters were very small and whereas Leoncio and Matt somehow remained still, Leoni's joints were so stiff she was unable to hold any position for more than a few moments. Yet as the hours of discomfort passed and the cold of the night settled into her bones she found an unexpected resolve. OK, she couldn't sleep but at least that meant Jack wouldn't get to her in her dreams.

Long before dawn they ate a scant breakfast of strange pungent fruits, slaked their thirst from a stream and were on their way again.

Leoni just kept on putting one foot in front of another, one foot in front of another, and the day wore on in a daze.

Finally, around mid-afternoon, they hit a definite track and straggled along it, Leoncio a few feet in front, Leoni leaning heavily on Matt. Soft dappled light came down through the canopy and a raucous flock of gaudy parrots, green with yellow heads, settled in a huge brazil-nut tree. They distracted Leoni for just a second but as she looked back to the trail a band of naked men, brown-skinned and barrel-chested, with hard, flat faces and suspicious eyes, stepped out of the forest and menaced them with blowpipes.

Chapter Eighty-Six

"Call me a bitch again and you'll have to fight me . . ."

After shouting the words in Merell, Ria repeated them in Naveen for the benefit of any of Balaan's men who might not have understood.

She intended the public ultimatum to be a challenge to his honor, but at first he laughed it off: "You? Fight me? A gnat would fight a mammoth sooner. Don't waste my time, little girl." In a ringing voice everyone could hear he addressed himself to Sebittu: "I repeat my offer: "get rid of the BITCH and we will unite our forces."

Ria felt the ranks of her Merell followers watching, waiting for their "Harbinger of Light" to prove herself. Failure would destroy her, but success would stamp her authority on the minds of everyone here – Merell and non-Merell alike – and that was a prize worth risking her life for.

"I'm challenging you to fight me, Balaan!" she yelled. "If you've got the stomach for it." She pulled one of her throwing stones from her pouch and showed it to him, and to the crowd: "Your spears against my stones," she said.

Balaan roared his laughter, tears of amusement dripping from his eyes: "Stones! Ha! Ha ha! What do you think you can do with those little things?"

"They're bigger than your balls," Ria answered, drawing back her arm. She repeated the words in Naveen and one of Balaan's braves gave a bark of laughter, cut short when the commander turned and glared. Another guffaw broke out behind Ria, from deep in her own column, and she saw Balaan flush and grind his teeth. "All right, bitch," he roared, "that's ENOUGH." But as he lunged at her with his spear Bont lumbered forward, slapped the point aside with the flat of his axe and stood eye to eye with him, daring him to strike again.

"Get out of the way, Bont," Ria snarled in the Clan tongue. She switched to thought-talk. "I have to fight this guy myself, you oaf. Don't you see that?"

Bont was swinging his axe, keeping Balaan at bay but not engaging him: "He's going to kill you," he pulsed to Ria, "that's all I know."

"Get OUT of the way," she yelled, reverting to out-loud speech. This time, shaking his head, Bont stepped aside.

Ria repeated her challenge to Balaan: "My stones against your spears," she screamed. "If you've got the balls for it, you piece of shit."

Rage and indignation flushed the Naveen leader's meaty face. Snarling his contempt, he spat a big gob of yellow phlegm at her, somehow missing. Then he stalked away, shifting his first spear from his left to his right hand.

"Get back," Ria pulsed to Bont and Driff as everyone else around her scattered. She dipped her hand into her pouch and pulled out a second stone.

Balaan was still walking. At fifty paces he spun on his heel and launched the spear with a roar of fury. It was a good throw, fast and powerful, but Ria trusted her eye. At the last moment she swayed aside and the missile shot past, burying itself in the ground behind her.

From the Merell ranks there came a sigh of appreciation.

"You spit better than you throw," Ria taunted as Balaan brandished his second spear. Twice he feinted – the man was not without some crude skill – but when he let fly she dodged again.

"In fact," she yelled, "you throw like a bitch."

The insult enraged him, as she had hoped, and he charged her with an explosion of energy, keeping hold of his last spear. As soon as he started to move Ria threw a stone with her right hand and – *CLUNK*! – it bounced off the side of his head just above the ear. A heartbeat later she hurled the second stone with her left arm, aiming for the same spot. *THWACK*! Another good hit.

He stopped in his tracks about thirty paces from her and touched his skull. He was bleeding, and there were more *oohs* and *ahs* from the crowd as he seemed to stumble and almost fall.

But Balaan was a big man and he kept on coming.

Ria snatched another stone from her pouch and threw it right-handed with all the force she could muster. It hit him between the eyes – *THWOCK*! Again he stumbled but again he failed to fall.

He kept on coming, just walking towards her, holding out his spear, blood gushing from his skull.

What was the matter with this guy? Was his head solid bone? Ria had already palmed her last two stones when he shook himself, spraying blood, and broke into a run. She threw fast. *CRACK*! – a punishing shot to the temple, enough to kill a normal man – and *CRUNCH*! – the final stone broke his nose. Then he was on top of her, his eyes rolling, somehow still finding the strength for a last desperate lunge with the spear. She danced aside, unsheathed her flint knife, thrust the blade between his ribs and jerked it out as his momentum carried him by.

Ria didn't need to look back as Balaan crashed to the ground behind her. She knew she'd found his heart.

Before high sun the column was on the move again, enlarged by the addition of Balaan's men. They'd agreed he'd been killed in a fair fight and they had sworn allegiance to Ria, accepting her as their leader in all matters of war against the Illimani. She could see from the slightly awestruck look on some of their faces they'd started to buy into the Merell belief that she was the chosen one – the Harbinger of the Light – handpicked by the spirits to lead the tribes in a time of darkness.

Ria saw no reason to disillusion them. At a quick count she now had close to four hundred braves taking orders from her – the beginnings of a real army to fight Sulpa – so the prophecy was doing what the blue woman intended.

But she also had more than a thousand women, children, elderly folk and other non-combatants who still had to be brought to safety. She glanced at the sun. Although the going was slow with such a large group, a positive spirit seemed to have seized everyone after her victory over Balaan and for a long while there were no interruptions. They simply marched, making good time, seeing nobody. There was a brisk east wind blowing that cut the heat, and by late afternoon Ria had begun to hope they might reach Secret Place before the night was out.

They had entered a green flower-strewn valley and were streaming across its floor when three young Naveen women, wailing and tearing their hair, rushed down the valley side towards them out of a small cave in which they had concealed themselves. They'd all been badly beaten and were streaked and smeared with blood from multiple flesh wounds. Their eyes were wild, their hair was matted and their clothing was torn.

Ria halted the column and brought forward other Naveen to comfort and succor the women.

When they were calmer she talked to them.
They had seen terrible things.

Their names were Moiraig, Aranchi and Noro and it seemed they had been part of a large Naveen band, more than a thousand strong, camped half a day's march to the southeast. With such numbers they had imagined themselves invulnerable to attack but early that morning, while most still slept, an Illimani force had fallen on them out of the mist and there had been a horrible massacre. It was clear from their descriptions that the attackers could only have been the five hundred of Martu and Sakkan.

Most of the Naveen hadn't been killed in the first onslaught and the adult male survivors and the older females had been rounded up and marched into a makeshift pen of uprooted thorn bushes the Illimani had erected. Brutally separated from their screaming children, Moiraig, Aranchi and Noro had been herded into a second pen with the remaining females over the age of twelve, including many other young mothers. A third pen held mothers with nursing babes, together with all the other children of the camp.

For some time the women in the second pen weren't clear about the function of the three enclosures. They took heart that sucklings had been allowed to stay at the breast – for surely their captors couldn't be as bad as they seemed if they were so careful to keep innocent babes alive. They didn't understand why they needed to be separated from their own children but at least nothing bad was actually being done to any of them.

Yet ominous preparations were under way. Around the camp the Illimani had forced a contingent of the male captives to chop down trees and strip trunks and branches to make sharpened stakes of different sizes. The smaller stakes, near the height of a man, were embedded point-up at random intervals across the camp's meeting ground. In amongst them a dozen larger and thicker posts, twice the height of a man, were sunk point-down, and generous piles of firewood the Naveen had been accumulating in preparation for winter were arranged around them.

When all was complete the captives who had done the work were seized, bound and impaled through the anus on the sharpened points of some of the shorter wooden stakes. As this was happening the entire

Illimani war band, five hundred strong, gathered round, laughing and roaring in the most horrible way at the victims' shrieks of torment. Having discovered the camp's large underground cache of water skins filled with Storl, the intoxicating fermented-apple drink of the Naveen, many of the victorious fighters were already very drunk.

It was around then, said black-haired, dark-eyed Aranchi, that they discovered what the separate women-only pen was for. There were two hundred of them in there and they all began to scream when a dozen blood-spattered Illimani braves suddenly barged through the gate, grabbed two women at random by the hair and dragged them outside. A terrible spectacle unfolded as they were punched and kicked to the ground, raped and then chopped to pieces with axes.

Reeking of Storl, a different group of men now appeared and two more women were dragged out of the guarded gate. Panic began to spread.

The treatment of the remaining men and older women from the first pen was even worse. On the shouted directions of a monstrous warrior in a bear-skull headdress, they'd been separated into different groups, just three or five in some, as many as fifty in others, and subjected to all the hideous tortures from the Illimani's gruesome repertoire that Ria was already familiar with – mass burnings at the stake, impalements, flaying alive, nailing to the few remaining large trees around the camp and so on and so forth. It was all done very slowly, one or two groups at a time, while the others, some voiding their bowels in terror, were forced to look on. It was obvious the Illimani took pleasure in inflicting pain and in magnifying the dread of those who were about to die.

And yet the children under twelve, and the babes in arms with their mothers, were still left unmolested.

Another group of drunken fighters burst through the gate of the women's pen causing a wild fear-driven stampede. A section of the thorn fence was trampled down in the confusion and Moiraig, Aranchi and Noro were amongst a very few who escaped, running for their lives and eventually finding their way to this valley.

Aranchi told Ria of their guilt at escaping. "But what else could we do?" she sobbed. "What else could we do?"

"We should have stayed for them," lamented Moiraig, who had not stopped weeping. She was chubby and earnest, with plain, simple features. "It was wrong to run."

"No," Ria said, putting a firm hand on her arm. "You would have gained nothing by staying and dying. At least you're alive now and I'm pretty certain your kids are still alive too."

Moiraig looked at her with sudden innocent hope: "Alive?"

"Alive?" echoed Noro. Her curly chestnut hair hung down over her shoulders, framing an anxious, pretty face.

"Yes, alive." Ria lowered her voice to a conspiratorial whisper that took in all three of them: "And I mean to get them back for you."

Chapter Eighty-Seven

"Thank goodness," said Leoncio. "We've arrived."

As he spoke, one of the Indians, a short, stocky, muscular man with a very flat face and straight black shoulder-length hair, lowered his blowpipe and uttered a few words in a strange language punctuated by clicks of the tongue – not Shipibo, Leoni thought, although she couldn't be sure. The man's fierce features, painted red and black with intricate geometrical designs, broke into a broad smile that seemed to signify amazement, delight and welcome all at the same time. He rushed forward and he and Leoncio embraced, both of them speaking in the curious click language. The other Indians had also lowered their blowpipes and now crowded close. Their bodies, all painted with the same fine red and black lines, had a curious buttery, smoky odor, which Leoni found extremely alien, but suspicion no longer glittered in their eyes and their initial hostility had vanished.

"Everything is good," Leoncio announced. "We're amongst the Tarahanua. The village is near."

Last night, before sleeping, as they sat under their improvised rain-shelters, Leoncio had spoken a little about the Tarahanua, the small tribe whose sanctuary they sought. Though not completely untouched by the forces of modernization, they had defended their independence and kept to their traditional ways, migrating deeper into the jungle whenever Christian missionaries or the Peruvian state became too bothersome. They grew beans, a little corn, manioc, plantains and bananas, fished the shallow streams that ran through their land (for they had deliberately kept their distance from any large river), and hunted tapir, peccary, deer, capybara, armadillos, monkeys and wild birds for their meat. They also hunted jaguar and ocelot, trading the skins through a chain of intermediaries for mirrors, pots, kerosene, cloth, soap, and the occasional shotgun, but otherwise had no contact at all with the outside world. "Unless *I* am to be counted as the outside world," Leoncio had added, "because I've been visiting them for years. They have two shamans, both powerful, and they've taught me many things."

He explained that the Tarahanua brewed a particularly potent form of Ayahuasca with an admixture of datura, a different visionary plant that sometimes had the effect of extending the trip for up to twelve hours. His own deepest trances had come in sessions with the Tarahanua and he was convinced that with the help of their shamans Leoni would be able to complete the work she'd been called to. "You do realize you've been called, don't you?" he said.

"Called to what?"

With the rain pattering down on their flimsy palm-leaf shelters and the dark jungle pressing close all around, Leoncio had paused, seeming to gather his thoughts: "Ayahuasca is a grace Our Lady of the Forest has bestowed on all mankind," he said at last, "a gateway to other worlds and times. Yet not one in a million of us – perhaps not even one in ten million – can make proper use of this amazing gift. Many are so frightened, so confused, so shattered by disconnection from the physical world, they gain nothing at all from the experience. Others have already dropped such strong anchors into material reality they never disconnect at all. Many do make the 'transit,' as I've heard you call it, and benefit greatly from access to other realms, but remain passive as the experience unfolds, as though it is something being done to them, not a process they can influence. Only a very few – and you are amongst them – can find their feet on the other side, remain functional, take control of situations that confront them, overcome the dangers that await them there, even obtain mastery over the spirits themselves. They're the ones who can become shamans. Some become *great* shamans . . ."

"And – sorry, but let me just get this clear – you're saying I'm one of those?"

"Much training and preparation will be required, but, yes, I'm saying you were *born* to walk in other worlds. You have amazing abilities. If you lacked them Our Lady of the Forest would not have selected you for this task."

Several knee-pounding miles up and down an endless series of forested hummocks and hollows still remained before they reached the Tarahanua village. As they walked, Leoncio brought up the subject of Leoni's last Ayahuasca vision which he had been forced to terminate with an antidote when his homestead was attacked.

On their trek through the jungle Leoni had already shared everything she could recall about the vision but Leoncio was now more interested in the next move. "From how you've described it," he said, "it seems Ria is in immediate danger from these Illimani . . ."

"Yes, immediate . . ."

"But the excellent thing is you are somehow able to communicate with her – that's difficult you know. I don't think you realize how difficult it is – not only to talk to matter from spirit but also to do it across the time barrier."

"The Blue Angel – Our Lady of the Forest – told me this kind of stuff happens because I'm entangled with Ria."

"In which case," said Leoncio, "I suggest you look out for other phenomena of your entanglement. They won't be confined to communication . . ."

"I don't understand . . ."

"Other powers you activate in each other. This will all be part of the the web Our Lady of the Forest is weaving by which Sulpa/Jack can be defeated."

The village of the Tarahanua was called Apo – a name that meant simply "home." It was set in a clearing in the heart of the jungle, a cluster of a dozen tall beehive-shaped huts with walls and roofs of banana-leaf thatch, surrounded by vegetable gardens. It would be mostly sheltered from aerial view by the overarching canopy, Leoni realized. A stream flowed nearby, noisy bright-eyed young children charged around, and one by one adults of all ages began to trickle out of the communal huts and stare first at the *gringos* and then, with joyful shouts of greeting, at Leoncio. So many of these naked, beaming folk came up to him to embrace him and shake his hand that it was obvious he was loved here.

Baido, the hunter whose band had found them, led them directly towards the largest beehive hut. Standing more than thirty feet tall, and perhaps as many across, the smooth convex curve of the continuous roof and walls was broken at the front of the building by a low doorway through which they now stooped to enter.

Inside it was dark and smoky, with two small cooking fires burning right and left, but there was a sense of lofty spaciousness in the gloom above. Several women, some with small children clustered round them, were at work preparing food. Hammocks hung from posts here and there, and at the back of the room an elderly man sat cross-legged on the earth floor, his face lit by a beam of light lancing through a smoke hole in the thatch.

Baido directed them towards this figure and, as they approached, Leoni saw he was blind, with milky cataracts over both eyes, and a lined and wizened face that seemed a million years old. Leoncio stooped and embraced him. A long dialogue of clicks followed, then Leoncio beckoned Leoni forward. "This is Buraya," he said, "chief of the Tarahanua. I'm going to introduce you now." More clicks. Finally, Leoncio asked Leoni to shake hands with Buraya who retained her hand in his own – she was surprised how firm his grip was – and made what seemed to be a short statement to her in his language, his voice rustling like dry leaves.

Then Matt was introduced and seconds later Baido ushered them all outside where a huge wooden bowl of a strange but somehow delicious and sustaining fermented banana drink was served to them.

"What did he say?" Leoni asked between gulps from the bowl.

"It's good news," said Leoncio. "He will summon his shamans and you will drink Ayahuasca tonight . . ."

"But he said something to me directly, right at the end. What was it?"

"I told him about our escape. He said that if this demon you're fighting has gone to so much trouble to stop you then you must be very dangerous to him."

They gathered at midnight in the same smoky communal *maloca* where Buraya had welcomed them. Tall thin Ruapa and short stocky Baiyakondi, the two ancient shamans of the Tarahanua, purified the space with the smoke from huge cigars of wild tobacco and sang *icaros* all around the room before the ceremony began. "I've told them about Jack," Leoncio whispered, "and they've taken special precautions. He won't be able to get his eye on us here."

Little by little, to Leoni's surprise the *maloca* filled up with what appeared to be the entire population of the village – more than a hundred men, women and children, all crammed in together cross-legged on the floor. She was even more amazed to learn that all of them – *all of them*, including the children – were about to drink Ayahuasca. "These group ceremonies where the whole tribe builds the energy have a magical effect," Leoncio explained. "Everyone here will play their part in helping your quest to succeed."

For some minutes Leoncio and Baiyakondi whispered in the click language before the stocky Tarahanua shaman used a wooden ladle to scoop a huge dose of Ayahuasca from a battered cooking pot and decant it into the grubby gourd that was to serve as Leoni's cup.

She held the gourd between her hands, looking down into the oily red-black sheen of the potion, her stomach already heaving and her eyes watering as the smell hit her. When the time came to drink, however – and the whole community drank at the same moment on Ruapa's signal – Leoni gulped down every drop, so eager was she to return to Ria's side.

The awful taste lingered, the liquid, thick as molasses, stuck to her teeth and lined her tongue and palate even as the mass of it burned its way down to her stomach. She suffered a moment of terrible nausea but this settled, and when she took a little water to rinse her mouth she didn't spit it out but swallowed it to ensure that none of the Ayahuasca went to waste.

In the lull before the storm hit her, Leoni summoned Ria's face to mind.

Chapter Eighty-Eight

While Ria listened to the three women's story, with cold fury building in her heart, part of her mind had been weighing up options.

Until this moment her only thought had been to lead her patchwork "tribe" of fifteen hundred refugees northwest, making a beeline for Secret Place. If the spirits were with them they would avoid Illimani scouts and war bands and she would bring them all to safety before the night was out. Even if they did encounter the foe, she had enough braves to deal with any but the largest force.

But a dizzying alternative had presented itself to her as she learnt of the horrifying aftermath of the attack on the Naveen camp, which lay nearly as far to the southeast of their present position as Secret Place lay to the northwest.

It was obvious from the women's report that Martu and Sakkan's five hundred weren't going anywhere tonight. They were so sure of their own power that they'd settled down to drink themselves into a stupor and enjoy an afternoon of torture, murder and rape. They would sleep it off in the ruins of the camp they'd destroyed, amidst the stiffening corpses of the people they'd murdered, and take their captive children down-country to Sulpa tomorrow.

Except, Ria had suddenly known, she wasn't going to allow that to happen and she had made her promise to the women. She did intend to get their kids back for them, if she could, and she wanted to give them hope. But she took the decision for other reasons.

Unless they were stopped, Martu and Sakkan were going to continue their rampage, annihilating other tribes and dragging even more children away for sacrifice. So running straight to Secret Place would simply condemn thousands more innocents to death. Sooner or later, Ria knew, she was going to have to fight the Illimani twins. It made sense to fight them now, on her terms, with the advantage of surprise.

And there was another larger issue in her mind.

Sulpa had used his forces to seize lands where there had been joy and abundance and transform them into charnel houses. Nobody had stood up to him as he destroyed their lives and ate their souls. And as misery, death and emptiness multiplied, his triumph grew. Although his ultimate target was the Uglies, whom the Illimani called the Light in the West, she knew from Driff that his former master gained power from every life he took and would keep on killing until all the people of these valleys were dead.

So far everything had been going his way.

But that was about to stop.

Martu was the demon's favoured commander, Driff had said, perhaps soon to be given command of the whole Illimani army. And right now Martu, Sakkan and their five hundred were just half a day's march distant.

Ria decided to kill them all.

It wasn't easy to explain the new plan to her companions.

Driff, as she had expected, was all for it. So, with some reservations, was Sebittu. But Ligar and Bont were both concerned the battle could not be won.

Ligar had walked up and down the column, making an accurate count, and they now knew that their whole fighting force amounted to three hundred and sixty-three braves, of whom two hundred and fourteen were archers and just a hundred and forty-nine were real hand-to-hand men. So it wasn't only that the Illimani five hundred outnumbered their total force but also that they outnumbered them by more than three to one in the front line. "That's going to make a huge difference when they close with us and our arrows are useless," said Ligar. "I don't see how we can beat them and it makes no sense to pick a fight we know we're going to lose."

"We're not going to lose," Ria huffed with exasperation. "We're going to win. Yes, we have two hundred archers – over half of our fighters – but that doesn't mean they can't handle themselves in close combat. They've got knives, spears, clubs. They'll know what to do if things get close up. And think of it, Ligar. Two hundred bowmen with, what, twenty arrows each? That's four thousand arrows. There's just five hundred Illimani and they don't have any bows at all. If we can get your men into the right position they shouldn't even have to do any close-up work."

"The Illimani don't use bows because they don't need them," Bont growled. "With those throwers their spears fly further than arrows. They'll skewer the lot of us before our archers even get into range."

Ria was trying hard not to get angry: "Obviously I've thought of that," she said. "We've got Moiraig, Aranchi and Noro to guide us. There's no reason why we shouldn't march on the Naveen camp tonight and have our archers in place before dawn. The Illimani have been drinking – they're not expecting any attack. With a bit of luck we'll slaughter them in their sleep."

"I still don't like the numbers," muttered Ligar. "Five hundred against three hundred and sixty. It doesn't add up."

"Your numbers are wrong . . ."

"Well OK, five hundred against three hundred and sixty-*three* – what difference does that make?"

"You're not understanding me. That's the number of *men* we have but we also have close to two hundred armed Merell women we can bring to the battle. They'll fight like wildcats."

The arguments, partly in thought-talk, partly in out-loud speech, went back and forth until the sun was low in the sky. The Uglies had so far expressed no opinion, but at last Ria insisted.

"It's obvious what we have to do," pulsed Grondin. "The spirits put Martu and Sakkan into our hands for a reason. Maybe we aren't ever going to get a chance as good as this again."

By sunset Ligar and Bont had been won over, but a final problem still had to be solved. What was to be done with the non-combatants in the column? There were close to a thousand of them – men, women and children – and they were slow-moving, noisy and hard to hide.

To send them back to Secret Place without an escort, guided perhaps by Jergat and Oplimar, would expose them to terrible risks. But an escort big enough to ward off all potential attackers in a land riddled with unknown numbers of Illimani war bands would fatally diminish Ria's force. Since she would need every man to beat Martu and Sakkan, it looked like nobody would be going back to Secret Place right now.

As darkness fell around them Ria asked her companions to marshal the column and she led the way towards the southeast and the Illimani.

Her people trusted her but what she was about to attempt could cost all of them their lives.

Chapter Eighty-Nine

Leoni spun out of the tunnel of light that had swept her from the Amazon jungle and was back in Ria's time, out of body in her transparent aerial form, flying very fast about fifty feet above the ground.

It was night. There was a big moon in the sky. And down below her, walking by its light, a huge column of people clad in simple plaids and skins were hiking into rough country. They were all ages, young and old, men and women, and hundreds of children. Many of the men were armed with crude weapons – spears and arrows tipped with flint, axes, knives, wooden clubs. Amongst the rearguard Leoni recognized three big Neanderthals who she'd seen with Ria before. And right at the front was Ria herself.

What had happened in the time they'd been apart to put her at the head of such a vast enterprise? Leoni was about to swoop down and try to speak to her when she noticed a flutter of movement just above the other girl.

She edged closer.

There it was again – very strange – as though a small piece of the night had rippled.

Closer still.

Another flutter.

Then the picture became clear. Flying a few inches above Ria's tousled head, as invisible to the physical eye as Leoni herself – and hard to detect even with her enhanced out-of-body senses – was one of Sulpa's monstrous little winged creatures.

Leoni glided up behind it, pinched its neck between her forefinger and thumb and plucked it, struggling, out of the air. It was about the size of a large bat and its repulsive gargoyle body, though transparent like her own, was scaly, hard and muscular to the touch. Its hind legs squirmed as it tried to rake her with its clawed feet and it beat at her hand with its leathery wings. Its blood-colored eyes swiveled towards her and it bared its needle-sharp teeth but she tightened her grip, grasped its head with her free hand and decapitated it with a vicious twist.

The creature dissolved into smoke, losing substance faster than a punctured balloon, and disappeared.

Gotcha!

But Leoni's moment of elation didn't last.

Some instinct made her look up.

There was a second creature about ten feet above, peering down at her. She caught the baleful red glint of its eyes as it shot away and she went right after it. But it was fast and agile and very hard to see against the background of the night.

With desperate sideways glances Leoni sought a landmark she could remember – there, a big old oak tree split by lightning – then put all else from her mind as she fought to keep the creature in sight. They wove through forests, across a lake, over hills and into valleys, sometimes hugging the contours of the ground, sometimes soaring up to the heights, as miles of country sped by beneath them.

They were never separated by much more or less than thirty feet and, try as she might, Leoni couldn't close the gap. Whenever she put on an extra burst of speed Sulpa's little gargoyle would sense it, peer over its shoulder, its eyes glinting red, and increase its own speed by the same amount.

Leoni wasn't sure how far they traveled like this – she guessed a hundred miles – or how she would find her way back to Ria amongst these savage hills and glens. Then she began to see armed men below her. At first there weren't too many of them, just little groups of three or five, all naked. But as she followed the creature out of the mouth of a valley and into the wide moonlit plain that lay beyond she found herself gazing down at a gigantic assembly of thousands of Illimani warriors, all armed to the teeth and standing in disciplined ranks as though awaiting an order to march.

The creature slowed to a stop and seemed to taunt her – perhaps it was feeling confident now that it was so near to its master – and Leoni struck at once, flinging herself at it in a last explosive effort.

WHACK! For a second she had it by the edge of one flapping wing, but it writhed away and sped off.

She went after it again – it was slower now she'd harmed it – and they were thirty feet in the air, streaking towards the front ranks of the army less than five hundred feet away, when she saw Sulpa. The moon was bright, but he had been concealed in shadow amongst his men. Now his beautiful body, his long flowing hair and his malice were all unmistakable as he took three graceful steps forward and stared right at her.

Leaving the little creature to alight on his shoulder and whisper in his ear, Leoni whirled in the air and shot away.

But it was too late. A dark cloud, boiling and agitated, surged out of Sulpa, out of his skin, out of his eyes, out of his mouth, and Leoni looked back to see it consisted of hundreds of his creatures, bat wings flapping, red eyes gleaming like laser spots in the dark.

He thrust his hands forward, fingers extended, and the cloud surged skywards and began to flow towards her.

Leoni paid attention to her direction of flight – back the way she had come, back to find that lightning-struck oak where she'd last seen Ria.

But her first concern was speed and escape.

Until now she'd only encountered Sulpa's little monsters in ones and twos. Though foul, they were quite small and easy to kill – if you could catch them.

But being pursued by a whole pack of them was quite another matter.

They were as non-physical as she was; yet if she could bash their smoky brains out and tear off their heads then what would they be able to do to *her* when they overtook her and swarmed her aerial body?

This wasn't the land where everything is known, nor Don Apolinar's dungeon, where consciousness was clothed in alternate physical forms. If the body you inhabited in such realms was destroyed, the Blue Angel had said, your soul was carried off to another domain. She had called it the "Between." You could get lost there for eternity. Or with skill you could find your way out and back to your body on Earth.

Was it the same deal if your aerial body was destroyed? Was it simply another form in which your soul was expressed – in some sense disposable like the avatars in the land where everything is known?

Or was it your soul itself?

The distinction was crucial because no matter how fast or high or far she flew, Sulpa's creatures continued to gain on her, red eyes gleaming, fangs bared in the moonlight. In the few seconds it had taken him to set them after her she'd already flown a thousand feet. Since then her lead had been cut to a tenth of that distance and glancing back over her shoulder she saw that three of the scaly little bastards were far in front of the others, just twenty feet behind her.

As always when she traveled in her aerial form, Leoni flew with her head forward, her arms folded across her chest, and her legs and feet stretched out. She was ten thousand feet up when two more of Sulpa's creatures – they must have dived like hawks from an even higher altitude – smashed into her at shocking speed. One sank its talons into her thigh, the other into her shoulder, and both held fast, beating their wings and rending her. She felt pain, sharp and hot, and then the other three were on her.

She plucked one from her side, wrung its neck, threw it away in a burst of smoke, snatched two more from her legs – their talons tore her as she ripped them loose – and crushed the little creatures in her hands. The gargoyle that had alighted on her shoulder, and the last one, which had anchored its talons in her back, she smashed together until they became smoke.

Before she could dart forward again the entire swarm caught her and fell upon her in a seething mass, covering her from head to foot. The sensation was a horrifying one of toxic suffocation, like being smothered in horse blankets impregnated with smallpox and razor blades, and she was overwhelmed by the foul smell of sulphur and burnt plastic that the creatures gave off.

She roared her anger and flailed her limbs, twisting and turning in her efforts to be free, but nothing she did made any difference. The monsters had deprived her of the power of flight and, no matter how hard she fought, she could feel her aerial body disintegrating under their sustained attack, slipping away from her little by little.

A terrible lassitude stole over her as the creatures bit and tore and she felt an overwhelming urge to sleep. Simply to sleep. Would that be so bad?

But then, faint as a radio signal from the dark side of the moon, she heard four words spoken deep inside her mind in the familiar voice of the Blue Angel: "Remember you are a lion."

And she remembered, when she'd fought Sulpa, how her aerial body had taken on the form of a mountain lion and broken free from his stranglehold.

She was a lion, not a victim.

A burst of pure, hot anger hit Leoni, giving her the strength to strike out one more time, and as she did so the process of transformation took hold, the outer human form of her aerial body began to shift and change, and she became once again a lioness. She was still cloaked in a boiling horde of Sulpa's creatures, but now she exploded into action, shaking herself, throwing off all but a handful of her attackers in an undulating wave and smashing them out of the air with great swipes of her paws.

Some could have escaped but it seemed their master had sent them on a suicide mission because they kept on attacking her, and she kept on destroying them, until she'd turned every one of them to smoke.

Leoni resumed her human form and paused to look down at herself.

She didn't like what she saw.

The tearing claws and teeth of the little creatures had drained her life-force, leaving her insubstantial as a ghost. The translucent envelope of her aerial body was faded, no longer a glittering evanescent soap-bubble but something dull and dim that seemed to flicker on the edge of complete fragmentation.

How far away was Ria?

At least a hundred miles from Sulpa, she was sure of it. And though the Illimani were obviously hard men she didn't think even they could march a hundred miles in a single night.

So her first mission – nothing else mattered if this failed – was to warn Ria that Sulpa's spies had found her, that one had lived to report her position to him, and that Sulpa himself was coming for her with all his forces.

Leoni searched for what seemed like many hours as the moon slowly tracked from east to west across the sky. But just as her energy had fallen to its lowest ebb, she recognized the lightning-struck oak she had chosen as her landmark and was soon streaking along the wide track that Ria's people had left in their wake.

It was hard to estimate distances, but after what she thought might have been another five miles Leoni came to a point where the trail forked. A very large group had turned off to the left of the main track and entered the pine forest that grew alongside it; a smaller group had continued straight ahead.

Leoni followed the broad trail into the trees and found herself amongst a thousand ragged, frightened-looking people, dressed in plaids and skins, pitching camp in the heart of the forest around the banks of a small hidden lake. A glance confirmed these were the women and children, as well as some of the older men, from the large band she'd seen Ria leading earlier. But Ria herself was missing.

Leoni streaked back to the fork in the trail and caught up with the smaller group five miles further along the track. At a quick count it consisted of more than three hundred men – all armed in their Stone Age way – plus a contingent of around two hundred women, also armed. Moving at a fast march, they had entered a long moonlit valley and seemed wary and nervous, primed for a threat, weapons held at the ready. Ria strode along in the lead with a determined look in her eye.

Still not attempting to tell Ria she was back, Leoni shot ahead to scout for danger and within two miles came to a place where the valley narrowed and avalanches of broken rock littered its floor amongst tumbled boulders piled into weird formations. Behind these, in the moonshadow, she found a small party of Illimani warriors – she counted fifteen – spread out at intervals, apparently on guard. They were facing the direction from which Ria was approaching and it could not be long before they detected her own much larger force.

The sentries were few, but what were they guarding?

Less than a mile further on Leoni found a ravaged and burnt-out nomadic camp by a river where the valley curved. Hundreds of bodies lay scattered about, hundreds of prisoners were penned inside thornbush enclosures, and lording it over them were hundreds of victorious Illimani. She recognized the bizarre headdresses of the huge warriors whom she thought of as Bear Skull and Bull. A small group of their men were butchering captive women amidst dreadful wails and screams. But many of the Illimani fighters were drunk, staggering around singing, and many more were already sprawled on the ground, snoring in pools of their own vomit.

As Leoni darted back along the trail to take the news to Ria another draining lurch of weakness hit her, the moon at last dropped below the horizon and complete, overwhelming darkness fell in an instant.

Chapter Ninety

The non-combatants had been left under cover of a forest, close to the edge of a small lake, and Ria and her five hundred fighters were far along the deep, steep-sided valley overgrown with tough grasses, gorse and heather that led to the Naveen camp. Guided by Moiraig, Aranchi and Noro, they had made good time while the moon was still in the sky. Now it had set, and the camp loomed close, they'd been forced to slow down.

Ria didn't think the Illimani conquerors, confident of their own power and most of them in a drunken stupor, would have troubled to post sentries. But she was about to send scouts forward to make sure when her senses tingled.

What was that?

The sensation hit her again and then it was almost as though a voice had whispered in her ear – yet no one had spoken. She stopped in her tracks, raised her hand, and hissed "*Halt*!" Bont, who was right behind, walked into her, treading on her foot, the front two ranks piled up, followed by the third and fourth, and several men fell with muttered oaths. Clunks and bangs could be heard all the way along the column as people and weapons collided.

"Stay here!" Ria pulsed to Bont. "Keep these fuckers quiet." And, without explaining, she strode a little way off and stood peering into the night right in front of her, her head tilted to one side.

It was a very strange moment, but she was certain the girl the blue woman had talked about, the girl from the future, the girl called Leoni, was present with her again.

More than that, she was pretty sure she could see her – or see something. How weird. Like a thin cloud of light.

"Hello," she pulsed. "Are you there?" She said these words in thought-talk, in the Clan language, and repeated them out loud in a friendly tone of voice. She felt Bont, Driff, Sebittu and many others close to the front of the column watching her – and listening – but she didn't care. This was important, and they already expected her to do odd things.

Ria tried the greeting and the question out loud in Merrell and Naveen as well before she realized the other girl was already speaking to her, in thought-talk, in what at first seemed a strange language but which she soon grasped. *"I don't understand you."* That was what the words meant. *"I don't understand you, Ria, and we need to understand each other. There are things you have to know."*

"Go ahead," Ria pulsed in the same language. "I understand you well enough."

She couldn't see Leoni's face but sensed her surprise and relief at being able to communicate at all.

"Go ahead," Ria repeated. "I have the gift of languages from the blue woman." She was in no doubt that Leoni would know who she meant. "Speak to me."

"Sulpa has these little creatures that fly around spying for him," said the other girl. "They look like this" – thought-pictures of the monsters came to life in Ria's mind, and with them a powerful pulse of the fear and horror Leoni felt for them. "Two of them found you. I killed one but the other got away. I followed it but I couldn't catch it and it got back to him – so he knows where you are." Into Ria's mind came an image of thousands of Illimani assembled under moonlight on a great plain, with Sulpa at their head. "He's gathered his whole army to come after you," Leoni said.

"How far?" Ria asked. It was the only important question. Regardless of its size, she wasn't frightened of Sulpa's army if she had time to finish her business here and be away before it arrived. "How far?"

"How far what?"

"How far is Sulpa from where we are now?"

"A hundred miles, maybe a little more."

"I don't understand 'miles,'" said Ria.

"It's a name we give to a distance. I guess a hundred miles is the kind of distance really tough people could walk in two days," Leoni said.

"Two days! Pah! In two days we'll be long gone from here. But there are five hundred Illimani up ahead I plan to kill first . . ."

"I've just seen them!" Leoni exclaimed, and a new thought-picture filled Ria's mind. This time what the other girl was showing her was a great camp of Naveen tepees, utterly destroyed, prisoners penned up in thorn-bush enclosures, corpses scattered everywhere, and the blood-smeared men of Martu and Sakkan's five hundred gorging on the fruits of victory. Some of the Illimani were still killing but many were dead drunk, staggering or already flat on the ground.

Ria took it all in with growing feelings of excitement. It was exactly as she'd hoped. "You bring me good news," she said.

"Good news?"

"Drunken men are easier to kill."

"I guess they are," said Leoni. "But be careful. They have sentries." Ria received a thought-picture of boulders piled across a narrow point of the valley floor and Illimani spearmen lurking in the shadows behind them. "Fifteen sentries," Leoni said. "I counted them."

Exchanging thoughts and images at great speed, Ria worked out a plan of action with Leoni to deal with the sentries.

"Started talking to yourself, have you?" said Bont when she returned to the column.

"Not to myself but to a spirit who will guide us."

"I don't believe in spirits."

"After tonight you will, Bont. After tonight you will."

Bowmen weren't needed for this mission in the dark, and spears would have been an encumbrance, so Ria went forward with Bont, Driff, Grondin, Oplimar and a squad of forty Merell woodsmen, hand-picked by Sebittu and armed with knives and tomahawks.

Everything – all their lives, the whole struggle against Sulpa – now depended on the accuracy of Leoni's information: that they had only fifteen sentries to deal with and no further obstacles or alarms before they reached the Naveen camp. But Ria believed in Leoni utterly – and besides, what she said made sense. The Illimani were so arrogant. Having slaughtered the Naveen they wouldn't imagine there was any force anywhere nearby that would be capable of hitting back.

She was wriggling on her stomach through tussocky marsh grass, soaking her belly and her leggings in cold water. Grondin and Bont were to her right, Driff and Oplimar to her left, each commanding eight of the Merell fighters, and all of them slithered forward silent as ghosts.

Everyone knew exactly where the sentries were and everyone knew exactly what they had to do.

Chapter Ninety-One

Despite the darkness, Leoni's out-of-body senses showed her more of what happened next than she really wanted to see.

The fifteen sentries had positioned themselves in five groups of three behind the boulders – some twice the height of a man, some tumbled on top of one another – that formed a natural obstacle course in this part of the valley floor. From time to time a two-man patrol armed with long stabbing spears made its way from group to group, exchanging muttered words and occasional guffaws of laughter.

The plan was to hit the entire guard detail at the same moment, giving no opportunity for any to flee into the darkness and raise the alarm. For this reason, after Leoni had put thought-images into her mind showing her the disposition of the sentries, Ria divided her force into five groups of nine. She herself led one group. In charge of the other four groups she placed two of the men and two of the Neanderthal males who Leoni had seen close to her on previous occasions.

The men, Ria told her, were Driff, a lean, intense, black-haired Illimani who had come over to her side, and the shaggy giant Bont, a member of her own Clan. The Neanderthals, who she called the Uglies, and Leoni could see why, were Grondin – Bont's size, built like a prize-fighter – and bushy-bearded, pot-bellied Oplimar. All of them were telepaths – Ria called it "thought-talk" – and so the attacks of all five groups would be coordinated in total silence.

Leoni admired the stealth with which the attackers squirmed through the wet grass and amongst the smaller rocks, worming ever closer to the positions of the sentries. She had not been able to reach the others with telepathy; but even if their minds had been open to her she suspected they did not have the Blue Angel's "gift of languages." Floating above the whole scene she pulsed directions to Ria as first Bont's group, next Oplimar's, then Grondin's and last of all Driff's arrived within twenty feet of their targets. Ria in turn must have signaled them because they all came to a halt, awaiting the order to attack.

Now two of the Illimani set off on patrol again, slowly crossing the narrow floor of the valley. They made their first stop and there were the sounds of muffled voices. At the second stop they paused for several minutes and Leoni flew over them to discover that the three sentries at their post had an animal skin, perhaps filled with liquor, which they were sharing with the other two. A few more minutes passed and though it was not yet dawn Leoni thought she could detect the faintest blush at the edge of the sky as the patrol at last moved on.

They were almost halfway to the next guard post when Ria's entire force rose to their feet and charged in grim silence.

The two patrolmen didn't see Bont coming and had no time to level their spears or cry a warning as his huge axe scythed out of the darkness. One fell grunting as the blade buried itself in his belly. With a jerk Bont withdrew it, unleashing a geyser of blood, and back-handed the weapon into the second man's face.

Darting forward, Leoni found Ria behind a boulder. She was stooped over a naked Illimani who lay face down, unconscious, on the ground. There was madness in her eyes and a stifled cry of wild joy burst from her lips as she pulled back a fistful of his hair and slit his throat with a long flint knife. The cut went so deep that his head came almost clean away from his shoulders.

Leoni saw Oplimar and Driff both kill men. Grondin picked one of the sentries up and smashed his spine across his knee. All along the line of guard posts it was the same story – the small number of defenders, surprised and utterly overwhelmed by the sudden unannounced attack, quickly fell and died under the brightening sky.

But one of the sentries, left for dead, leapt to his feet despite a jagged wound in his side and ran zigzag like a hare towards the camp. He was very fast and though Driff pursued him he had a good lead.

Leoni couldn't understand why Ria also took off after the escaping Illimani because he was at least a hundred feet ahead of her, just a faint white blur in the pre-dawn shadows, and she'd never catch him. But then she snatched at a pouch hanging by her side, drew back her arm and threw a stone at him. Leoni lost sight of the little missile as it flew through the air. It must have whizzed right past Driff's ear before – *CLUNK*! – it bounced off the back of the fleeing man's skull and dropped him to the ground in a heap.

Driff reached him first, hatchet raised, but Ria wasn't having it. She barged her friend aside, jerked back the Illimani's head and cut his throat.

With the sentries disposed of and more light seeping into the sky, Leoni scouted the way forward while Ria brought up her whole force at the double as far as the boulders. From there it was about a mile to the camp but because the valley ahead took a sharp curve to the left the place wouldn't be visible to the Illimani, even in daylight, and provided good shelter to muster for the final attack. Not until they had rounded the curve would Ria's fighters come into view. Even so they would still have to cover at least quarter of a mile in the open before reaching the camp and a small nagging voice at the back of Leoni's mind told her this would not be good.

She explored both sides of the valley for alternatives, but the slopes were too steep to be climbed by a large force without attracting attention. What she did find was a narrow path, angling up to the left, that a small group walking in single file might scale. Better still, the path led to the ridge directly overlooking the sector of the camp where the Illimani had kept their prisoners. Leoni remembered many of Ria's fighters carried bows. She'd never got closer to a battle than *World Of Warcraft* but something told her this would be a good spot to put some archers.

She glanced to the sky. It was still more night than dawn but in half an hour – an hour at most – the sun would be above the horizon and all the advantages of darkness would be lost.

She darted down to get a closer look at the camp.

Behind it ran a fast-flowing mountain river channeled in a rocky gorge that intersected the main valley from the right. It had been a large camp, consisting of hundreds of tall conical shelters of skins stretched over wooden frames, like Native American tepees, ranged across the valley floor almost to the river's edge. But the Illimani had burned everything to the ground. What stood out now were the three thorn-bush stockades they'd set up amongst the ashes to hold their prisoners.

For a few moments Leoni was dizzied by the nightmare horror of it all.

The stockade at the extreme left of the group was empty, but a little beyond it was a large cleared area in which the Illimani had burned at the stake, crucified and tortured to death several hundred men – probably the entire adult male population of the camp.

A second stockade at the extreme right of the group was crammed with young children. All were alive but milling in terror and crying out.

In the third stockade, between the other two, the bodies and body parts of a great many women lay strewn in the dust as casually as animal carcasses in an abattoir. About a hundred still lived but Leoni saw a small group of bloodstained and filthy Illimani on the rampage amongst them – ten brutal naked men finishing off the orgy of violence that had obviously continued throughout the night. It was a horrific scene, made worse by the pitiful screams of the victims.

But something even more disturbing was happening. When Leoni had first flown over the camp, perhaps an hour before, many of the Illimani who weren't raping and butchering women had been sprawled out, dead drunk. Now most of them were on their feet, some rubbing their heads but obviously alert and responding to an order to form up. Hundreds had already assembled in the cleared area and more were joining them every moment.

Leoni saw the warrior she thought of as Bull swaggering around, kicking and beating men who were still sleeping. His twin, Bear Skull, had assembled a mob of twenty and now led them, knives unsheathed, to join the other murderers already at work in the women's enclosure.

If Ria was going to attack she must do so at once, while the shadows were still deep in the last exposed quarter-mile of the valley, and before the Illimani finished their killing and marched out of the camp.

As she hurried back to Ria's side, Leoni was conscious once again of the numbing weakness spreading like poison through her aerial body, and when she looked down at herself she saw . . . almost nothing.

Chapter Ninety-Two

Arrayed on the stony valley floor beyond the line of huge boulders where the Illimani sentries had been killed, Ria's entire force of more than five hundred waited for her command, while she herself stood alone, fifty paces to the fore, peering into the darkness ahead.

Though there was no thin cloud of light to announce the other girl's presence, as there had been earlier, Ria knew that Leoni had returned to her side. She also sensed – she felt it in her own breath and heartbeat – that Leoni was in terrible danger. "Sister," she pulsed – it was the only word that did justice to the strength of the bond she felt – "what has happened to you?"

Leoni's thought-voice was weak, barely audible, seeming to emanate from somewhere very far away: "No time to explain," she said. "I won't be able to stay with you long. I'm going to be taken back." Then Ria felt a flood of words and thought-images wash over her as Leoni shared everything she'd observed during her reconnaissance – the Illimani forces mustering on the meeting ground of the Naveen camp, the pitiful condition of the surviving captives, the disposition of the stockades and the trail leading to a promising ridge that overlooked them.

As she took all this in Ria's mood darkened. The prospect that had lured her to this place was of drunken and disorganized enemies who could be surrounded in the dark by archers and shot like fish in a pool. Instead it was close to sunrise and the five hundred Illimani she confronted were alert and would soon be on the march. These were men who had dedicated their lives to violence and fought side by side in many battles. Her men were hunters first, fighters second, and the women might be hard as flint around hearth and home but none of them knew war.

Ria thought of retreat but rejected the idea. The Illimani would pursue them and catch them before they could make good their escape, probably even before they reached their waiting non-combatants, and certainly when they did. Better by far to force the fight now while they still had surprise on their side.

All at once, so bright and obvious it dazzled her, a plan began to take shape in her mind: "Can I get two hundred of my archers into place to the side of the meeting ground?" she asked Leoni. "Is there a chance they could approach without being seen? Is there enough cover there to hide them?"

There was no reply and Ria almost choked with frustration. She needed a clearer picture! "Leoni! Please! Help me."

Again she was met by silence – and, worse, her sense of the presence of the invisible girl, so strong moments before, had now evaporated. She shifted to out-loud speech. "Sister, are you there?" she asked. "Are you with me?"

When no answer came, Ria understood her ally had truly gone. Perhaps she had simply been snatched back into her body the way she herself had been snatched back at the end of her two journeys with the Little Teachers? But she couldn't rid herself of the intuition that some greater danger was involved.

The intelligence Leoni could have brought in from different parts of the battlefield would have been invaluable, but Ria was ready to improvise. She had the whole plan of the fight worked out in her mind now. All she had to do was get her archers into place, and persuade two hundred proud Merell women to strip naked, and she could yet win the day.

She called Moiraig, Noro and Aranchi forward, together with Bont, Ligar, Driff, Sebittu, Grondin, Jergat and Oplimar. In less than the count of a hundred she explained her plan to them and their parts in it. Then at once, under cover of the little dark that remained, she sent Ligar, Sebittu and Jergat off with the archers, primed Bont, Grondin and Driff for their missions, and summoned the women to their task.

The sun would rise soon. The valley's rugged sides were already emerging from the darkness in shades of black and gray.

"Have courage," Ria whispered. "We will win."

She was walking with Sebittu's wife Tari amongst the two hundred Merell women she had brought up to the elbow of the valley, just a few bowshots from the destroyed Naveen camp and the Illimani. Some of the women, though not Tari herself, were trembling at the prospect of a pitched battle so Ria sought to reassure them: "Have courage – the spirits are with us."

There was a commotion. A girl pushed through the ranks, and a pair of wild green eyes and a snub nose confronted her under a disordered thatch of red Merell hair.

Birsing!

"What are you doing here?" Ria demanded. "You're supposed to be with the kids."

"I followed you," said the eleven-year-old. "I don't want to hide in the forest. I want to fight the Evil One. I want to kill the Illimani." Her face was covered in freckles and she clutched a little flint dagger, more a toy than a weapon, in her small white fist.

Ria considered sending her back but decided not to. Birsing's arrival like this, so full of fighting spirit, was an omen. An excellent omen. "If you want to fight these bastards then I won't stop you," she said. She took the girl's fist between her own hands, still clenching the dagger: "See you blacken that pretty blade in Illimani blood."

Birsing grinned: "We're going to beat them, aren't we? I can feel it."

"We're going to fucking destroy them."

Tari and Ria walked on." "Do you really believe that?" Tari whispered. "Will we truly win?"

"I'm certain of it," Ria answered. They had reached the curve of the valley, and she would show no weakness now. But the truth, despite the beauty of her plan, was that her confidence had begun to ebb.

She glanced up to the valley sides again. The light had risen enough to reveal the silver threads of a dozen descending streams and she knew it was time – past time – to mount the attack. What held her in check was Ligar and Jergat who had been out of contact, stubbornly unreachable by thought-voice, since she had sent them on their missions. This was worrying, and weird. Were they too far away for thought-talk to carry? Were they dead? Were they prisoners? Without word from them, or Leoni to confirm they were in position, Ria knew she was taking a terrible risk.

But to do nothing now was out of the question.

"Wait," she told Tari. "Bring them forward on my signal." Stooping, she jogged twenty paces ahead, took cover behind a gorse bush and looked long and hard at the camp.

It was closer than she had imagined, a great deep crescent-shaped scar of burnt-out tepees following the continuing left curve of the valley, bounded on the far side by a rushing river and on the near side sprawling across the valley floor almost to the foot of the steep slope. Above, Ria very much hoped, Jergat and twenty of the best Naveen archers had already been guided into position by Noro who claimed to know the track Leoni had found. Again she pulsed a message to Jergat, and again she got no reply.

Amongst the ashes of the tepees she saw the three bulky thorn-bush pens the Illimani had built to hold their prisoners. The pen nearest to her, on the right side of the row, was filled with children and nursing mothers and their cries of terror were awful to hear. Next to it, as Leoni had described, a pen containing only women seethed with furious activity, where thirty Illimani braves were running amok and blood-curdling screams left no doubt that a mass slaughter was under way.

Ria hated to stand by and let this happen but a mistake now would be fatal for her whole force and there was still no contact with Jergat and Ligar.

The third enclosure was furthest from her and empty. Beyond it, in the camp's extensive meeting ground, she could see the mass of the Illimani – hundreds of warriors formed up in disciplined ranks amidst burnt-out bonfires and the piled corpses of their victims. Although the camp was large, and the meeting ground was far away, she recognized the tall figure of Martu with his headdress of aurochs horns. He seemed to be making a speech to his warriors.

"Keep talking," Ria whispered. With luck their leader's words of wisdom, and the slaughter of the women, would occupy the Illimani for a little longer. Patches of morning mist had risen to cover parts of the valley floor and there were still some areas of deep shadow that greatly served her purpose.

She beckoned to Tari, who at once led the little army of women forward. Ria looked them over, reminded them to keep total silence until she gave the signal, nodded in friendship to those she'd talked with, and ruffled Birsing's hair. Then she raised her fist above her head and led the charge down the valley.

As she ran they all ran in a pack alongside her, teeth bared, faces set, and it was good to be alive and in such company.

The sun touched the hilltops. Ria felt the cool morning breeze on her skin and heard the distant screech of a golden eagle.

It was another excellent omen.

Chapter Ninety-Three

Leoni hated the fact that she'd been swept away from Ria, without warning, at the vital moment.

Except, of course, there *had* been warnings – the growing weakness, the spreading numbness, the gossamer lightness of her aerial body following the attack of Sulpa's creatures.

Leoni's eyes blinked open, but she didn't move. She was lying on her back. Four beings were hunched around her but their shapes were indistinct and above them, from a dark vault, beams of dazzling celestial light shone down.

"The wanderer has returned," said a familiar voice.

Don Leoncio's voice!

And in a flash Leoni realized she had returned to her body, the celestial lights were nothing more than the sun streaming through the smoke holes in the roof of the *maloca,* and the beings hunched over her were Matt and Don Leoncio on her left and the two Tarahanua shamans, Ruapa and Baiyakondi, on her right.

She sat up: "I can't leave Ria where she is," she said clutching Leoncio's sleeve. "You've got to give me more Ayahuasca. I have to get back to her right now."

He placed the palm of one warm, dry hand on her brow as though testing her temperature. "I don't think so," he said after a few moments.

"What do you mean, you don't think so?"

"You have suffered a very grave psychic attack," he replied. "Am I correct?"

Leoni shrugged: "I suppose you could call it that." She described how Sulpa's creatures had swarmed over her and how she had broken free. She had no doubt that her aerial body had been damaged in the encounter and that some vital energy had been drained.

"If you hadn't escaped when you did," said Leoncio, "you would certainly have been killed." He breathed out emphatically through his nose: "That's what happens when the etheric energy structure that you call your aerial body is destroyed. First your physical body falls into a deep coma, respiration and heartbeat slow, brain activity ceases. Within a space of hours – in some rare cases days – you are dead."

"And your soul? What happens to your soul?"

Leoncio wrinkled his brows: "The worst possible fate. Your soul is taken to the underworld, and from there it can never return."

Leoni shivered. She didn't want to know about the underworld. "Sounds bad," she said.

"Very bad. Much worse than you can imagine." Leoncio rested a sympathetic hand on her shoulder: "And it would be madness now, with your subtle energies so utterly depleted, to venture at once out of the shelter of the flesh. You must wait – you must restore yourself – before you attempt such a thing again."

Leoni shook her head: "You don't understand! I *can't* wait." She had raised her voice: "I left Ria in the middle of a battle with the Illimani. I was her eyes and ears, Leoncio! She can't beat them without me."

His features, already set in an expression of intense concentration, seemed to betray some inner conflict, but at last he said: "I will not stop you if this is something you are called to do."

"I *am* called! Yes. Definitely."

"But if you decide on this course of action," Leoncio continued, "you must understand what you face. A single psychic assault from the least of the demon's servants will send you to the underworld. Game over, Leoni. Game over forever! Are you sure you want to risk that?"

Leoni thought about it.

She was very much tempted not to go back, and especially not in her present weakened condition. But she was also amazed and overawed by Ria, and in love with her for her beauty and style and courage and sheer *balls.*

Her sister in time? Yes, truly. It felt like they'd been separated at birth and had just found each other again.

More than that, the way they'd worked together to destroy the sentries and put Ria's desperate battle plan into action had, Leoni realized, been the most amazing and exhilarating experience of her life – bar none. All barriers and differences had evaporated and in those moments of danger and fear they had shared a complete understanding.

So there was no way, no way at all, she would turn her back on her now.

"This is something I have to do," she told Leoncio. "I understand the risks, but I'm going through with it. I've never been more sure of anything in my life."

Leoni turned to Matt and put her arms around his neck. "Just hold me," she said. "Just hold me for a little while before I go."

Chapter Ninety-Four

The closer Ria could get her force to the prisoner enclosures before they were seen the better chance there was that her plan might succeed, so they charged in absolute silence, making the most of the deep shadows and patches of mist that shrouded this part of the valley floor. Yet the nearer they came, the more they saw of the terrible deaths the Illimani were inflicting on the helpless Naveen women still left alive in their enclosure.

"*Ligar*!" Ria pulsed as she ran, "*Jergat*! *Speak to me*!" But still there came no reply and she felt a growing dread. She saw that Birsing, clutching her little dagger, was running at her left side. She gave a smile of encouragement but the girl's face was dead white, her eyes fixed on the women's enclosure ahead. Tari was on her right and all around and behind them, hair flying in the wind, weapons in hand, came the rest of the two hundred. They were terrified, every one of them – it was painted on their faces – but they didn't falter.

The murders in the women's enclosure were being organized by Sakkan – his height and his bear-skull headdress were unmistakable – and the idea seemed to be for each death to be brutal and drawn out, which was why it was all taking so long. The Illimani didn't just want these women to die. They wanted them to die in a state of absolute horror and fear. No more than thirty braves were at the work. Here and there knots of them were hacking prisoners limb from limb with axes, or beating them to death with clubs, or hanging them from racks and skinning them alive. Some of the executioners simply darted into the thinning crowd of survivors, stabbing and slashing with spears and knives, spreading pandemonium. Ria saw Sakkan snatch up a small cowering woman and pound her down on a sharpened stake he had set into the ground. Everywhere there were blood-curdling screams and bellows.

As the edge of the sun appeared above the eastern ridge, flooding the valley with light, Ria and her fighters streamed towards the first enclosure, raising sudden cries of hope from the crowd of children penned within and yells of alarm from the single guard left on duty. "*Ligar*!" she pulsed again, "*Jergat*! *Be ready. We are upon them.*" Then, because the time had come whether they were ready or not, she gave the signal and in unison her two hundred women yelled, at the tops of their voices, the single word of the Illimani language she had taught them – the word *kharga* that meant "death."

It sliced through the still morning air like an axe and caught the attention of the thirty Illimani in the women's enclosure and close to five hundred more on the meeting ground, making them all look up at once in surprise.

"*KHARGA*!" "*KHARGA*!" "*KHARGA*!"

These swaggering men, Ria had calculated, would not expect to hear their own battle cry, in their own language, hurled at them by a horde of women, armed with hatchets and knives, running towards them stark naked – for she and her entire force had stripped down to their moccasins before the charge. She'd hoped the unusual spectacle of foes as naked as themselves – and women into the bargain – might gain her some small advantage.

Now she found she'd been right. The two groups of Illimani seemed to relax when they saw they were under attack by a force of less than half their numbers consisting entirely of women. With a dismissive gesture Martu sent a hundred braves jogging out of the meeting ground to support the thirty executioners in the enclosure and resumed his speech. In the same instant – at last – Ria heard Ligar's thought-voice, faint but clear: "*We are in place. May the spirits protect us all.*"

The first flight of arrows erupted into the air out of the sector of rough gullies and hollows, overgrown with bracken and gorse, that lay between the meeting ground and the steep slope of the valley's western side. Ria and her fighters surged past the captive children and bore down on the slaughterhouse enclosure, screaming their defiance. There the massacre of the women had stopped and the Illimani were witnessing, with obvious disbelief, the utter destruction that two hundred arrows had wrought on the detachment supposed to reinforce them. Halfway out of the meeting ground, moving in tight formation, they had been cut down in their tracks, almost every one of them; less than twenty were still on their feet.

With fierce satisfaction Ria saw a second flight of arrows start up like a flock of birds, blacken the air directly above the meeting ground and smash down into Martu's remaining force of three hundred and fifty men. After that she lost sight of what was happening there but she was confident of Ligar and Sebittu and focused herself on the task of obliterating Sakkan and his thirty braves.

While the sky was still dark and sufficient cover remained to move a large group down the valley unseen, Ria had sent Ligar and Sebittu ahead with their mixed troop of nearly two hundred Merell and Naveen archers. They had been guided by Moiraig and Aranchi who'd said they could bring them close to the meeting ground without being seen and had proved as good as their word.

Ria had done what she could to prepare her own force for the task of breaching the thorn-bush walls of the women's enclosure. The Illimani inside would expect them to try and enter by the gate, so that wasn't her plan. Fifty women in five groups of ten would form scrums around the walls and everyone else would climb up over them and leap from their shoulders. There had been no opportunity to practice the maneuver, only to select the groups and hastily brief her whole force, but now as Ria sprinted towards the enclosure she felt proud as the women she'd selected surged forward and formed up where they should.

Ria's knife hung in its sheath at her waist, alongside her deerskin pouch. As she jumped up onto the shoulders of the nearest scrum, with women streaming after her, she filled her hands with stone and her heart with hate and leapt over the thorn-bush stockade.

Chapter Ninety-Five

WHOOMF! Leoni was back.

Before Baiyakondi had given her the gourd of vile-tasting Ayahuasca he had sat over her for what had seemed like an age, singing a strange and mournful *icaro* while Ruapa had moved around enveloping her in fragrant clouds of tobacco smoke and the constant susurration of his *chacapa* rattle. "This ritual will cleanse some of the contamination that your etheric body has suffered," Don Leoncio explained, "and restore a little of your strength. We can only hope it will be enough."

Then she drank and it seemed seconds later that her spirit soared up with the joy of a caged bird at last set free. She fixed her intent firmly, summoning Ria's image to mind, and a tunnel of pure white light blinked open beside her. Leoni surrendered, allowing herself to be drawn into it and carried away and now, feeling her aerial body somewhat restored, she hovered thirty feet above Ria's head.

It was full daylight, the sun was over the ridge of the valley and the entire scene was brightly lit and crystal clear as Leoni watched Ria clamber onto the shoulders of a cluster of women and leap like an acrobat into the thorn-bush stockade, strewn with bodies, where the Illimani had been raping and murdering female prisoners. The stockade formed a large square, two hundred feet on each side, and now only thirty of the women who'd been held captive still lived. Crowded screaming into a corner, they were being butchered by a tight mass of ten braves led by the monstrous figure who Leoni thought of as Bear Skull. Elsewhere within the enclosure were three smaller groups of Illimani clustered round the bloody bodies of more women – some of whom had been hung from racks and skinned alive.

But right now none of the executioners were going about their business. Many had expressions of astonished stupidity on their brutal faces as four from the group nearest to Ria charged towards her. Dozens of other women – Leoni hardly registered they were all naked

– began to stream into the stockade from various points around its perimeter.

She saw Ria hurl two stones in quick succession, one with her left hand, one with her right, and two of the charging warriors fell in mid-stride as though they'd been shot. A howling mob of naked women swarmed over the other two, hacking them down with knives, cutting them to bloody shreds in seconds. Ria threw twice more, bringing two more Illimani crashing down, drew her own knife and hurled herself at a third, spilling his bowels before whirling around with the pure joy of battle dancing in her eyes. All the action was in the physical realm – mercifully, it seemed that none of Sulpa's aerial creatures had yet found their way here – and Leoni would not distract Ria in the midst of a fight for her life, so for the next few moments she could only watch and hope.

Across the enclosure the Illimani were being overrun by packs of armed women pouring in over the thorn-bush barriers and the prisoners had at last turned on their captors. Many of Ria's force were killed and injured by the huge warriors but the women's numbers were overwhelming and they could not be stopped. In seconds only Bear Skull and six of the executioners were still on their feet, clearing their way to the gate of the stockade with savage sweeps of their axes.

Through all this Leoni had been aware the battle was not confined to the enclosure. She soared high into the air to try to understand what was happening and to find a way to be useful.

The battlefield followed the curve of the valley, bounded by the river that ran behind the destroyed camp, and thus formed roughly the shape of a crescent. The "horn" that curved to Leoni's right contained the three thorn-bush stockades, with the children's enclosure furthest down the valley in the direction from which Ria and her fighters had come. Now they saw the Illimani fully occupied with the attack and no longer watching them, some of the older children had forced open the gate of their prison and overwhelmed the lone guard.

The women's enclosure came next, a scene of utter carnage and horror. Having fought their way out, leaving a trail of women's bodies behind, Bear Skull and his gang of six were now reinforced by twenty more Illimani, some pierced by arrows, who came pounding round the corner of the final – empty – stockade that formed the rough center point of the battlefield.

Tracking to her left from there, into the other horn of the crescent, Leoni saw the newcomers were the survivors of a bigger group sent to rescue Bear Skull. Bristling with arrows, eighty of them lay dead or crippled in a compact mass between the empty stockade and the wide cleared area a few hundred feet beyond it where the male prisoners had been tortured to death the night before. It seemed that Bull and the main Illimani force had formed up there, only to be caught in the same devastating ambush. More than half the warriors were down, many with multiple arrow wounds, but the two hundred or so who were still in the fight had unslung their atlatls and now sent a black wall of spears whirring back towards the archers. Within seconds the Illimani had launched two more volleys and then, yelling with fury, a hundred of them charged the archers' positions in the rough land near the side of the valley.

The archers didn't run. Many had been hit by spears but those who remained now burst from the cover of thorn bushes, fired one more withering volley, then laid down their bows and charged the advancing Illimani, brandishing axes and knives. The two groups were of roughly equal size and they met with a frightful clash at the edge of the cleared ground across a front hundreds of feet long. A desperate and frenzied fight to the death began.

Behind them, Bull and the other hundred Illimani had charged in the opposite direction and were now smashing Ria's women aside to reach the beleaguered defensive circle formed by Bear Skull and his warriors. But before the two forces could join up – there were still a hundred feet between them – the women seemed to panic and Leoni watched in horror as they broke and ran.

Chapter Ninety-Six

Ria hung to the rear of the wild flight from the Illimani. A throng of sweating braves roared battle cries right behind her, as her force of women, bloody and battered – more than fifty had already fallen – pounded back down the valley, taking losses every step of the way.

Their flight, like their naked attack, was a ruse. The Illimani enjoyed hunting and terrorizing people so much, and were so accustomed to victory, that Ria hoped they wouldn't even suspect they were being lured into a trap. Besides, they had every reason to believe they were dealing only with women and a good number of archers. Nothing could have led them to guess she'd held almost a hundred and fifty fighting men in reserve. They were under Bont's command, hidden just ahead around the elbow of the bend, with Driff, Grondin and Oplimar stiffening the front line.

Since the ability to use thought-talk had returned, even if reduced in strength, it had become much easier for Ria to get things done the way she wanted. As the battle developed she'd repeatedly pulsed to Bont to hold his men back – she'd sensed his eagerness – but it looked like the time had come at last. The first ranks of the women had already reached the bend and she herself was almost upon it.

"*Now*!" she pulsed. "*Now*!" Bont's warriors surged out and smashed into the flank of the Illimani pack, catching them perfectly off guard and spreading mayhem. Ria whirled round, dodged between a pair of pursuing braves and hurled her last stone at Martu, hitting him full in the brow and dropping him to his knees. Oplimar ran up, snatched off his horn headdress, and dashed his brains out with a single blow of his club.

It was the same all across the elbow of the valley. Outnumbered and overmatched, the Illimani were smashed down and ground into the dirt. Ria saw Grondin and Bont in the thick of it, striking out left and right with their huge war-axes, both spattered from head to foot in enemy blood. But every man of every tribe played his part and the women, having lured the Illimani here, now turned on them and teemed over their fallen and injured, knives and cleavers flashing.

Ria saw that Driff had found Sakkan, the smaller man's slim build and tomahawks at first seeming puny against the giant warrior swinging a big double-headed axe.

But Driff was agile and fearless, darting in under his opponent's blows to cut him with his blades, opening dripping wounds between his ribs, gashing his thighs and shoulders, driving him to madness. In an explosion of rage, Sakkan charged him, sweating, his massive chest heaving, but Driff slipped aside and cut him again as he pounded past, leaving a slab of bloody flesh flapping loose from his back.

In a circle around them, as the last of the Illimani were dispatched, Ria's fighters, men and women, began to gather to watch. But she could not spare them for this. Not yet. "*Finish him, Driff*!" she pulsed. "*The battle isn't over.*"

Driff didn't seem to hear her. He was laughing at Sakkan, shouting insults at him, and now he lunged forward again under a sweep of the axe, leapt into the air and dislodged the bear-skull headdress, sending it rolling. With a roar the big man swung wildly but was overcommitted to the blow and stumbled when he missed. Instantly Driff was on him. He hammered his first hatchet – *CRUNCH*! – between the vertebrae at the base of his enemy's thick neck and buried the second – *SMACK*! – in the top of his skull.

"*Finished*!" he pulsed to Ria who was already leading the charge back towards the camp, leaving behind a battlefield strewn with Illimani dead.

So great was the advantage of surprise that only a handful of Bont's men fell in the ambush, and a hundred of the Merell women were still able to fight, so it was a large force that Ria took back down the valley to relieve the hard-pressed archers. More than half of them still lived, and they were locked in hand-to-hand combat with the Illimani all along the far side of the meeting ground where it gave way to uncleared land filled with gorse and bracken.

The distance between Ria's force and the battle on the meeting ground was closing fast. Urging her fighters to a charge, she led them straight across the curve of the valley and the whole mass thundered between the empty thorn-bush stockades to their right and the escaped children who had gathered in the shade of a copse of bushes and small trees along the valley side to the left. A ragged cheer went up from the children and, ahead, there came an immediate change in the character of the battle as the Illimani – who had the upper hand – discovered they were doomed.

Some ran at once, seeking cover and escape through the gorse.

Others, turning to face the new threat, were struck down from behind.

A few of them regrouped and attempted to form defensive circles but broke under the massive force and numbers of Ria's attack and were cut to pieces. Many of the rest, scattered in ones and twos along the battlefront, attempted to surrender, and many of the fallen had been injured but were not dead. "What shall we do with them?" asked Bont.

"Kill them all," said Ria. "That's the only thing we came here to do."

While Bont gave the orders for execution squads to comb the battlefield and sent other men to hunt down runaways, Ligar and Sebittu walked up arm in arm. They were both covered in blood – mostly not their own, as they themselves had survived the thick of the fight with only minor injuries. "I owe you an apology," Ligar said to Ria as he embraced her. "I didn't think we could do this, I tried to talk you out of it, but I couldn't have been more wrong. You've won us a fantastic victory here! A fantastic victory! It's the stuff of legend – a legend, by the way, in which I myself plan to be remembered as Ligar the Great. I think that will suit me well. Or perhaps Ligar the Slayer?" He gestured to the battlefield where more than half of the dead, lying in thick heaps, had been killed by arrows.

Sebittu was more serious – as well he might be, Ria thought, since many of his archers had died in this fight. She wondered if he would upbraid her for not reinforcing him sooner. But instead he fell on one knee before her, which made her feel uncomfortable.

Men and women, some Merell, some from other tribes, were gathering round. Amongst them Ria's heart leapt to see Birsing. Still clutching her little flint knife, she was covered in cuts and bruises but there was joy in her eyes.

Sebittu raised his voice: "Hail to Ria," he declaimed, "the Harbinger of the Light. After such a victory none may doubt who you are. The foe has run proudly through our valleys scattering us to the four directions, but you have united the tribes to stop him . . . Triumph is yours this day, Ria. You have bloodied the Evil One."

Only the Merell could have understood his words but Ria saw everyone gazed at her with the same rapt intensity. For a moment there was total silence. Then in a swirl of movement Sebittu was back on his feet and he and Ligar stooped and lifted Ria, surprised and laughing, onto their shoulders. Bont and Grondin, Driff and Oplimar linked arms with them and they carried her through the crowd.

She didn't know who shouted her name first, although she was sure it was a woman, but very soon hundreds of people, wearied and bloodied, were chanting – "RIA! RIA! RIA!" – and she was looking down at a sea of faces raised towards her in something very like adoration. Many were the hands that reached out to touch her as she was carried past, as though they might absorb from her the blessing of the spirits.

Ria's head felt light. All through the battle she had not thought for a moment what it might mean to win. But now, with the flash of a blinding revelation, it came to her that victory meant power.

Not personal power over others – she cared nothing for that – but the power to move men's minds, to overcome their differences, to inspire them to action, and to bind them together into an unstoppable force. Today she had fought the Illimani in their hundreds and proved they could be beaten. But the time was not far off, she knew, when she would have to face Sulpa and thousands more of his warriors on the battlefield.

He wasn't going to let her get away with what she'd done to him today – which was why she'd done it. She would need more men – a lot more men – but she had an idea where she might find them.

Still on her friends' shoulders, still being carried through the crowd to roars of acclamation, she was lost in her plans for Sulpa's destruction when she sensed Leoni's presence again, just a shimmer on the morning air. "There are twenty Illimani you didn't see," Ria heard her say. "They're going to kill the children. You've got to stop them."

Ria looked back to the little stand of bushes and trees a thousand paces away where the prisoners were sheltering. A great outcry of children's voices rose up.

Chapter Ninety-Seven

As the battle unfolded fifty feet below her Leoni saw the whole mechanism of Ria's plan: an ambush within an ambush, a powerful enemy caught off balance and fatally duped into dividing his force. The naked women were the bait, the archers the spring and Bont's men the hammer in a perfect trap.

While it lasted, the battle moved too fast for Leoni to risk distracting Ria. Besides, although Ria often seemed in danger as the fighting swirled around her, she was astonishingly agile and deadly and had uncanny survival instincts. Again and again she dodged lethal blows by a hair's breadth, and her lean body – naked, dusty and blood-smeared after the fight – had suffered just one new wound. Some jagged edge, perhaps a knife or a spear point, had sliced open her left breast from nipple to armpit. The gash was ugly, and oozed blood, but Ria seemed unaware of it as her triumphant warriors carried her across the battlefield shoulder-high, and cheers and shouts of victory rose all round her.

Leoni was in far worse shape. Since she'd made the choice to return, she'd known that the restoration of her aerial body by Ruapa and Baiyakondi could only be temporary. As she hovered over the battle, following its shifting fortunes, she once more become aware of the awful lassitude and creeping numbness that had afflicted her before, and of the frightening thinness and attenuation of her aerial form which seemed to be slowly evaporating and drifting away. It was difficult to resist the warm shelter of her meat body and the call of her own place and time. She felt its strong pull upon her and sensed she needed only to unlock her focus from Ria and she would be back in an instant with Don Leoncio and the Tarahanua shamans who would heal her wounds.

As though triggered by her thoughts of return, a tunnel of light opened in the air a few feet in front of her. It was inviting and she began to drift towards it when a distant flutter of movement – that yet had a sort of *purposive* flow about it – made her look off to her right.

A thousand feet back across the curve of the valley, near the stockades, she saw a group of men, crouched low, running.

The tunnel would have to wait. With the power of flight Leoni reached the place in an instant and swooped down amongst twenty Illimani who all Ria's forces had somehow failed to root out. Some were armed with axes, some with long flint knives, and as she watched they ducked out of sight between two of the stockades and squirmed forward.

What were they doing? Leoni soared higher and saw their target could only be the two hundred women and children, formerly their prisoners, gathered in the shade of the bushes and small trees growing along the opposite side of the valley. It seemed crazy for these warriors to take time out for murder when they had a real chance to slip away and escape, but no doubt these were the kinds of decisions people made when they'd sold their souls to a demon.

Leoni darted down to Ria, where her men still carried her on their shoulders, and projected the thought urgently: "There are twenty Illimani you didn't see." With every atom of her will she fought the weakness spreading across her aerial body: "They're going to kill the children. You've got to stop them."

"Sister!" exclaimed Ria. "It's so good to have you back." In the same instant her gaze swept towards the valley side where a distant chorus of screams now rose up and figures could be seen scattering. Her expression changed to one of fury and as she sprang to the ground, yelling orders, Leoni streaked back along the valley, expecting the bloodbath to have begun.

Instead she saw flights of arrows pouring down off the ridge above the copse sheltering the women and children and thudding into the twenty Illimani where they'd charged across the open ground from the stockades. All but three were already down, two more fell in the next second and only the last one got anywhere near the copse before a dozen arrows smashed him off his feet. Another flight arched from the ridge, thudding into the lifeless and bloody bodies, then another, and then it was all over. Not a woman or child had been harmed.

Leoni soared up to take a look at the rescuers. There were twenty of them, under the command of the third Neanderthal – the one whose name she didn't know – and they occupied the very position she'd suggested to Ria as a good spot to place some archers. They'd got here late, it seemed, because they'd missed the main fighting, but that had put them in exactly the right place at exactly the right time to save the innocents.

Ria was coming down the valley at a run with fifty of her fighters, but when they saw the threat had been dealt with they slowed to a walk. Hovering transparent and invisible above the ridge, Leoni watched as a milling joyous crowd streamed towards them from all sides, victorious warriors mingled with the women and children they had saved, and whirling dances broke out amidst wild hand-clapping and exultant whoops.

A tunnel of light blinked open again at Leoni's side and in the same instant she saw that two of Sulpa's little creatures had appeared in the valley – no doubt he had sent them out in their hundreds to search the countryside. The gargoyles flew closer but they didn't seem to see her, perhaps because she was now so insubstantial or because their eyes were fixed on Ria. Leoni made no movement to attract their attention. She only knew she must catch them and kill them. All would be lost, and Ria would be followed and hunted down wherever she tried to flee, if she failed to do that.

Leoni stayed above the ridge while the creatures flew past and watched as they descended to hover directly over Ria's head.

Now!

She dived, swept up behind them and snatched them out of the air.

That was the easy part, but she feared that her hands and fingers might no longer have enough substance to hold them as they lashed and squirmed away from her. She tried smashing them together as she'd done before but couldn't get the same degree of force – *SMACK*! *SMACK*! It just seemed to make them more angry. Then *SMACK*! *SMACK*! *SMACK*! – one of the creatures burst apart in a puff of smoke.

Now she could deal with the other one. She wrenched its head away from its body with her free hand, but even as it died it raked its talons down her side, filling her with a stabbing mortal pain.

There was no time to explain to Ria.

Leoni felt an instant shocking drain of power and all at once, like a cloud of mist in a breath of wind, her aerial body gave up the unequal struggle to remain whole, was scattered into gossamer threads and vanished.

The last thing she knew was falling away into nothingness.

Chapter Ninety-Eight

The labyrinth of caves that led from the outside world into Secret Place was an impressive and terrible obstacle. Without personal knowledge of it, or a guide, or sorcery, it was difficult to see how attackers could ever find their way through its confusing twists and turns, dark deadfalls, circuitous tunnels and blind passages. Still Ria was surprised and concerned to discover Brindle had posted no sentries to guard the exit. As she started the process of leading her horde of injured and exhausted refugees out onto the hillside she reflected they might as easily be Illimani warriors ready to sweep down on the campfires of Secret Place that twinkled in the night just a few bowshots below. With an enemy like Sulpa it was best to take nothing for granted, but now was not the time to scold her friend for this lapse: "Brindle." She sent out her thought-voice: "I'm back! We're all back. We all made it. Something amazing happened."

There was no reply and Ria became alert. "What's up, Grondin?" she asked. "Why can't I reach Brindle?"

The big Ugly looked worried: "Don't know. I too cannot reach him."

It wasn't the same sort of interruption of thought-talk they'd experienced during the battle at the Naveen camp. Then it had been lost to all of them; they still didn't know why. But now Oplimar, Jergat and Grondin reported open contact with friends and relatives below in Secret Place, and already figures could be seen running up the hillside to greet them – so this was a problem with Brindle alone.

"No problem with Brindle," Grondin announced a moment later. "He's busy. Working in the Cave of Visions. Can't talk to us right now."

Busy? Ria was outraged. How dare Brindle be busy? Didn't he know – didn't he want to know – about her incredible victory? What could he possibly be doing that was more important than that?

After the battle, and a long day's forced march, Ria had brought almost two thousand refugees to Secret Place. It was a huge number.

Fear had kept them silent and biddable until now but they hailed from a dozen different tribes, with different languages and customs, and their group behavior tended towards chaos. Getting them out of the labyrinth and marshaling them on the hillside in the darkness was already taking a very long time and then the Uglies would have to find them food, shelter, sleeping spaces and other necessities of life on the terraces below.

Ria felt weary at the prospect. She'd done enough. Her companions could organize the refugees without her help. "Sort it all out," she told them. "I'm going to find Brindle."

Making her way through the crowd of Uglies streaming up to welcome the new arrivals, she set off downhill towards Secret Place.

Most evenings the broad natural platform in front of the Cave of Visions was packed with little groups of Uglies sitting around fires, cooking, eating, talking and dancing. Tonight the space was deserted except for four guards, armed with spears, who stood at the entrance to the cave.

"What are you doing here?" Ria asked as she approached.

"Keeping everyone out," one of the guards replied. He was young, with heavy brow ridges and wispy hair on his chin.

"I'm going in," said Ria.

"Cannot let you in . . ." A second guard was speaking now. Older, gray-haired, with large drooping leathery ears, he had a stubborn slow-moving look about him.

Ria sighed: "Don't even think of stopping me. I've killed more men today than I can count." She didn't want to hurt these Uglies but she would not allow them to thwart her. She stepped forward, the older guard tried to block her and in a flash she unsheathed her knife and held its blade to his throat. "I'm going in," she pulsed again, gritting her teeth. She pushed him aside and walked into the vast cave.

It was midnight black within, but Ria knew from her previous visits that the floor of the Cave of Visions was roughly circular. It extended more than eight hundred paces from side to side under a huge vaulted roof that rose at its peak to a height of almost two bowshots. She paused to be sure the guards hadn't followed her through the entrance tunnel and to get her bearings. Up ahead she could hear a large group of Uglies giving out a strange, hooting chant – quite different from the one they used for healing – but the echoes in the chamber and the thick darkness made it impossible to be sure where the sound was coming from.

Ria walked slowly towards the center of the cave – ten paces, thirty, sixty, a hundred – feeling her way over the uneven floor with the toes of her moccasins. There was no light from outside, and no lamps were burning, yet every step forward seemed to offer her tantalizing glimpses through the absolute blackness of . . . something.

She squinted and stooped, felt some disturbance in the air.

There! What was that?

Lit by a faint ghostly radiance, a giant fang of rock went flying past her with its base a hand's breadth above the floor. It was bigger and faster than a charging rhino and she was close enough to touch it. *Fuck*! She just had time to realize she would have been dead if she'd got in front of it when another massive rock hurtled out of the darkness and shot past – *WHOOSH*! – followed by another, and another. They all seemed to be moving in the same direction, not randomly, and not even in a straight line, like an avalanche, but in a weird and unnatural whirling circle.

Then it dawned on her. This was the outer ring of Brindle's stone circle – the idea the blue woman had given him in a vision that she'd said would help to fight Sulpa. He must have built it. But how was he keeping the stones off the ground? How was he making them fly?

WHOOSH! *WHOOSH*! Two more of the megaliths whizzed past just in front of her nose.

"Where are you, Brindle?" Ria pulsed. "Let me through."

There came a change in the pitch of the Uglies' chant, from an irregular, snarling rumble to a steady sonorous roar. At the same moment the big stones ceased their restless whirling and froze in place. Either their inner radiance was growing, or her eyes were becoming more accustomed to the darkness, but Ria found she could see all of them now – all thirty of them – even the ones farthest away. They were arranged in a circle a hundred paces from side to side, and they surrounded the two inner circles of stones exactly as Brindle had shown her.

She heard his thought-voice. "I can't stop the stones dancing for long, Ria. It would be a good idea if you came through now."

She stepped between two of the huge gray megaliths, towering over her head. No sooner had she passed them than there was a further change in the pitch of the chant and the outer circle once more began to rotate rapidly – *WHOOSH*! *WHOOSH*! *WHOOSH*! *WHOOSH*!

Still frozen in their places, the inner ring of twenty black stones now loomed before Ria. Again, as soon as she had stepped through between two of them, the entire circle resumed its rotation.

The light radiated by all the stones had increased to such a level that Ria could see Brindle. He stood at the center of the innermost ring of eight gigantic white megaliths, each four times the height of a man. He had undergone an incredible transformation. His body was skeletal and dirty. His hair was matted. His eyes, hollow and dark-shadowed under his brow ridges, gleamed with feverish heat.

A few more paces and Ria was at his side. "What's happened to you, old friend?" she asked.

"I've made this marvellous thing," Brindle replied, with an excited grin. There was a further change of pitch in the chanting deep in the cave, becoming more insistent, more urgent, and the inner circle began to rotate rapidly again, a hand's breadth above the floor, until all was a blur and the individual stones could no longer be seen.

Chapter Ninety-Nine

Ria watched the revolving circles with amazement – three circles, fifty-eight huge upright stones all suspended a hand's breadth above the ground, all glowing with inner light and hurtling at tremendous speed around the still point at the center where she stood with Brindle. The chanting that filled the cave continued to rise in intensity, and in the growing illumination cast by the stones Ria saw four separate groups of Ugly males gathered at intervals beyond the outer circle. As was their custom when they performed healings, they stood in knots of ten or so, their arms linked around each other's shoulders, chanting in unison. But this was no healing ceremony. It was obvious the sounds they were making – not lulling and restorative but stirring and inflammatory – were powering the headlong rush of the stones. Ria also sensed an intense pattern of mental concentration linking them with Brindle and saw that although they were the source of the power it was he alone who was directing and controlling it.

"Where did the stones come from?" she asked him. "How did you get them here?"

"They're magic stones," he said. "Our Lady of the Forest told me where to find them, and taught me the song that makes them fly. All the time you've been away I've been bringing these stones here."

"And now?"

"I'm making them dance," Brindle said. His thought-voice was no more than a whisper: "Our Lady of the Forest told me they have to dance before I set them in the earth." An anxious look crossed his face: "That's why I was busy before. I hope you understand."

"But you've got time to talk to me now?"

The rhythm of the chant was rising towards a crescendo. "The dance is finished," said Brindle. He stretched his hands above his head and thrust them down, pointing his index fingers to the ground. The chant stopped and the whirling of the circles ceased. For an instant the fifty-eight stones hung poised in absolute silence and stillness. Then, with a tremendous crash, they plunged down, driving themselves like huge spears hip deep in the floor of the Cave of Visions. Not all pointed straight up, some were skewed at crazy angles, but within heartbeats they became still and the cracked earth out of which they jutted like giant teeth seemed to harden to rock around them, encasing them rigidly in place.

"Come on," said Brindle. Glowing with pride and satisfaction, he took Ria's hand and led her on a slow walk around each of the three concentric circles of standing stones. From time to time he would stop and place his hands or his forehead against one. Twice – seemingly fruitlessly – he threw his shoulder against stones as though trying to force them into new positions. Finally he brought her back to the edge of the inner ring of eight white megaliths and directed her attention towards the center of the circle where they'd stood before. "Now I've set the stones in the earth all their power should be channeled here," he said.

He didn't sound very sure of himself.

Ria peered in: "I don't see anything," she said.

She took a step forward.

Nothing.

Another step.

WHOOSH!

She was falling through a tunnel of light.

When she spilled out onto a hillside under the twin suns of the spirit world, the blue woman was waiting for her, wearing a tunic of some strange supple material that gleamed like fire.

"Shit," said Ria. "What the fuck happened? How can I be here?"

"I opened a stone gateway for you," said the blue woman. With her words she sent an image of the megaliths set into the floor of the Cave of Visions.

"Brindle's stones!" Ria exclaimed. "He said they'd help us fight Sulpa."

"That was my intention," said the blue woman. "But unfortunately a vital element of the plan has failed. We're going to have to rethink."

"Vital element? What vital element?"

"I speak of Leoni, the one with whom you are entangled. Without her to help us, in her own time, the gateway cannot serve its purpose. Do you forget her so quickly?"

Ria was stung by the question. She didn't think of herself as the sort of person who forgot her friends, but she didn't know what to do about Leoni: in their last fleeting encounters she'd sensed that her time-sister was in danger. She'd vanished in the thick of things, returned to warn of the sneak attack on the Naveen women and children, and then vanished again. After that Ria had heard no more from her. Had she simply been called back into her Earth body? Surely this was the most likely explanation? Nonetheless her disappearance had haunted Ria's thoughts throughout the long day as she'd trekked the vulnerable column of refugees across country and up to Secret Place.

"What's happened to her?" she asked, with dread in her heart.

"Leoni has fallen into the underworld," replied the blue woman. "She gave her life for you."

A flood of memories and images filled Ria's mind and she saw what she had not seen and learned what she had not been told.

She saw again how Leoni had come to her in the valley before the Naveen camp and told her of the little winged creatures Sulpa used as his spies. Two of them had found Ria, Leoni said. She'd killed one and pursued the other but it got back to its master before she could catch it.

What Leoni had not mentioned was that she herself had been attacked by hundreds of Sulpa's monstrous little creatures and been weakened by them. Nor had she told how she had overcome her weakness by force of will in order to help Ria long after she should have fled back to the safety of her Earth body. In mortal danger, she had stayed to pinpoint the locations of the Illimani sentries guarding the neck of the valley and to supply the vital intelligence Ria had used to plan her assault on the camp.

Leoni's strength had given out before the attack began – hence her sudden disappearance. She'd been pulled back into her Earth body but had put her life at risk again and returned to perform one last service. In thought-images filled with emotional power Ria witnessed the arrival over the battlefield of two more of Sulpa's spy creatures, Leoni's unhesitating courage in grappling with them despite her feeble and damaged state, and the fight to the death that had followed.

"There has to be a way to bring her back," said Ria as the last images faded. "That wasn't her Earth body I saw killed. That was some other part of her."

"That was her spirit, Ria. That was her soul. She walks the dark road now, in the company of ghosts."

"So that's it? That's the fucking END? Is that what you're telling me?"

The blue woman's gaze was penetrating. "It need not be the end. Alone amongst all humankind your entanglement with Leoni gives you the power to bring her back. But you must journey to the underworld and seek her out on the dark road. Are you ready to do that?"

"I'm ready," Ria said.

"Monsters will confront you there. Can you master them? Loss of heart and madness will assail your wits. Can you overcome them? Perils and difficulties will crowd in on you from all sides. Can you defeat them?"

"I can try."

"Even so, it may be too late. If a morsel of food has passed Leoni's lips in the underworld it will be impossible for her to leave."

"Then we have to hope she hasn't eaten yet . . ."

"There is one other matter. It is the weightiest."

"Yes?"

"Bring Leoni back and your own life becomes forfeit. You will live only for a year and a day. Do you accept?"

Ria thought about it. She wasn't going to turn coward and leave her sister in the lurch, no matter what the cost. Besides, a year and a day was a long time. Long enough to defeat Sulpa.

"Of course I accept," she said.

With a flash and a swirl, a tunnel of light opened at her feet.

Also From GRAHAM HANCOCK

SUPERNATURAL: Meetings with the Ancient Teachers of Mankind

LESS THAN 50,000 YEARS AGO, humankind had no art, no religion, no sophisticated symbolism, no innovative thinking. Then, in a dramatic and electrifying change, described by scientists as the "greatest riddle in human history," all the skills and qualities that we value most highly in ourselves appeared already fully formed, as though bestowed on us by hidden powers.

In ***Supernatural***, Hancock sets out to investigate this mysterious "before-and-after moment" and to discover the truth about the influences that shaped the modern human mind.

His quest takes him on a journey of adventure and detection from the stunningly beautiful painted caves of prehistoric France, Spain and Italy to remote rock shelters in the mountains of South Africa where he finds a treasure trove of extraordinary Stone Age art.

He uncovers clues that lead him to travel to the depths of the Amazon rainforest to drink the powerful plant hallucinogen Ayahuasca with Indian shamans, whose paintings contain images of "supernatural beings" identical to the animal-human hybrids depicted in prehistoric caves and rock shelters. And in Western laboratory experiments hallucinogens also produce visionary encounters with exactly the same beings. Scientists at the cutting edge of consciousness research have now begun to consider the possibility that such hallucinations may be real perceptions of other "dimensions."

Could the "supernaturals" first depicted in the painted caves and rock shelters be the ancient teachers of mankind? Could it be that human evolution is not just the "blind," "meaningless" process that Darwin identified, but something else, more purposive and intelligent, that we have barely even begun to understand?

Trade Paperback * History/Spirituality * ISBN: 978-193257-84-9
*** 480 Pages/Over 120 Photos & Illustrations * $18.95 (U.S.)**